CN
CARTOON NETWORK

DISTILLATORIA

OVER THE GARDEN WALL: DISTILLATORIA, November 2018. Published by KaBOOM!, a division of Boom Entertainment, Inc. OVER THE GARDEN WALL, CARTOON NETWORK, the logos, and all related characters and elements are trademarks of and © Cartoon Network. A WarnerMedia Company. All rights reserved. (S18). KaBOOM!™ and the KaBOOM! Logo are trademarks of Boom Entertainment, Inc., registered in various countries and categories. All characters, events, and/or institutions depicted herein are fictional. Any similarity between any of the names, characters, persons, events, and/or institutions in this publication to actual names, characters, and persons, whether living or dead, events and/or institutions is unintended and purely coincidental. KaBOOM! Does not read or accept unsolicited submissions of ideas, stories, or artwork.

For information regarding the CPSIA on the printed material, call: (203) 595-3636 and provide reference #RICH - 816415.

BOOM! Studios, 5670 Wilshire Boulevard, Suite 400, Los angeles, CA 90036-5679. Printed in USA. First Printing.

ISBN: 978-1-68415-268-1, eISBN: 978-1-64144-130-8

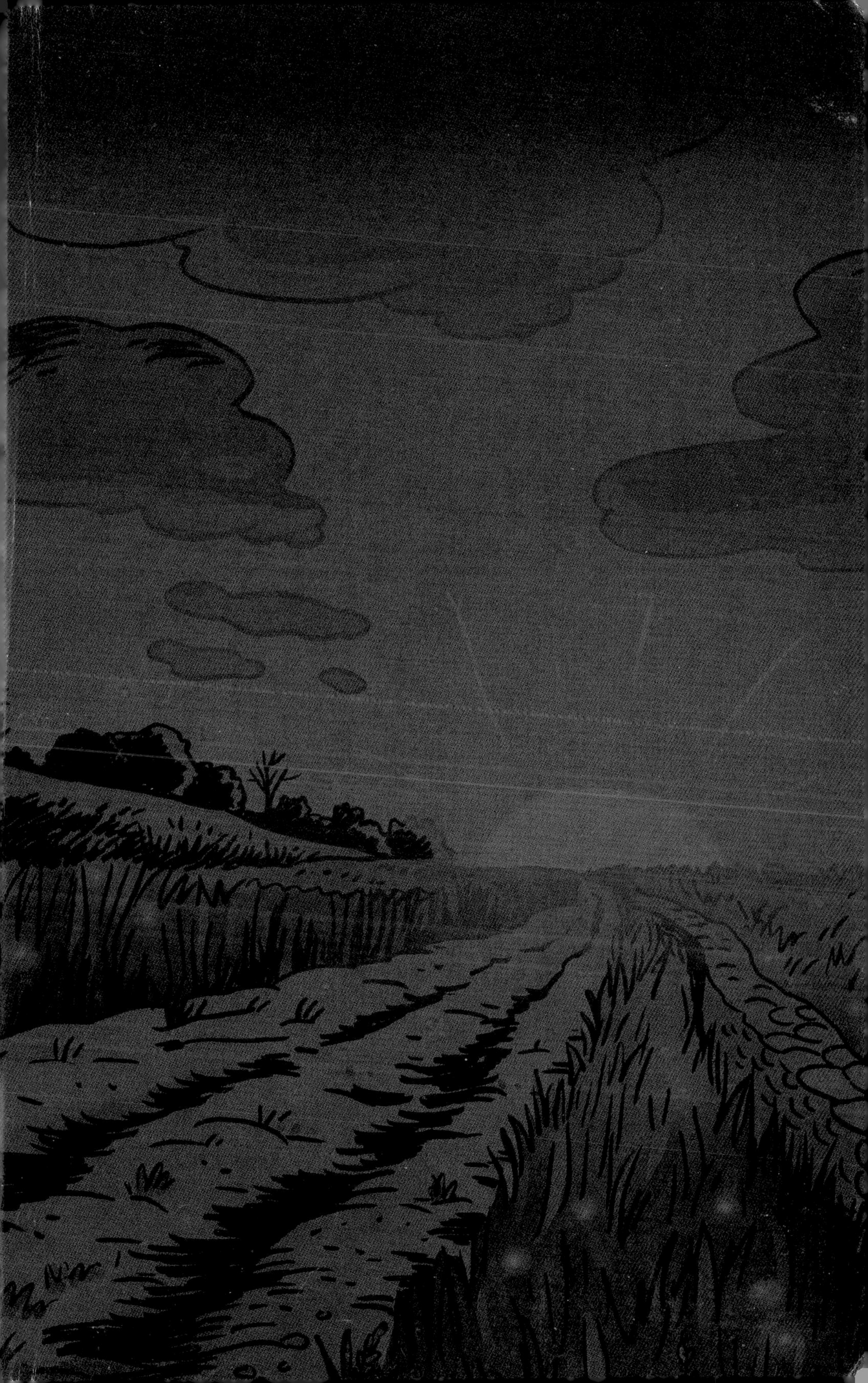

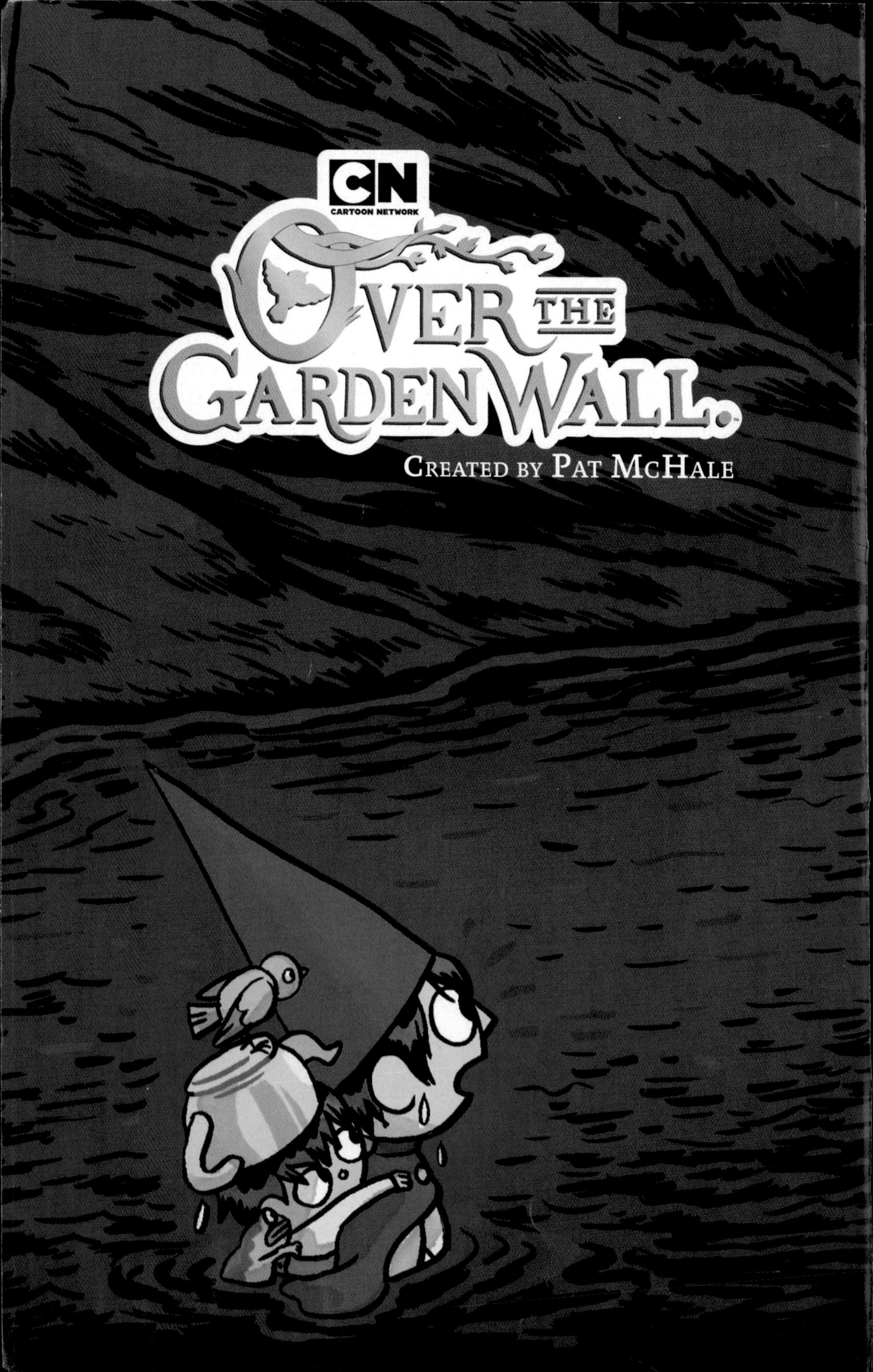
CARTOON NETWORK
OVER THE GARDEN WALL
CREATED BY PAT MCHALE

"DISTILLATORIA"

WRITTEN BY
JONATHAN CASE

ILLUSTRATED BY
JIM CAMPBELL

COLORS BY
SJ MILLER

LETTERS BY
MIKE FIORENTINO

COVER BY JIM CAMPBELL

DESIGNER KARA LEOPARD
ASSISTANT EDITOR MICHAEL MOCCIO
EDITOR WHITNEY LEOPARD

WITH SPECIAL THANKS TO MARISA MARIONAKIS,
JANET NO, BECKY M. YANG, CURTIS LELASH,
PERNELLE HAYES AND THE WONDERFUL FOLKS AT
CARTOON NETWORK.

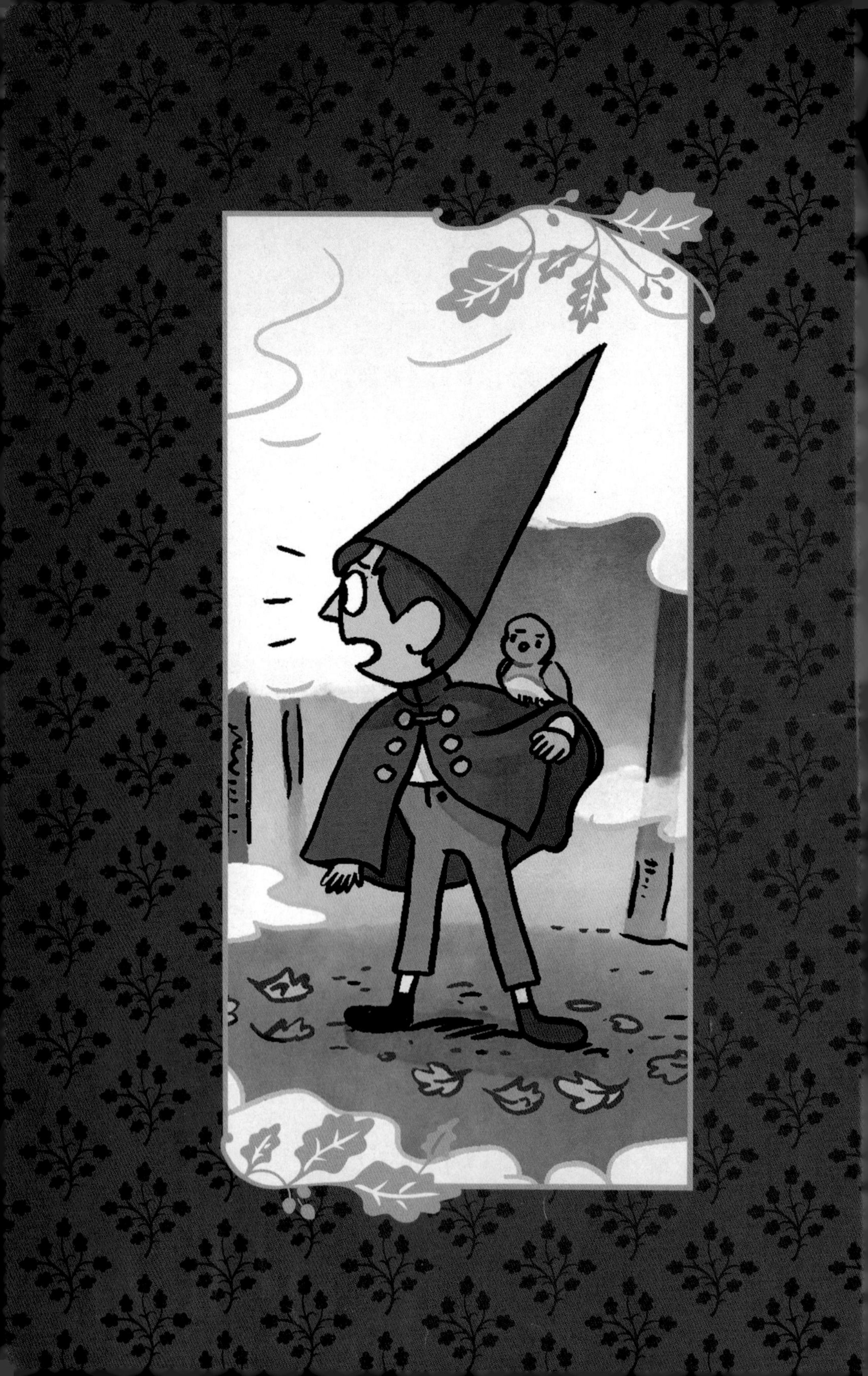

ACT ONE

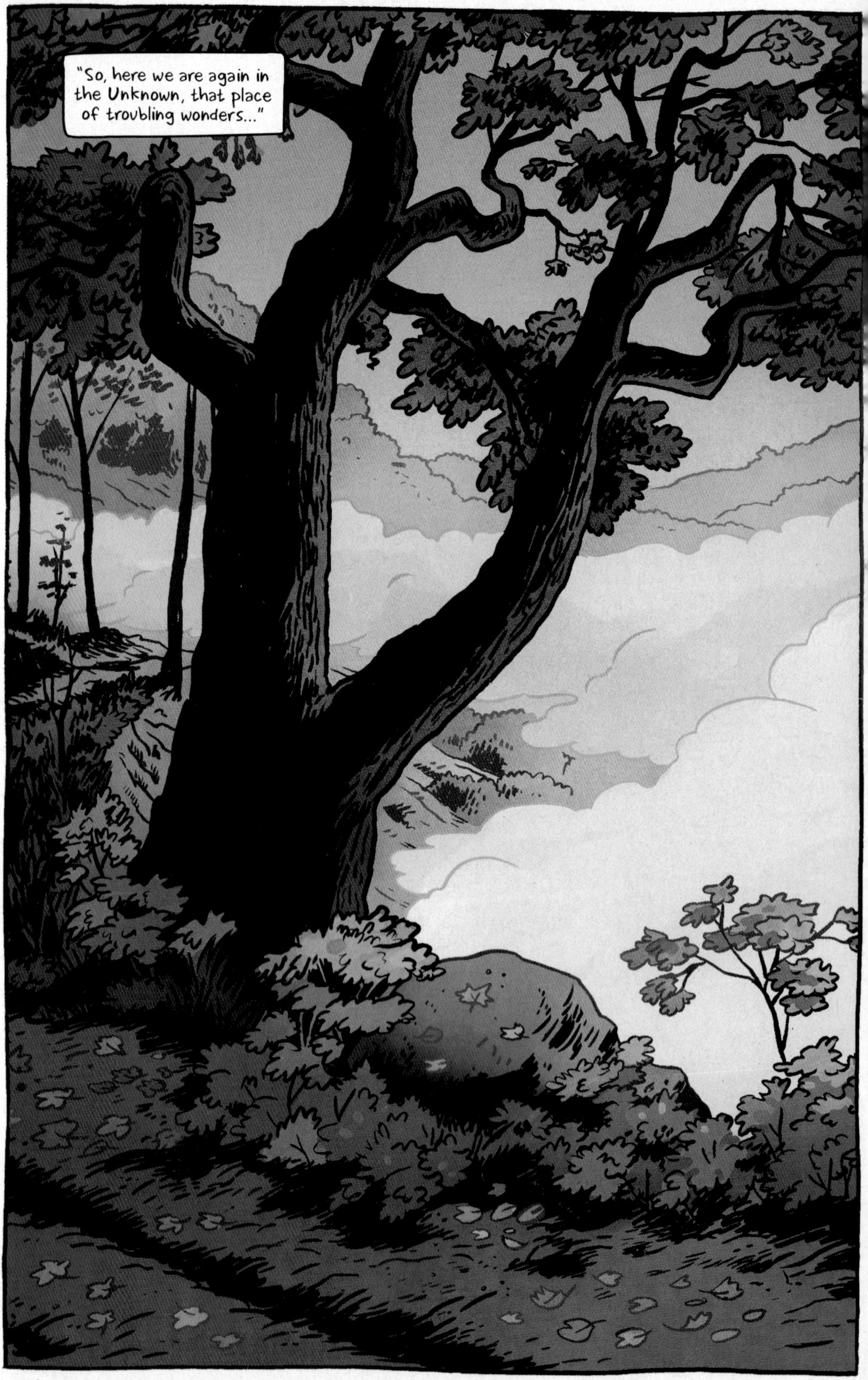
"So, here we are again in the Unknown, that place of troubling wonders..."

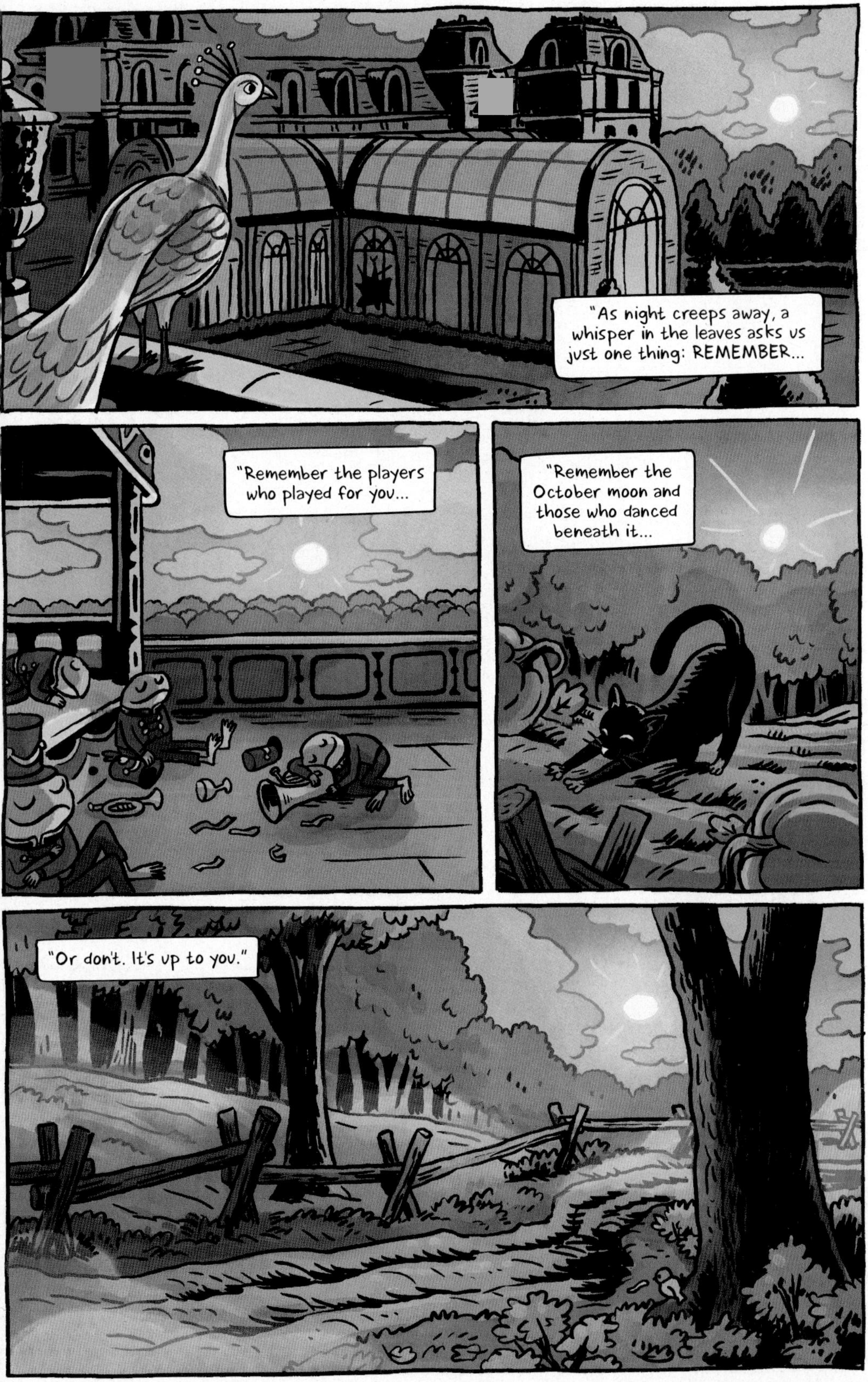
"As night creeps away, a whisper in the leaves asks us just one thing: REMEMBER...
"Remember the players who played for you...
"Remember the October moon and those who danced beneath it...
"Or don't. It's up to you."

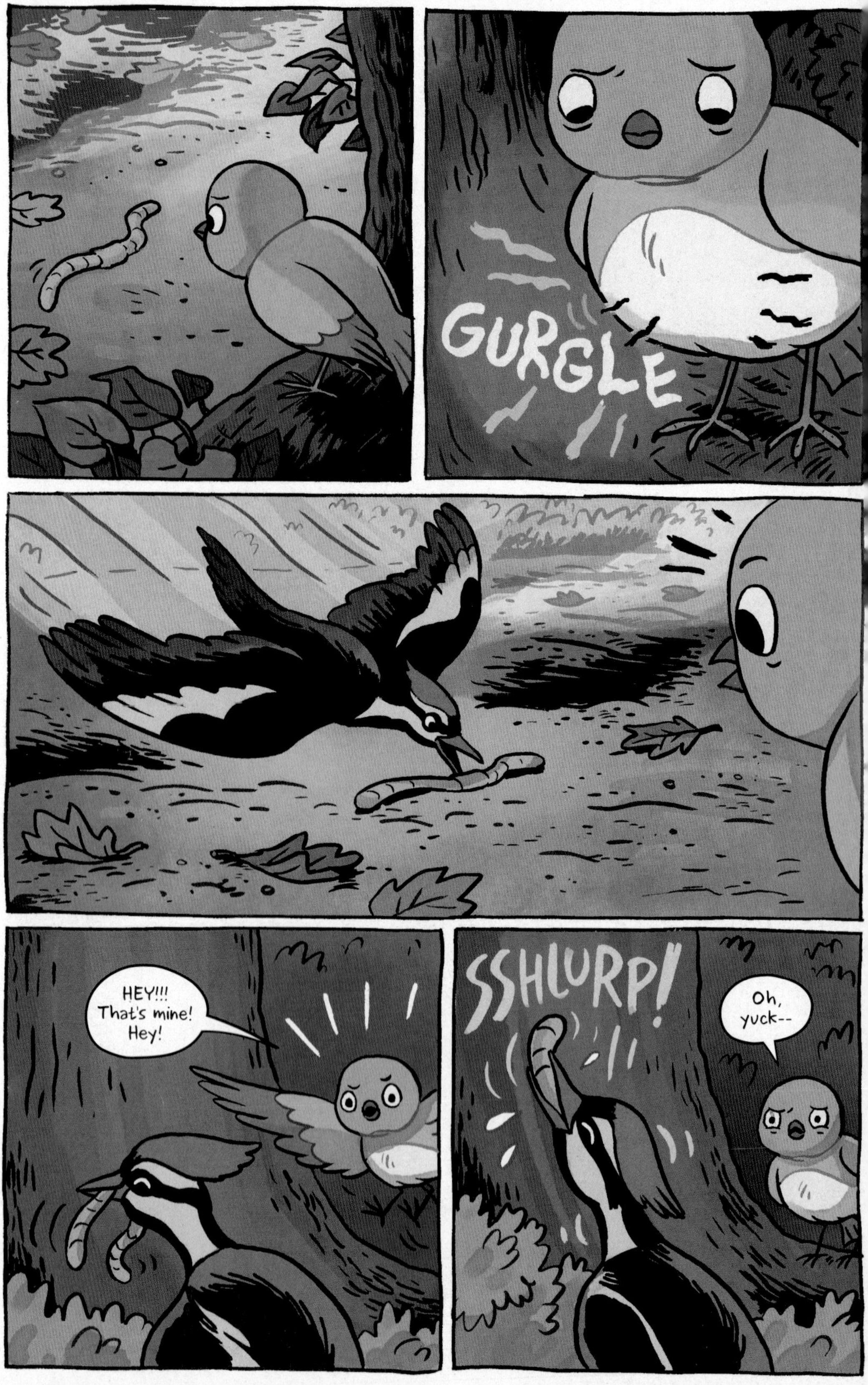
GURGLE
HEY!!! That's mine! Hey!
SSHLURP!
Oh, yuck--

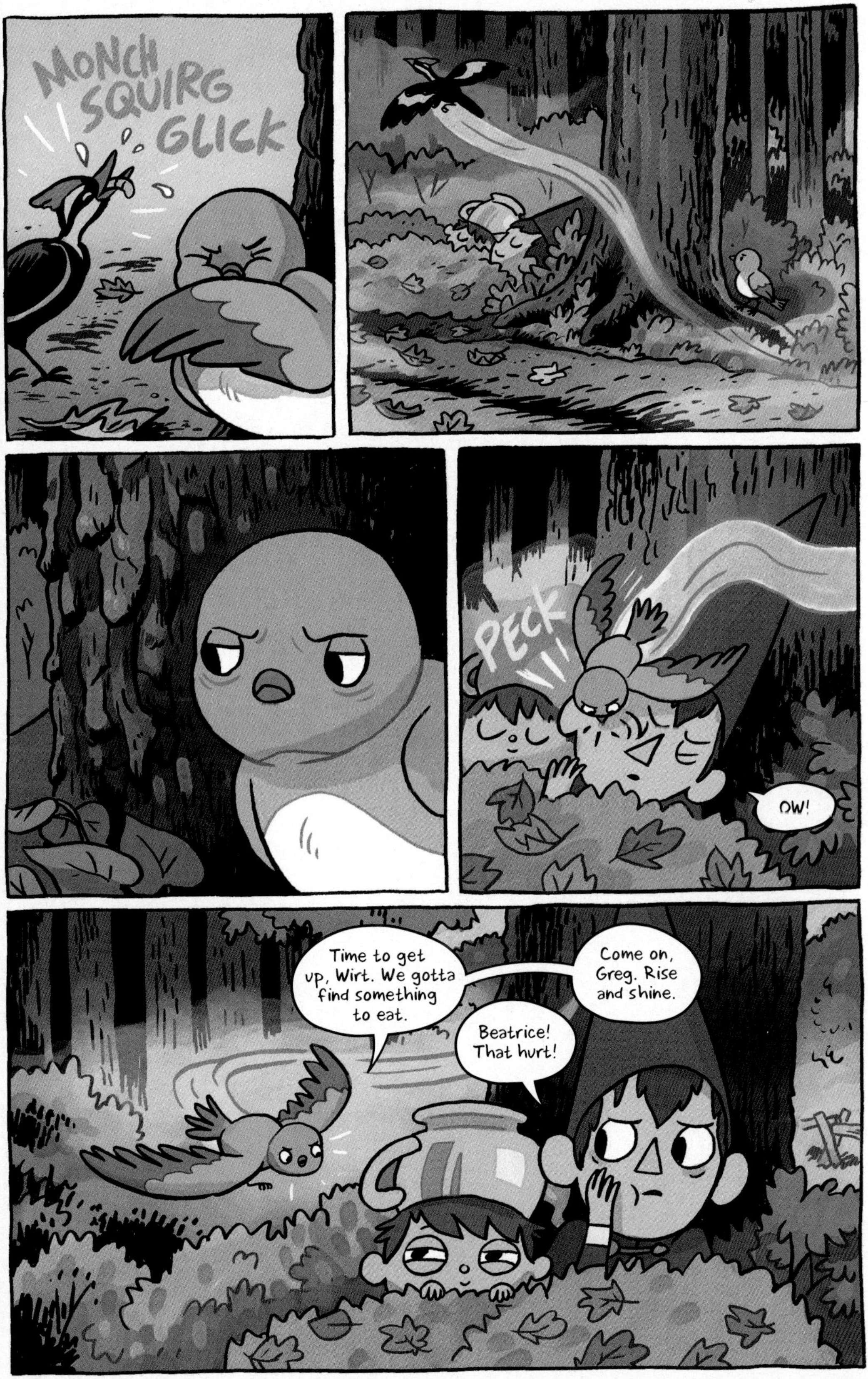
MONCH
SQUIRG
GLICK
PECK
OW!
Time to get up, Wirt. We gotta find something to eat.
Come on, Greg. Rise and shine.
Beatrice! That hurt!

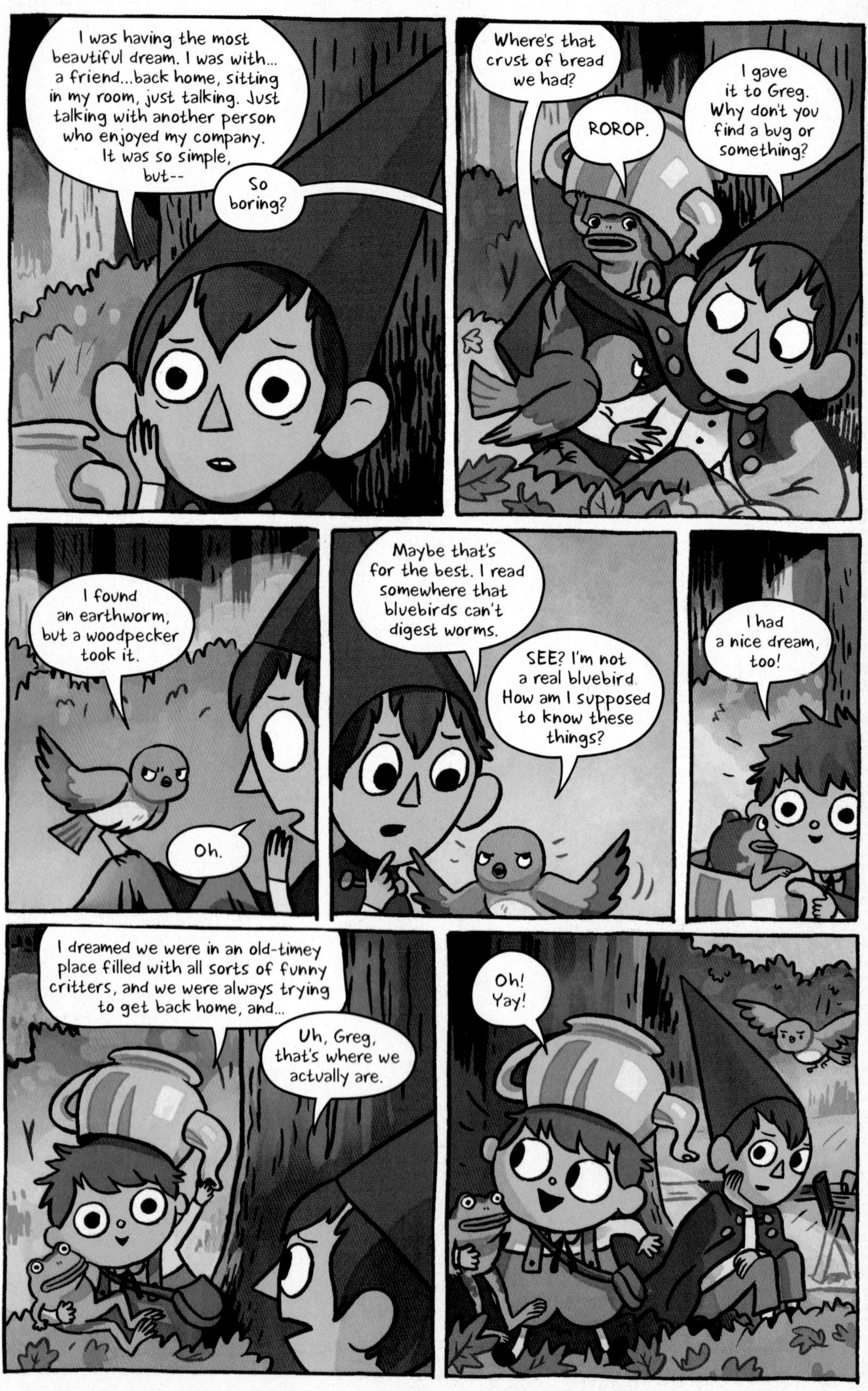
I was having the most beautiful dream. I was with... a friend...back home, sitting in my room, just talking. Just talking with another person who enjoyed my company. It was so simple, but--
So boring?
Where's that crust of bread we had?
ROROP.
I gave it to Greg. Why don't you find a bug or something?
I found an earthworm, but a woodpecker took it.
Oh.
Maybe that's for the best. I read somewhere that bluebirds can't digest worms.
SEE? I'm not a real bluebird. How am I supposed to know these things?
I had a nice dream, too!
I dreamed we were in an old-timey place filled with all sorts of funny critters, and we were always trying to get back home, and...
Uh, Greg, that's where we actually are.
Oh! Yay!

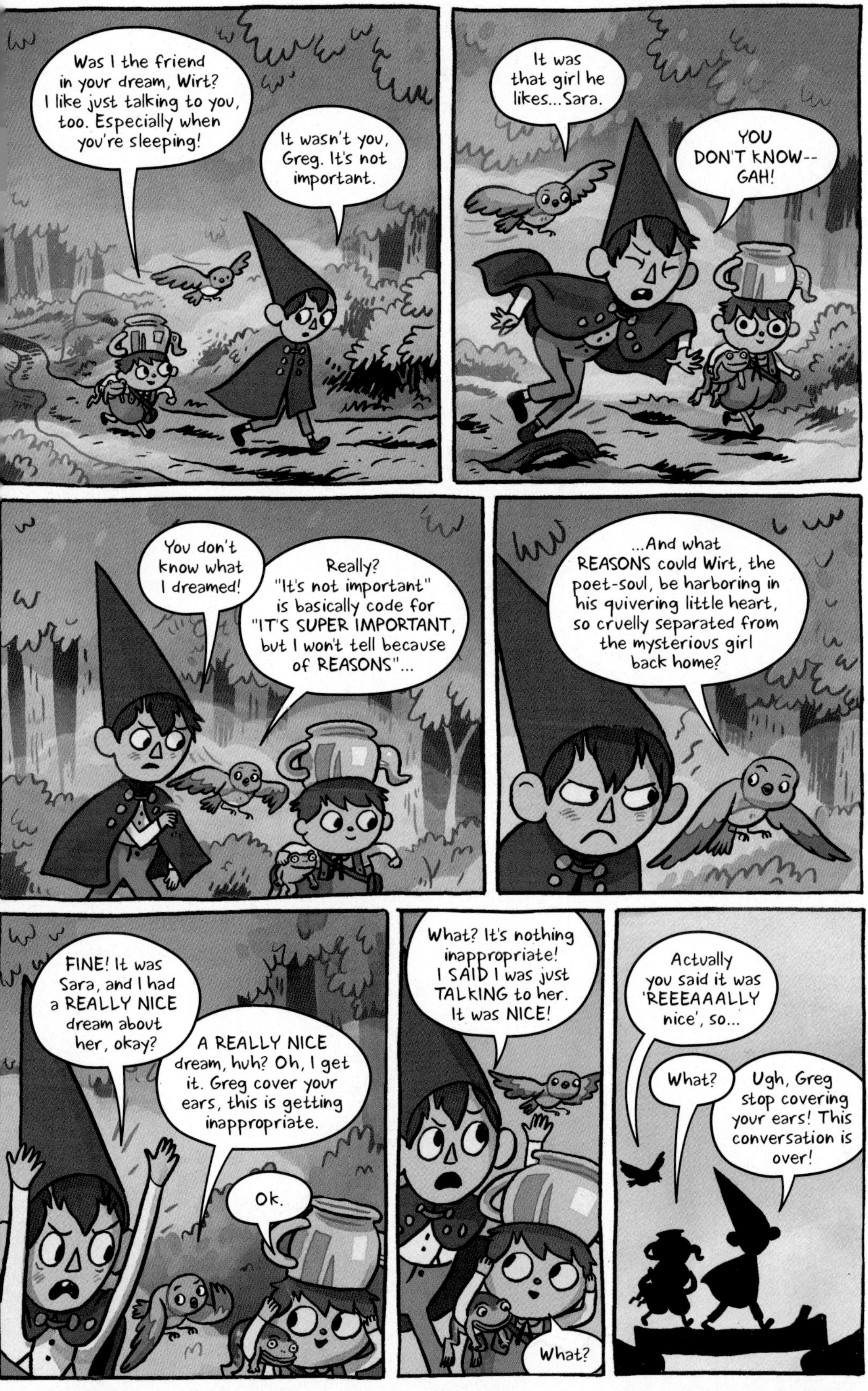
Was I the friend in your dream, Wirt? I like just talking to you, too. Especially when you're sleeping!
It wasn't you, Greg. It's not important.
It was that girl he likes... Sara.
YOU DON'T KNOW-- GAH!
You don't know what I dreamed!
Really? "It's not important" is basically code for "IT'S SUPER IMPORTANT, but I won't tell because of REASONS"...
...And what REASONS could Wirt, the poet-soul, be harboring in his quivering little heart, so cruelly separated from the mysterious girl back home?
FINE! It was Sara, and I had a REALLY NICE dream about her, okay?
A REALLY NICE dream, huh? Oh, I get it. Greg cover your ears, this is getting inappropriate.
Ok.
What? It's nothing inappropriate! I SAID I was just TALKING to her. It was NICE!
What?
Actually you said it was 'REEEAAALLY nice', so...
What?
Ugh, Greg stop covering your ears! This conversation is over!

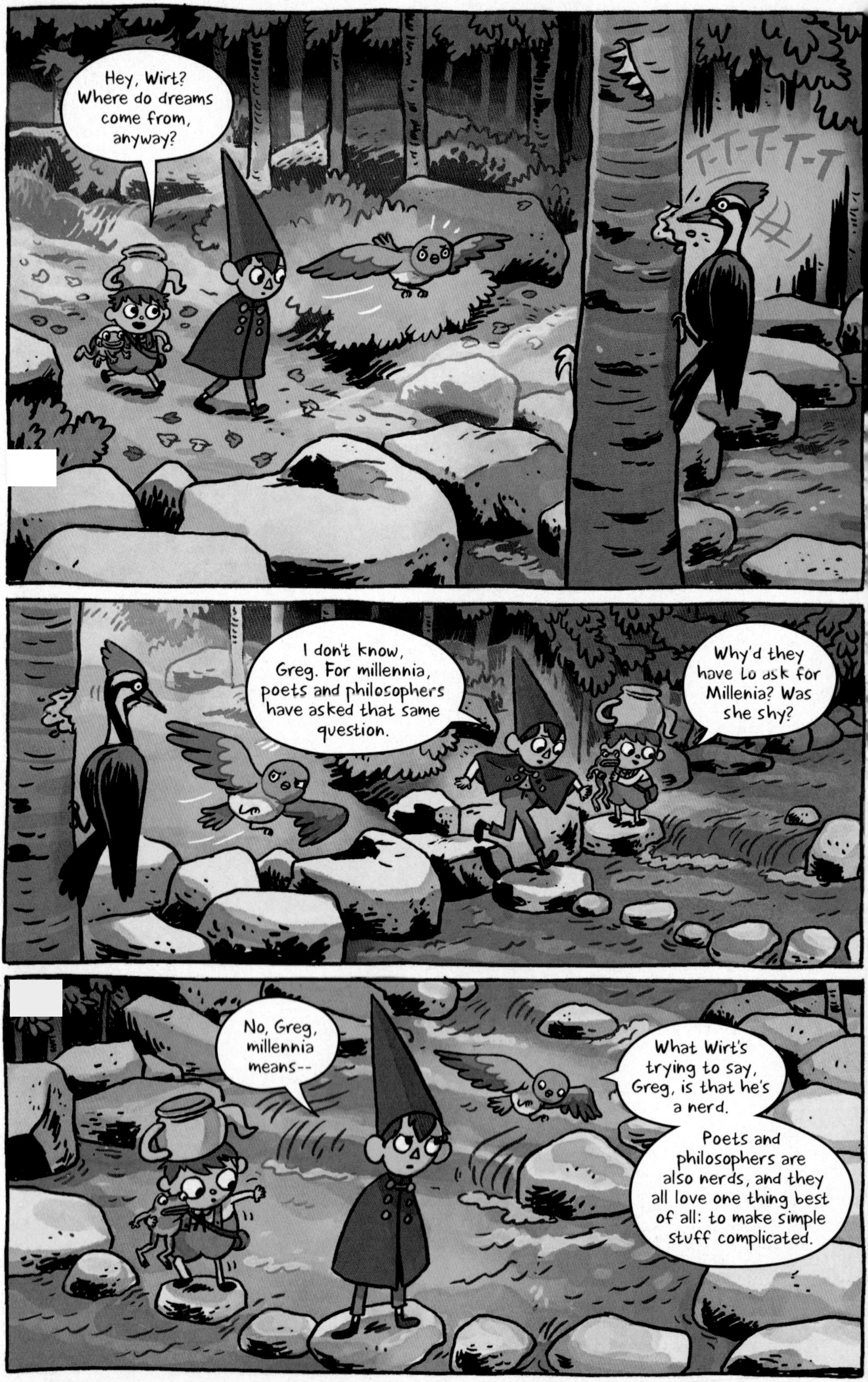

Hey, Wirt? Where do dreams come from, anyway?
T-T-T-T-T
I don't know, Greg. For millennia, poets and philosophers have asked that same question.
Why'd they have to ask for Millenia? Was she shy?
No, Greg, millennia means--
What Wirt's trying to say, Greg, is that he's a nerd.
Poets and philosophers are also nerds, and they all love one thing best of all: to make simple stuff complicated.

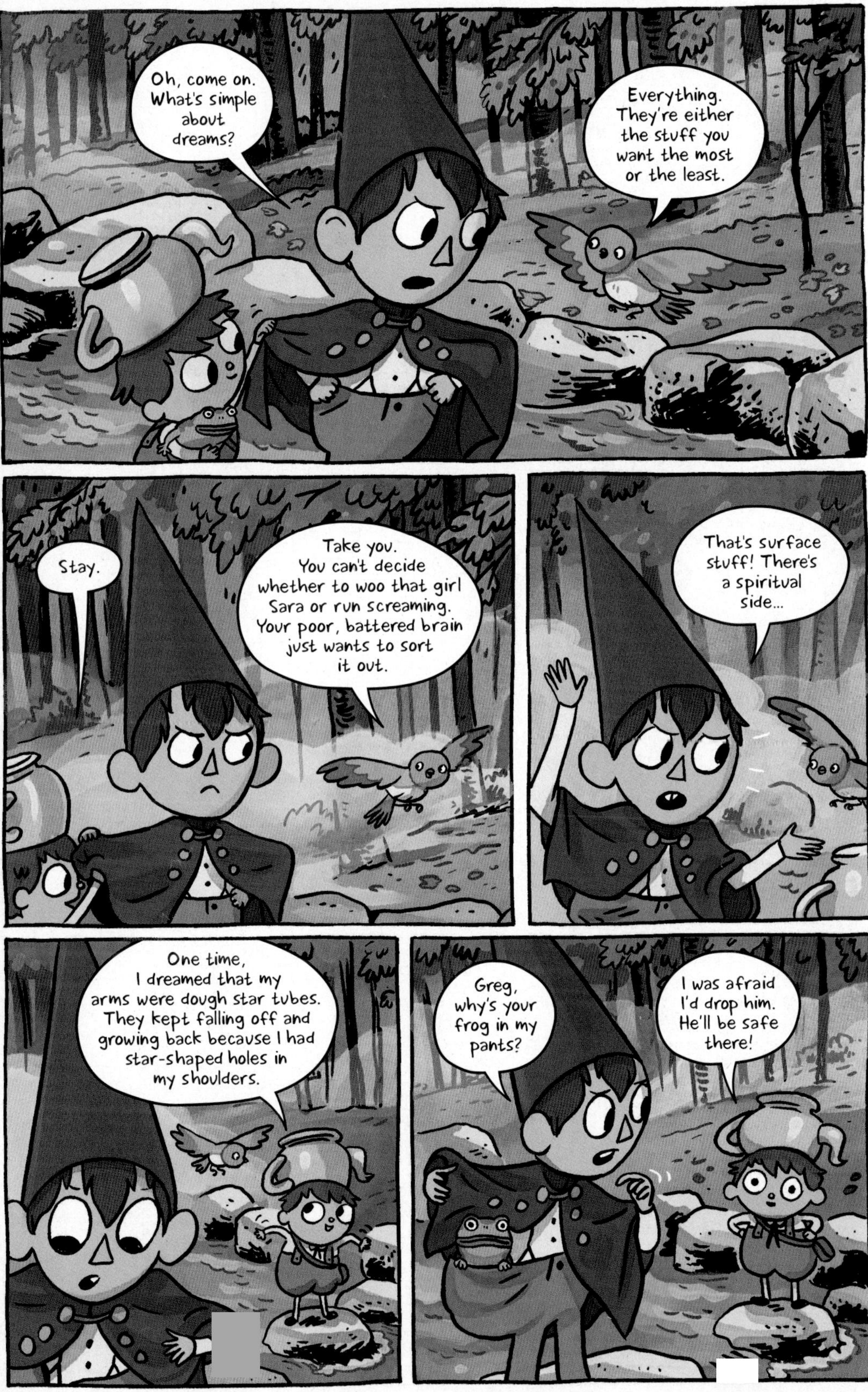

Oh, come on. What's simple about dreams?
Everything. They're either the stuff you want the most or the least.
Stay.
Take you. You can't decide whether to woo that girl Sara or run screaming. Your poor, battered brain just wants to sort it out.
That's surface stuff! There's a spiritual side...
One time, I dreamed that my arms were dough star tubes. They kept falling off and growing back because I had star-shaped holes in my shoulders.
Greg, why's your frog in my pants?
I was afraid I'd drop him. He'll be safe there!

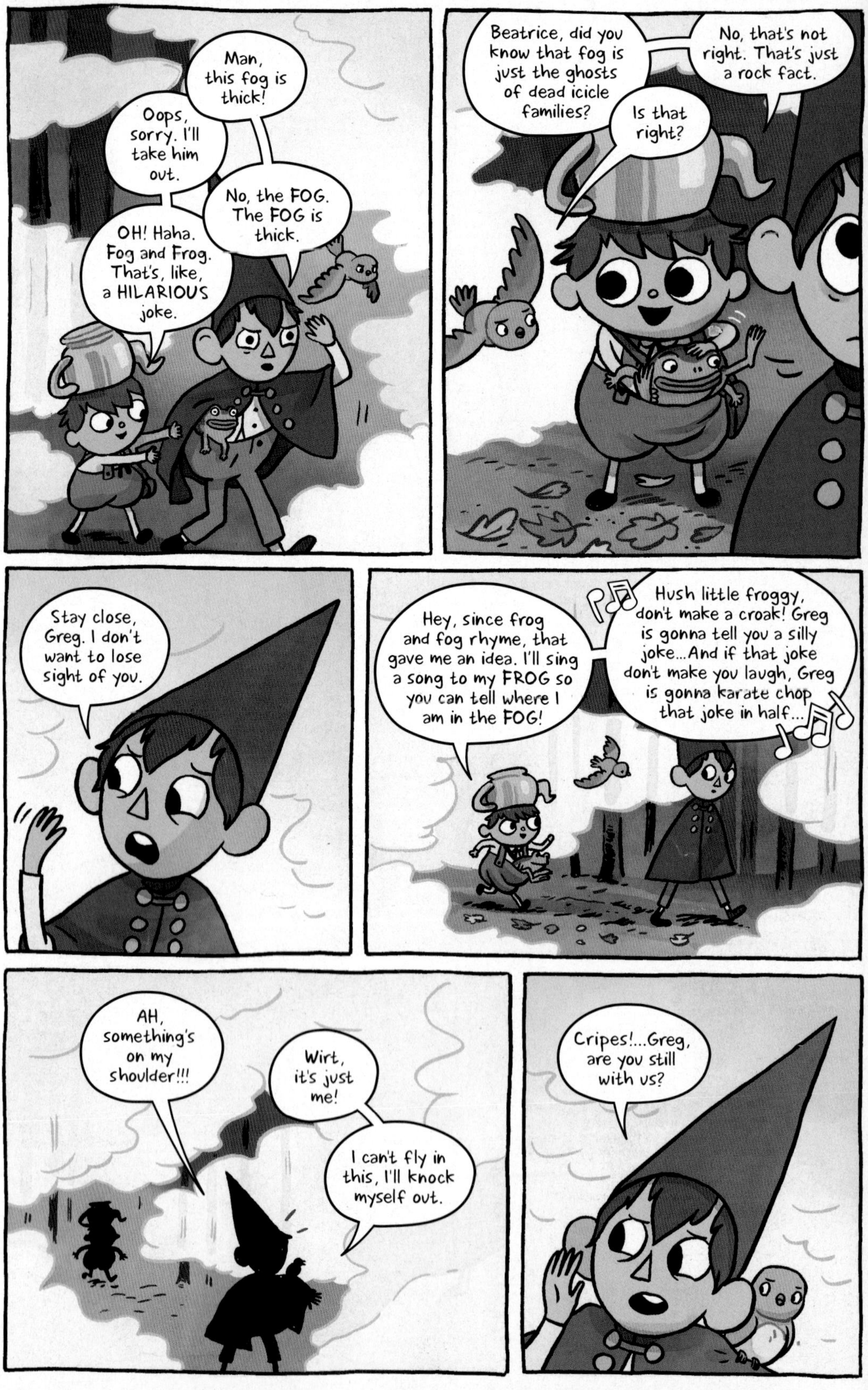
Man, this fog is thick!
Oops, sorry. I'll take him out.
No, the FOG. The FOG is thick.
OH! Haha. Fog and Frog. That's, like, a HILARIOUS joke.
Beatrice, did you know that fog is just the ghosts of dead icicle families?
Is that right?
No, that's not right. That's just a rock fact.
Stay close, Greg. I don't want to lose sight of you.
Hey, since frog and fog rhyme, that gave me an idea. I'll sing a song to my FROG so you can tell where I am in the FOG!
Hush little froggy, don't make a croak! Greg is gonna tell you a silly joke...And if that joke don't make you laugh, Greg is gonna karate chop that joke in half...
AH, something's on my shoulder!!!
Wirt, it's just me!
I can't fly in this, I'll knock myself out.
Cripes!...Greg, are you still with us?

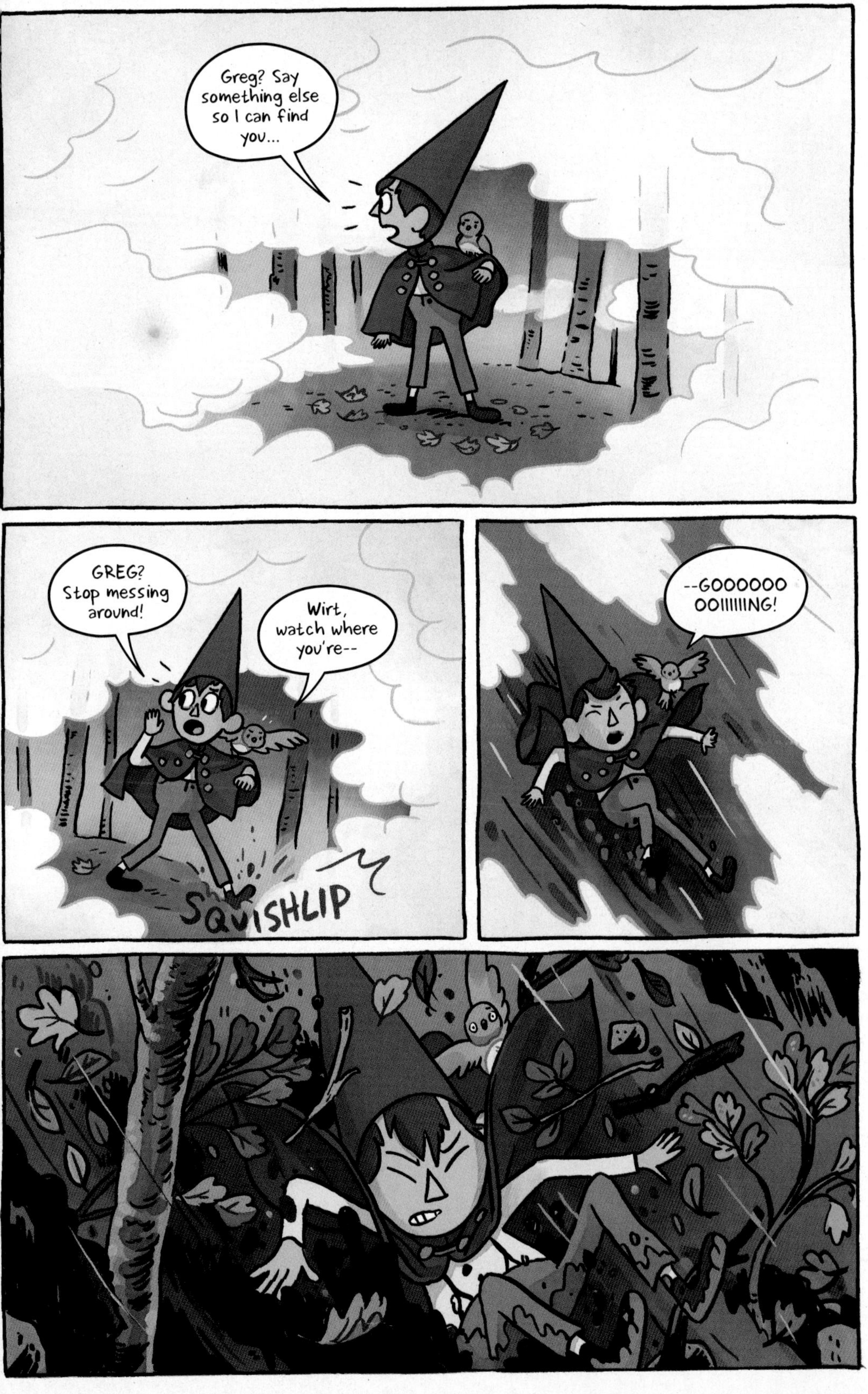
Greg? Say something else so I can find you...
GREG? Stop messing around!
Wirt, watch where you're--
SQUISHLIP
--GOOOOOO OOIIIIIING!

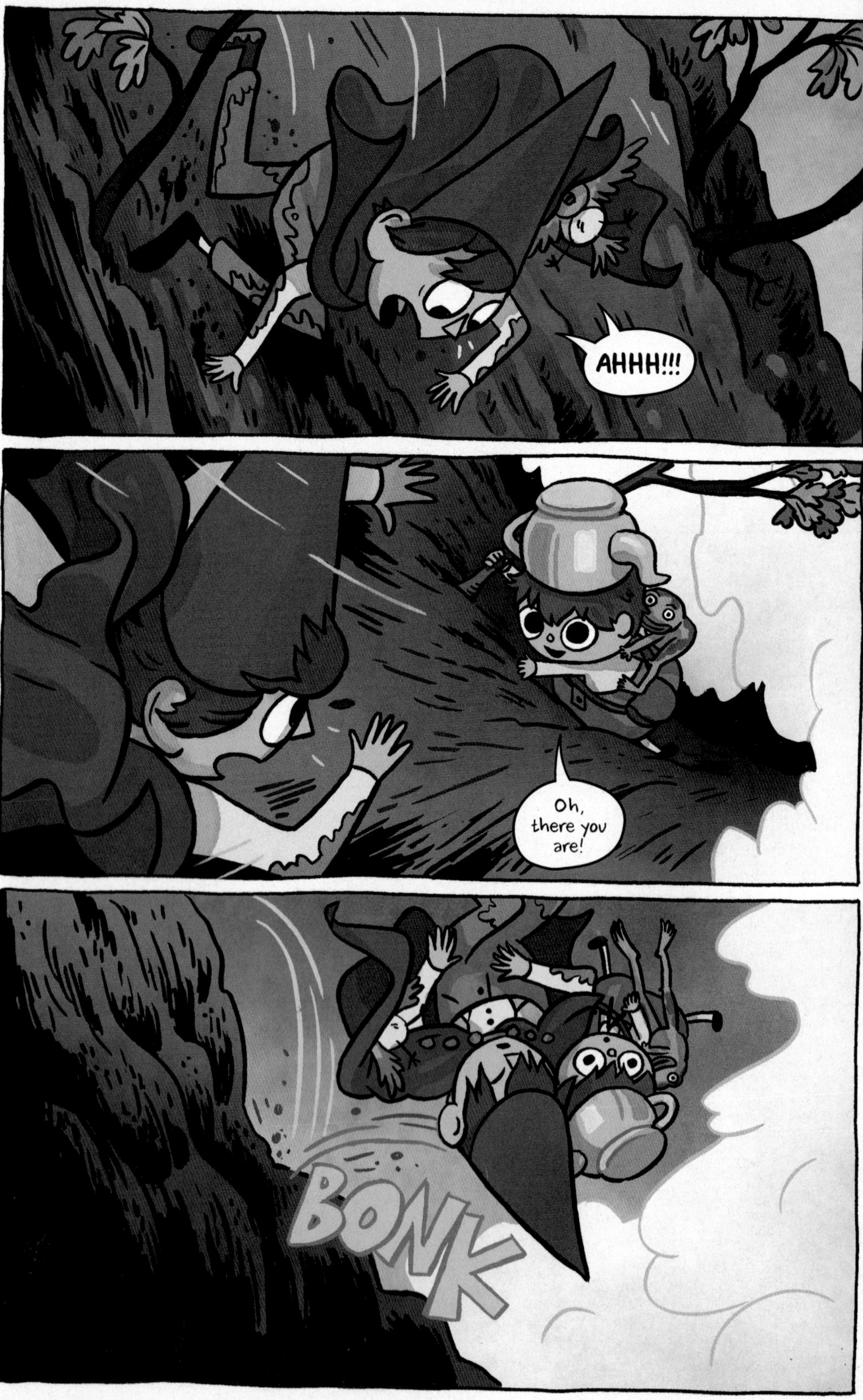
AHHH!!!
Oh, there you are!
BONK

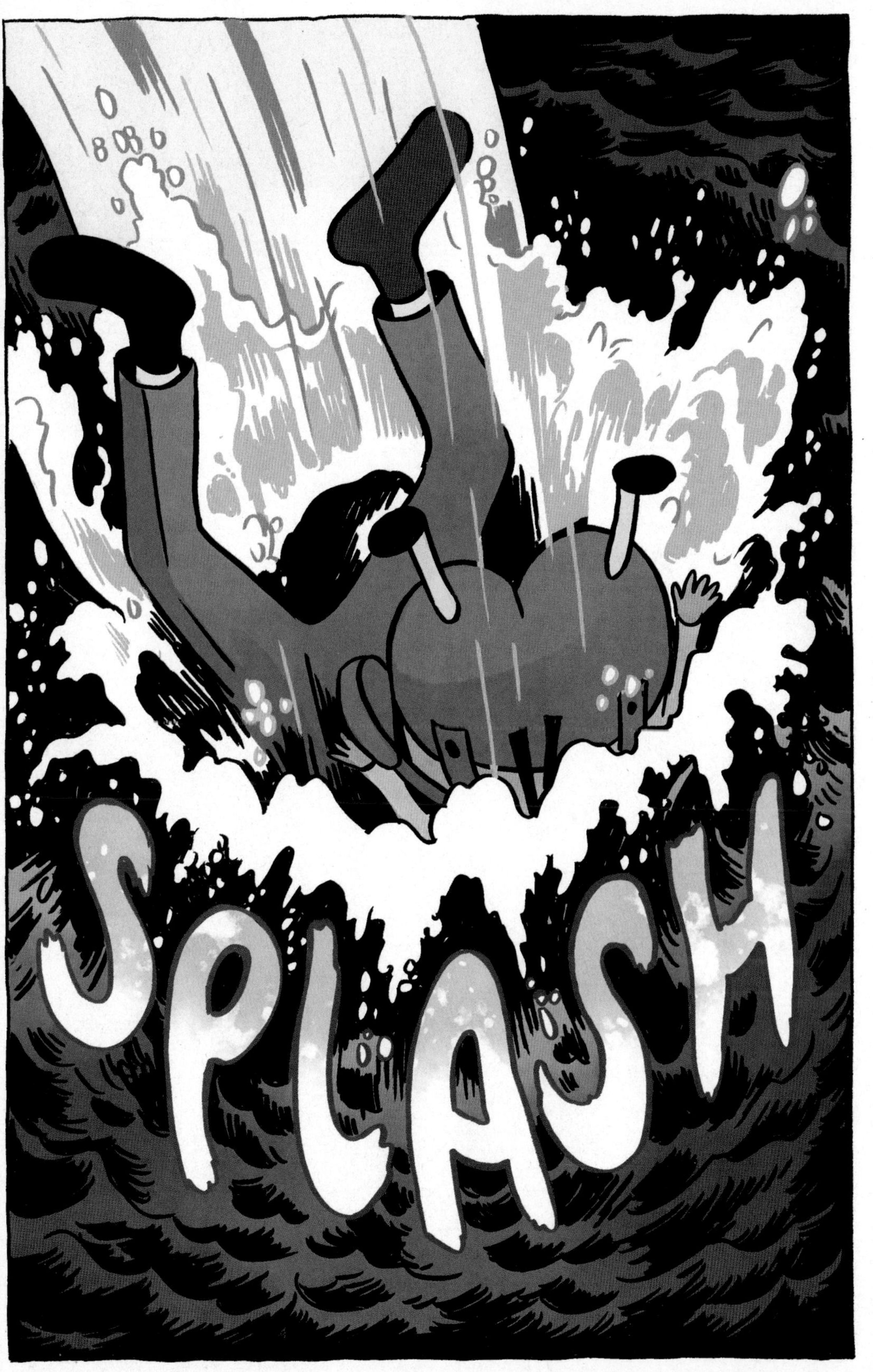
SPLASH

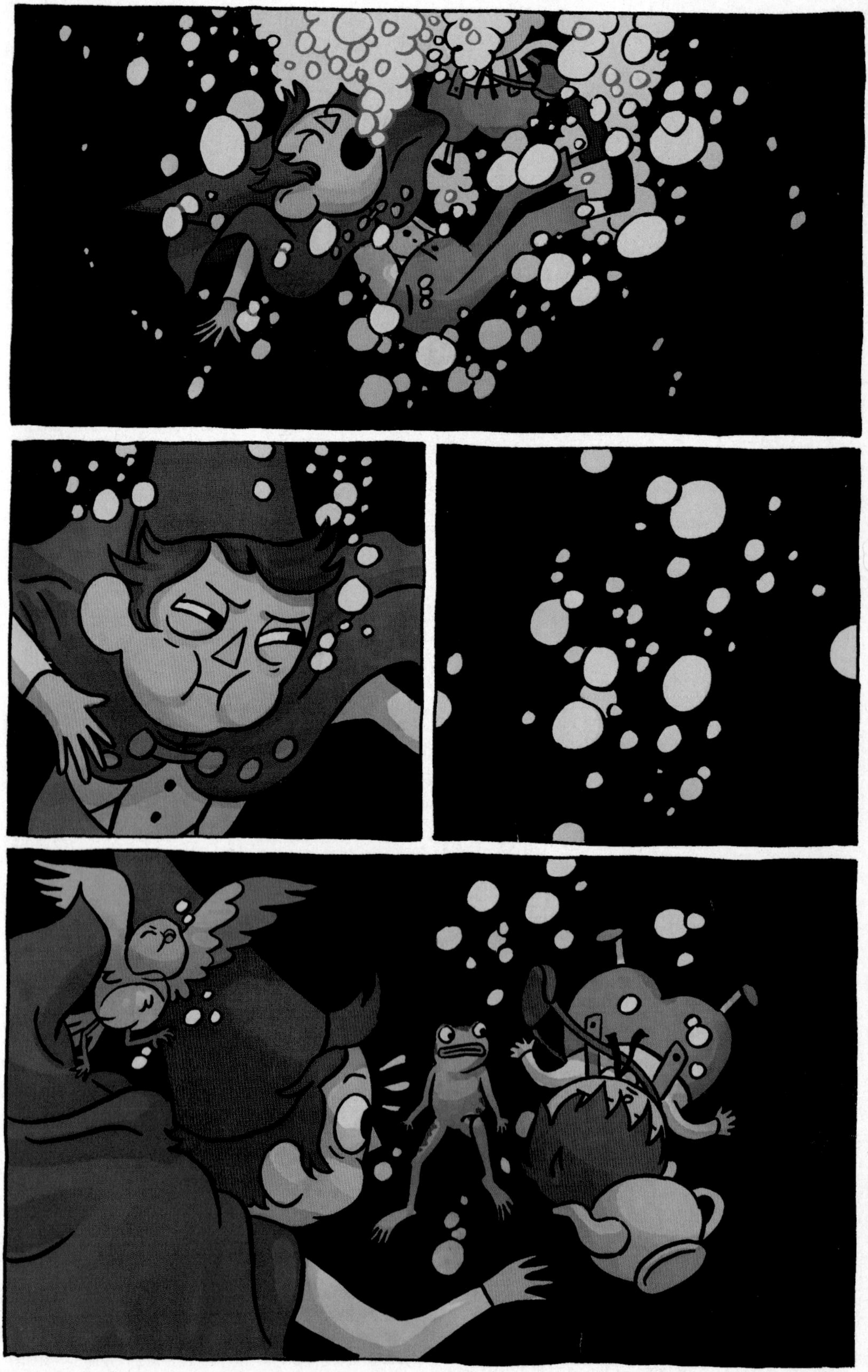

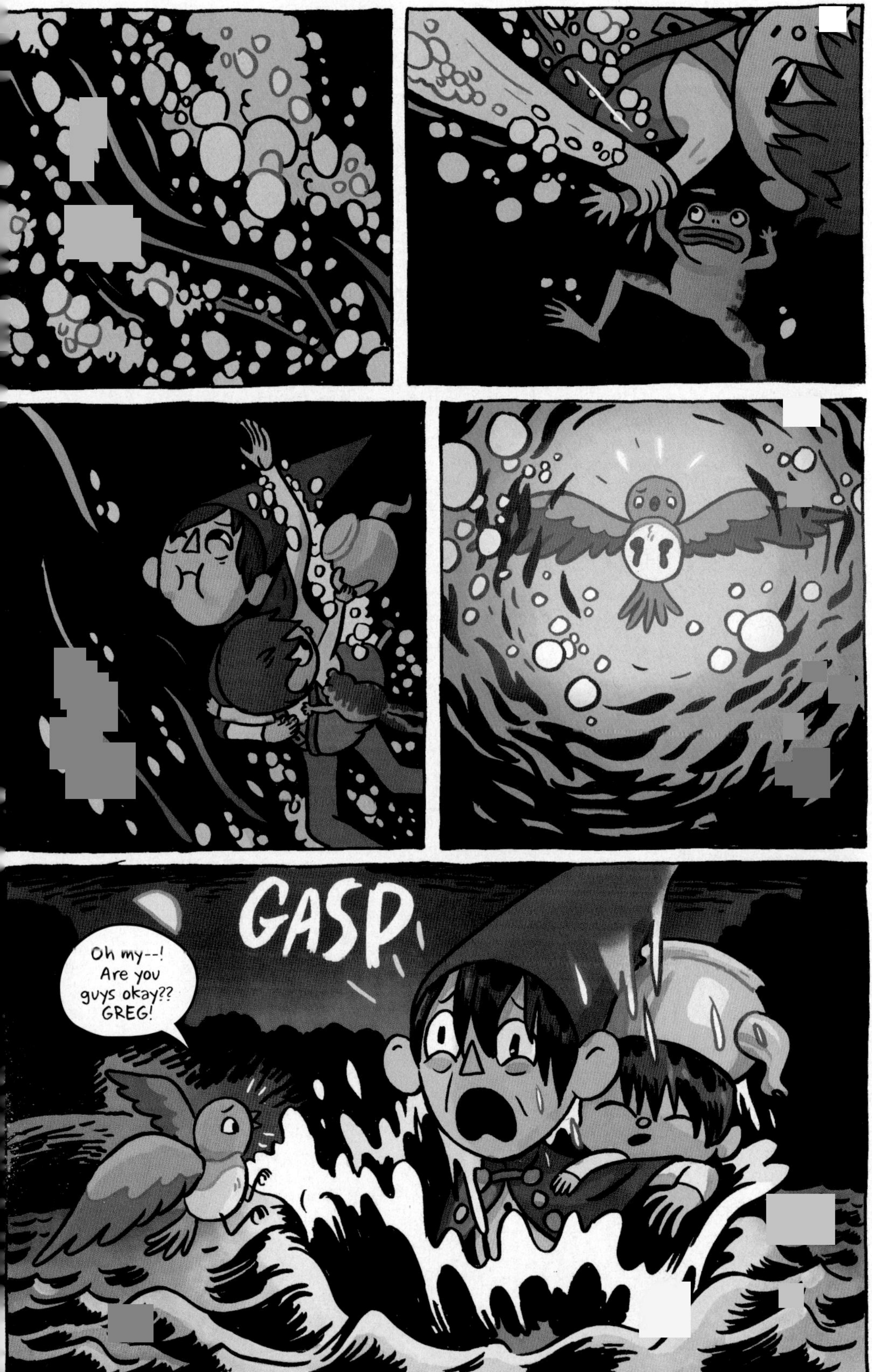
GASP
Oh my--! Are you guys okay?? GREG!

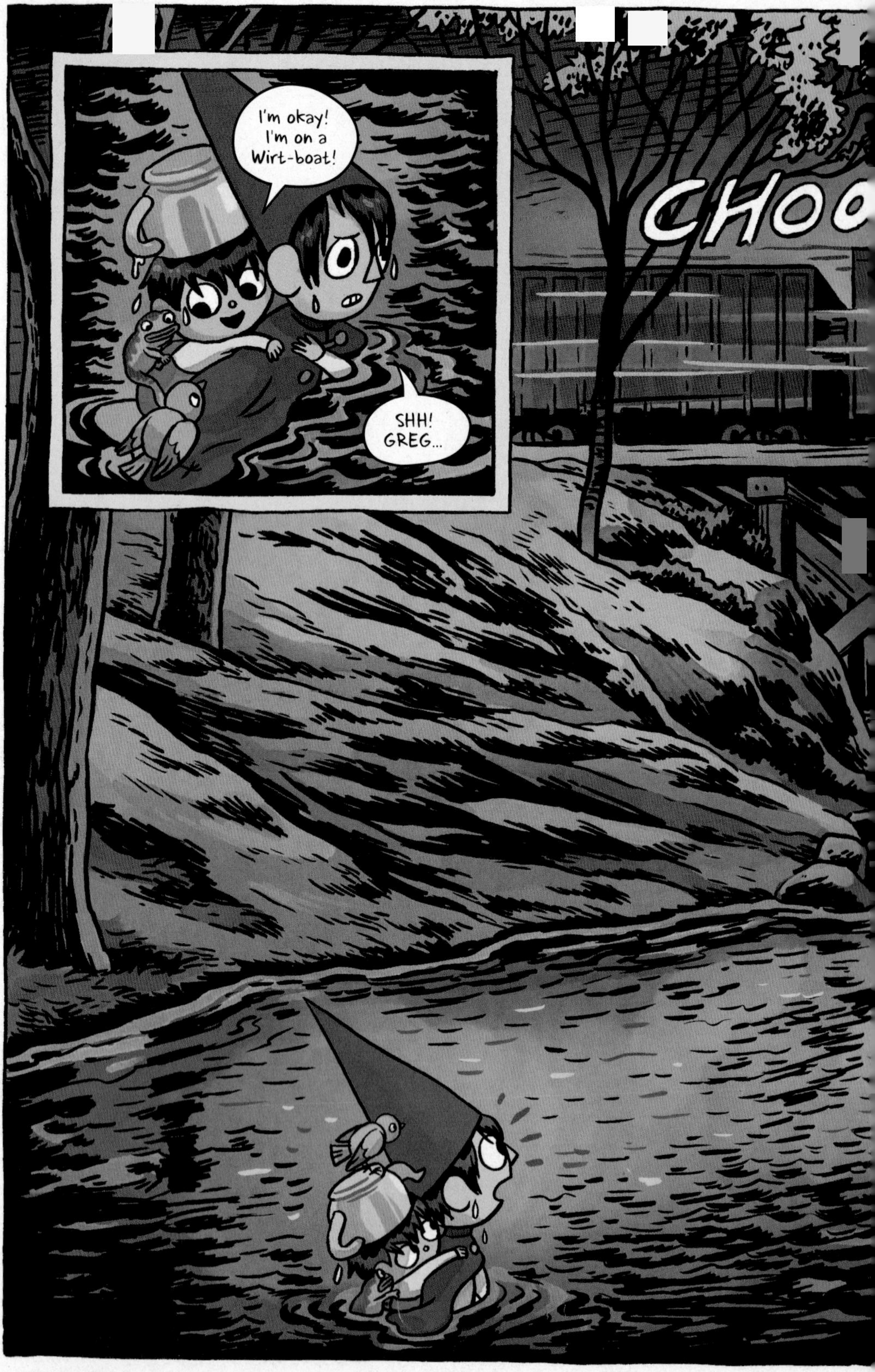
I'm okay! I'm on a Wirt-boat!
SHH! GREG...
CHOO

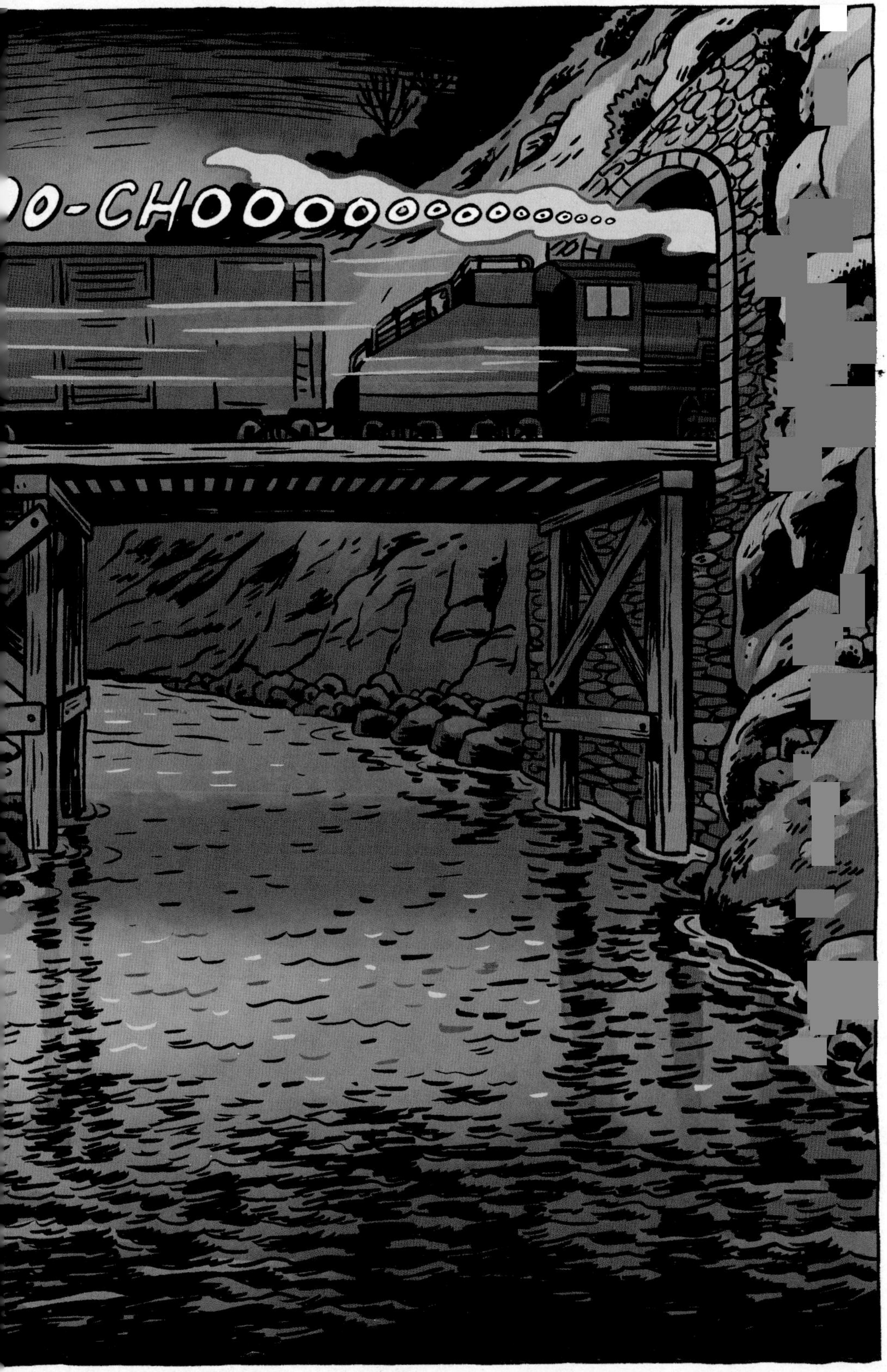
O-CHOOOOOOOOOOOO...

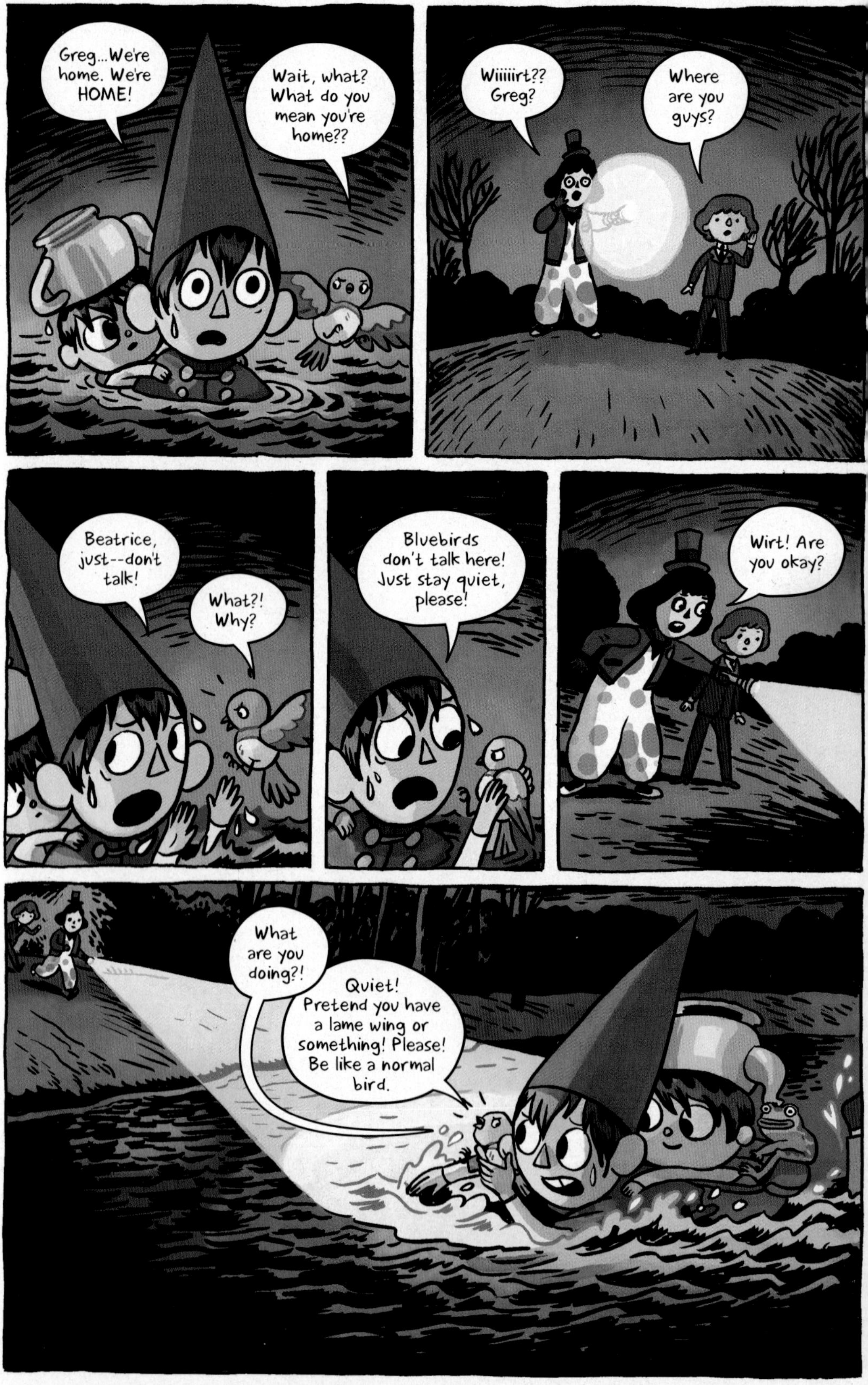
Greg...We're home. We're HOME!
Wait, what? What do you mean you're home??
Wiiiiirt?? Greg?
Where are you guys?
Beatrice, just--don't talk!
What?! Why?
Bluebirds don't talk here! Just stay quiet, please!
Wirt! Are you okay?
What are you doing?!
Quiet! Pretend you have a lame wing or something! Please! Be like a normal bird.

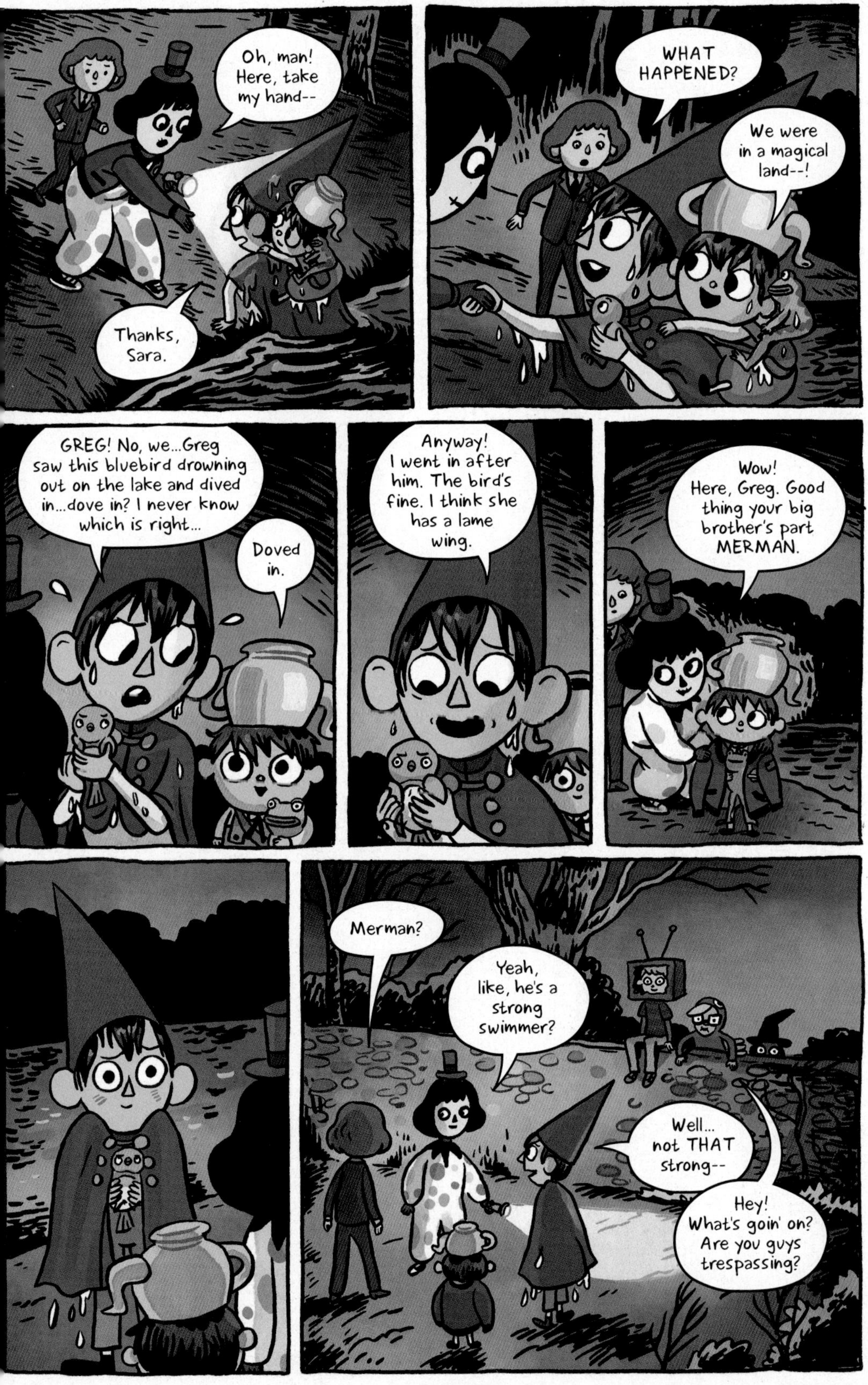
Oh, man! Here, take my hand--
Thanks, Sara.
WHAT HAPPENED?
We were in a magical land--!
GREG! No, we...Greg saw this bluebird drowning out on the lake and dived in...dove in? I never know which is right...
Doved in.
Anyway! I went in after him. The bird's fine. I think she has a lame wing.
Wow! Here, Greg. Good thing your big brother's part MERMAN.
Merman?
Yeah, like, he's a strong swimmer?
Well... not THAT strong--
Hey! What's goin' on? Are you guys trespassing?

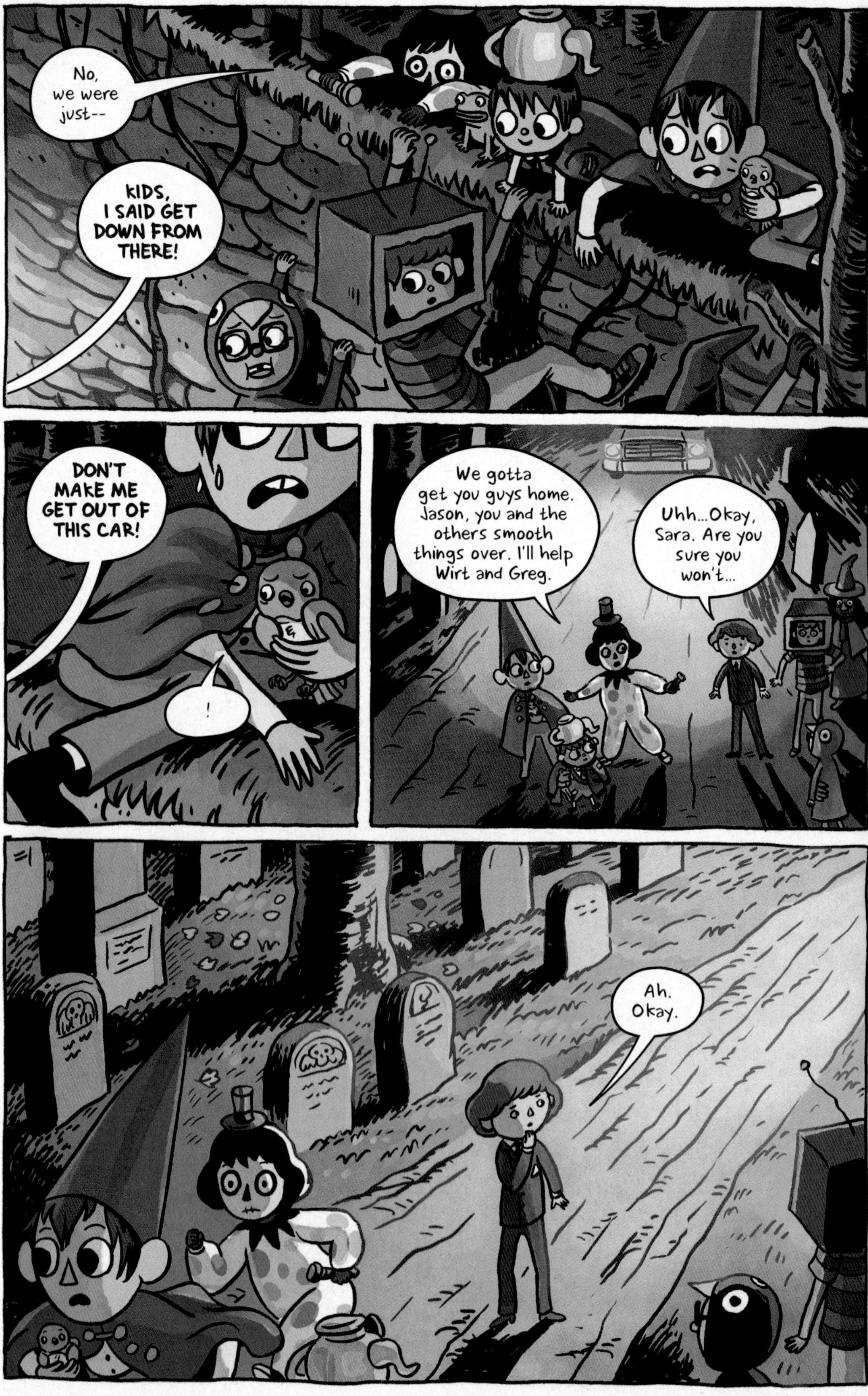
No, we were just--
KIDS, I SAID GET DOWN FROM THERE!
DON'T MAKE ME GET OUT OF THIS CAR!
!
We gotta get you guys home. Jason, you and the others smooth things over. I'll help Wirt and Greg.
Uhh...Okay, Sara. Are you sure you won't...
Ah. Okay.

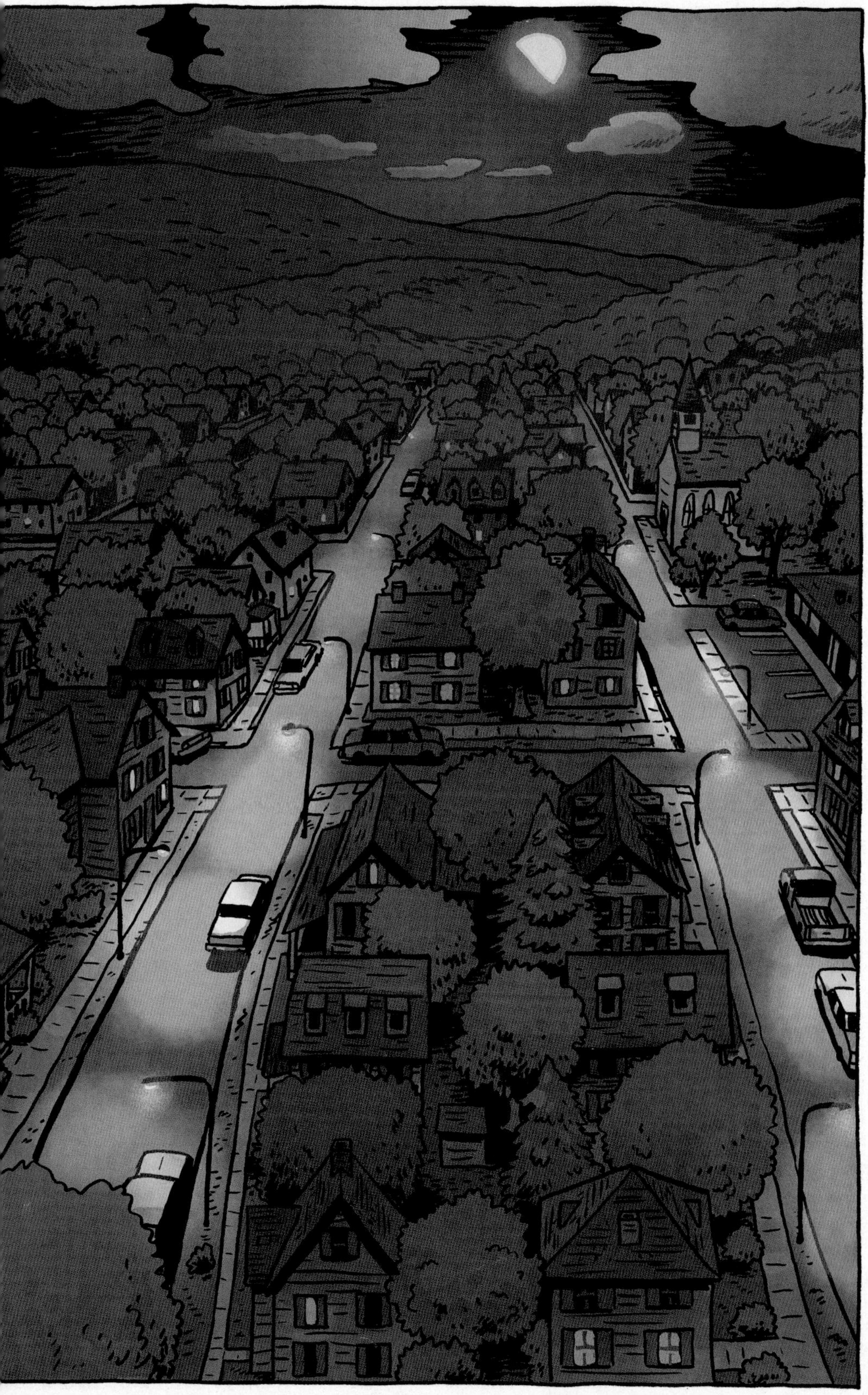

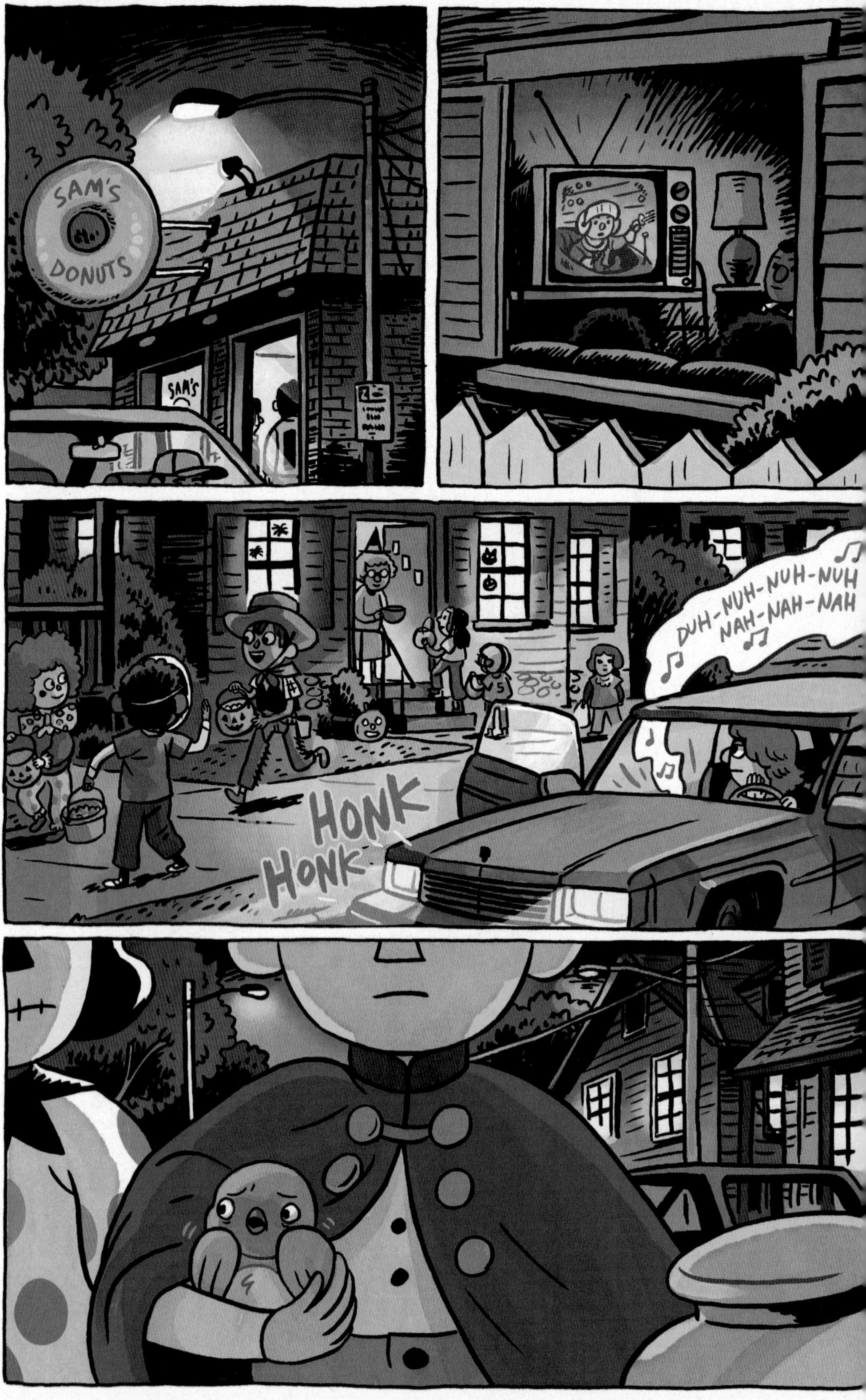
SAM'S DONUTS
SAM'S
DUH-NUH-NUH-NUH NAH-NAH-NAH
HONK HONK

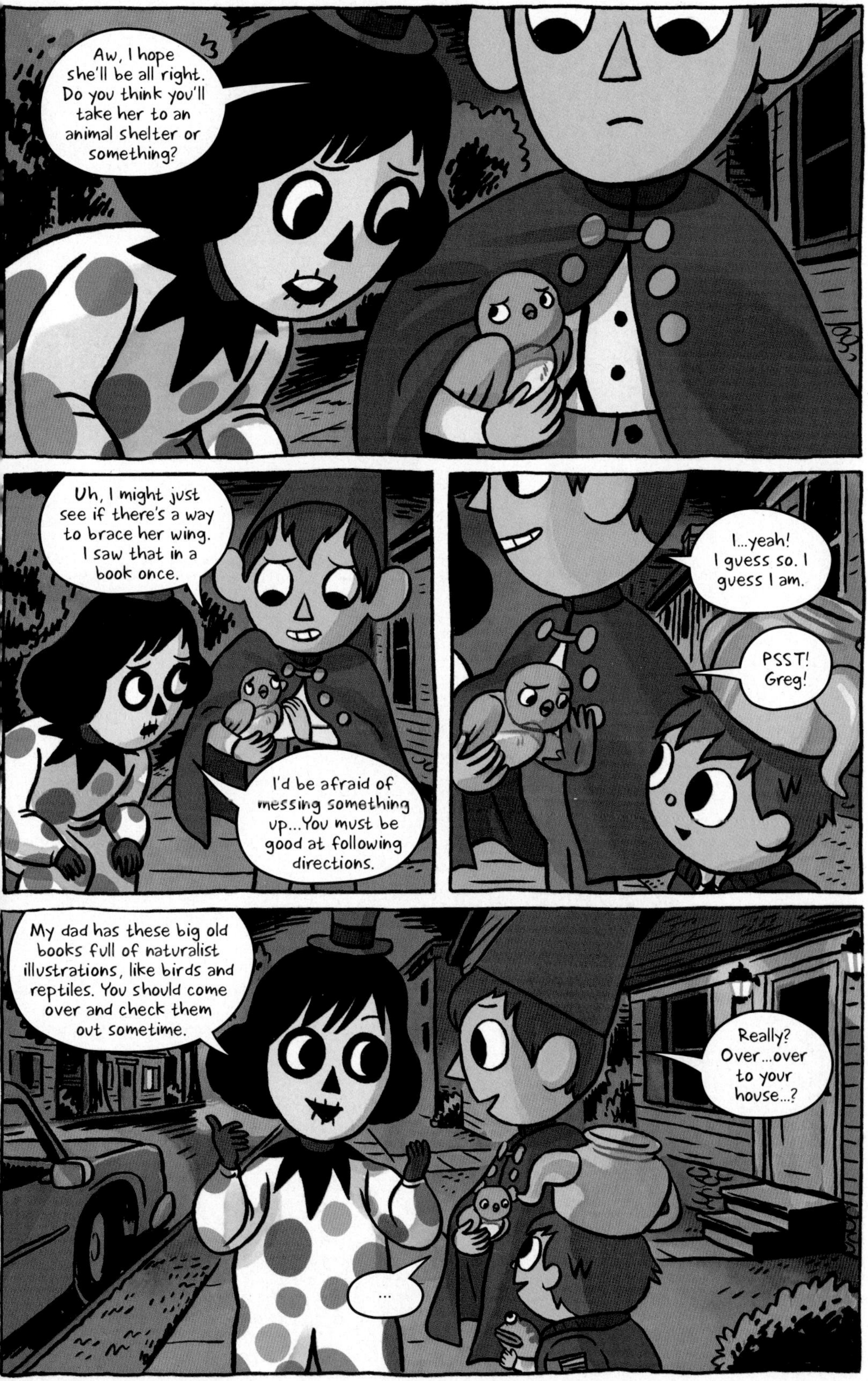
Aw, I hope she'll be all right. Do you think you'll take her to an animal shelter or something?
Uh, I might just see if there's a way to brace her wing. I saw that in a book once.
I'd be afraid of messing something up... You must be good at following directions.
I...yeah! I guess so. I guess I am.
PSST! Greg!
My dad has these big old books full of naturalist illustrations, like birds and reptiles. You should come over and check them out sometime.
Really? Over...over to your house...?
...

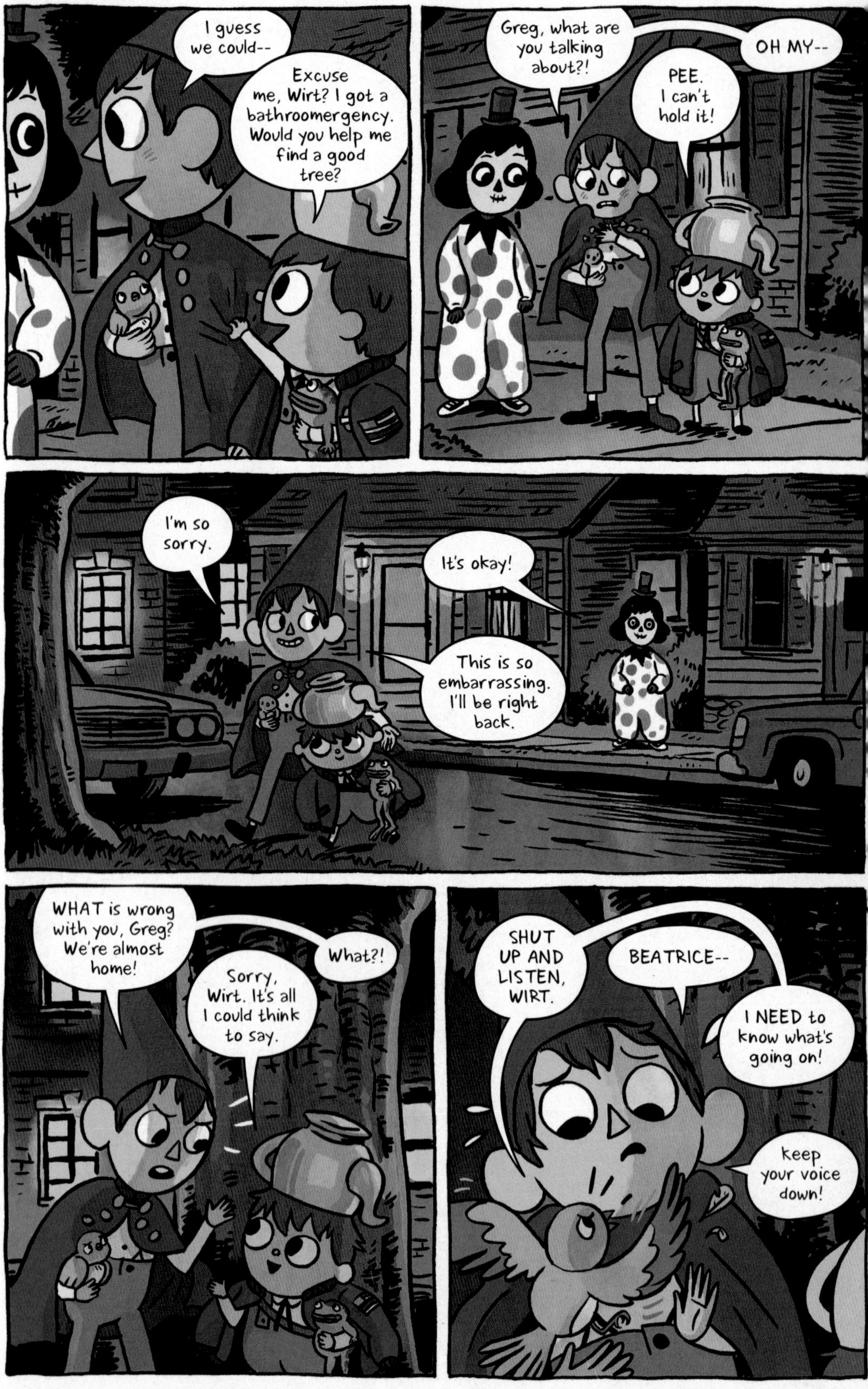
I guess we could--
Excuse me, Wirt? I got a bathroomergency. Would you help me find a good tree?
Greg, what are you talking about?!
OH MY--
PEE. I can't hold it!
I'm so sorry.
It's okay!
This is so embarrassing. I'll be right back.
WHAT is wrong with you, Greg? We're almost home!
What?!
Sorry, Wirt. It's all I could think to say.
SHUT UP AND LISTEN, WIRT.
BEATRICE--
I NEED to know what's going on!
Keep your voice down!

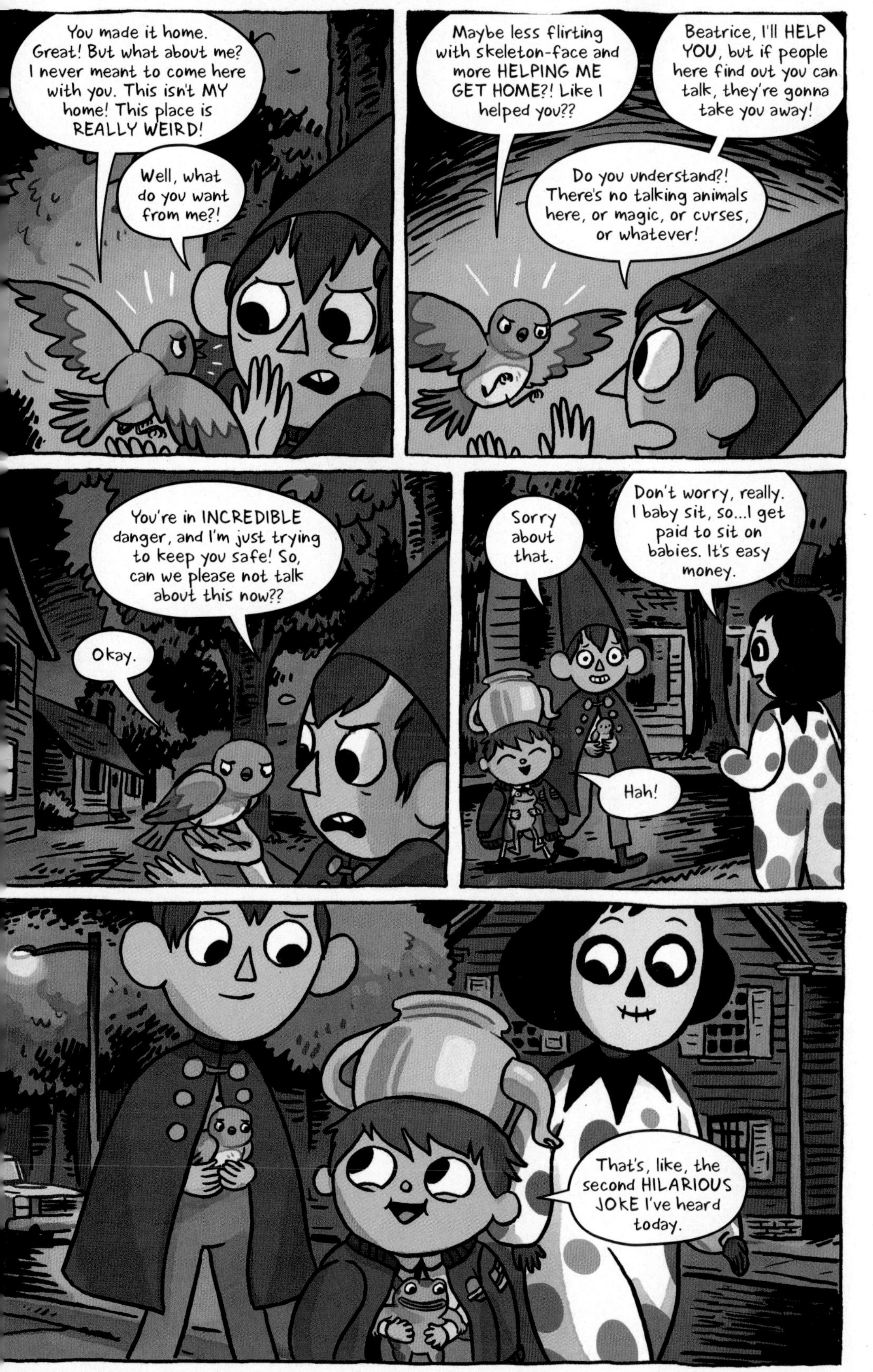
You made it home. Great! But what about me? I never meant to come here with you. This isn't MY home! This place is REALLY WEIRD!
Well, what do you want from me?!
Maybe less flirting with skeleton-face and more HELPING ME GET HOME?! Like I helped you??
Beatrice, I'll HELP YOU, but if people here find out you can talk, they're gonna take you away!
Do you understand?! There's no talking animals here, or magic, or curses, or whatever!
You're in INCREDIBLE danger, and I'm just trying to keep you safe! So, can we please not talk about this now??
Okay.
Sorry about that.
Don't worry, really. I baby sit, so...I get paid to sit on babies. It's easy money.
Hah!
That's, like, the second HILARIOUS JOKE I've heard today.

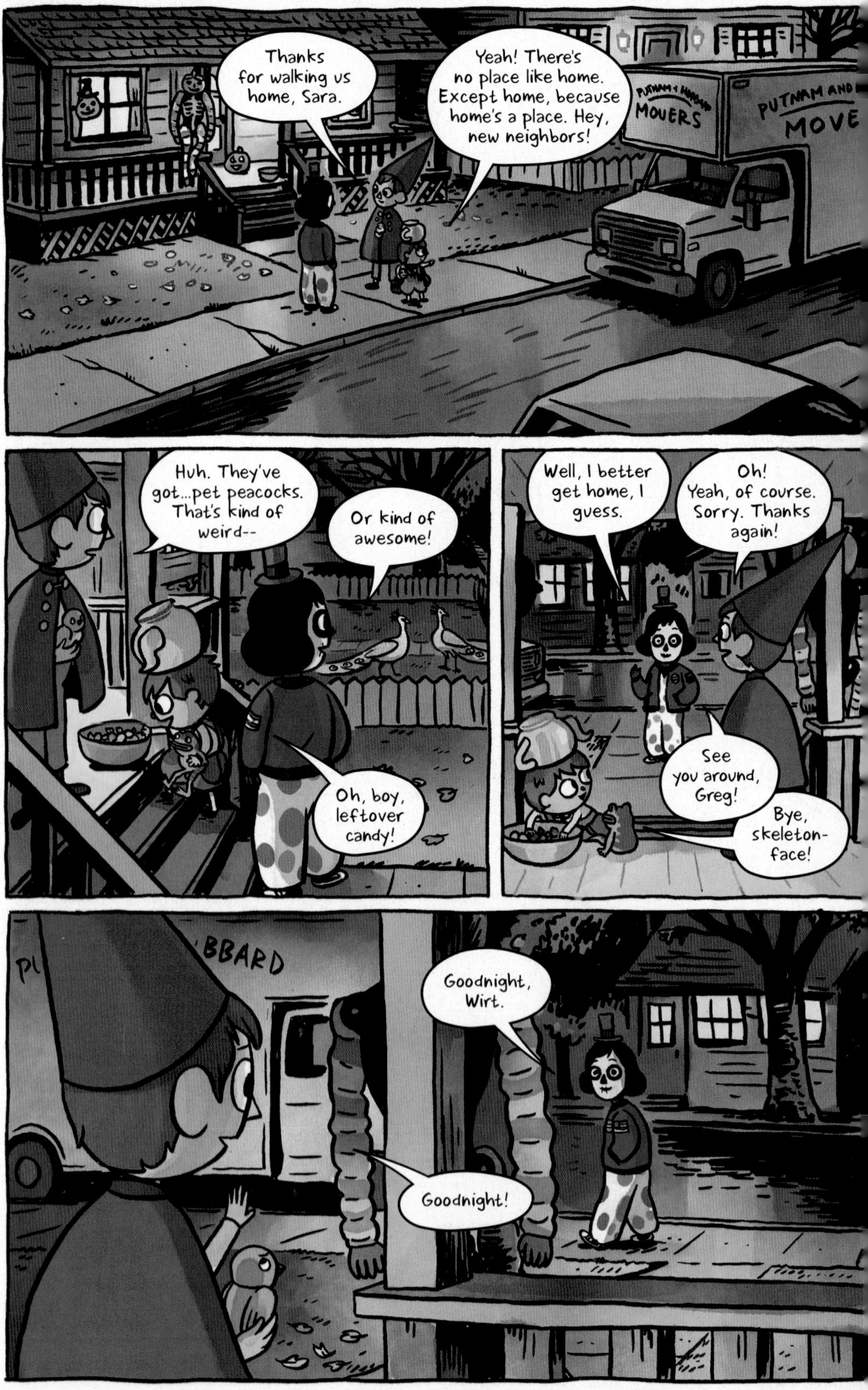
PUTNAM & HUBBARD MOVERS
Thanks for walking us home, Sara.
Yeah! There's no place like home. Except home, because home's a place. Hey, new neighbors!
PUTNAM AND HUBBARD MOVERS
Huh. They've got...pet peacocks. That's kind of weird--
Or kind of awesome!
Oh, boy, leftover candy!
Well, I better get home, I guess.
Oh! Yeah, of course. Sorry. Thanks again!
See you around, Greg!
Bye, skeleton-face!
BBARD
Goodnight, Wirt.
Goodnight!

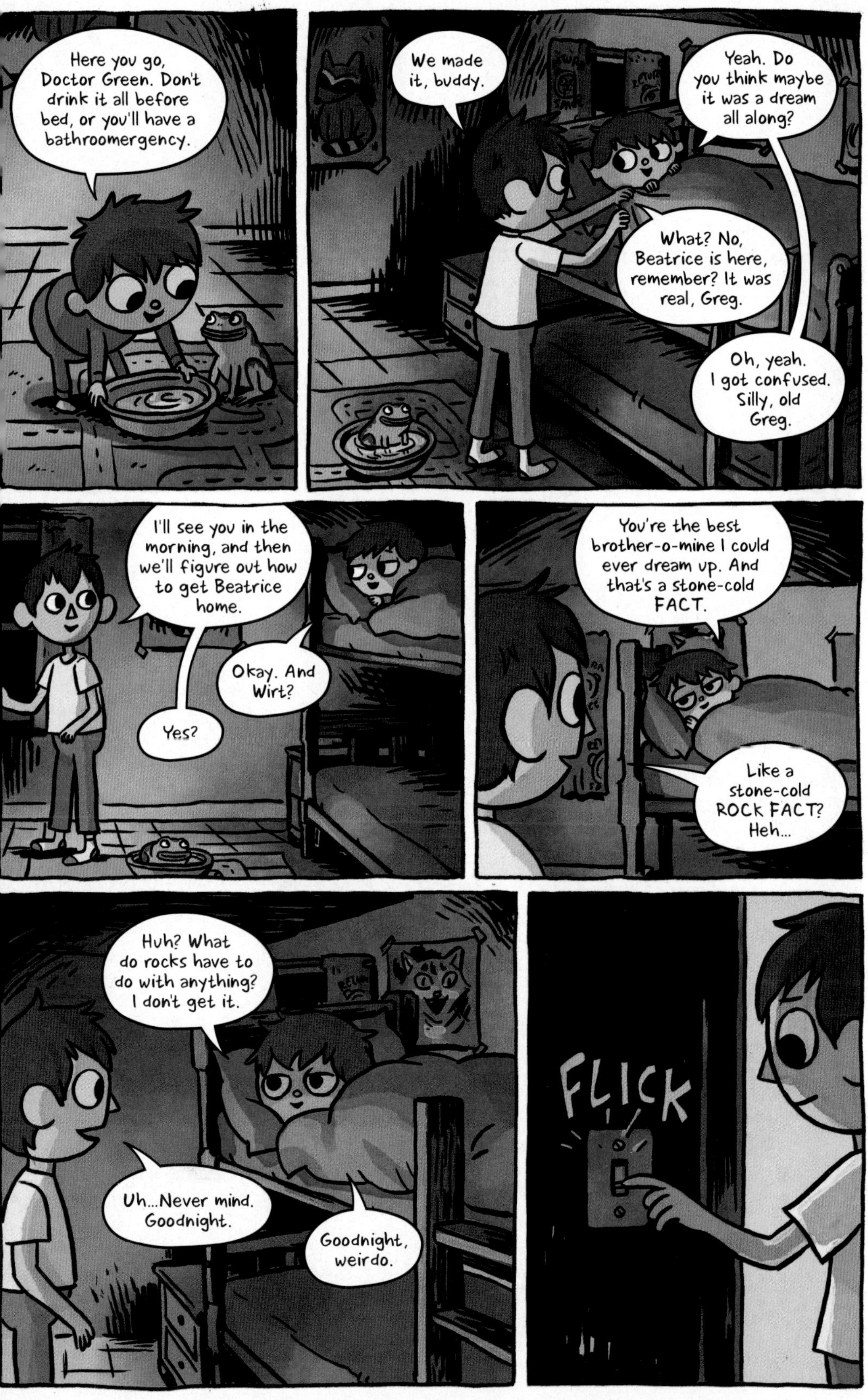
Here you go, Doctor Green. Don't drink it all before bed, or you'll have a bathroomergency.
We made it, buddy.
Yeah. Do you think maybe it was a dream all along?
What? No, Beatrice is here, remember? It was real, Greg.
Oh, yeah. I got confused. Silly, old Greg.
I'll see you in the morning, and then we'll figure out how to get Beatrice home.
Okay. And Wirt?
Yes?
You're the best brother-o-mine I could ever dream up. And that's a stone-cold FACT.
Like a stone-cold ROCK FACT? Heh...
Huh? What do rocks have to do with anything? I don't get it.
Uh...Never mind. Goodnight.
Goodnight, weirdo.
FLICK

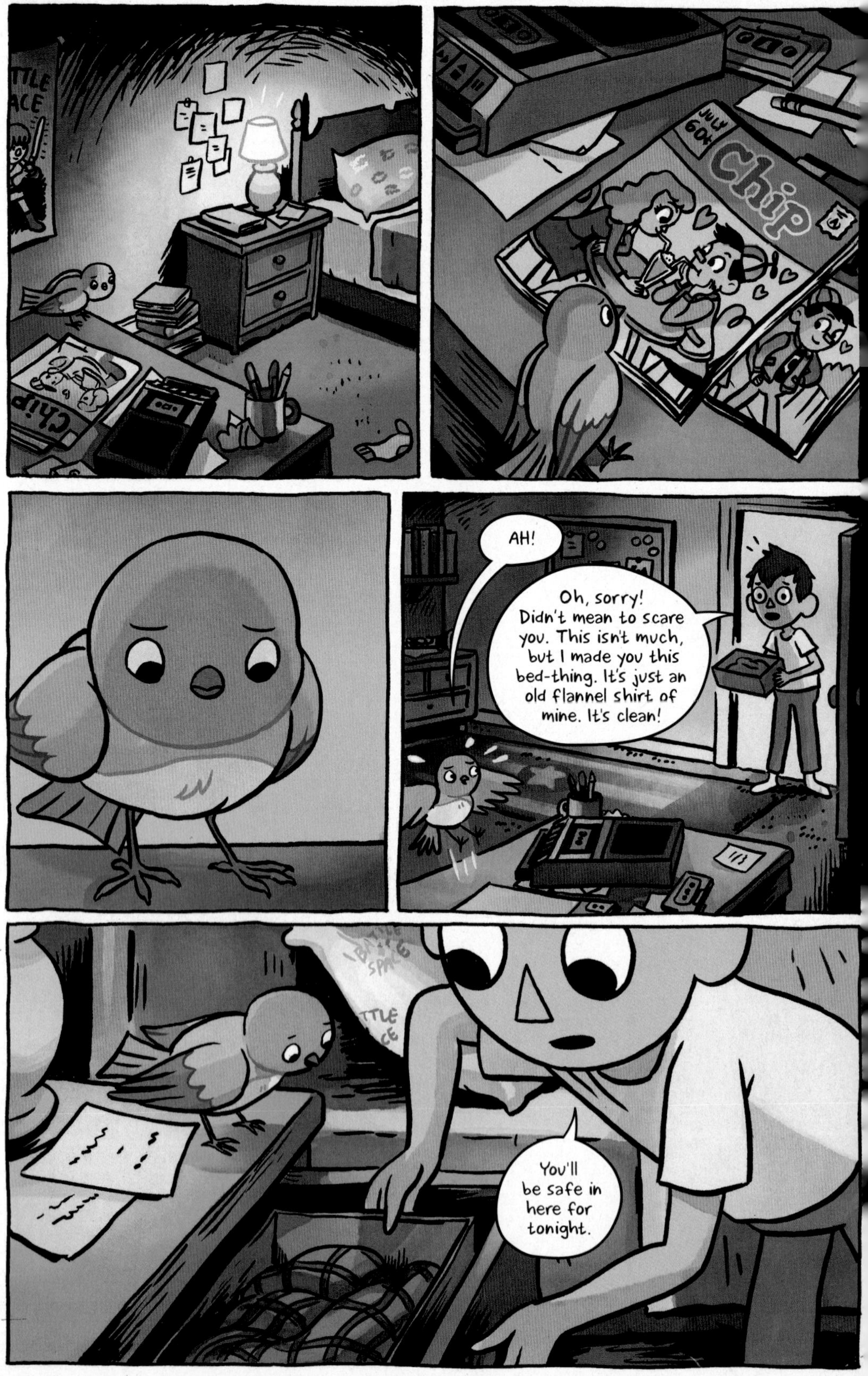
AH!
Oh, sorry! Didn't mean to scare you. This isn't much, but I made you this bed-thing. It's just an old flannel shirt of mine. It's clean!
You'll be safe in here for tonight.

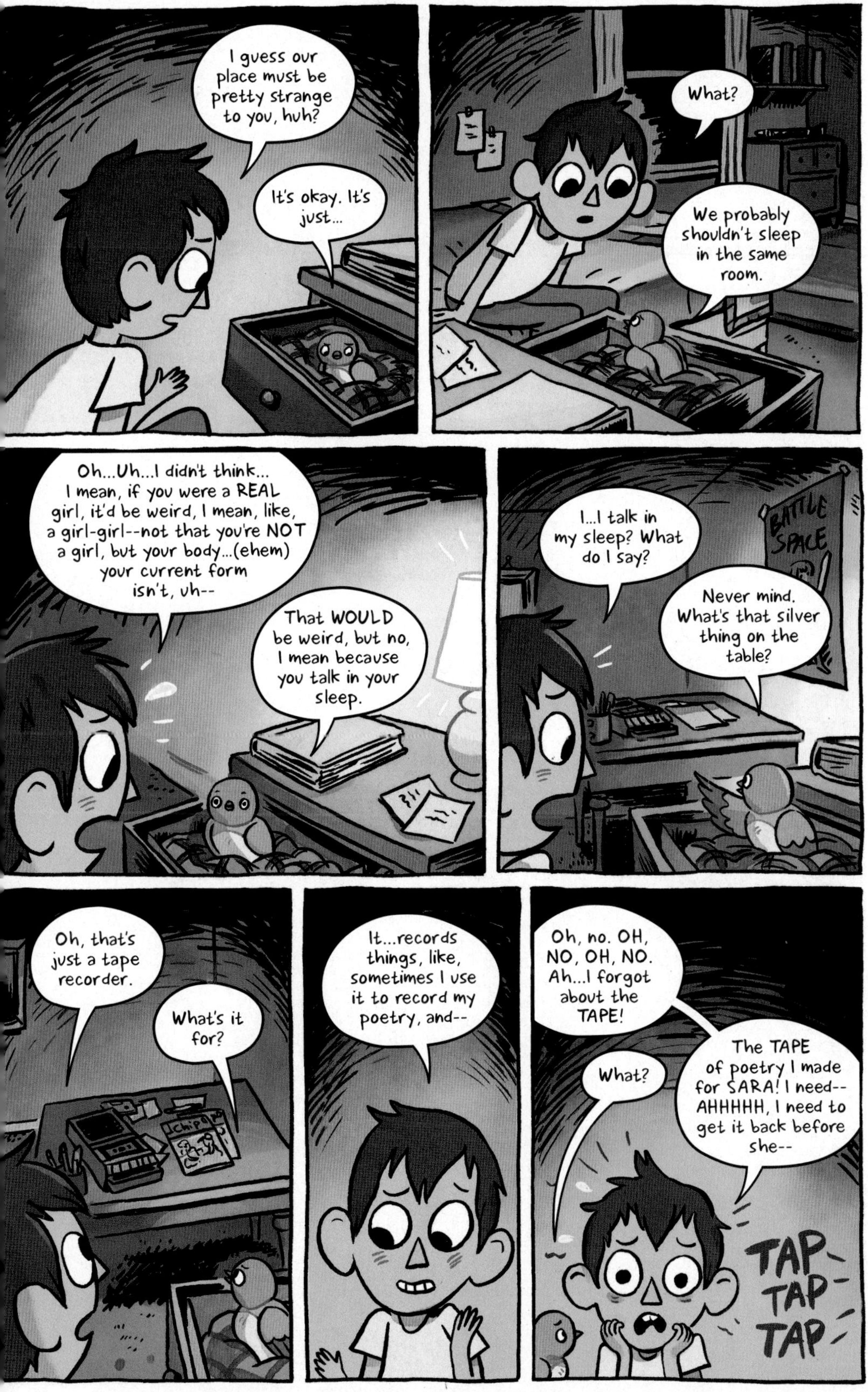
I guess our place must be pretty strange to you, huh?
It's okay. It's just...
What?
We probably shouldn't sleep in the same room.
Oh...Uh...I didn't think... I mean, if you were a REAL girl, it'd be weird, I mean, like, a girl-girl--not that you're NOT a girl, but your body...(ehem) your current form isn't, uh--
That WOULD be weird, but no, I mean because you talk in your sleep.
I...I talk in my sleep? What do I say?
BATTLE SPACE
Never mind. What's that silver thing on the table?
Oh, that's just a tape recorder.
What's it for?
It...records things, like, sometimes I use it to record my poetry, and--
Oh, no. OH, NO, OH, NO. Ah...I forgot about the TAPE!
What?
The TAPE of poetry I made for SARA! I need-- AHHHHH, I need to get it back before she--
TAP TAP TAP

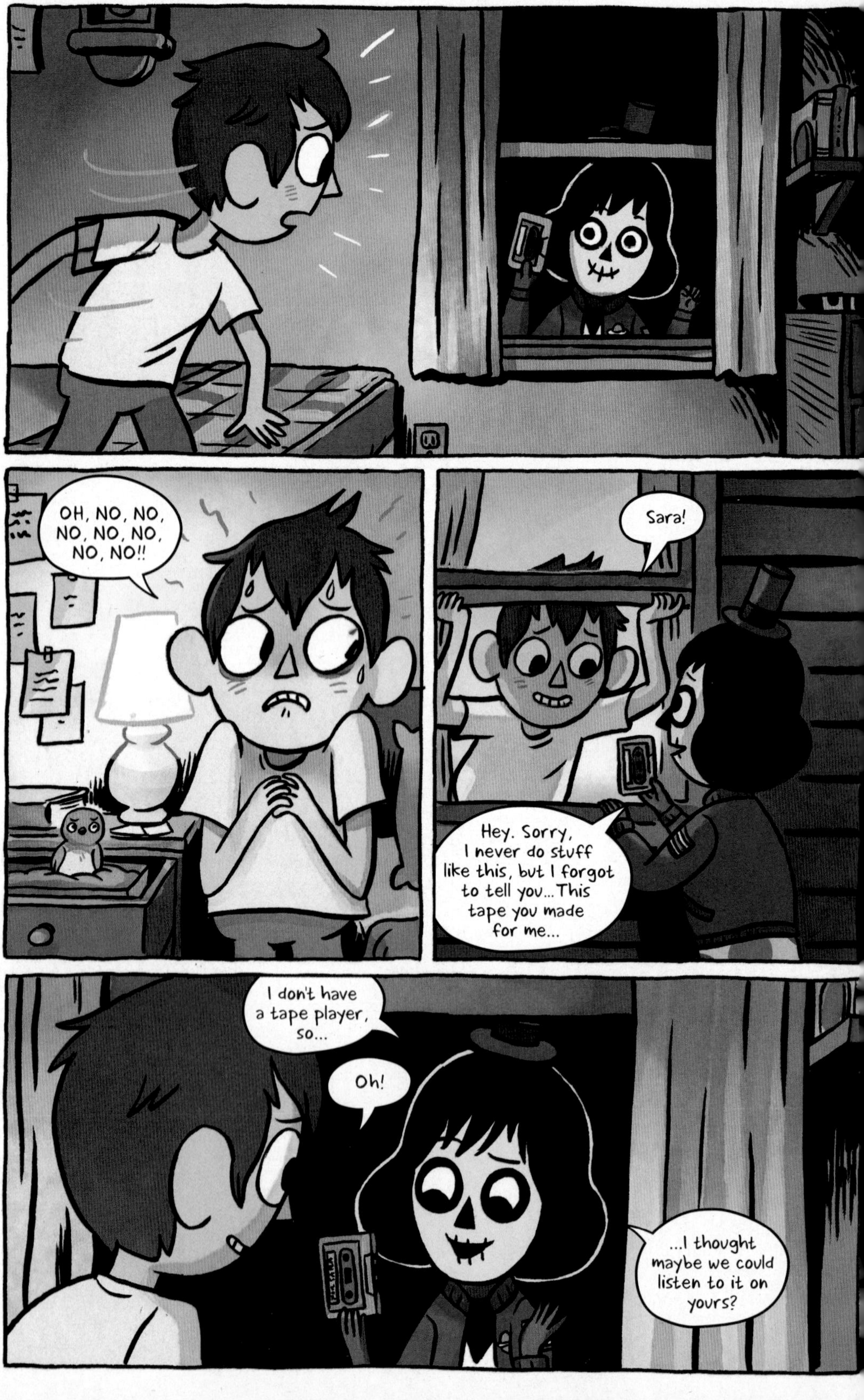
OH, NO, NO, NO, NO, NO, NO, NO!!
Sara!
Hey. Sorry, I never do stuff like this, but I forgot to tell you... This tape you made for me...
I don't have a tape player, so...
Oh!
...I thought maybe we could listen to it on yours?

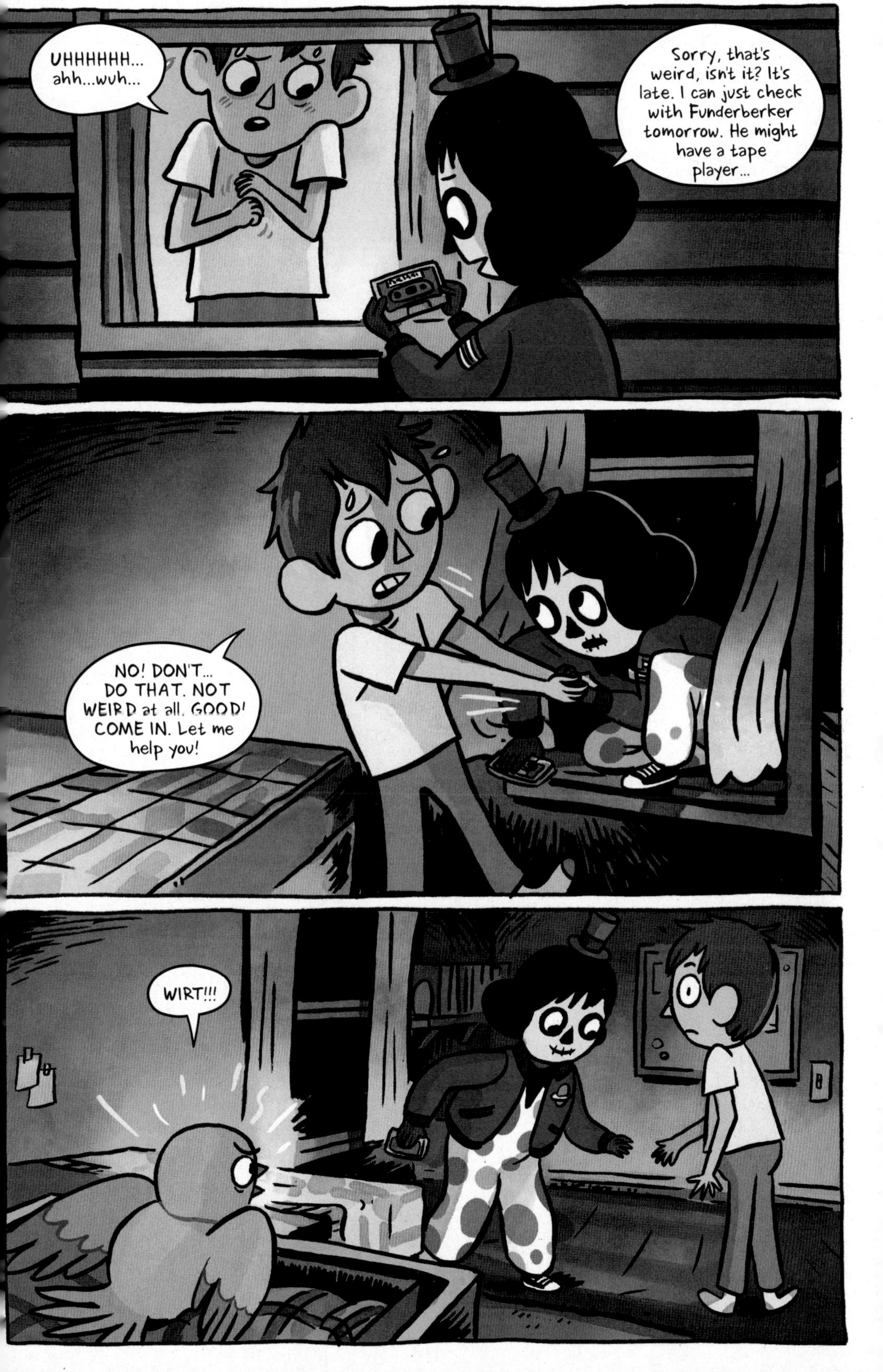
UHHHHHH... ahh...wuh...
Sorry, that's weird, isn't it? It's late. I can just check with Funderberker tomorrow. He might have a tape player...
NO! DON'T... DO THAT. NOT WEIRD at all. GOOD! COME IN. Let me help you!
WIRT!!!

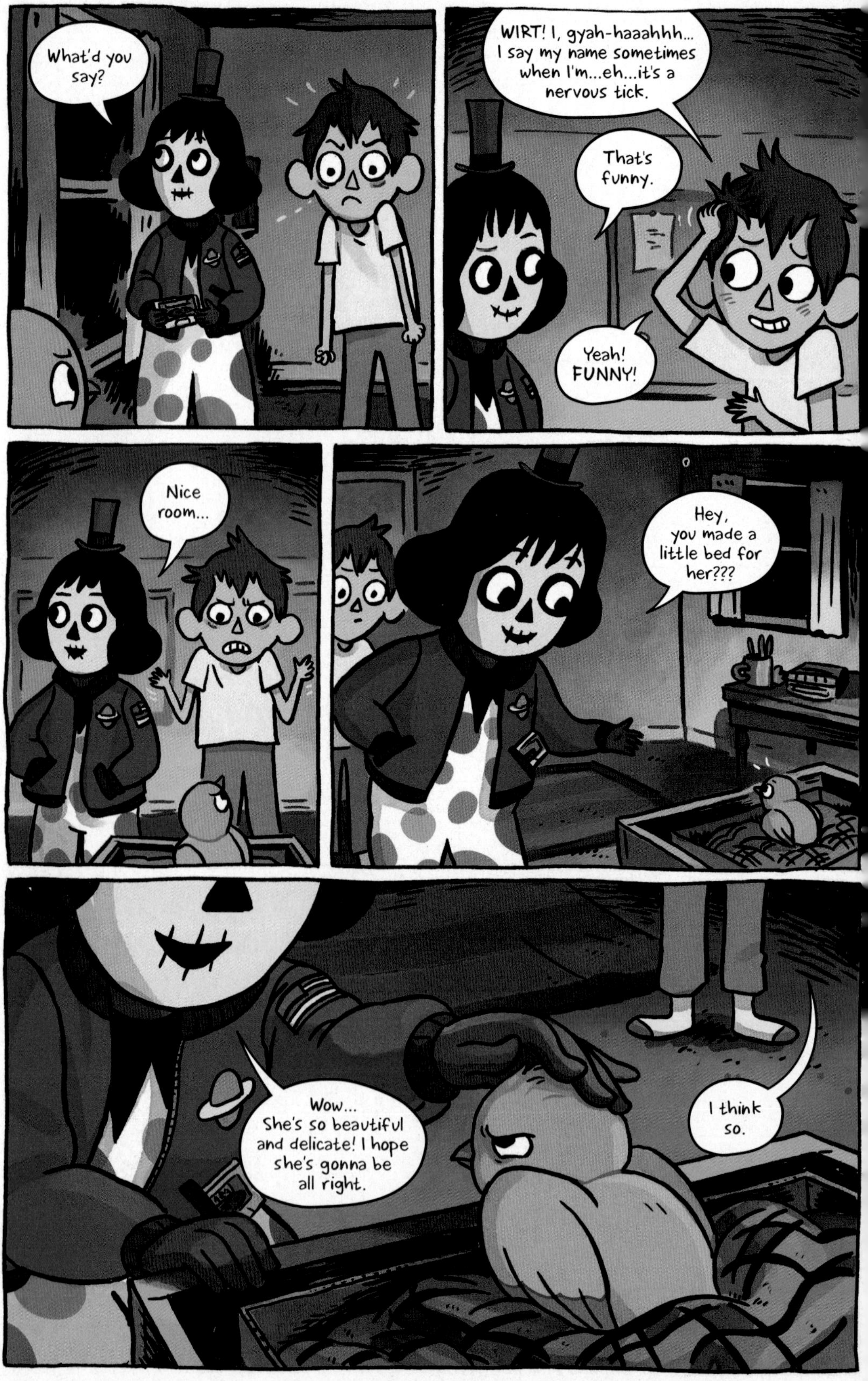
What'd you say?
WIRT! I, gyah-haaahhh... I say my name sometimes when I'm...eh...it's a nervous tick.
That's funny.
Yeah! FUNNY!
Nice room...
Hey, you made a little bed for her???
Wow... She's so beautiful and delicate! I hope she's gonna be all right.
I think so.

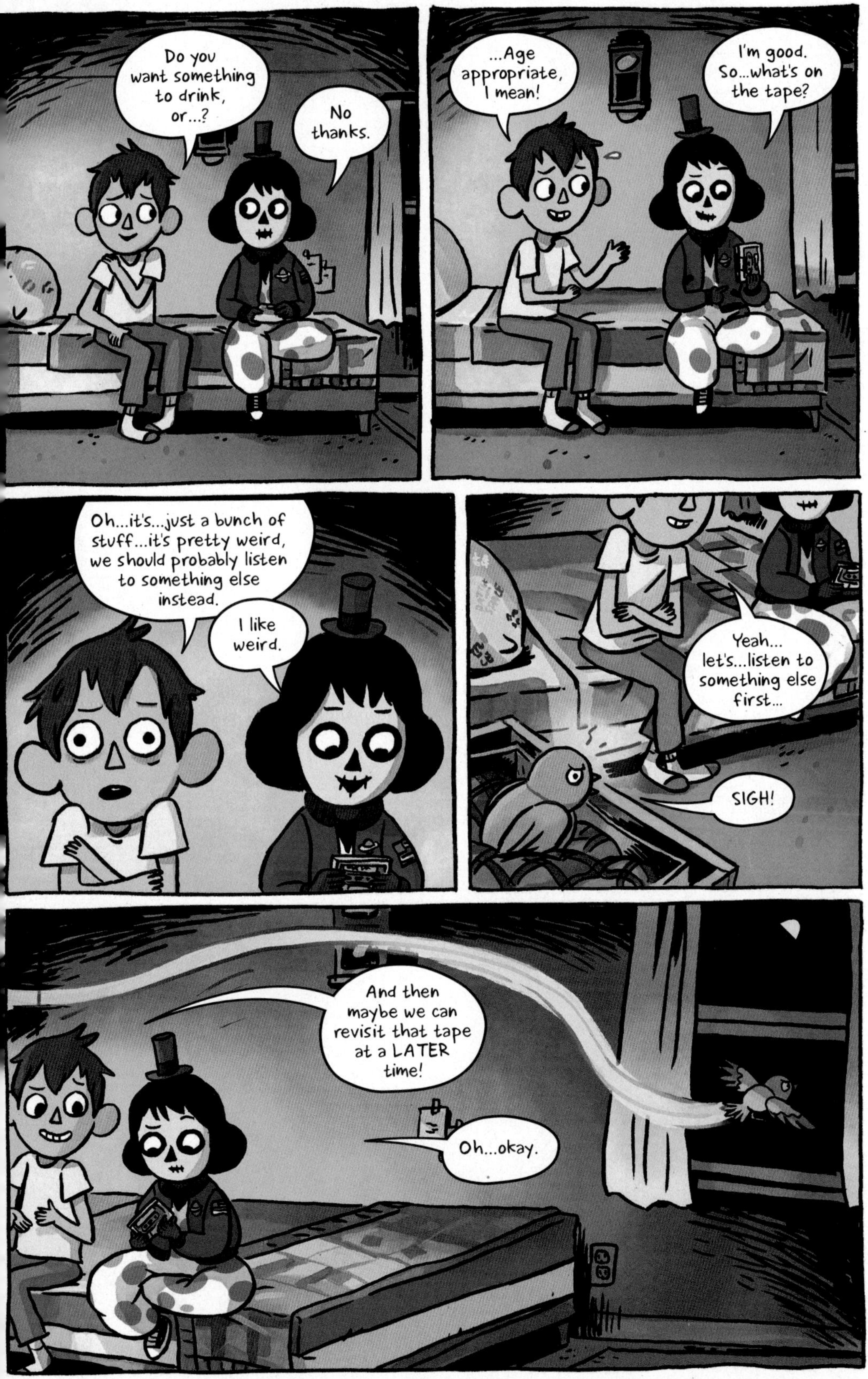
Do you want something to drink, or...?
No thanks.
...Age appropriate, I mean!
I'm good. So...what's on the tape?
Oh...it's...just a bunch of stuff...it's pretty weird, we should probably listen to something else instead.
I like weird.
Yeah... let's...listen to something else first...
SIGH!
And then maybe we can revisit that tape at a LATER time!
Oh...okay.

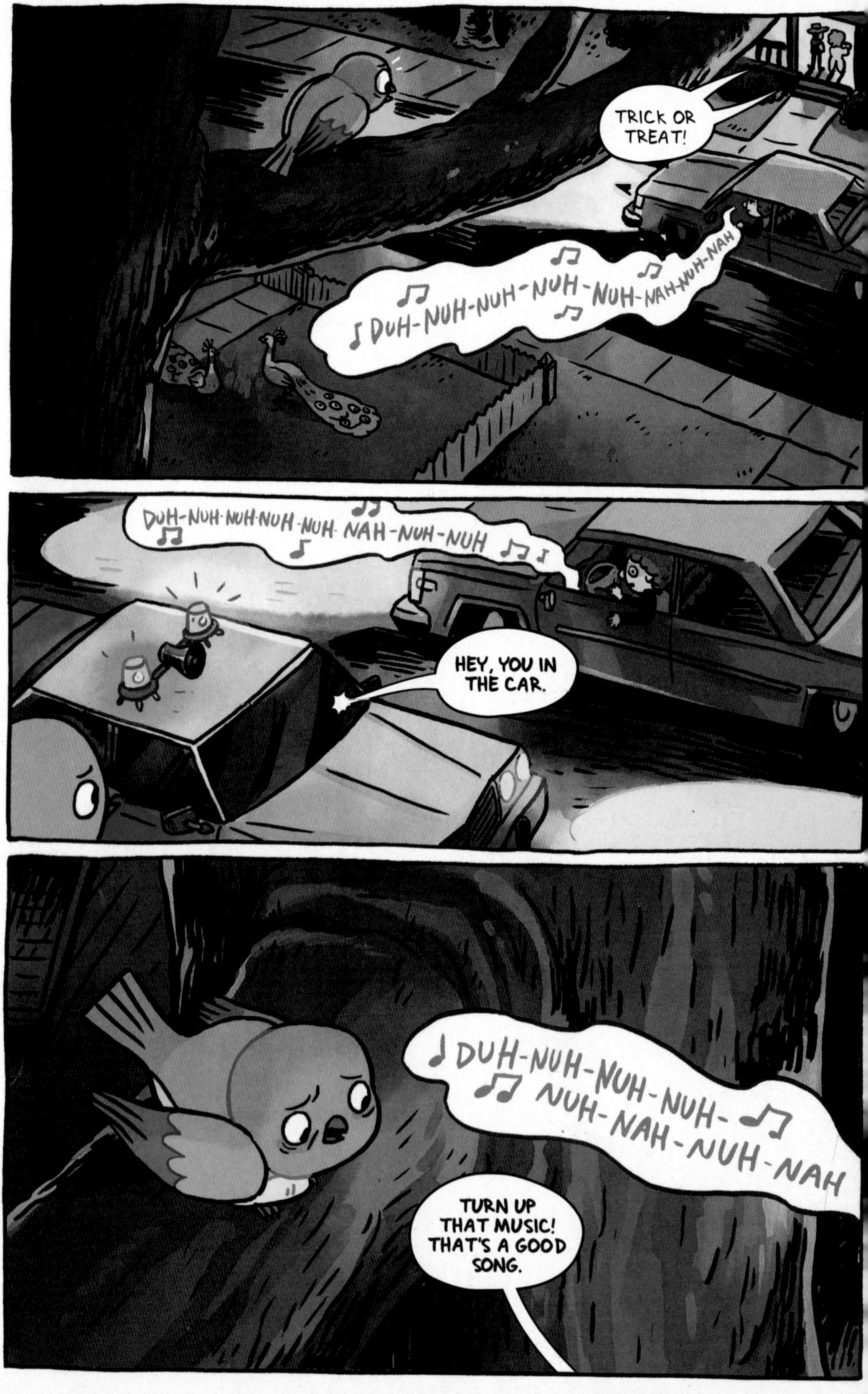
TRICK OR TREAT!
DUH-NUH-NUH-NUH-NUH-NAH-NUH-NAH
DUH-NUH-NUH-NUH-NUH-NAH-NUH-NUH
HEY, YOU IN THE CAR.
DUH-NUH-NUH-NUH-NUH-NUH-NAH-NUH-NAH
TURN UP THAT MUSIC! THAT'S A GOOD SONG.

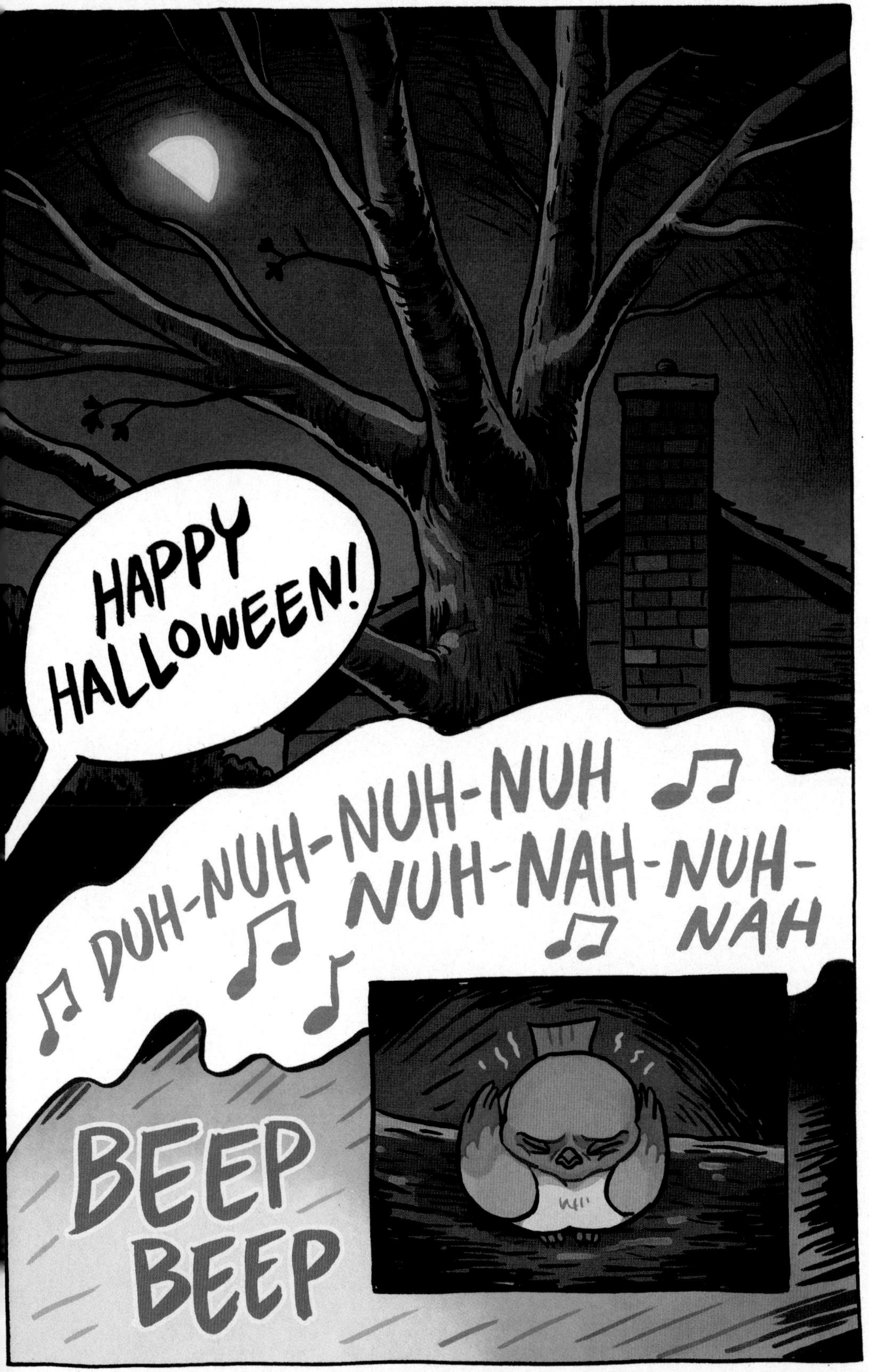
HAPPY HALLOWEEN!
♫ DUH-NUH-NUH-NUH ♫ NUH-NAH-NUH-NAH ♫
BEEP BEEP

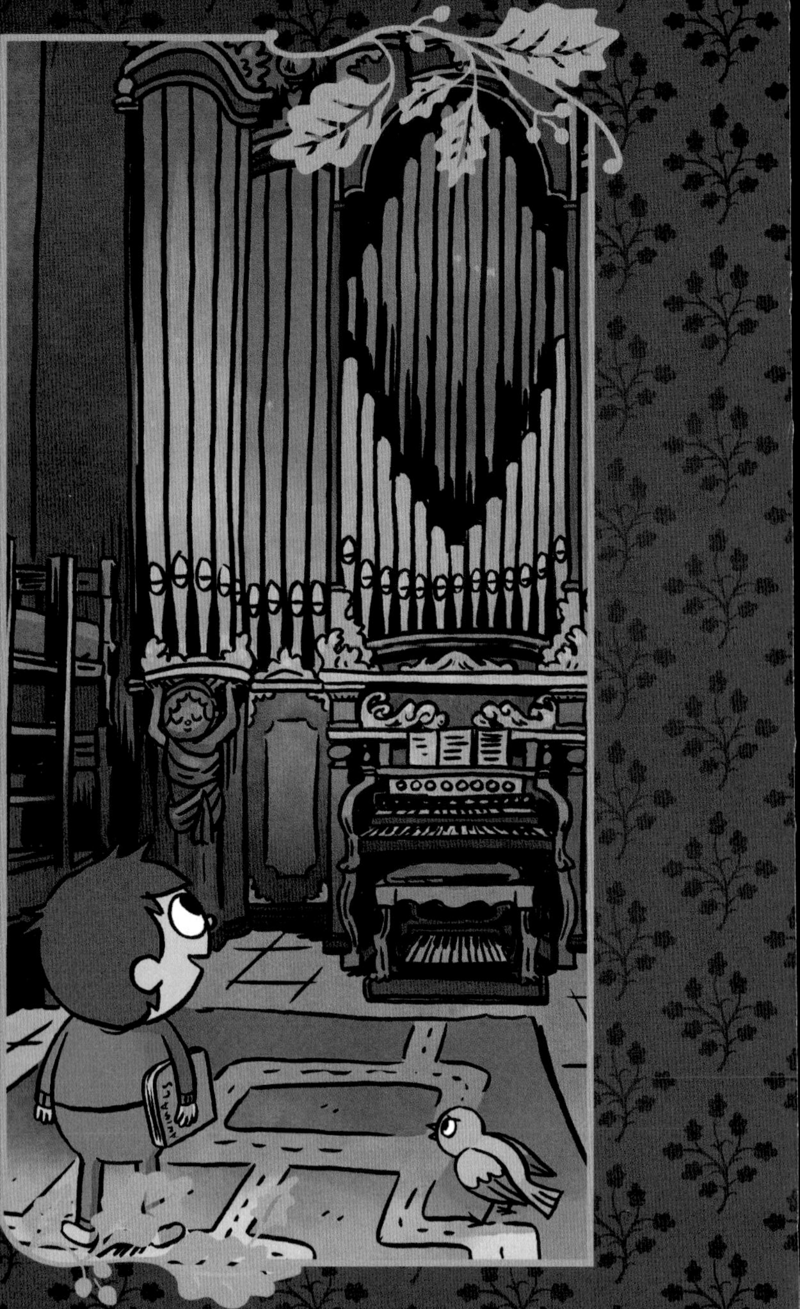
ANIMALS

ACT TWO

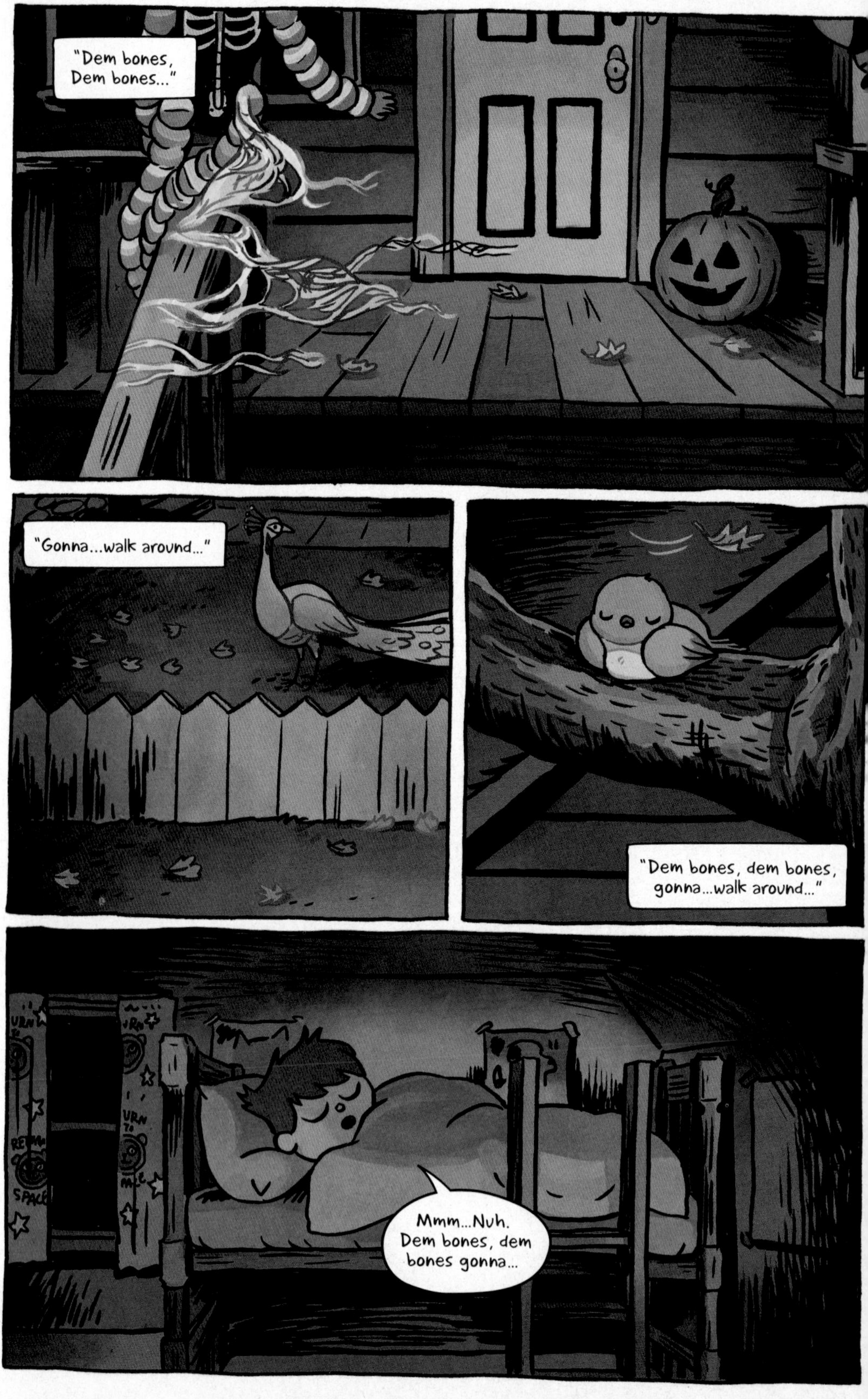
"Dem bones, Dem bones..."
"Gonna...walk around..."
"Dem bones, dem bones, gonna...walk around..."
Mmm...Nuh. Dem bones, dem bones gonna...

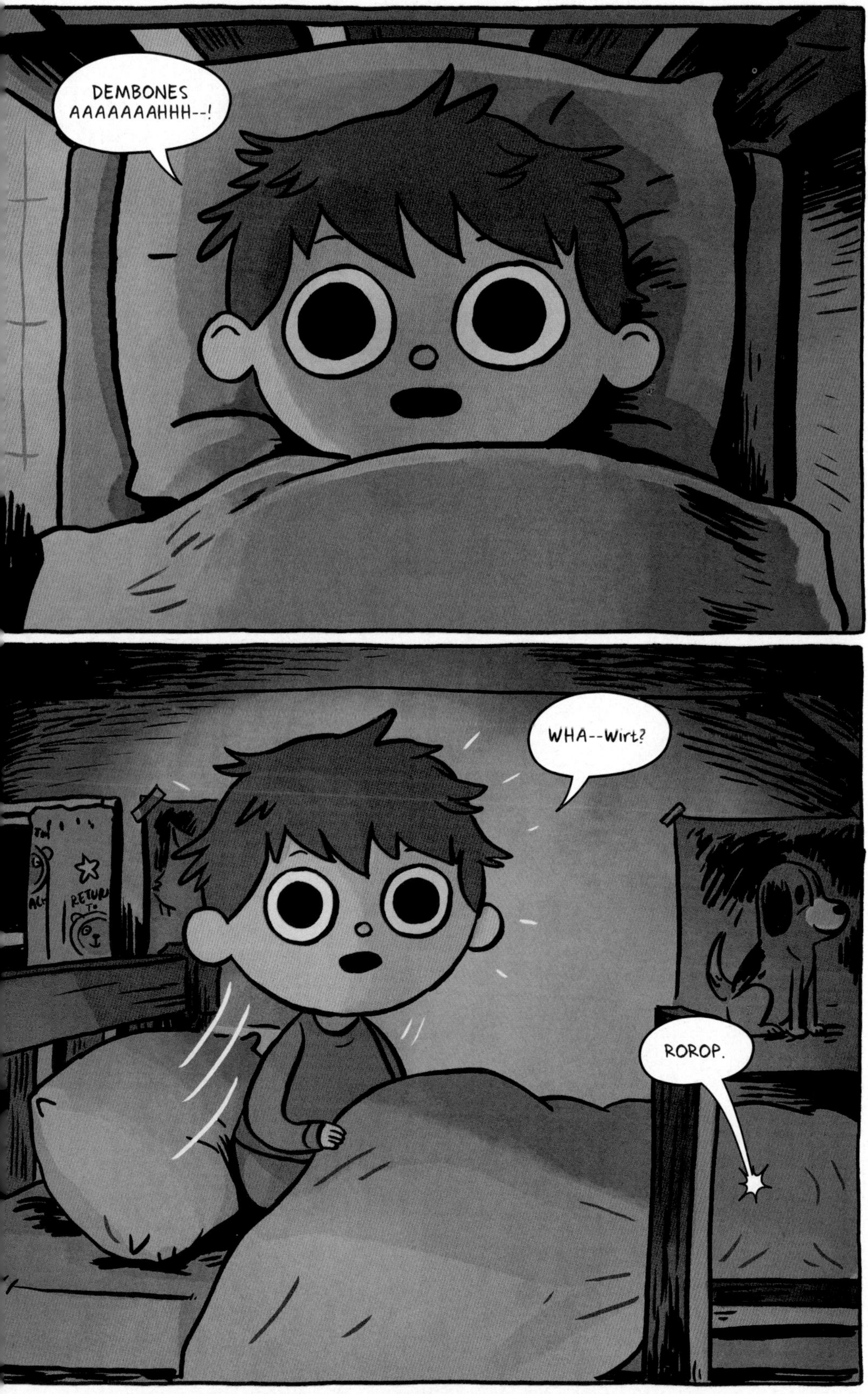
DEMBONES AAAAAAAHHH--!
WHA--Wirt?
ROROP.

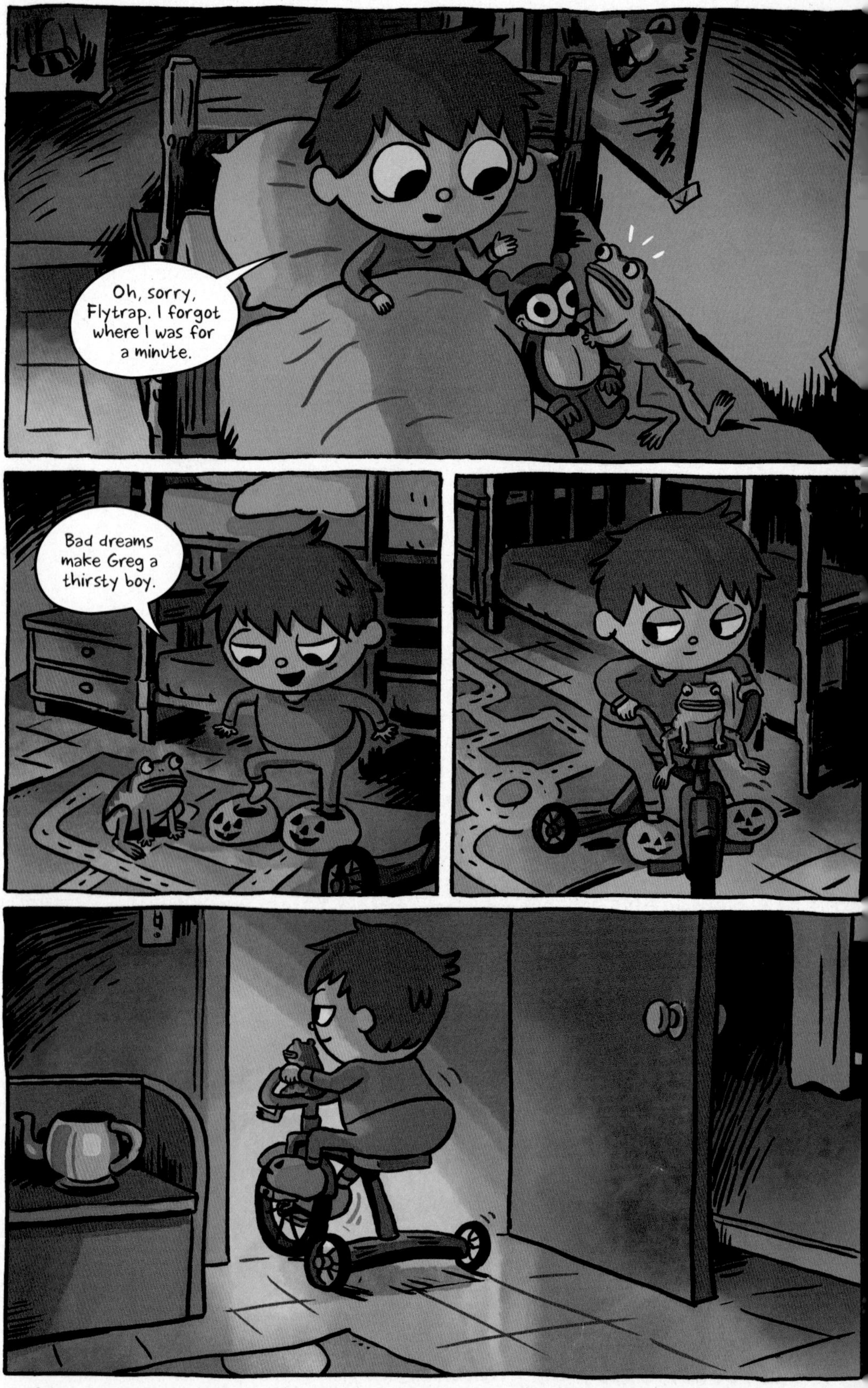
Oh, sorry, Flytrap. I forgot where I was for a minute.
Bad dreams make Greg a thirsty boy.

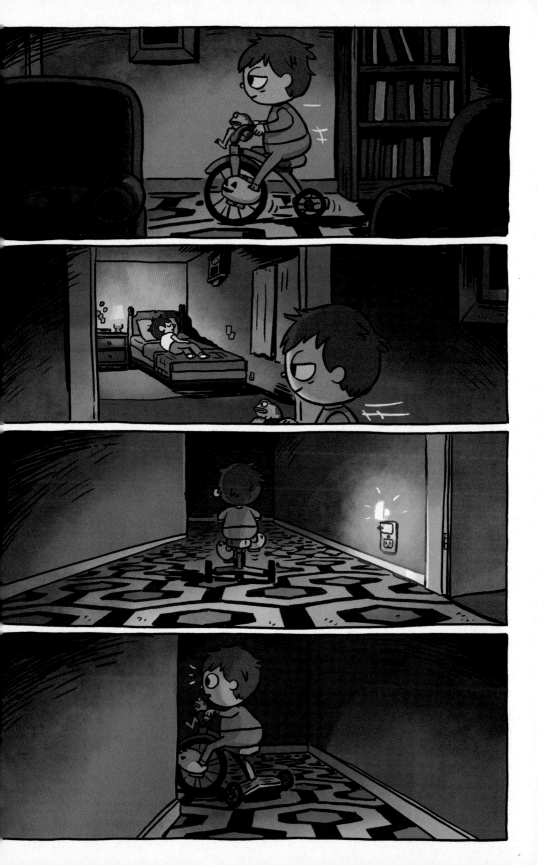

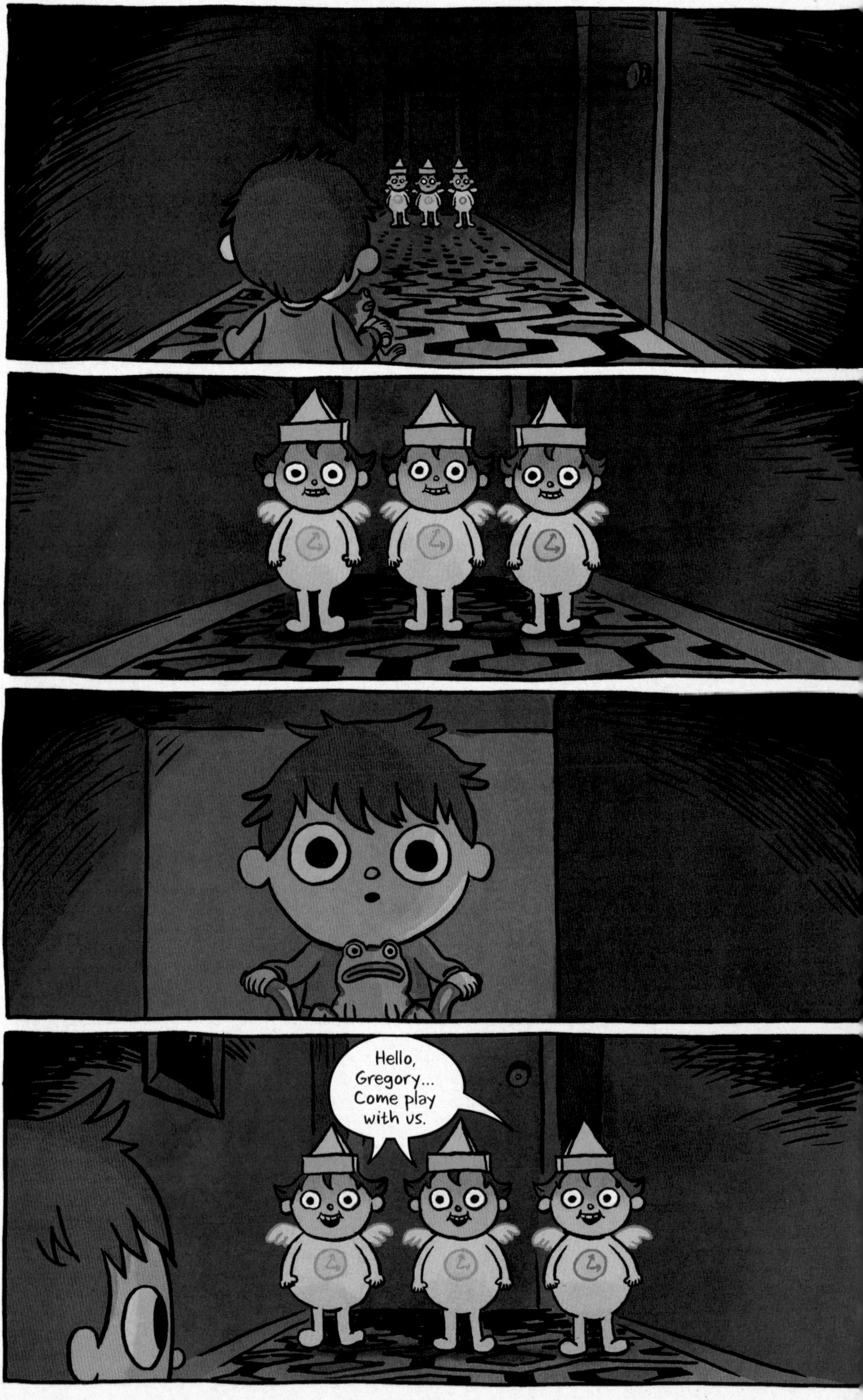
Hello, Gregory... Come play with us.

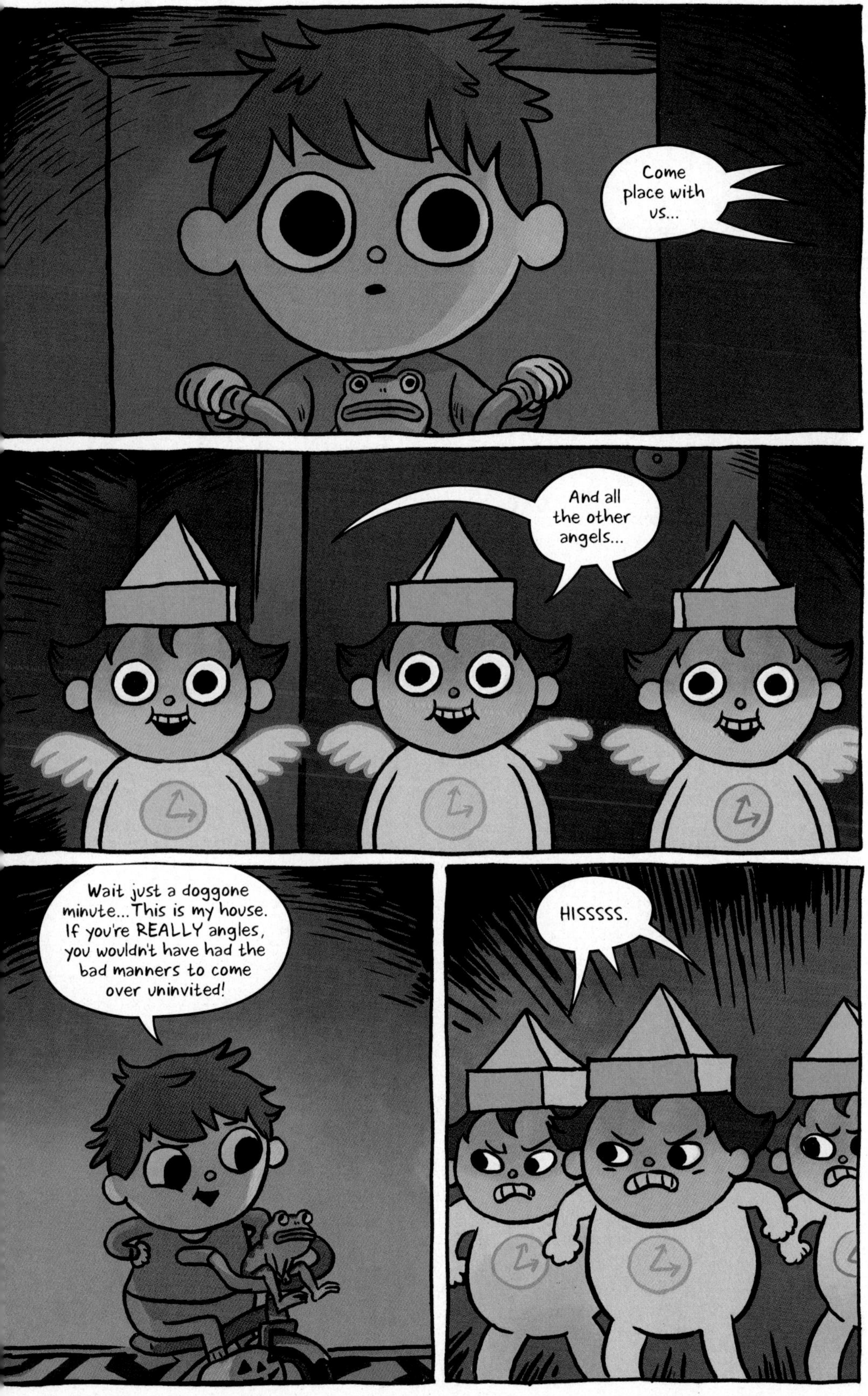
Come place with us...
And all the other angels...
Wait just a doggone minute... This is my house. If you're REALLY angles, you wouldn't have had the bad manners to come over uninvited!
HISSSSS.

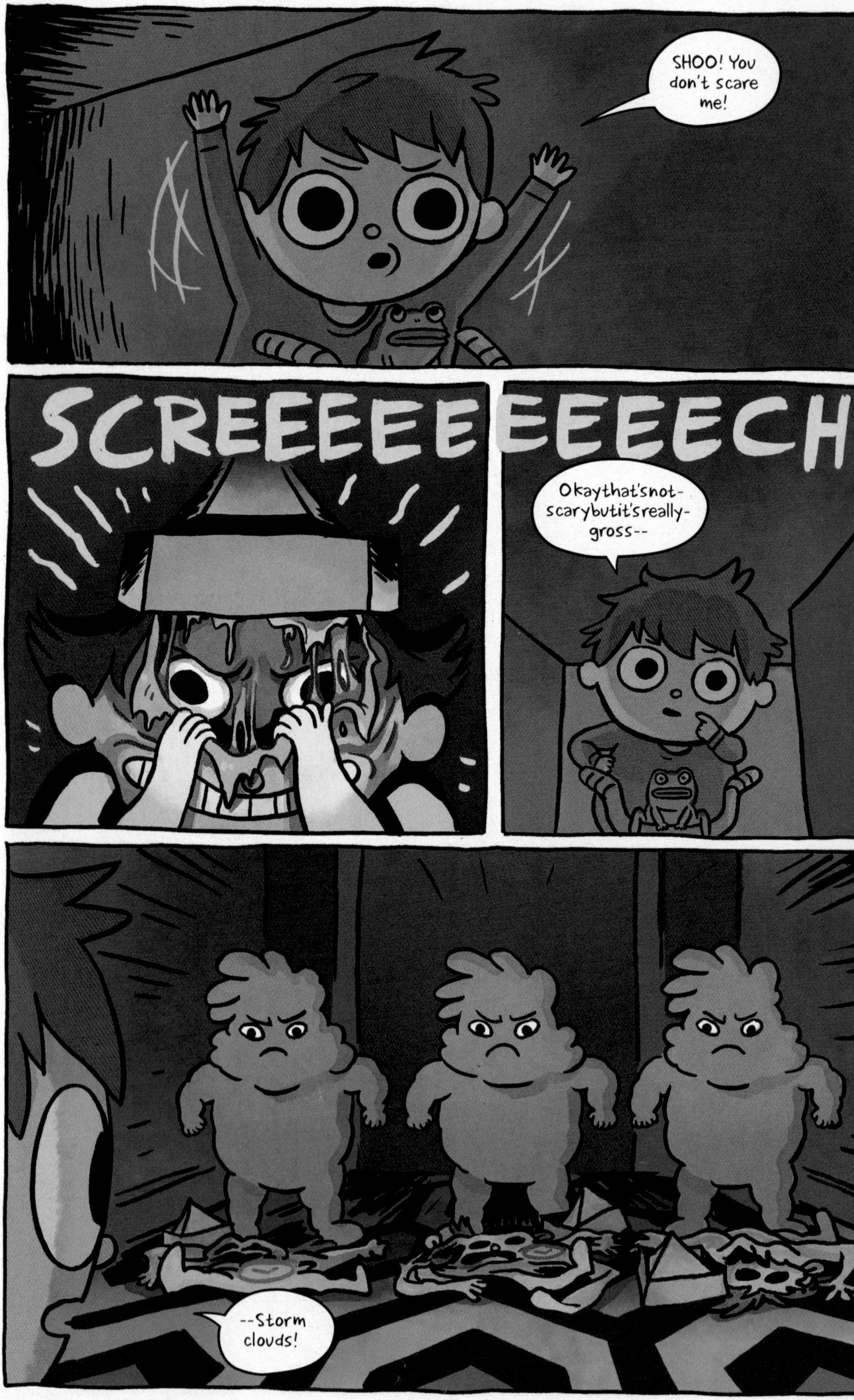
SHOO! You don't scare me!
SCREEEEEEEEEEECH
Okaythat'snot-scarybutit'sreally-gross--
--Storm clouds!

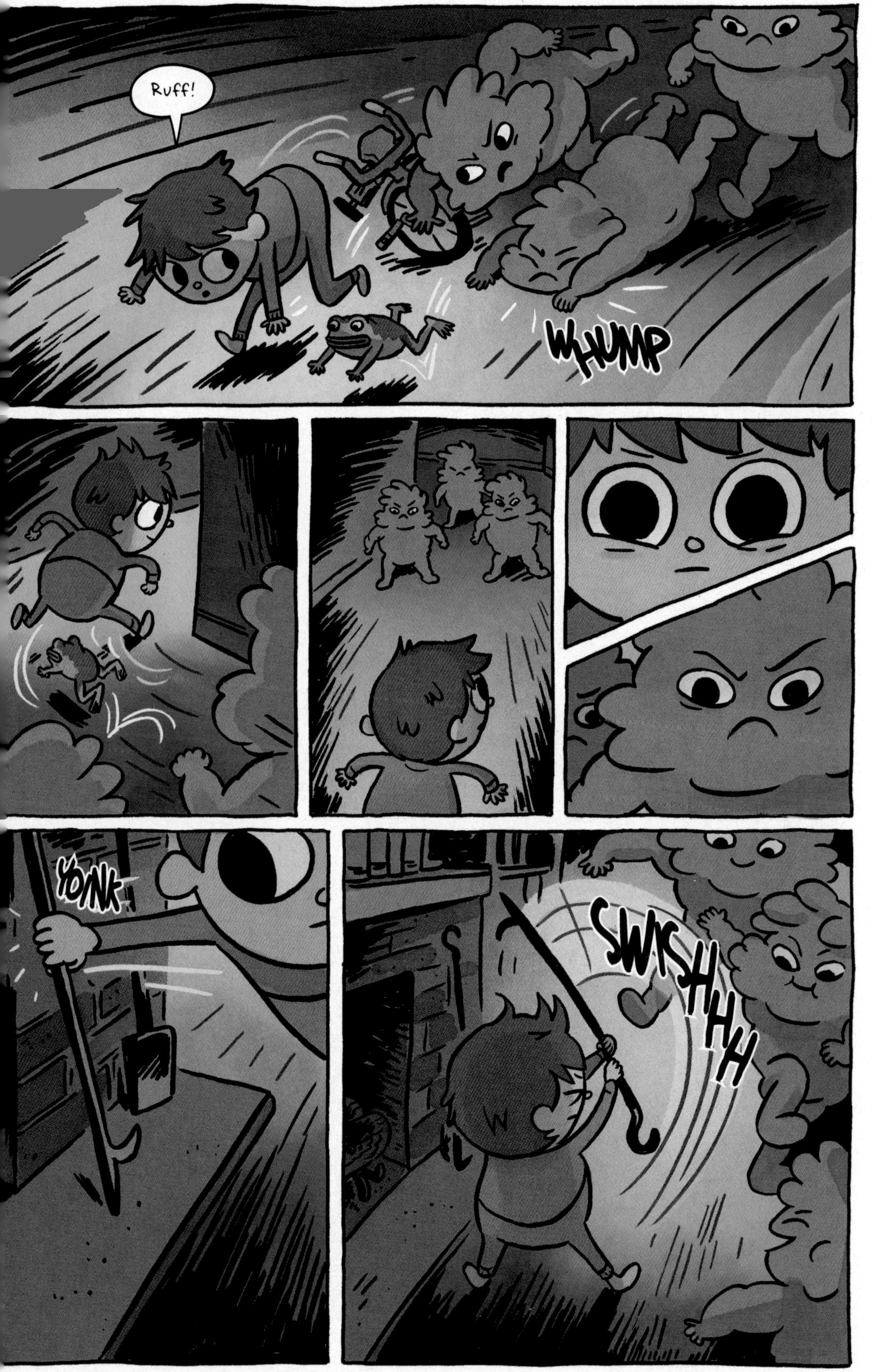
Ruff!
WHUMP
YOINK
SWISHHHH

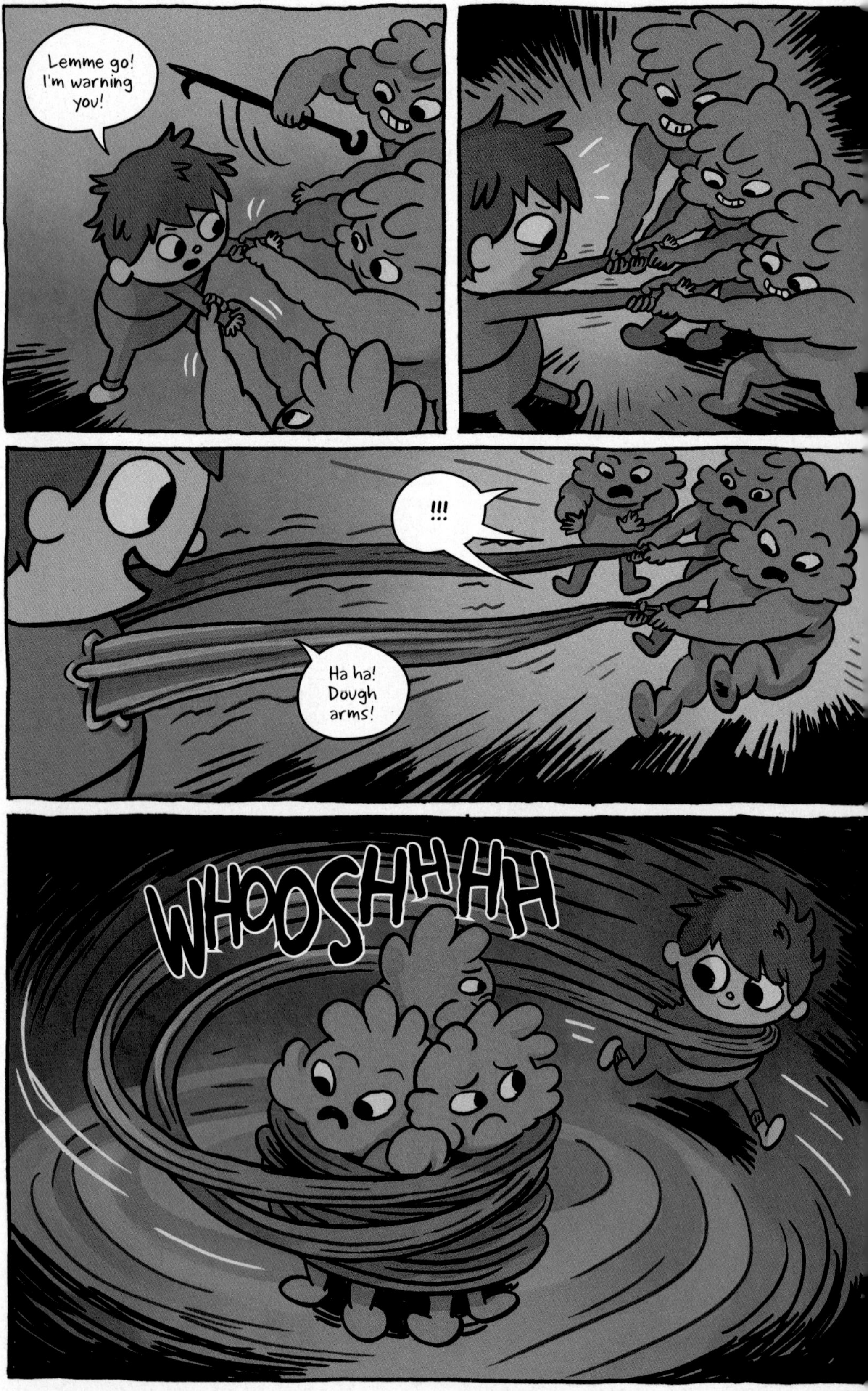
Lemme go! I'm warning you!
!!!
Ha ha! Dough arms!
WHOOSHHHH

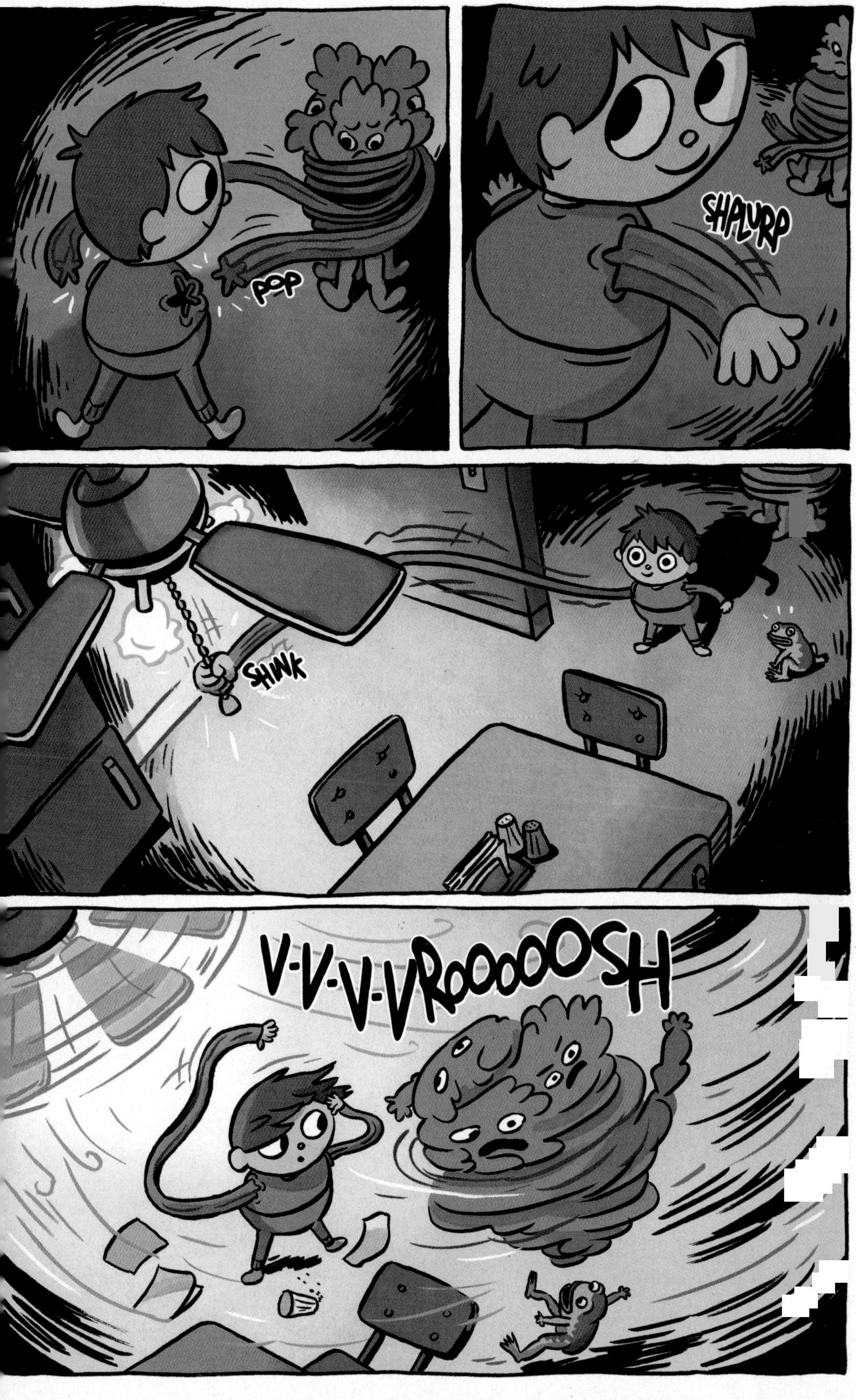
POP
SHPLURP
SHINK
V-V-V-VROOOOOSH

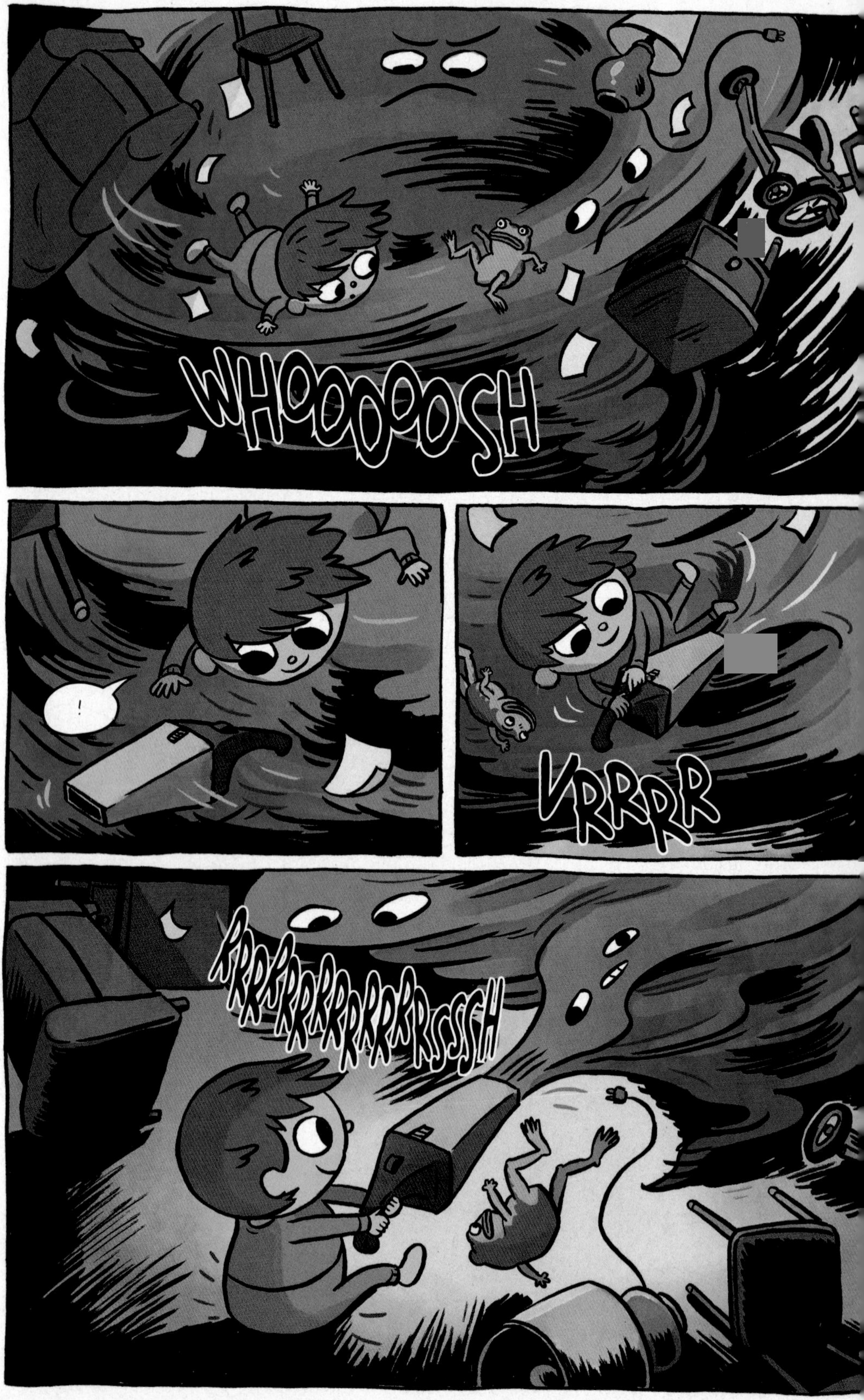
WHOOOOOSH
!
VRRRR
RRRRRRRRRRRRRSSSH

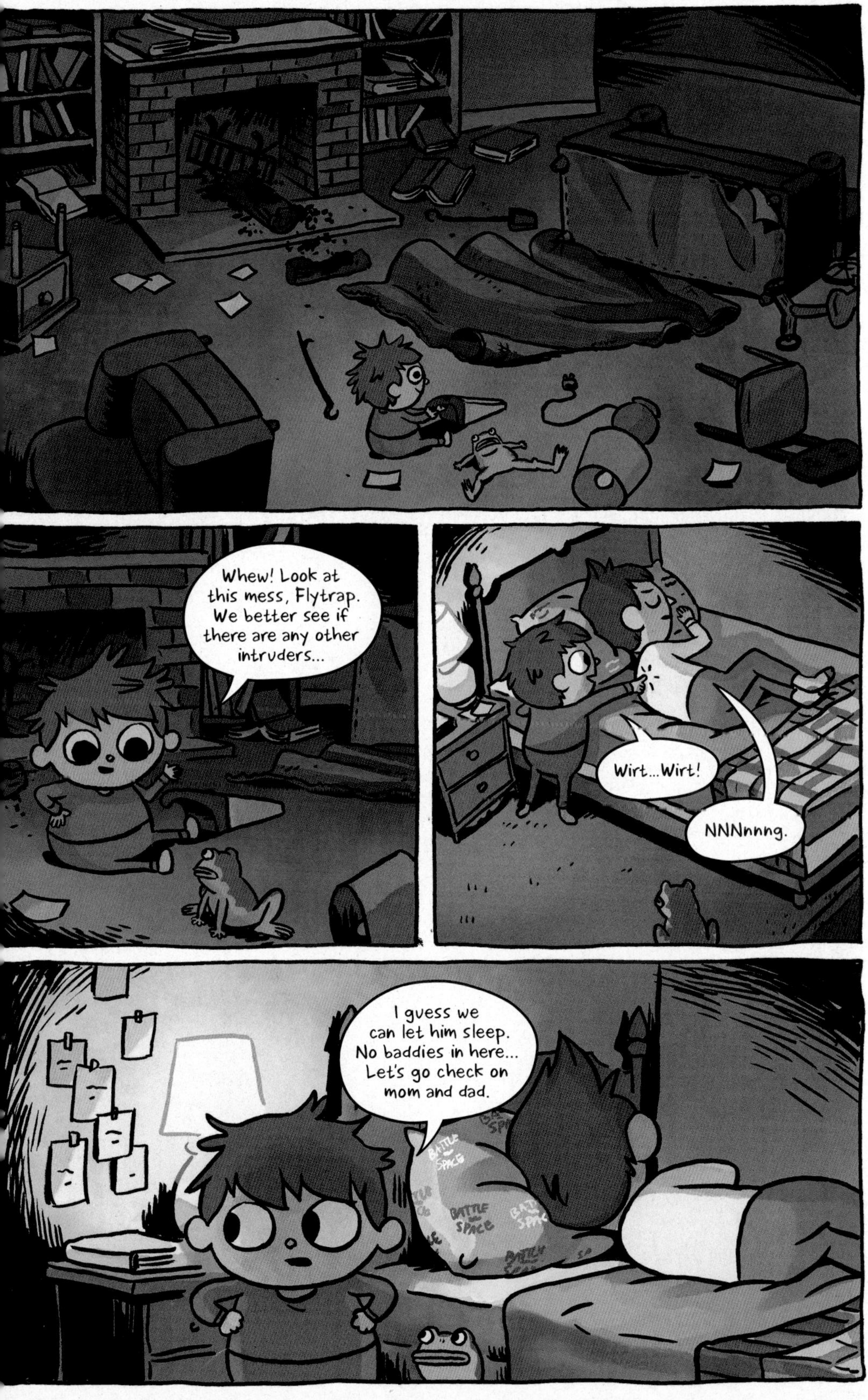
Whew! Look at this mess, Flytrap. We better see if there are any other intruders...
Wirt...Wirt!
NNNnnng.
I guess we can let him sleep. No baddies in here... Let's go check on mom and dad.
BATTLE SPACE

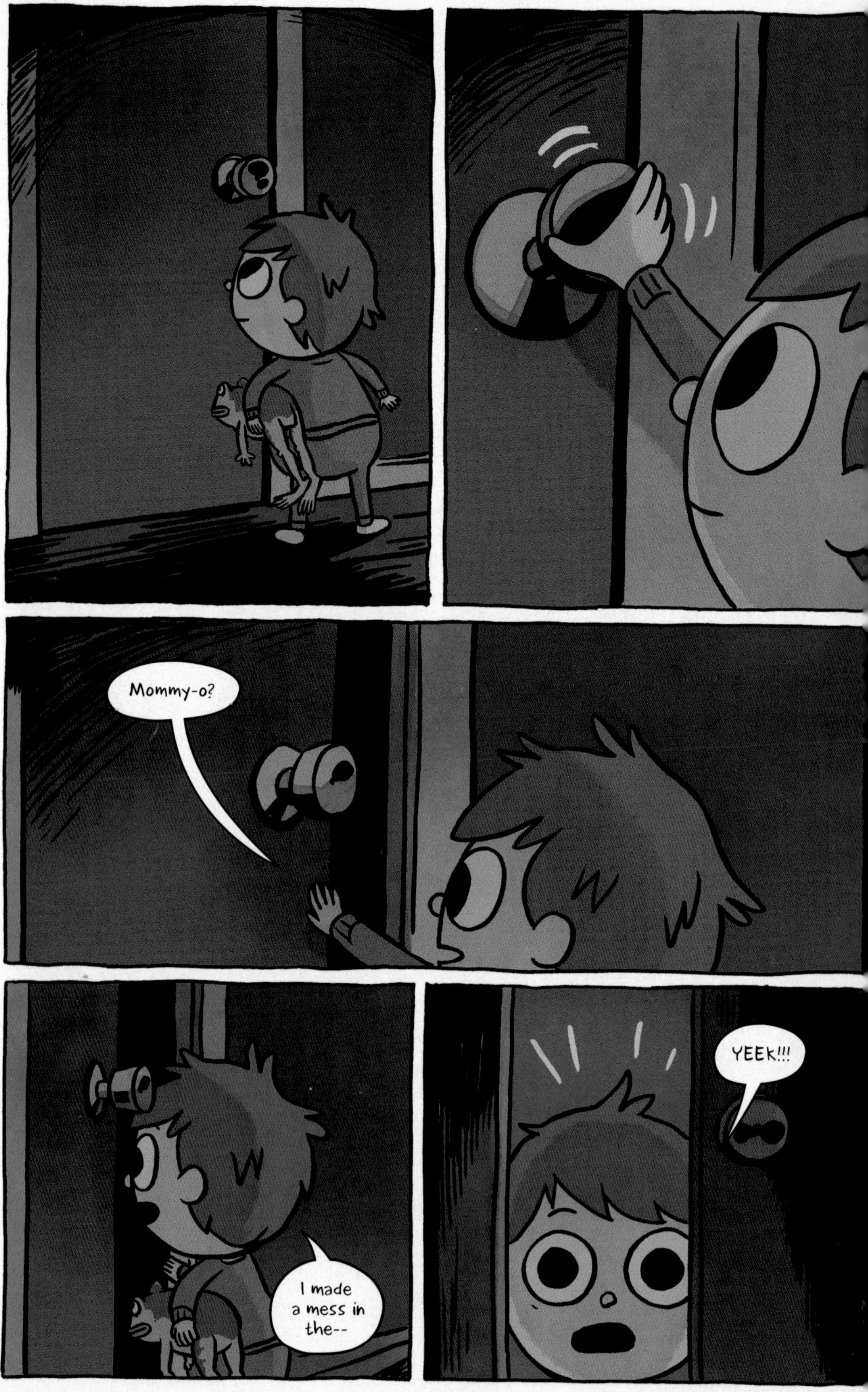
Mommy-o?
I made a mess in the--
YEEK!!!

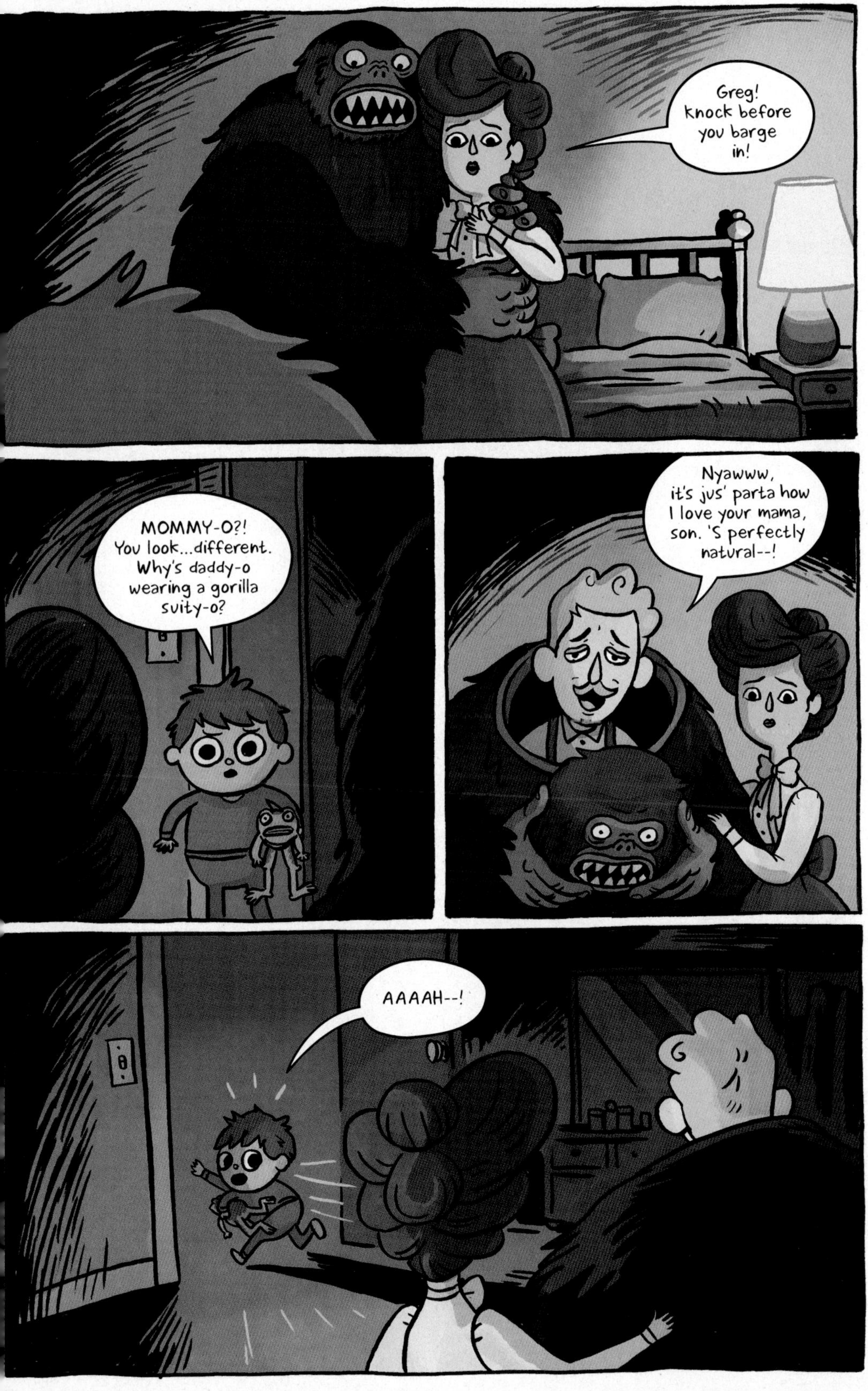
Greg! knock before you barge in!
MOMMY-O?! You look...different. Why's daddy-o wearing a gorilla suity-o?
Nyawww, it's jus' parta how I love your mama, son. 'S perfectly natural--!
AAAAH--!

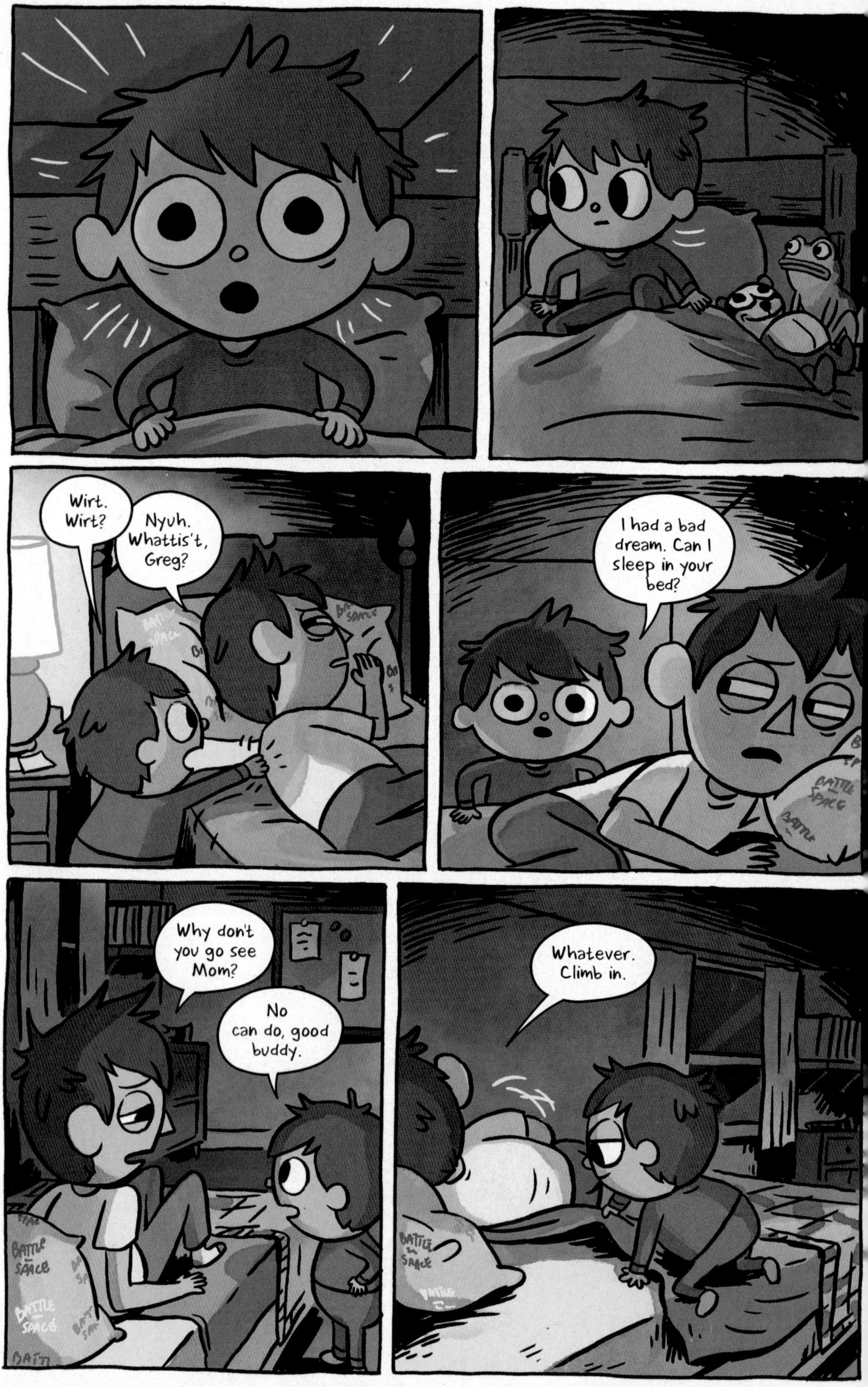
Wirt. Wirt?
Nyuh. Whattis't, Greg?
I had a bad dream. Can I sleep in your bed?
Why don't you go see Mom?
No can do, good buddy.
Whatever. Climb in.

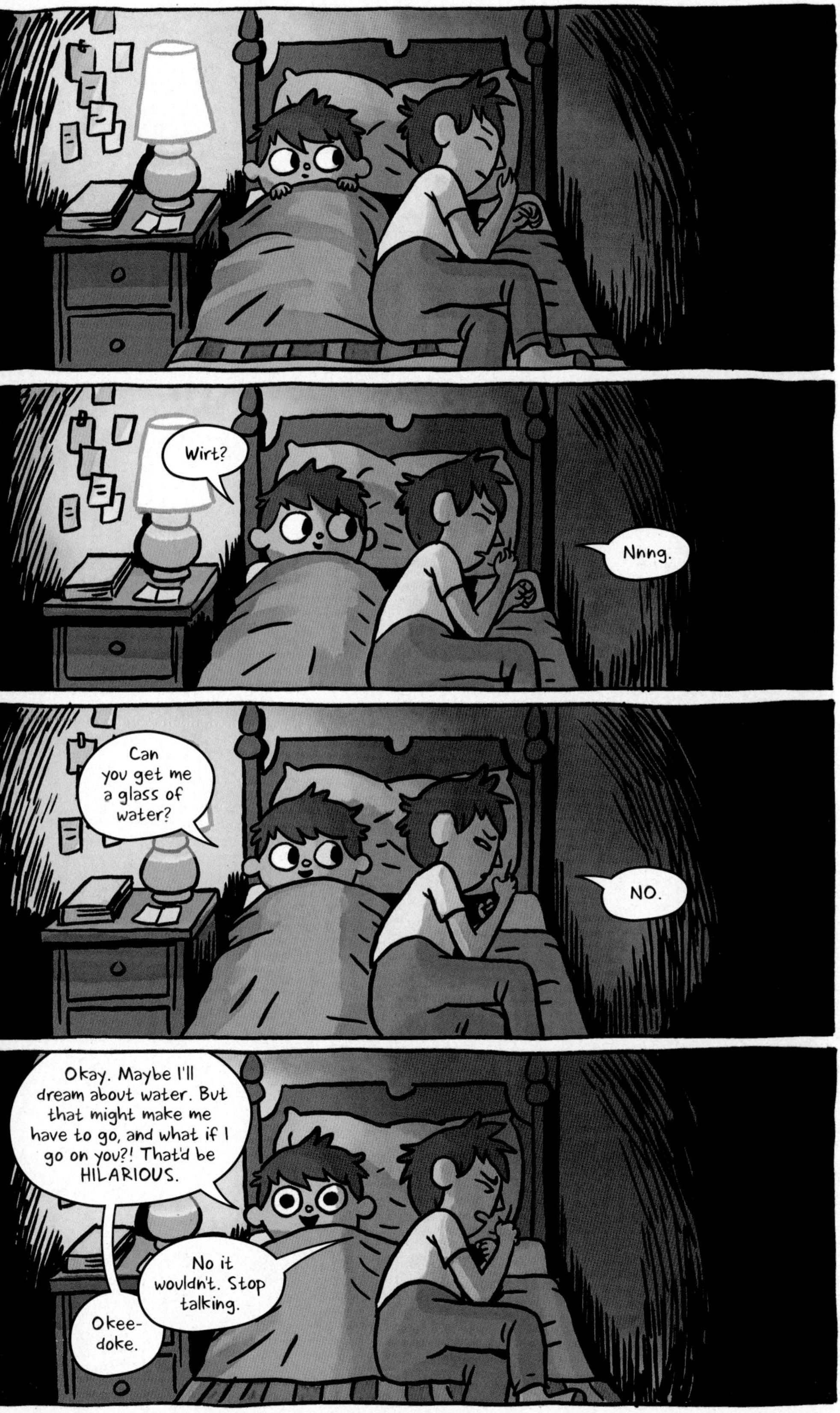
Wirt?
Nnng.
Can you get me a glass of water?
NO.
Okay. Maybe I'll dream about water. But that might make me have to go, and what if I go on you?! That'd be HILARIOUS.
No it wouldn't. Stop talking.
Okee-doke.

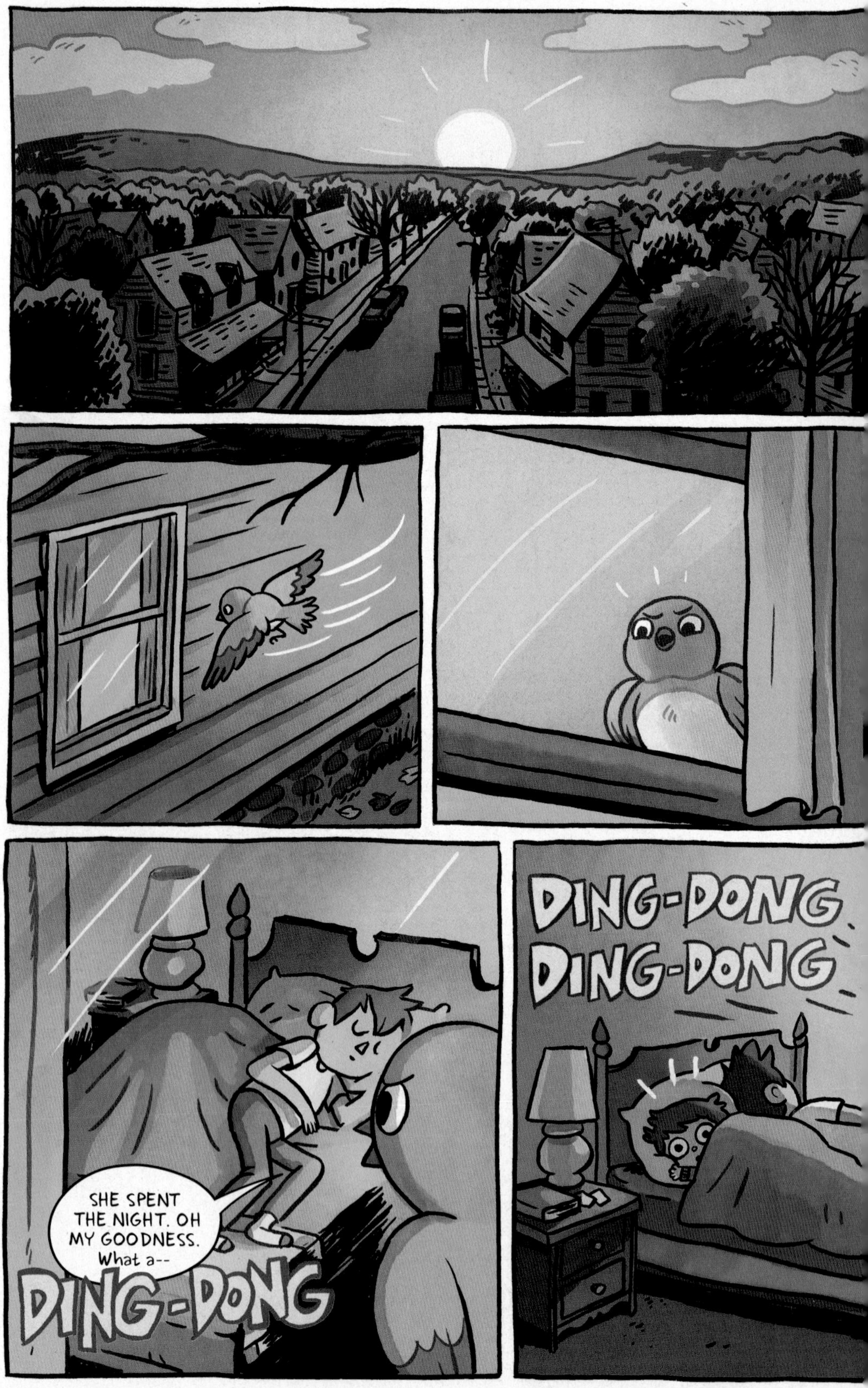
SHE SPENT THE NIGHT. OH MY GOODNESS. What a--
DING-DONG
DING-DONG
DING-DONG

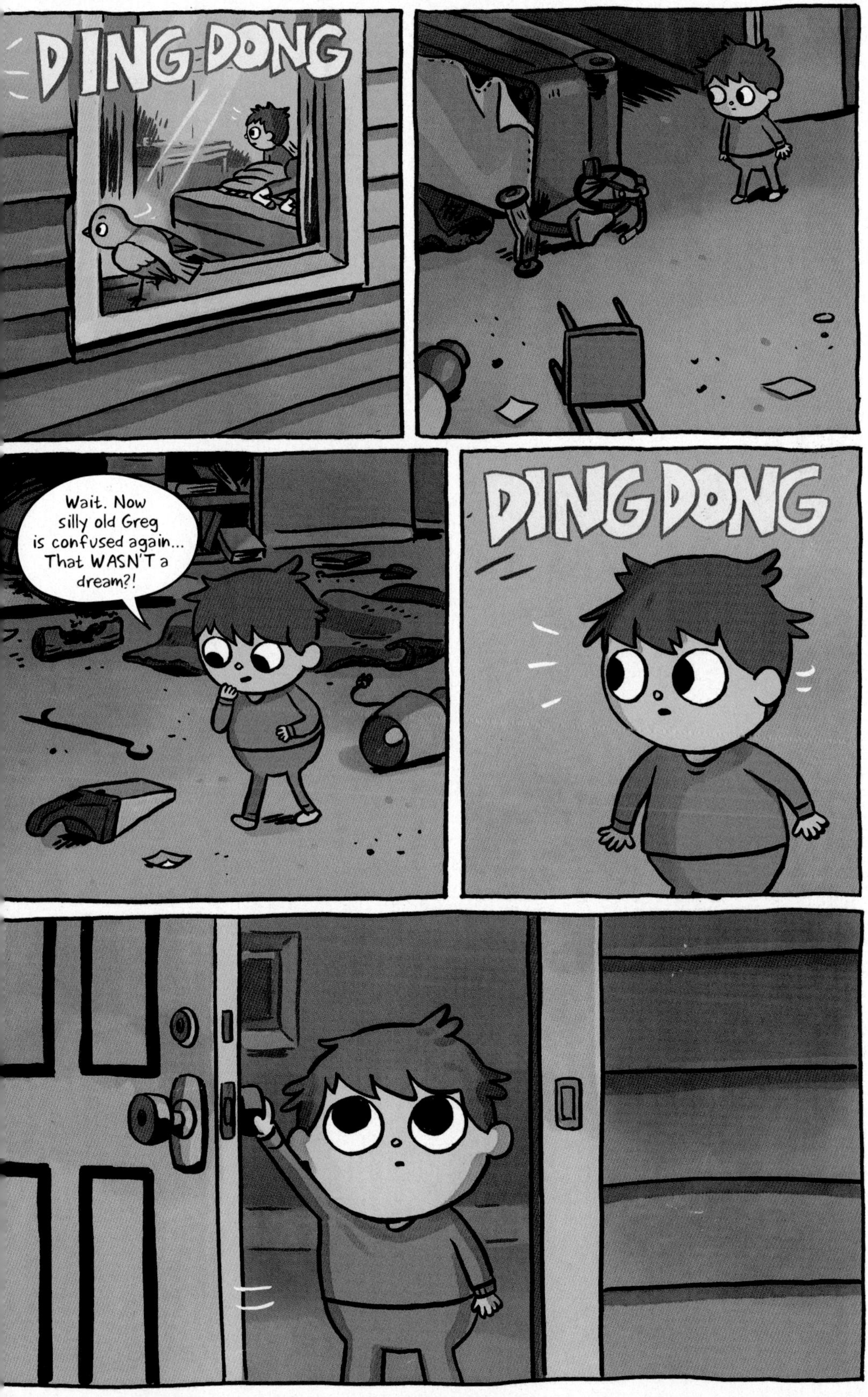
DING DONG
Wait. Now silly old Greg is confused again... That WASN'T a dream?!
DING DONG

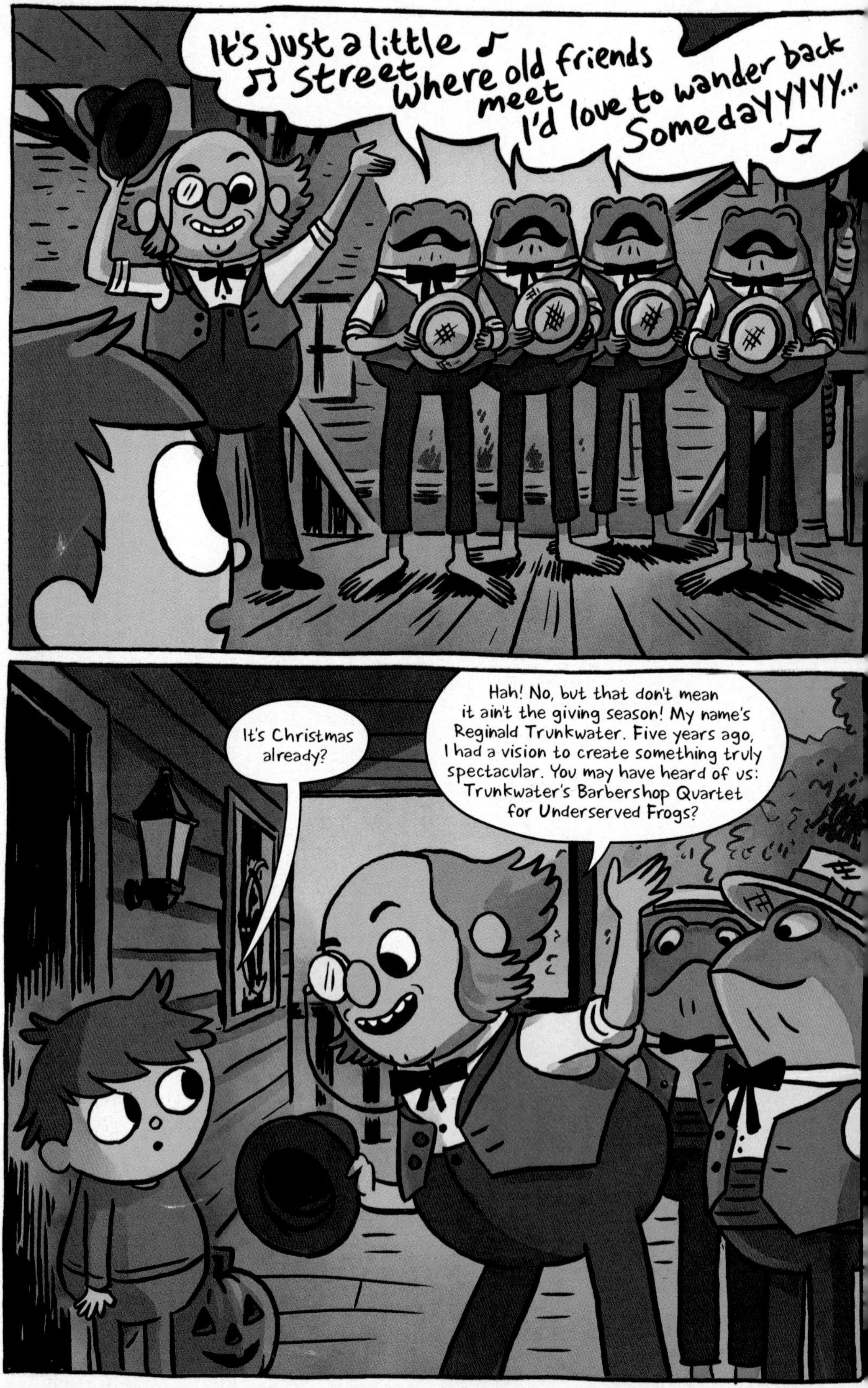
It's just a little ♪ Street where old friends meet I'd love to wander back SomedaYYYYY... ♪
It's Christmas already?
Hah! No, but that don't mean it ain't the giving season! My name's Reginald Trunkwater. Five years ago, I had a vision to create something truly spectacular. You may have heard of us: Trunkwater's Barbershop Quartet for Underserved Frogs?

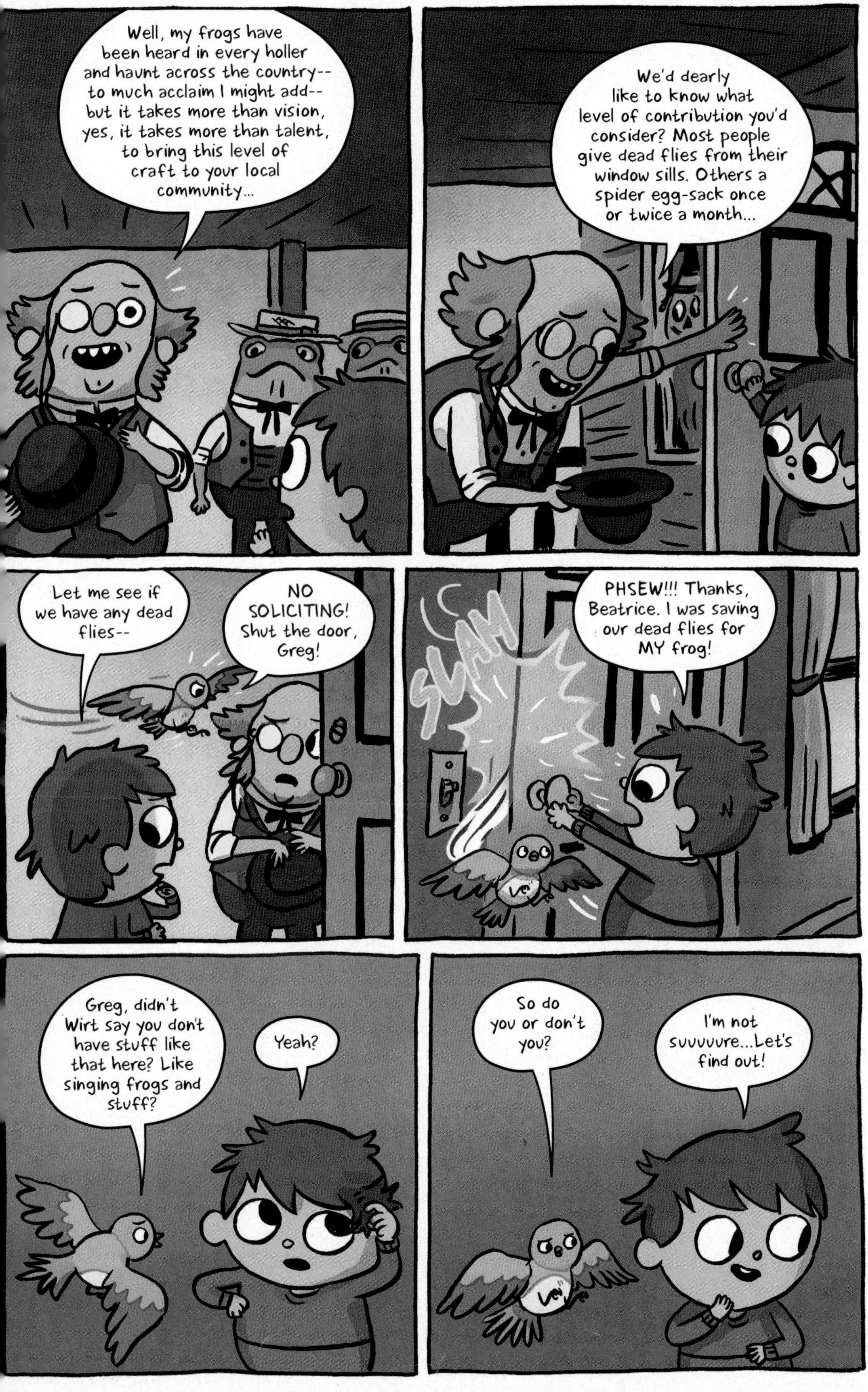
Well, my frogs have been heard in every holler and haunt across the country--to much acclaim I might add--but it takes more than vision, yes, it takes more than talent, to bring this level of craft to your local community...
We'd dearly like to know what level of contribution you'd consider? Most people give dead flies from their window sills. Others a spider egg-sack once or twice a month...
Let me see if we have any dead flies--
NO SOLICITING! Shut the door, Greg!
SLAM
PHSEW!!! Thanks, Beatrice. I was saving our dead flies for MY frog!
Greg, didn't Wirt say you don't have stuff like that here? Like singing frogs and stuff?
Yeah?
So do you or don't you?
I'm not suvvvure...Let's find out!

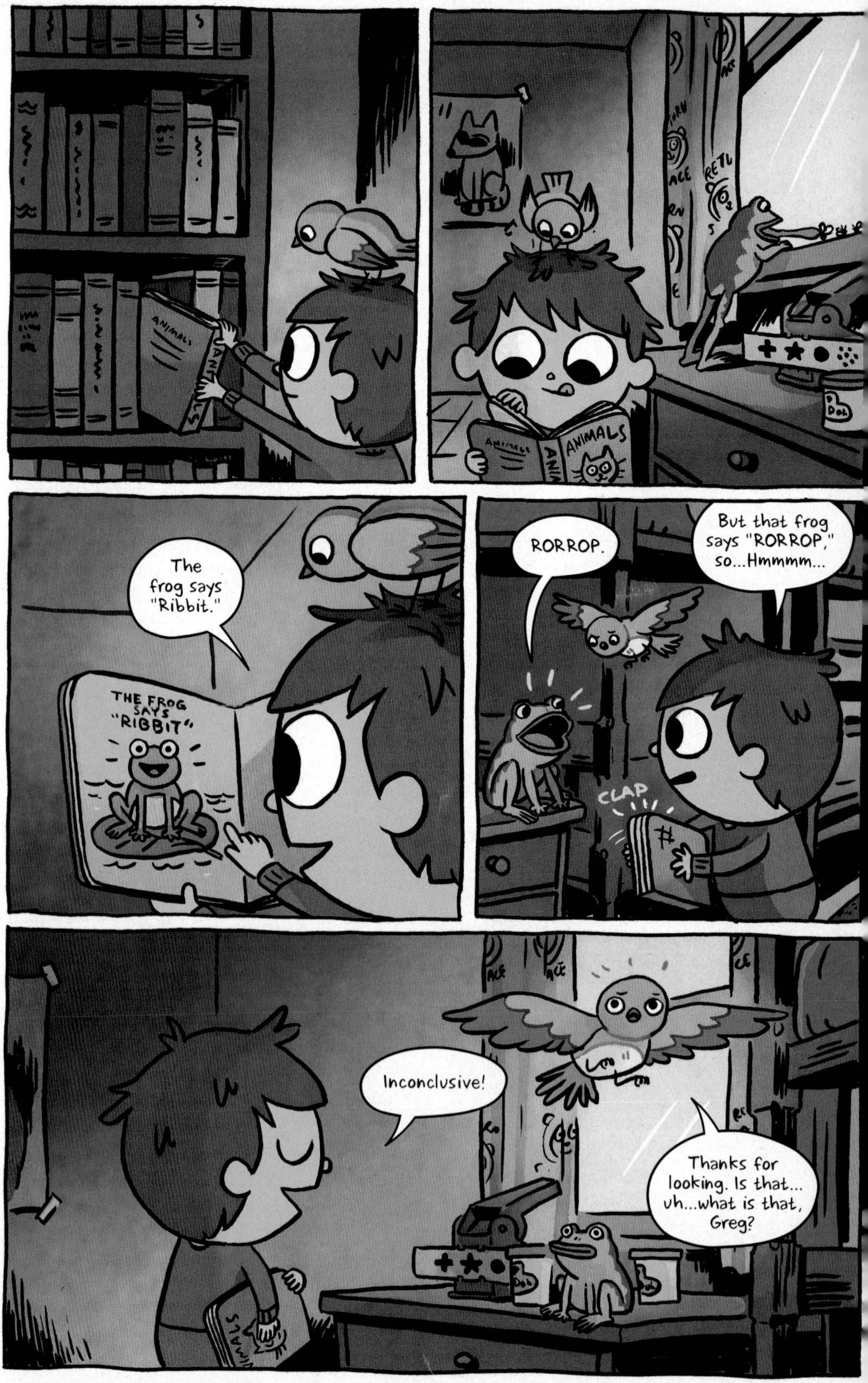

ANIMALS
ANIMALS
The frog says "Ribbit."
THE FROG SAYS "RIBBIT"
RORROP.
But that frog says "RORROP," so...Hmmmm...
CLAP
Inconclusive!
Thanks for looking. Is that... uh...what is that, Greg?

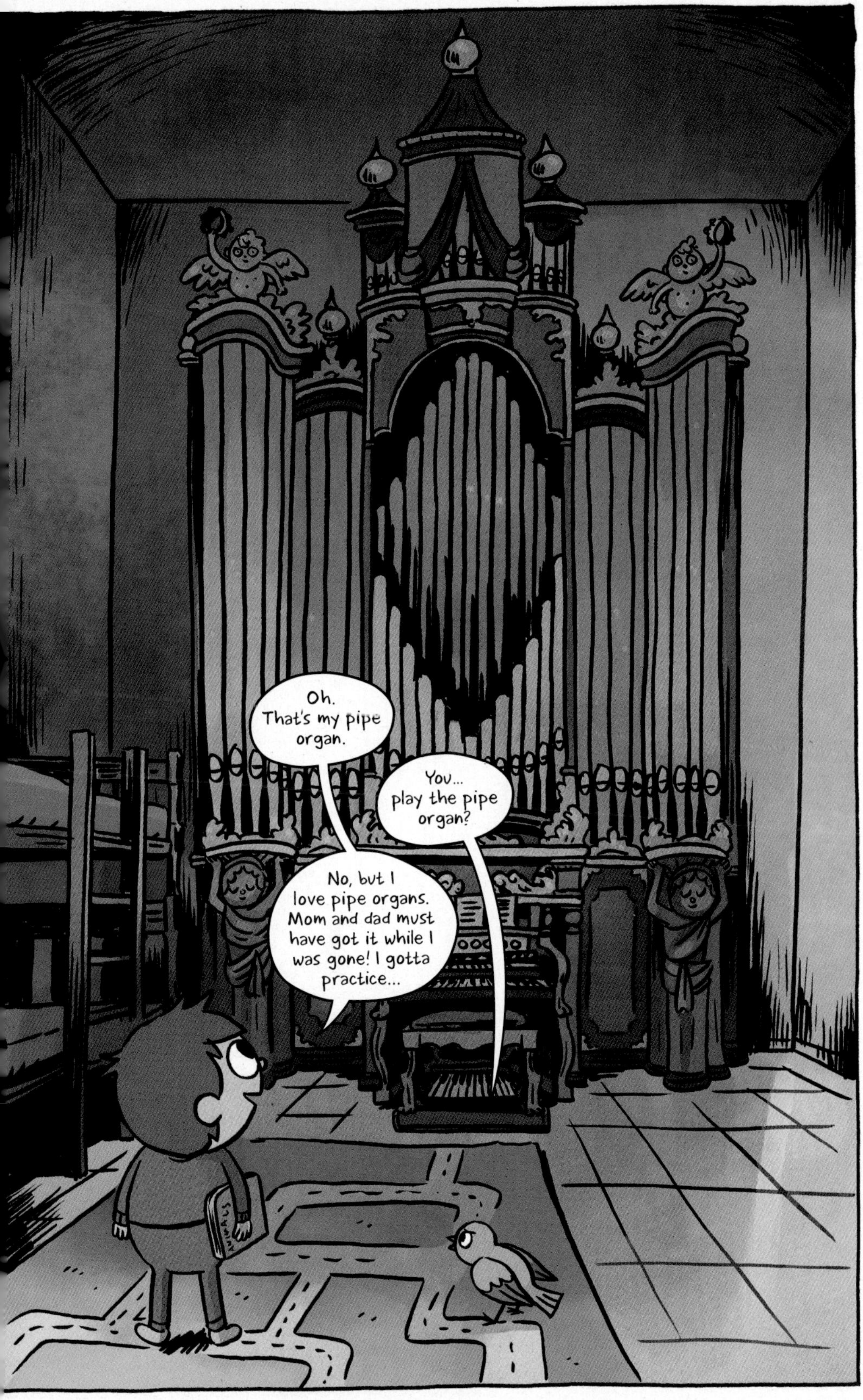
Oh.
That's my pipe organ.
You... play the pipe organ?
No, but I love pipe organs. Mom and dad must have got it while I was gone! I gotta practice...
ANIMALS

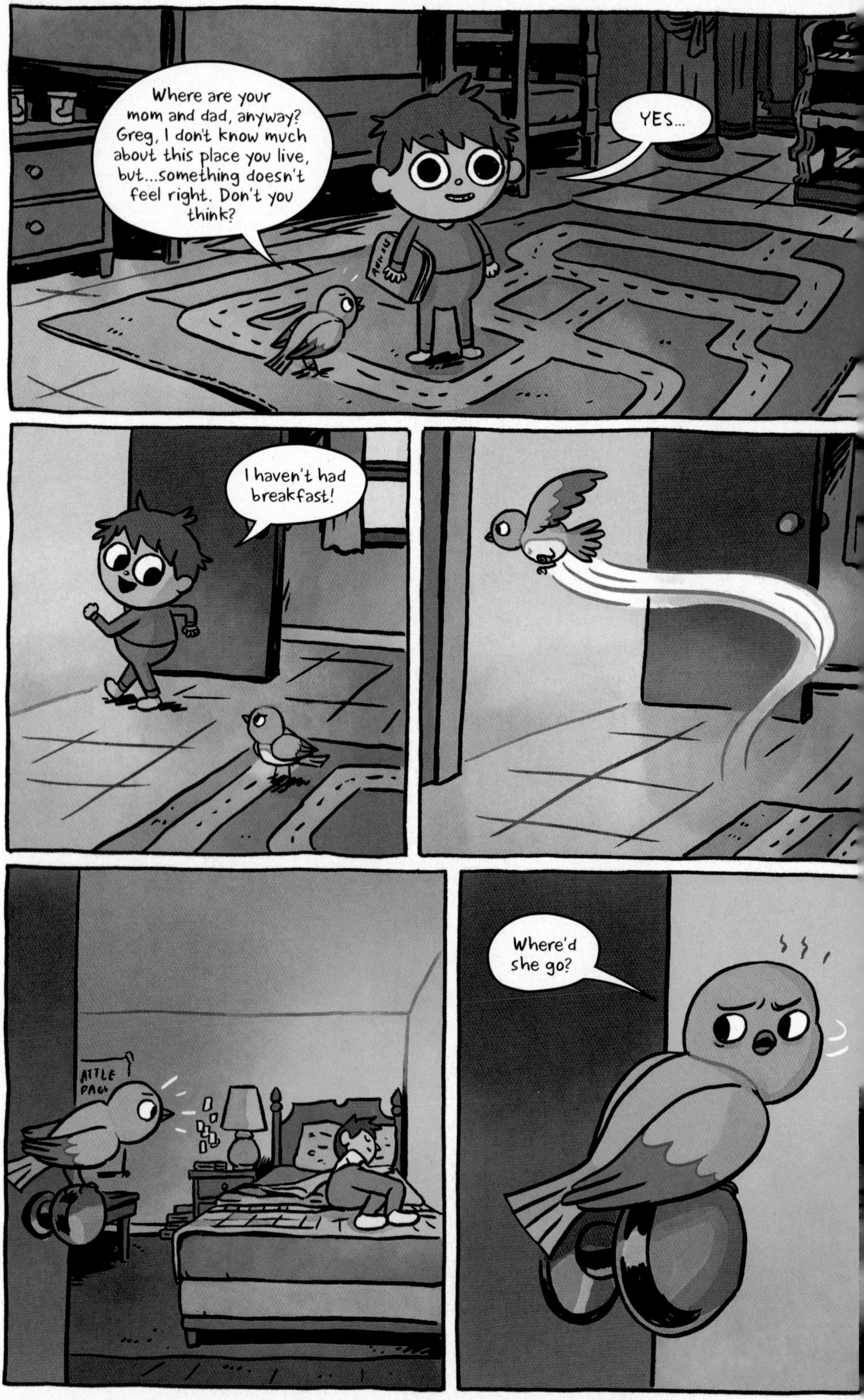
Where are your mom and dad, anyway? Greg, I don't know much about this place you live, but...something doesn't feel right. Don't you think?
YES...
I haven't had breakfast!
Where'd she go?

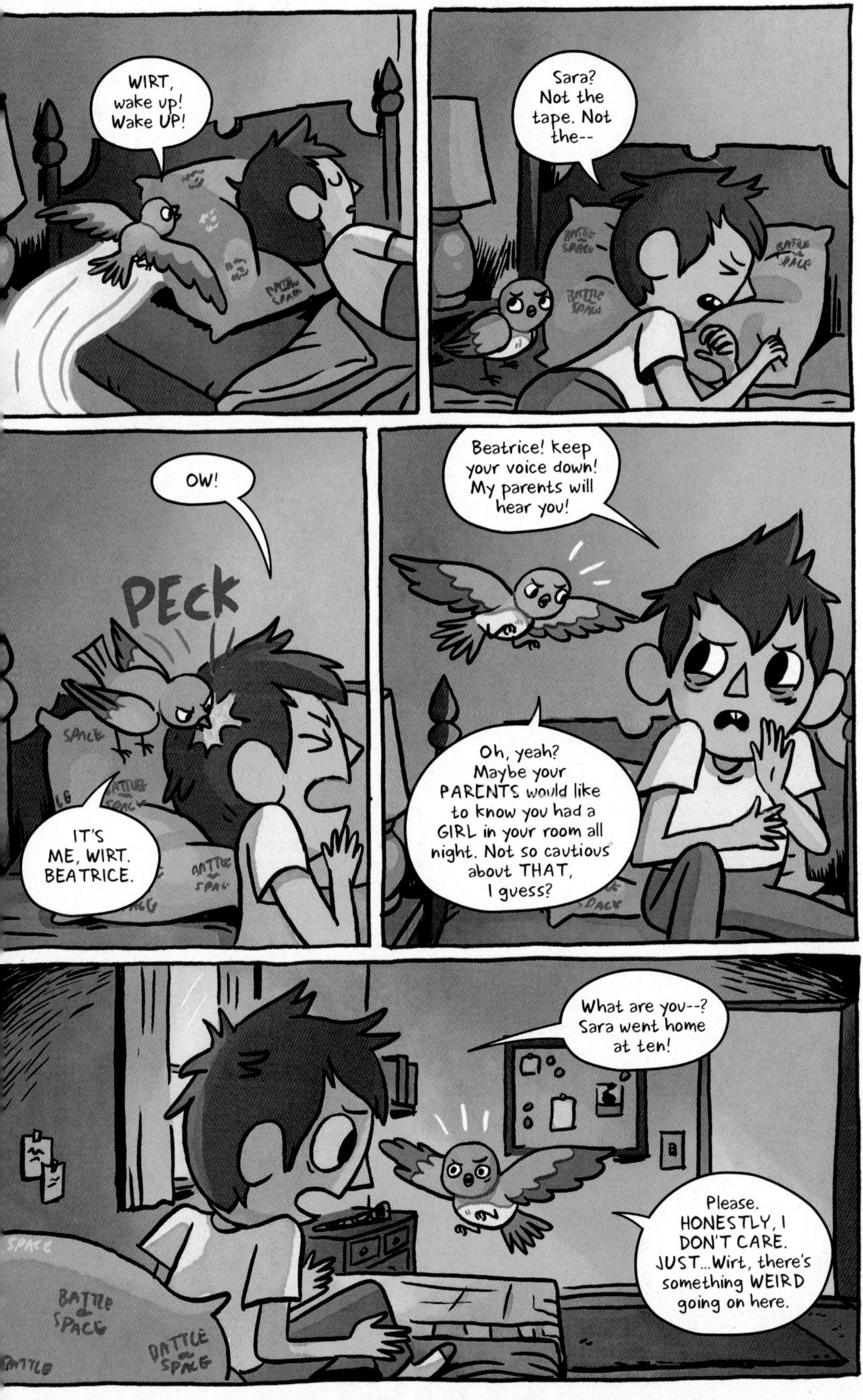
WIRT, wake up! Wake UP!
Sara? Not the tape. Not the--
OW!
PECK
IT'S ME, WIRT. BEATRICE.
Beatrice! Keep your voice down! My parents will hear you!
Oh, yeah? Maybe your PARENTS would like to know you had a GIRL in your room all night. Not so cautious about THAT, I guess?
What are you--? Sara went home at ten!
Please. HONESTLY, I DON'T CARE. JUST...Wirt, there's something WEIRD going on here.

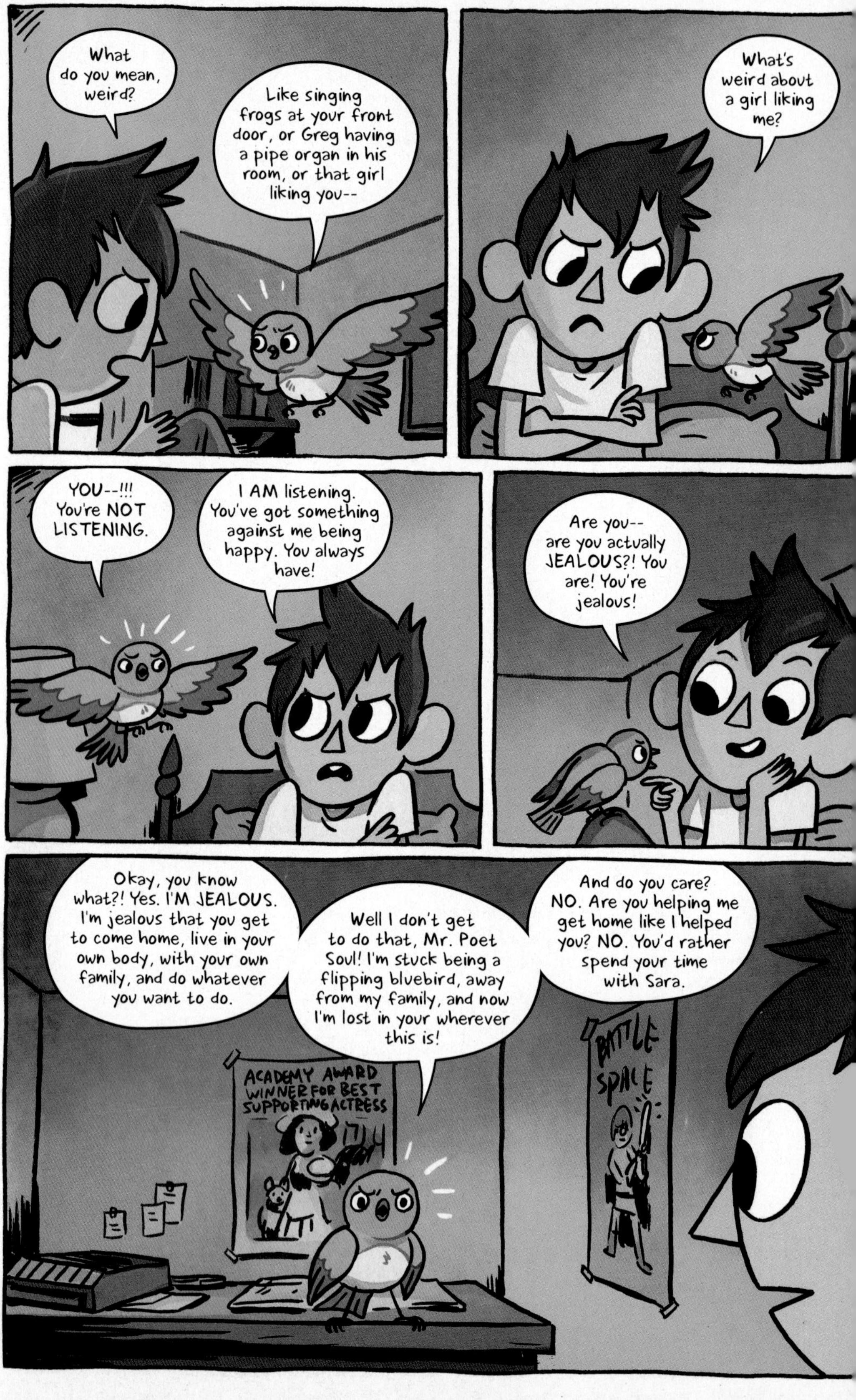
What do you mean, weird?
Like singing frogs at your front door, or Greg having a pipe organ in his room, or that girl liking you--
What's weird about a girl liking me?
YOU--!!! You're NOT LISTENING.
I AM listening. You've got something against me being happy. You always have!
Are you-- are you actually JEALOUS?! You are! You're jealous!
Okay, you know what?! Yes. I'M JEALOUS. I'm jealous that you get to come home, live in your own body, with your own family, and do whatever you want to do.
Well I don't get to do that, Mr. Poet Soul! I'm stuck being a flipping bluebird, away from my family, and now I'm lost in your wherever this is!
And do you care? NO. Are you helping me get home like I helped you? NO. You'd rather spend your time with Sara.
ACADEMY AWARD WINNER FOR BEST SUPPORTING ACTRESS
BATTLE SPACE

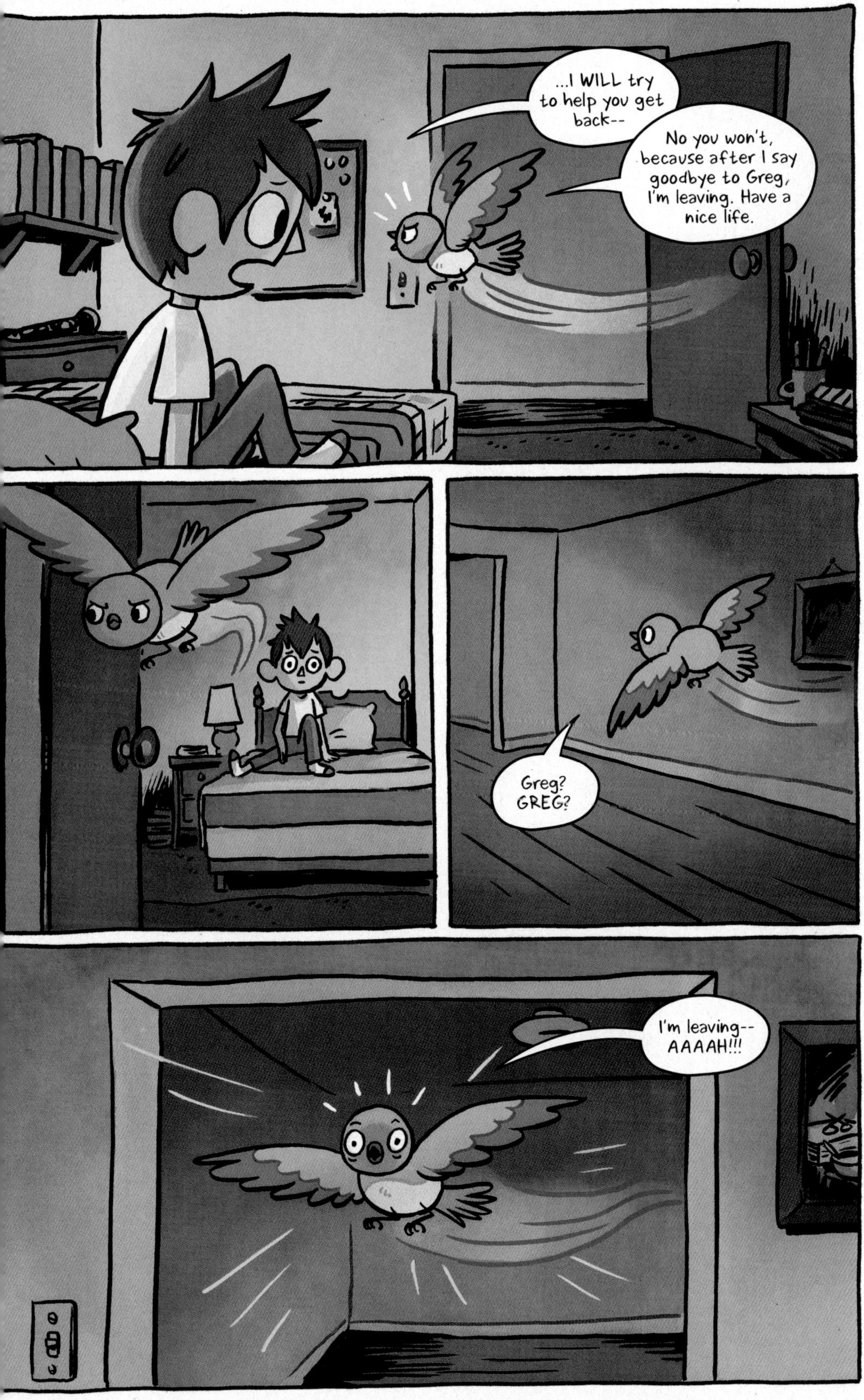
...I WILL try to help you get back--
No you won't, because after I say goodbye to Greg, I'm leaving. Have a nice life.
Greg? GREG?
I'm leaving-- AAAAH!!!

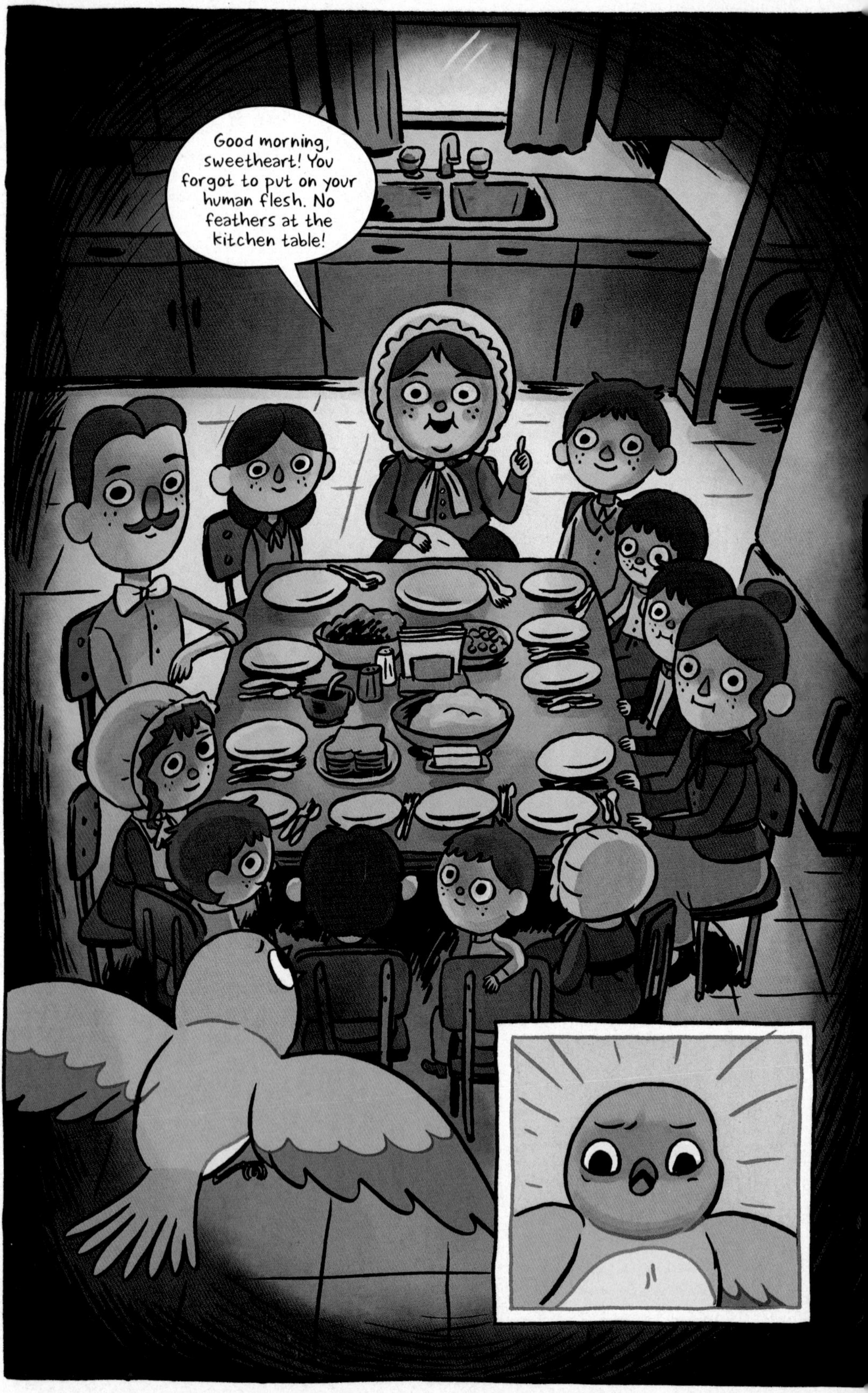
Good morning, sweetheart! You forgot to put on your human flesh. No feathers at the kitchen table!

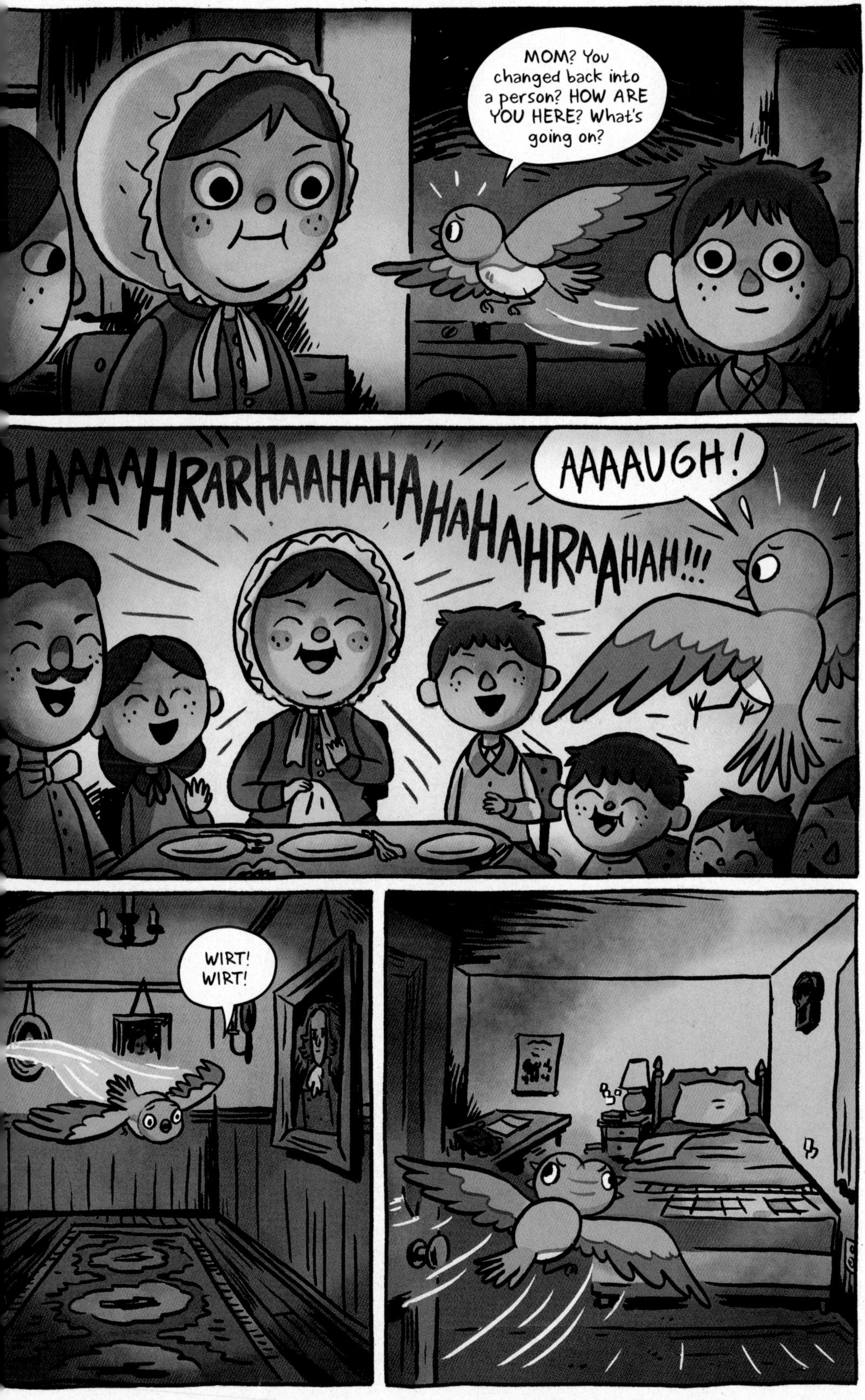
MOM? You changed back into a person? HOW ARE YOU HERE? What's going on?
HAAAAHRARHAAHAHAHAHAHRAAHAH!!!
AAAAUGH!
WIRT! WIRT!

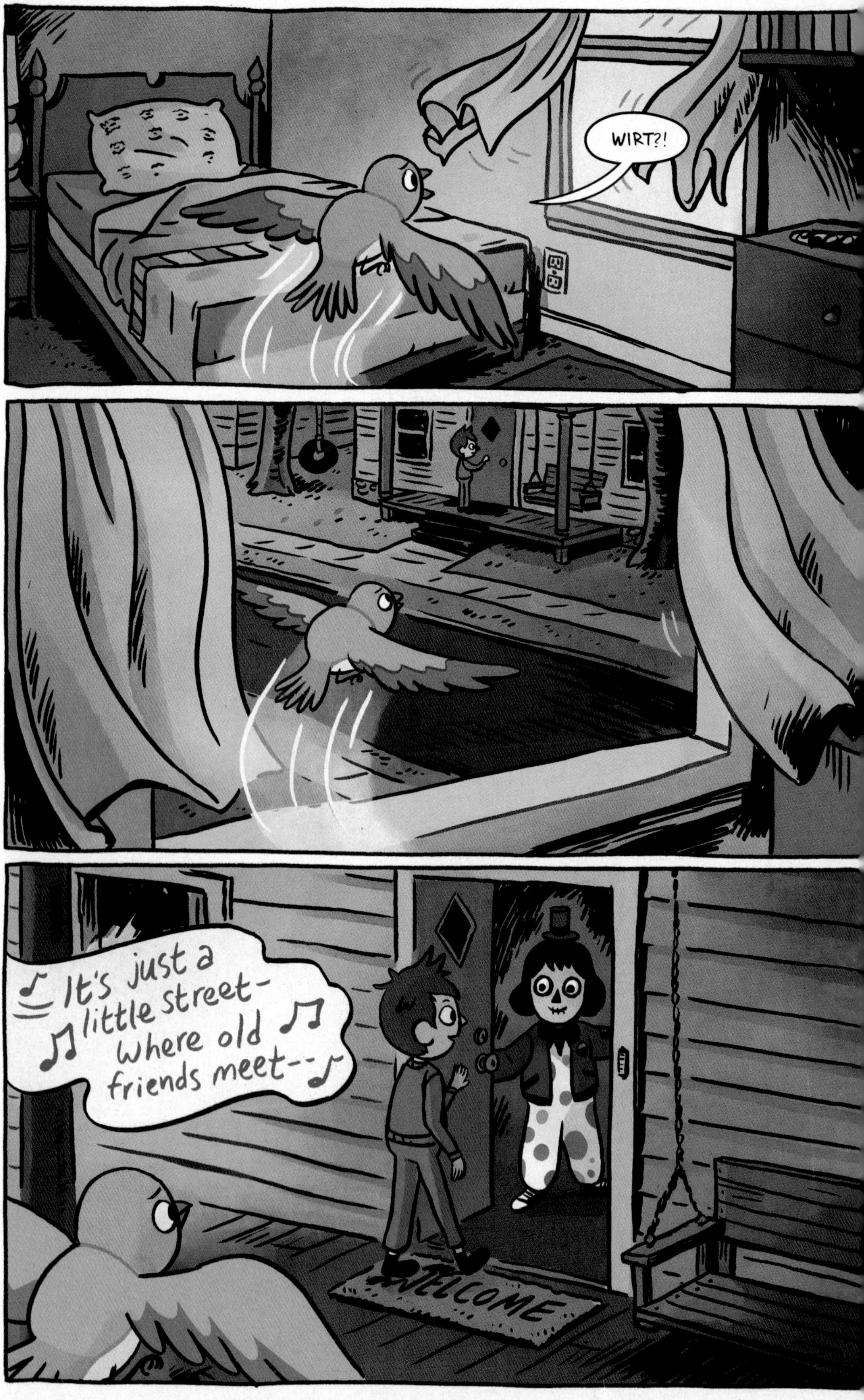
WIRT?!
It's just a little street- where old friends meet--

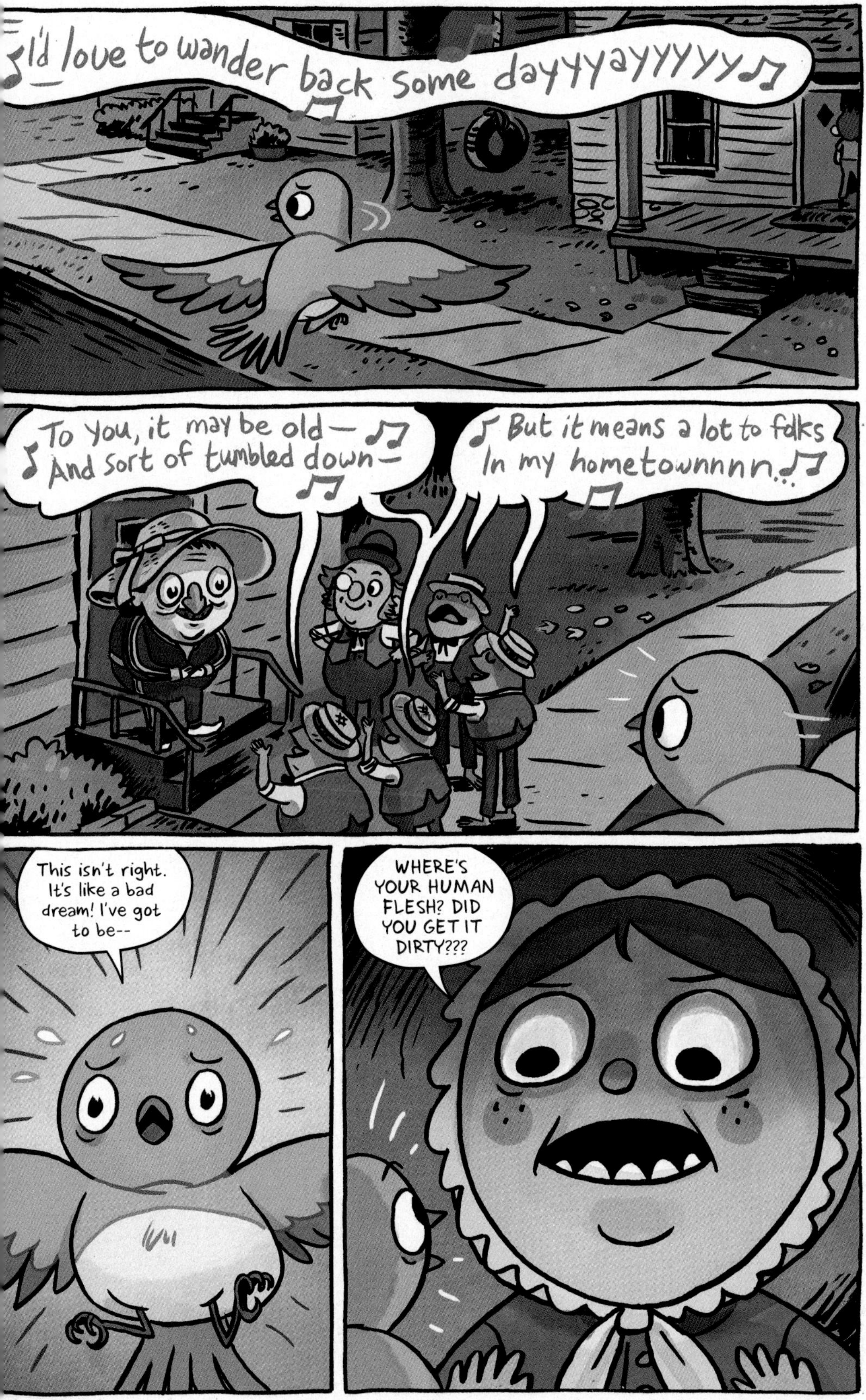
I'd love to wander back some dayyyayyyyy
To you, it may be old— And sort of tumbled down—
But it means a lot to folks In my hometownnnnn...
This isn't right. It's like a bad dream! I've got to be--
WHERE'S YOUR HUMAN FLESH? DID YOU GET IT DIRTY???

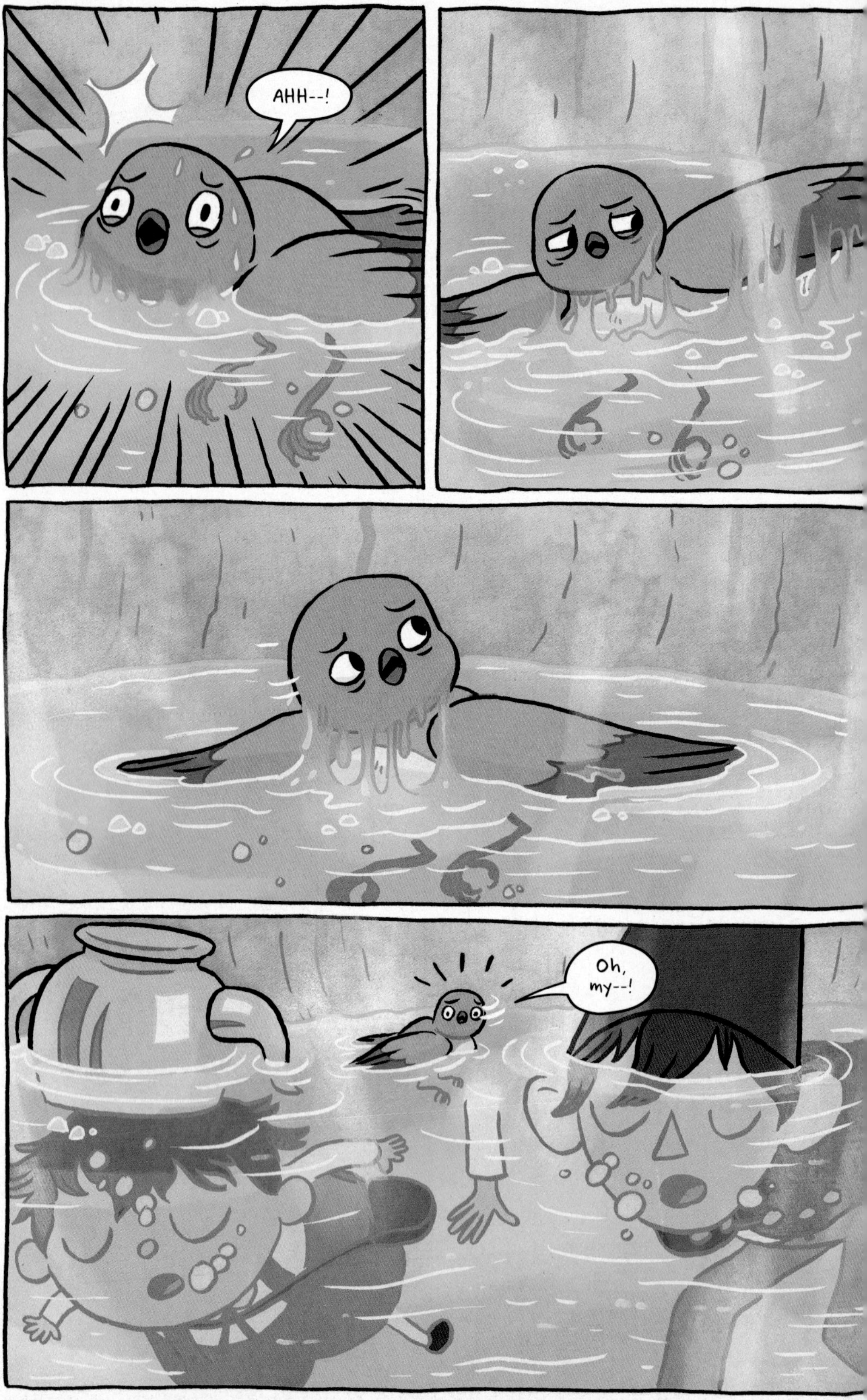
AHH--!
Oh, my--!

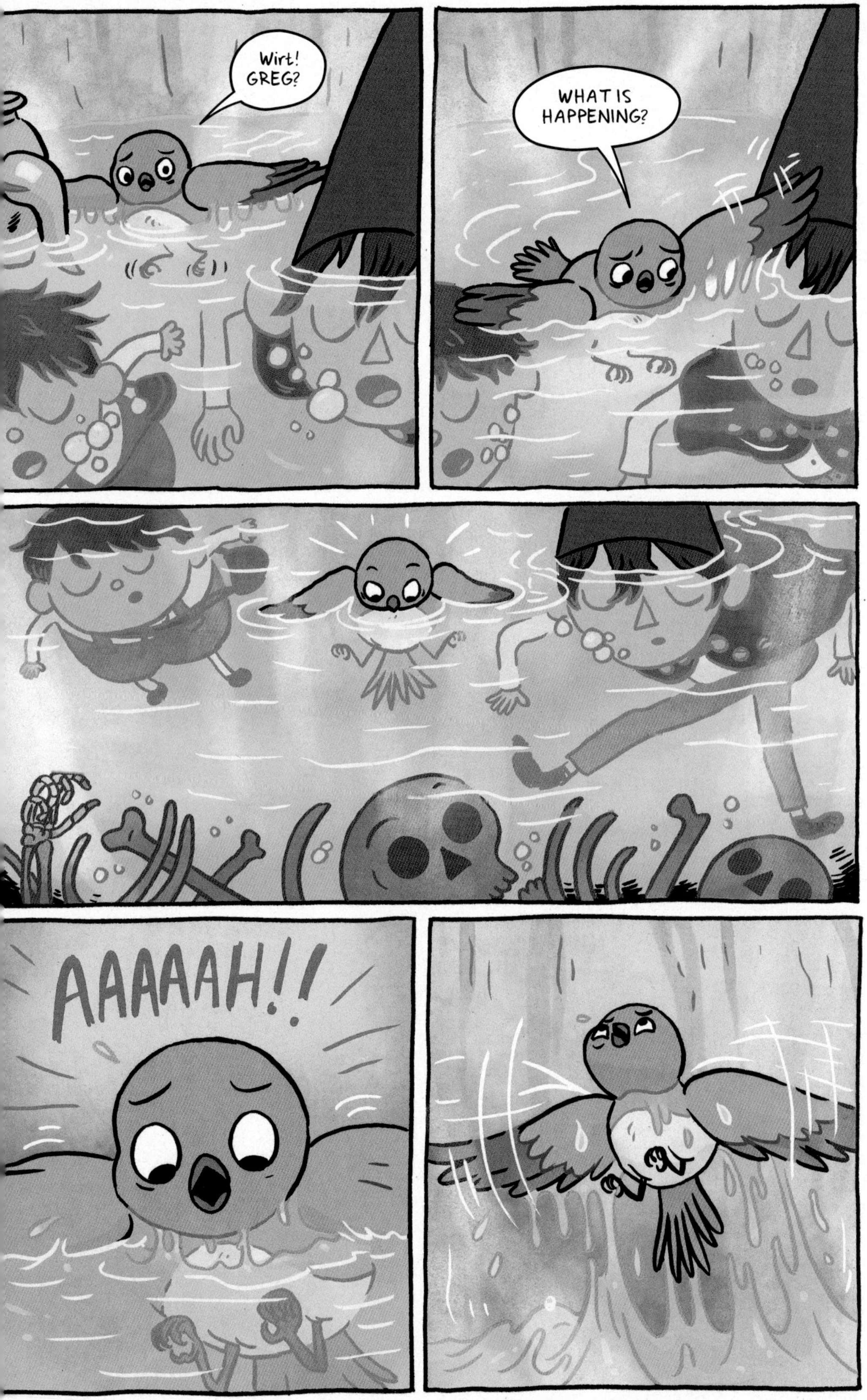
Wirt! GREG?
WHAT IS HAPPENING?
AAAAAH!!

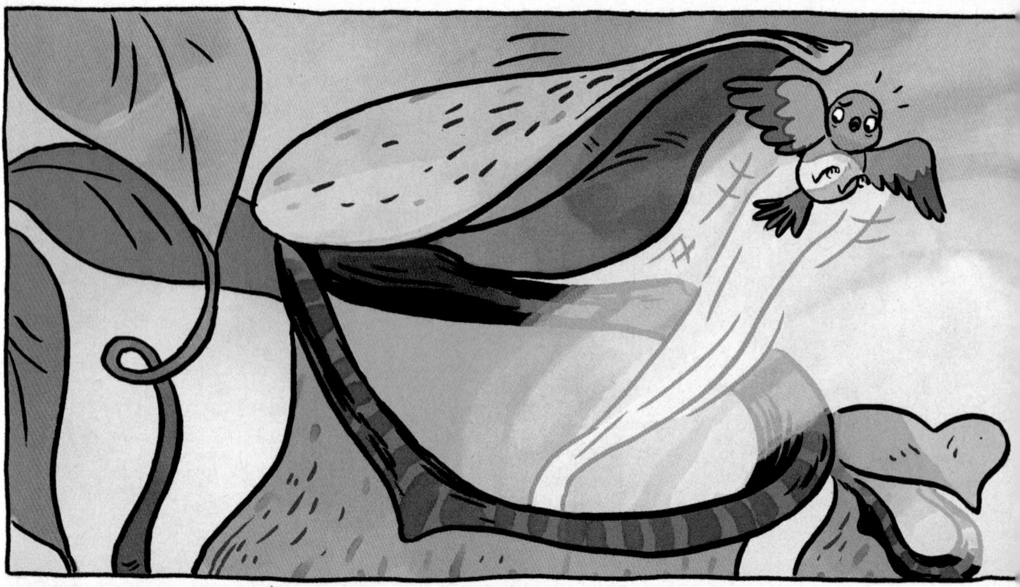

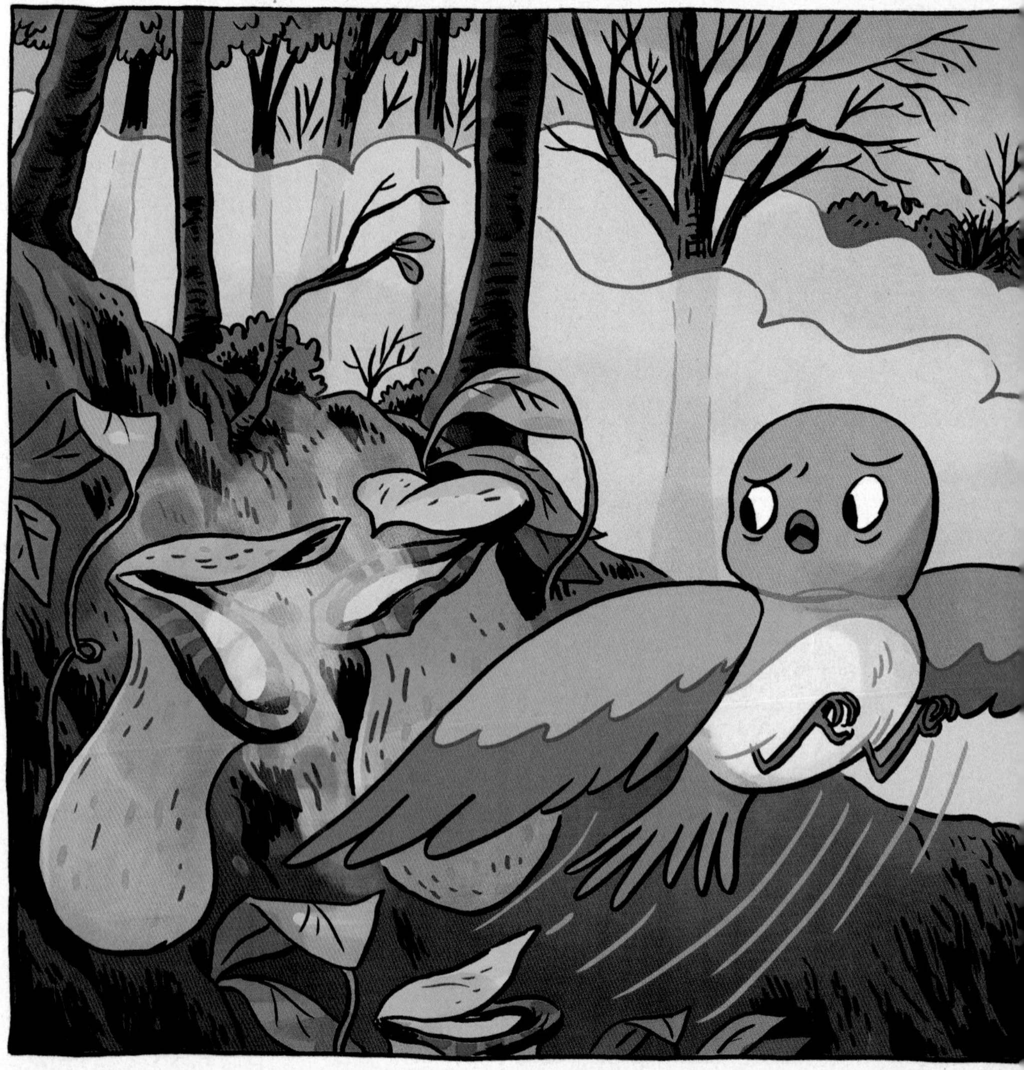

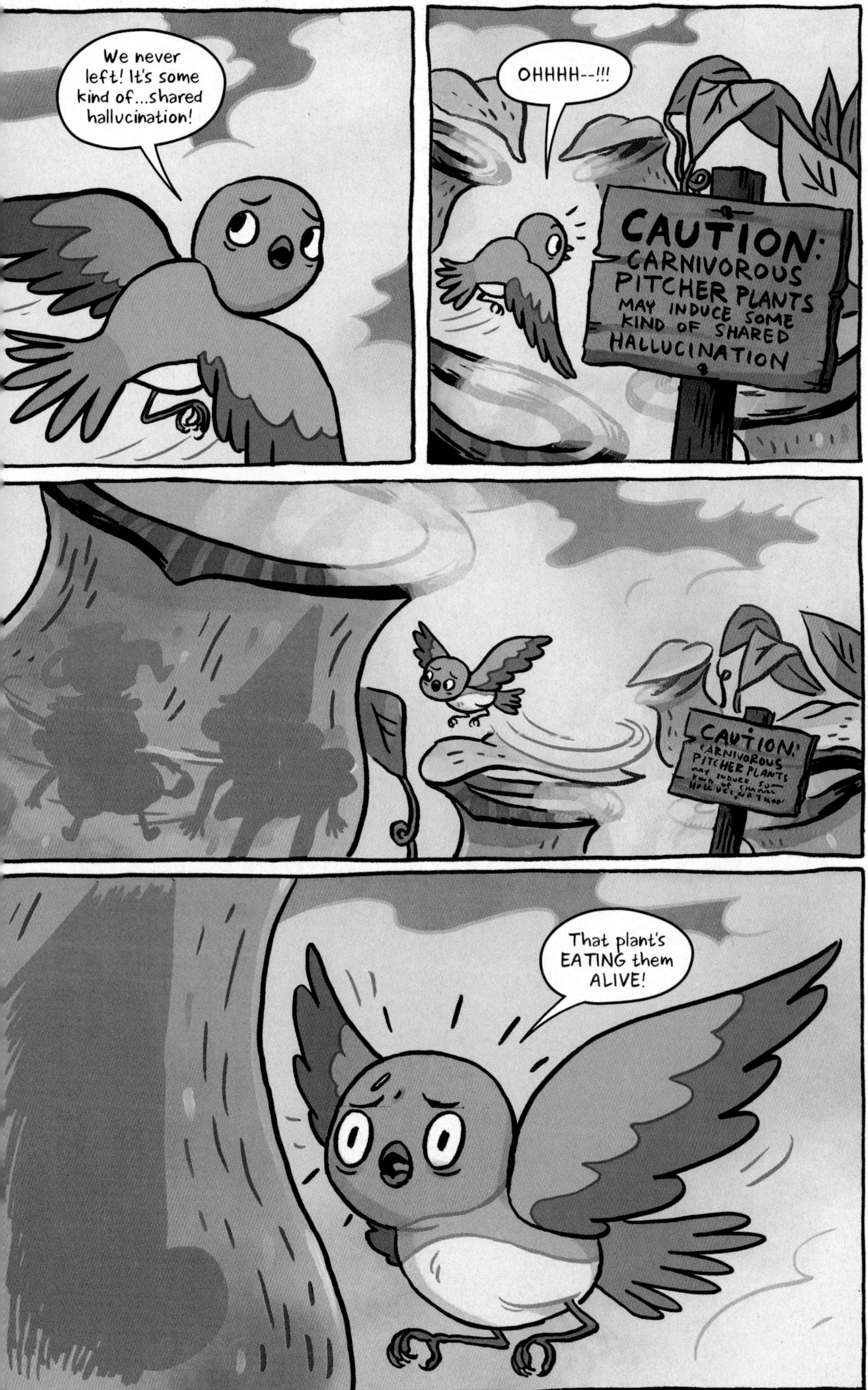
We never left! It's some kind of...shared hallucination!
OHHHH--!!!
CAUTION: CARNIVOROUS PITCHER PLANTS MAY INDUCE SOME KIND OF SHARED HALLUCINATION
CAUTION: CARNIVOROUS PITCHER PLANTS
That plant's EATING them ALIVE!

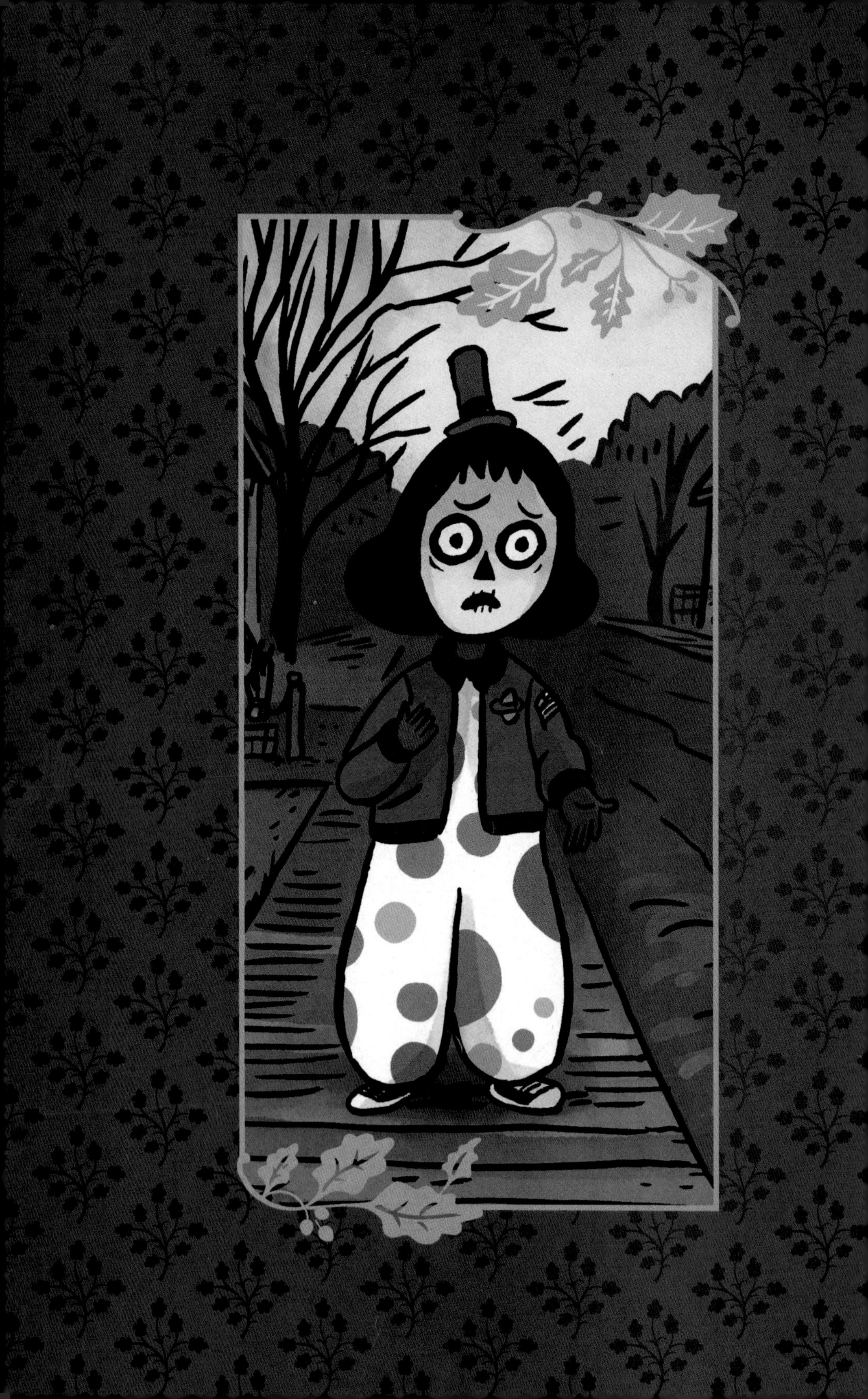

ACT THREE

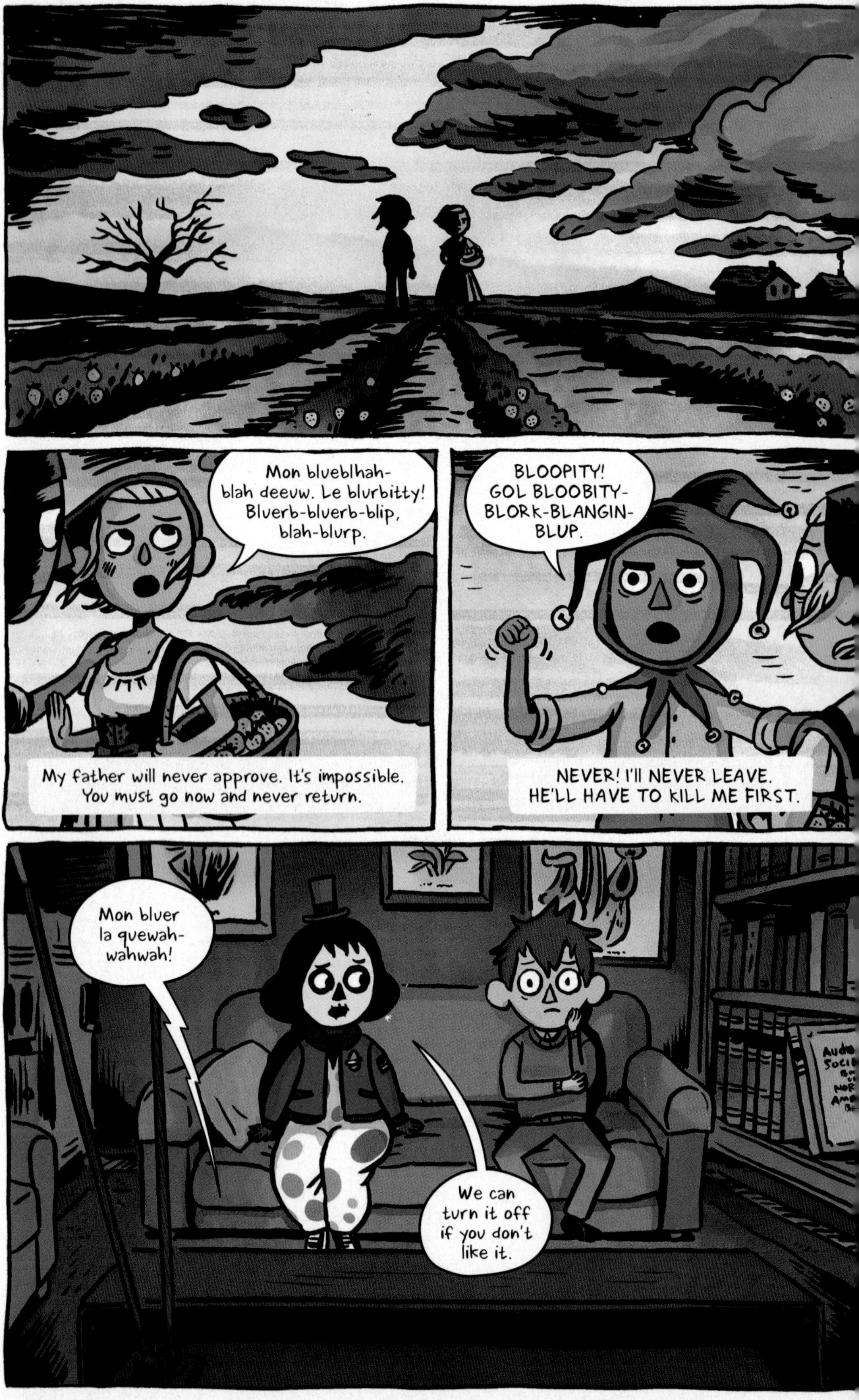
Mon blueblhah-blah deeuw. Le blurbitty! Bluerb-bluerb-blip, blah-blurp.
My father will never approve. It's impossible. You must go now and never return.
BLOOPITY! GOL BLOOBITY-BLORK-BLANGIN-BLUP.
NEVER! I'll NEVER LEAVE. HE'LL HAVE TO KILL ME FIRST.
Mon bluer la quewah-wahwah!
We can turn it off if you don't like it.

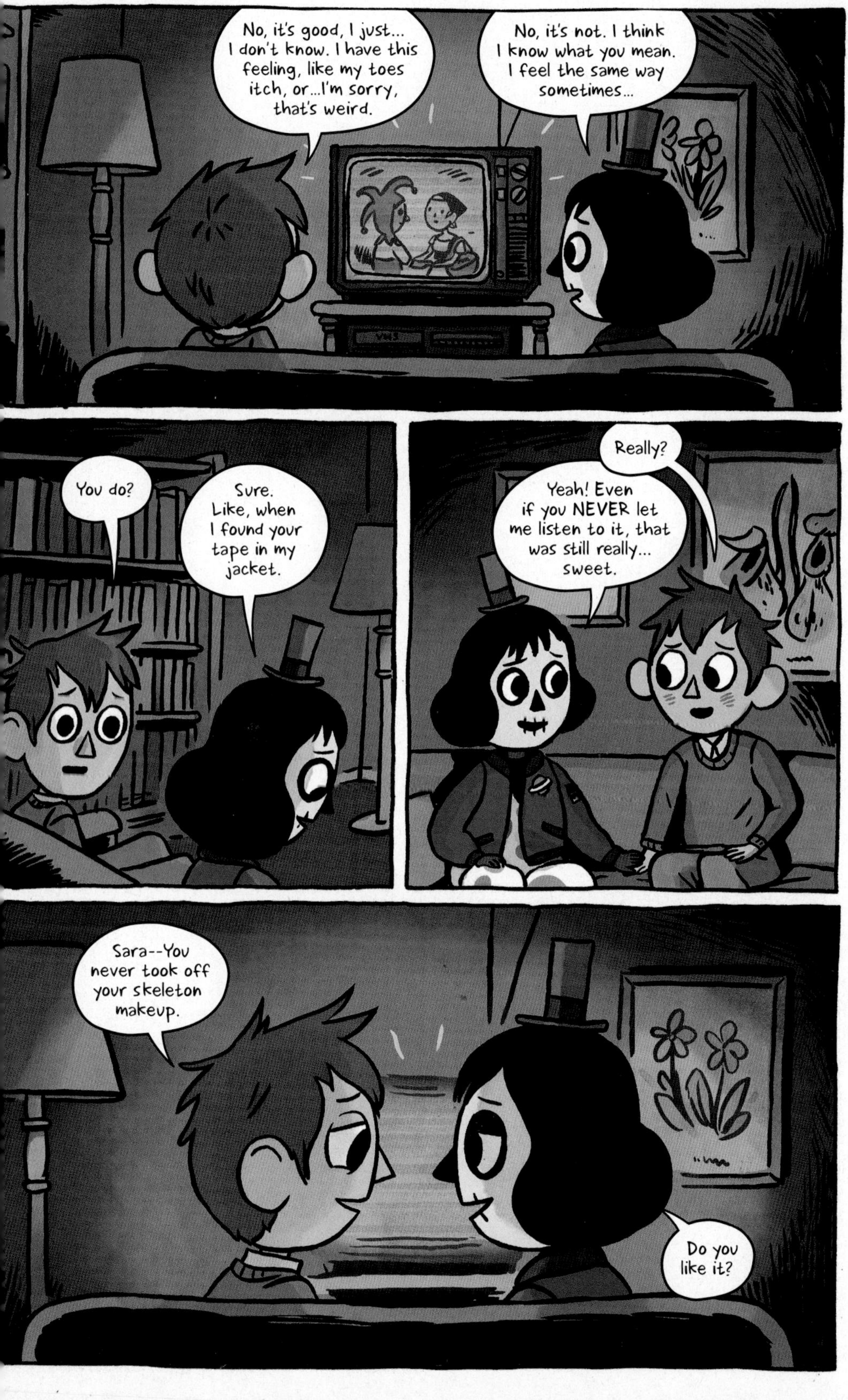
No, it's good, I just... I don't know. I have this feeling, like my toes itch, or...I'm sorry, that's weird.
No, it's not. I think I know what you mean. I feel the same way sometimes...
You do?
Sure. Like, when I found your tape in my jacket.
Really?
Yeah! Even if you NEVER let me listen to it, that was still really... sweet.
Sara--You never took off your skeleton makeup.
Do you like it?

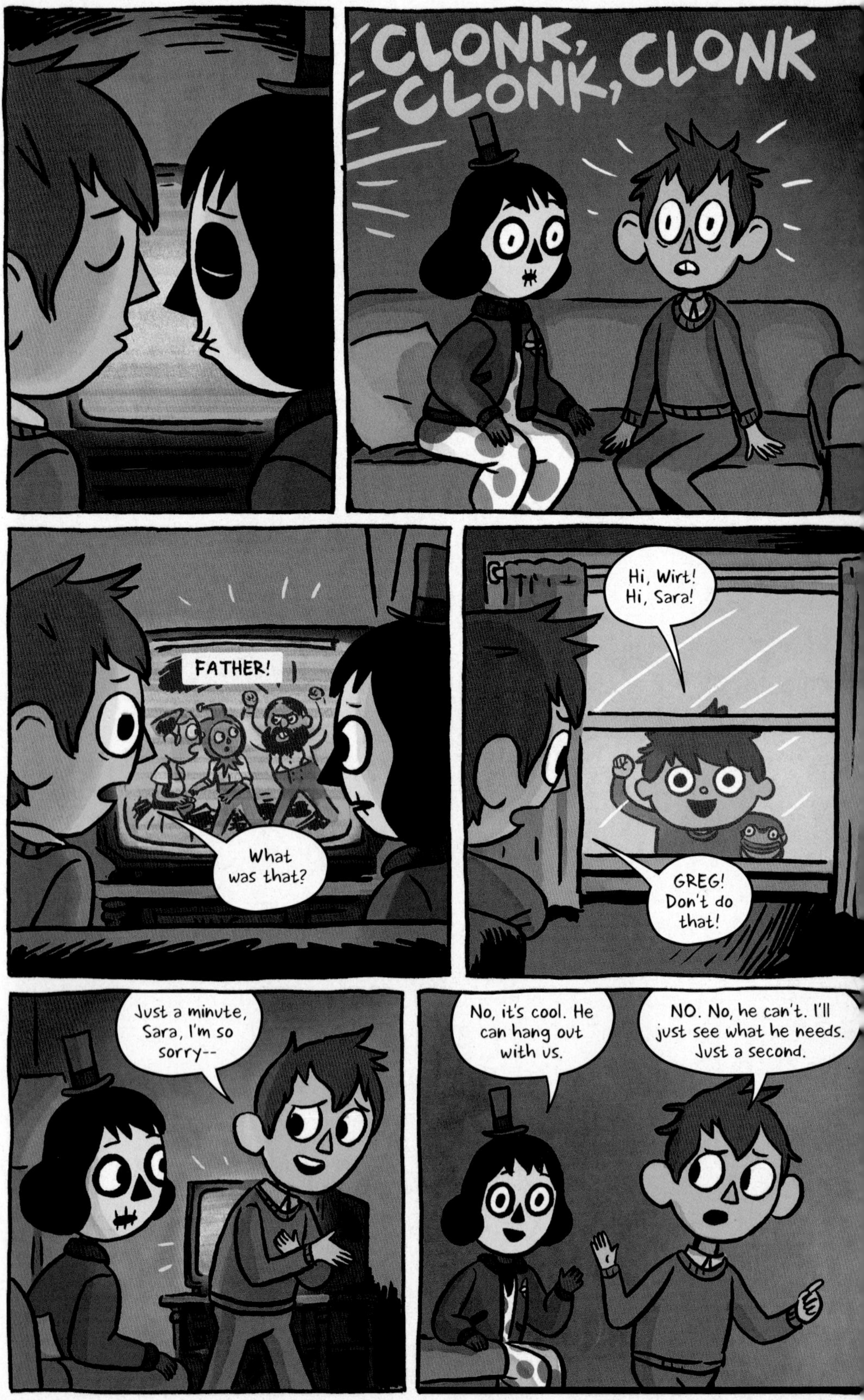
CLONK, CLONK, CLONK
FATHER!
What was that?
Hi, Wirt! Hi, Sara!
GREG! Don't do that!
Just a minute, Sara, I'm so sorry--
No, it's cool. He can hang out with us.
NO. No, he can't. I'll just see what he needs. Just a second.

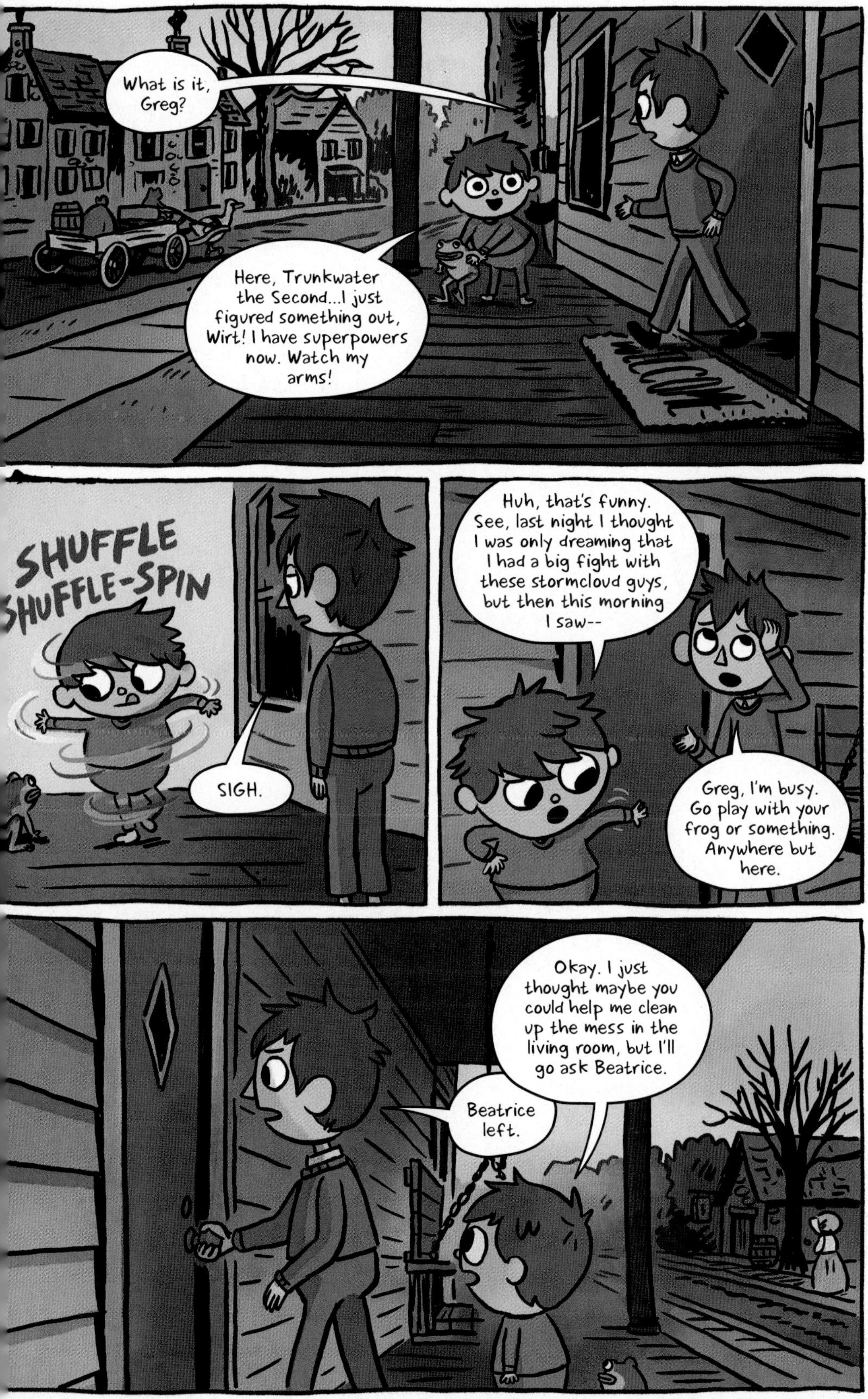
What is it, Greg?
Here, Trunkwater the Second...I just figured something out, Wirt! I have superpowers now. Watch my arms!
SHUFFLE SHUFFLE-SPIN
SIGH.
Huh, that's funny. See, last night I thought I was only dreaming that I had a big fight with these stormcloud guys, but then this morning I saw--
Greg, I'm busy. Go play with your frog or something. Anywhere but here.
Okay. I just thought maybe you could help me clean up the mess in the living room, but I'll go ask Beatrice.
Beatrice left.

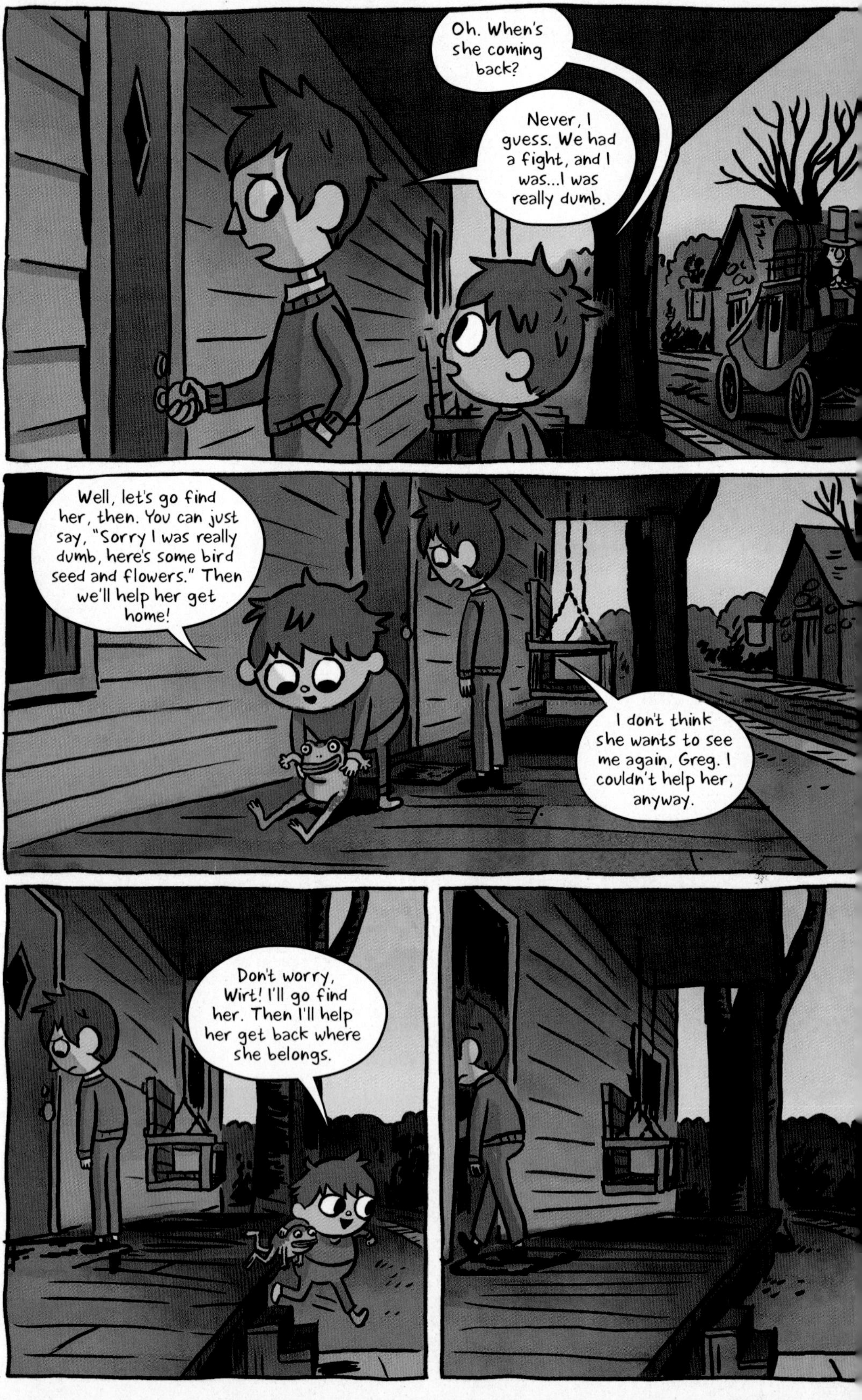

Oh. When's she coming back?
Never, I guess. We had a fight, and I was...I was really dumb.
Well, let's go find her, then. You can just say, "Sorry I was really dumb, here's some bird seed and flowers." Then we'll help her get home!
I don't think she wants to see me again, Greg. I couldn't help her, anyway.
Don't worry, Wirt! I'll go find her. Then I'll help her get back where she belongs.

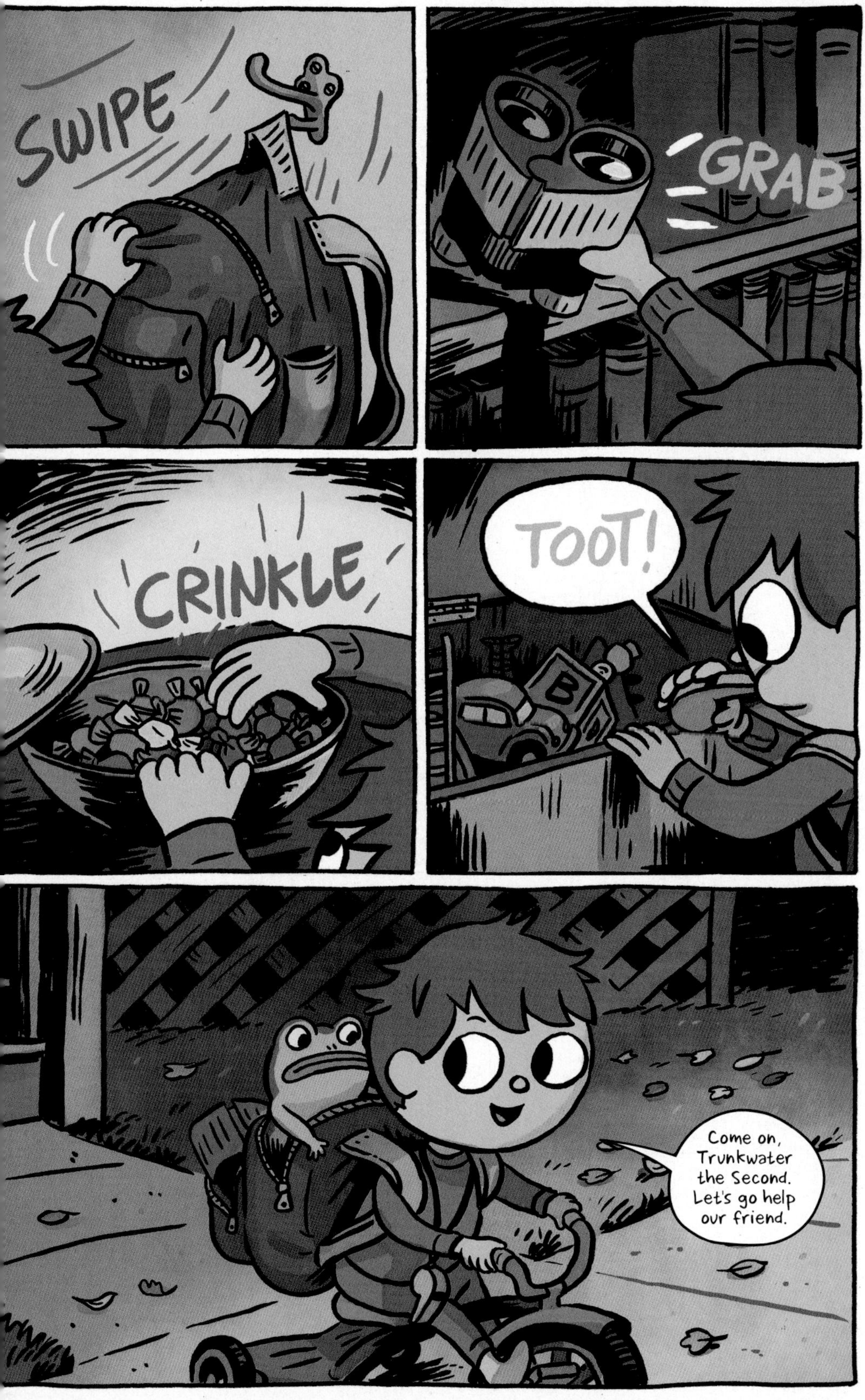
SWIPE
GRAB
CRINKLE
TOOT!
Come on, Trunkwater the Second. Let's go help our friend.

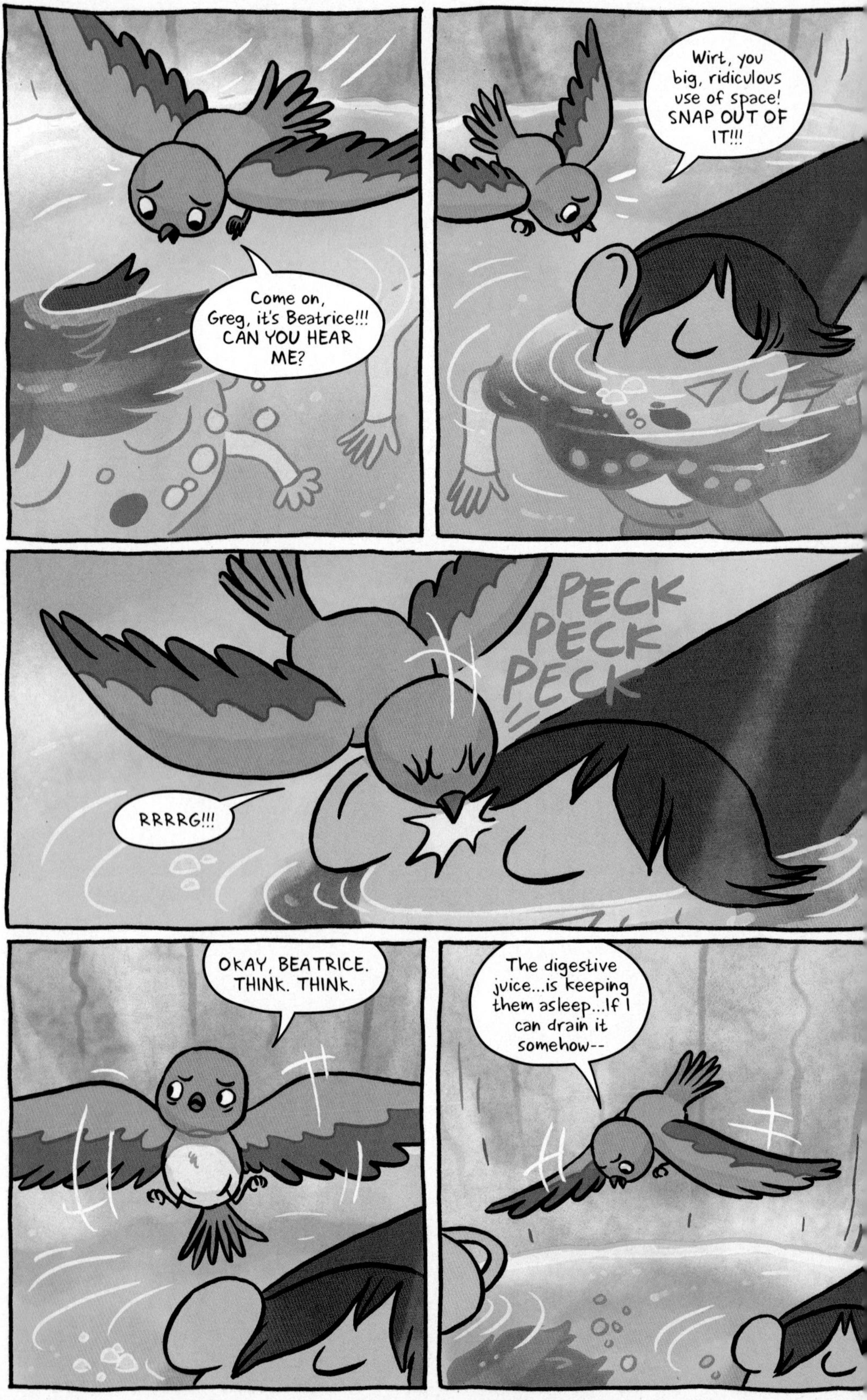
Come on, Greg, it's Beatrice!!! CAN YOU HEAR ME?
Wirt, you big, ridiculous use of space! SNAP OUT OF IT!!!
PECK PECK PECK
RRRRG!!!
OKAY, BEATRICE. THINK. THINK.
The digestive juice...is keeping them asleep...If I can drain it somehow--

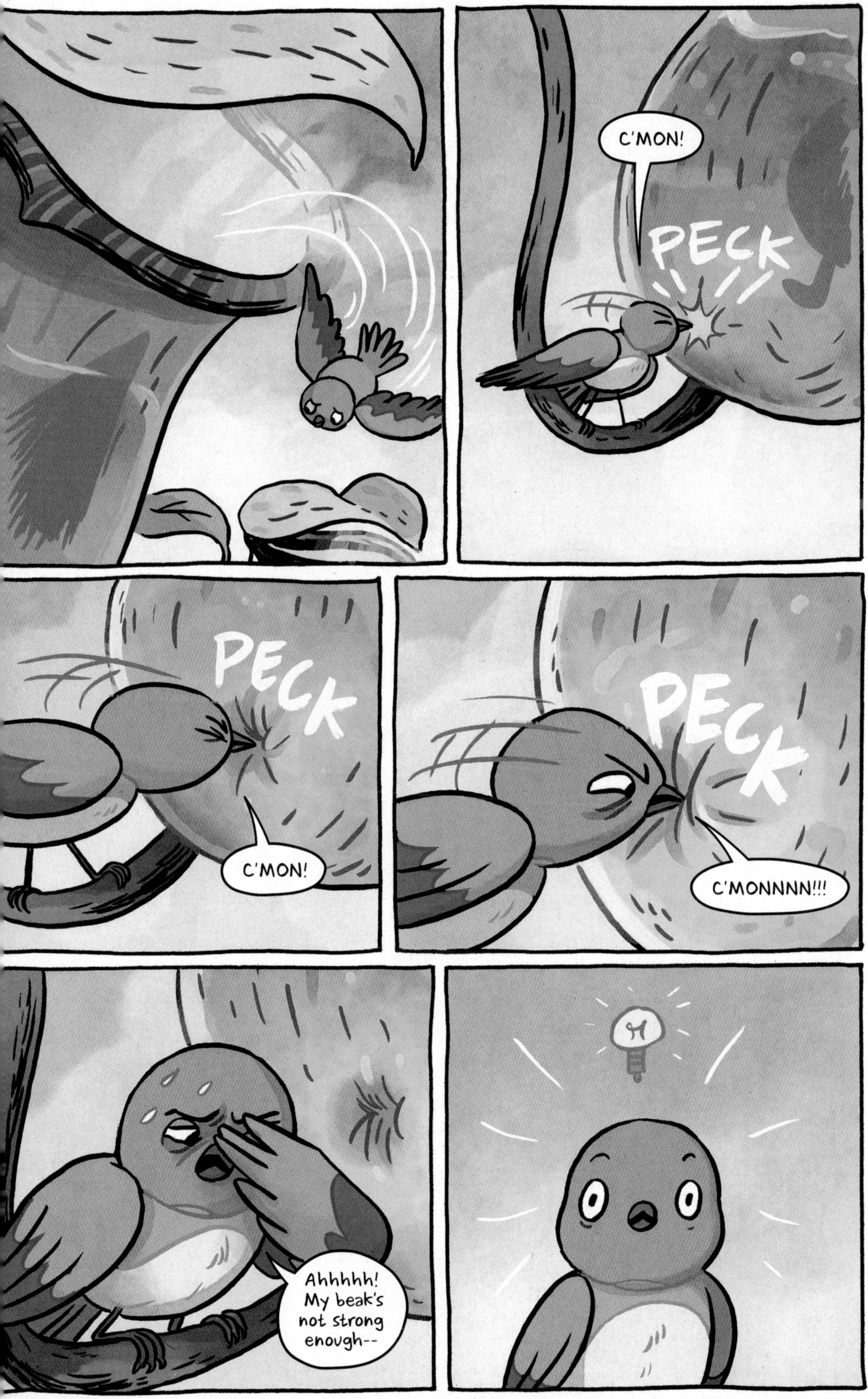
C'MON!
PECK
PECK
C'MON!
PECK
C'MONNNN!!!
Ahhhhh! My beak's not strong enough--

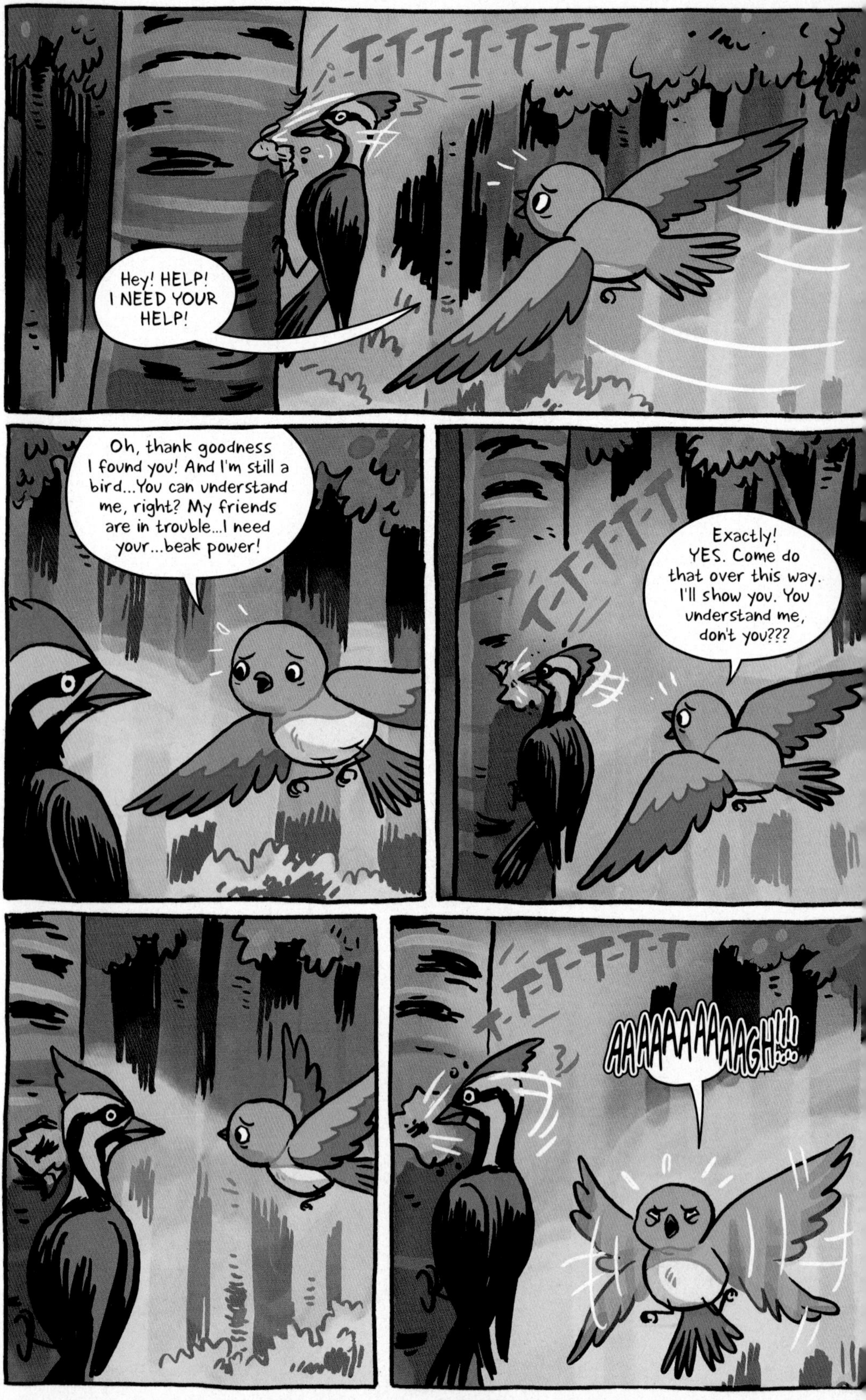

T-T-T-T-T-T-T-T
Hey! HELP! I NEED YOUR HELP!
Oh, thank goodness I found you! And I'm still a bird...You can understand me, right? My friends are in trouble...I need your...beak power!
T-T-T-T-T-T
Exactly! YES. Come do that over this way. I'll show you. You understand me, don't you???
T-T-T-T-T-T-T
AAAAAAAAAGH!!!...

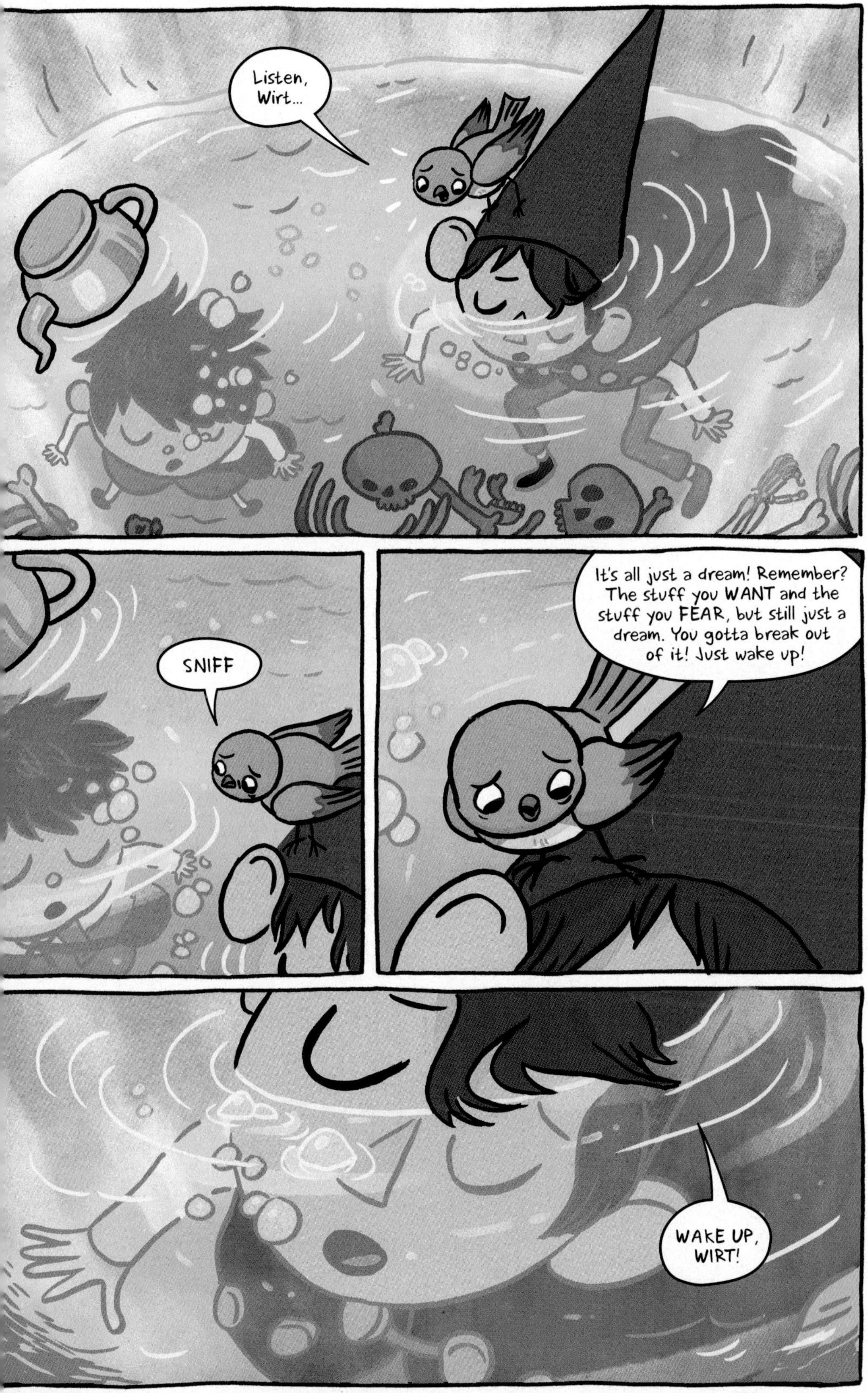
Listen, Wirt...
SNIFF
It's all just a dream! Remember? The stuff you WANT and the stuff you FEAR, but still just a dream. You gotta break out of it! Just wake up!
WAKE UP, WIRT!

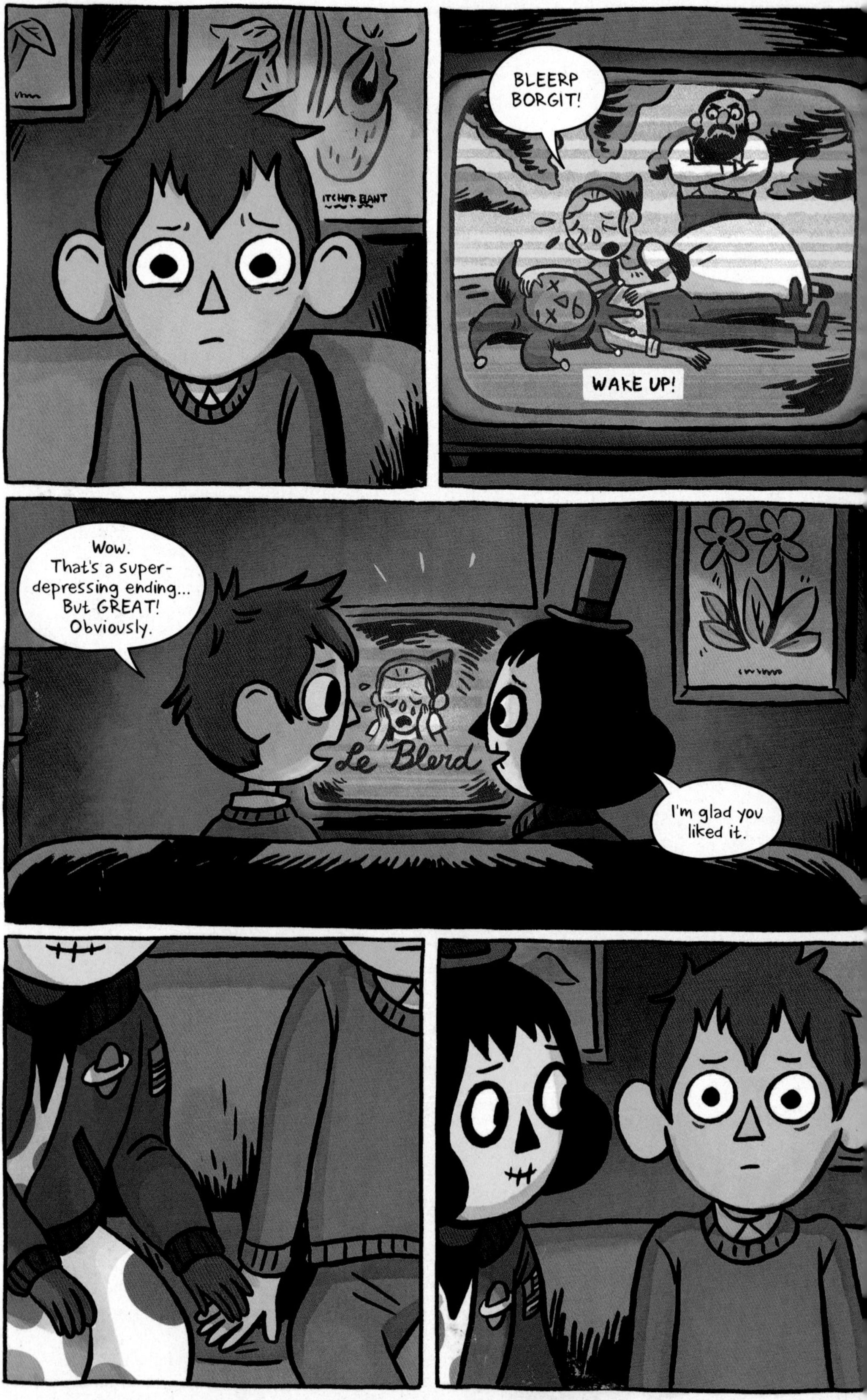
BLEERP BORGIT!
WAKE UP!
Wow. That's a super-depressing ending... But GREAT! Obviously.
Le Blerd
I'm glad you liked it.

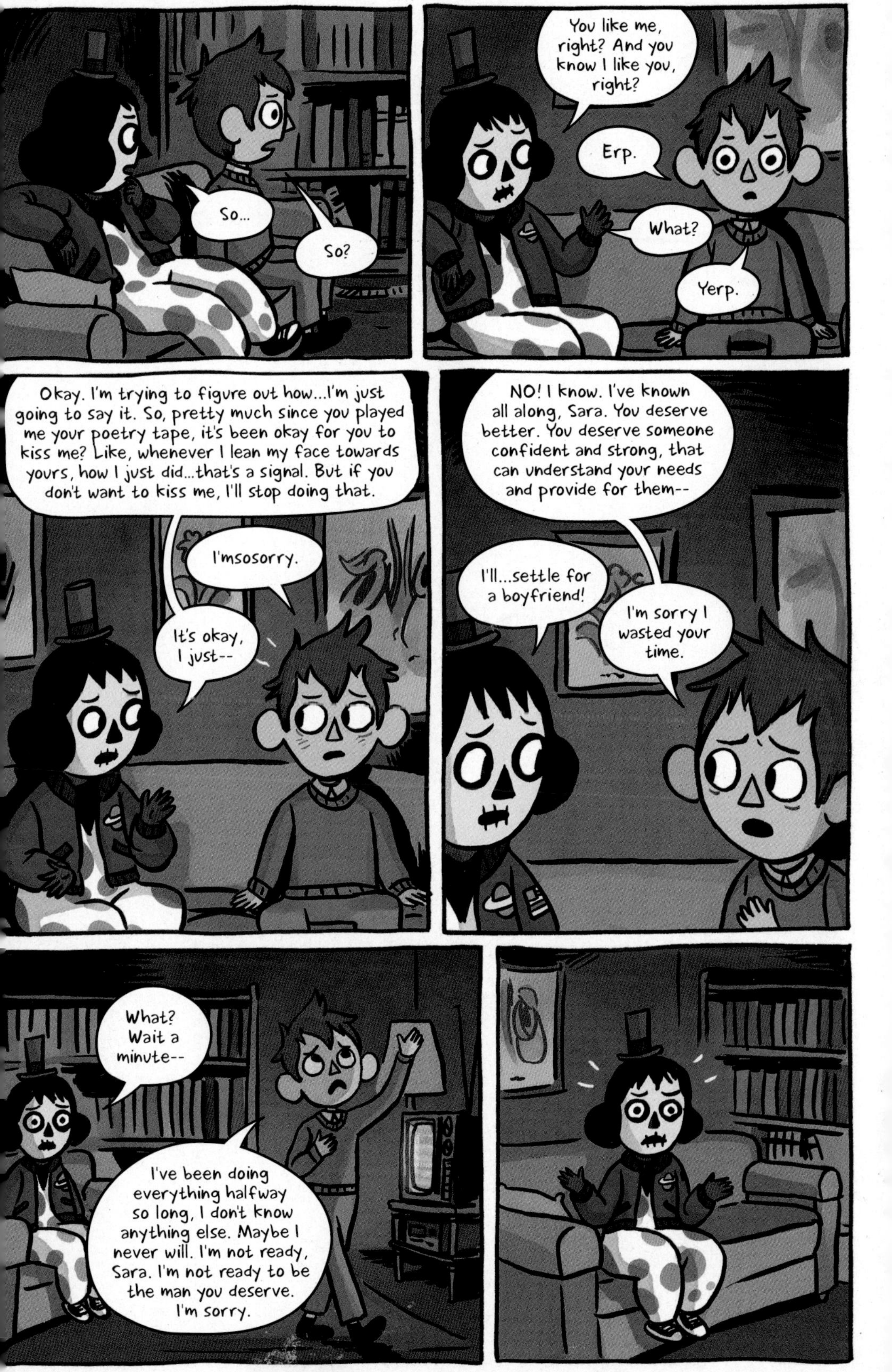

So...
So?
You like me, right? And you know I like you, right?
Erp.
What?
Yerp.
Okay. I'm trying to figure out how...I'm just going to say it. So, pretty much since you played me your poetry tape, it's been okay for you to kiss me? Like, whenever I lean my face towards yours, how I just did...that's a signal. But if you don't want to kiss me, I'll stop doing that.
I'msosorry.
It's okay, I just--
NO! I know. I've known all along, Sara. You deserve better. You deserve someone confident and strong, that can understand your needs and provide for them--
I'll...settle for a boyfriend!
I'm sorry I wasted your time.
What? Wait a minute--
I've been doing everything halfway so long, I don't know anything else. Maybe I never will. I'm not ready, Sara. I'm not ready to be the man you deserve. I'm sorry.

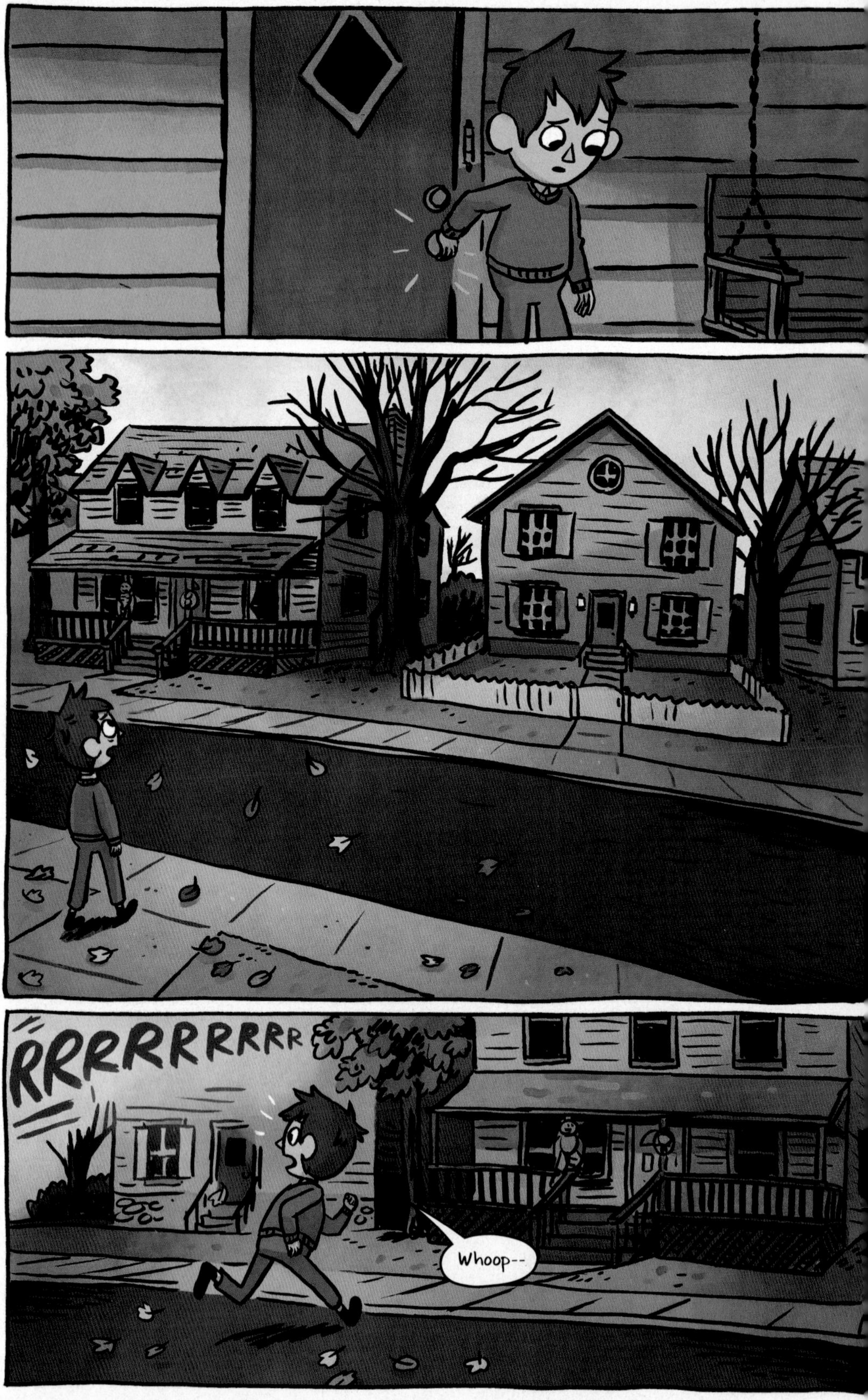
RRRRRRRRR
Whoop--

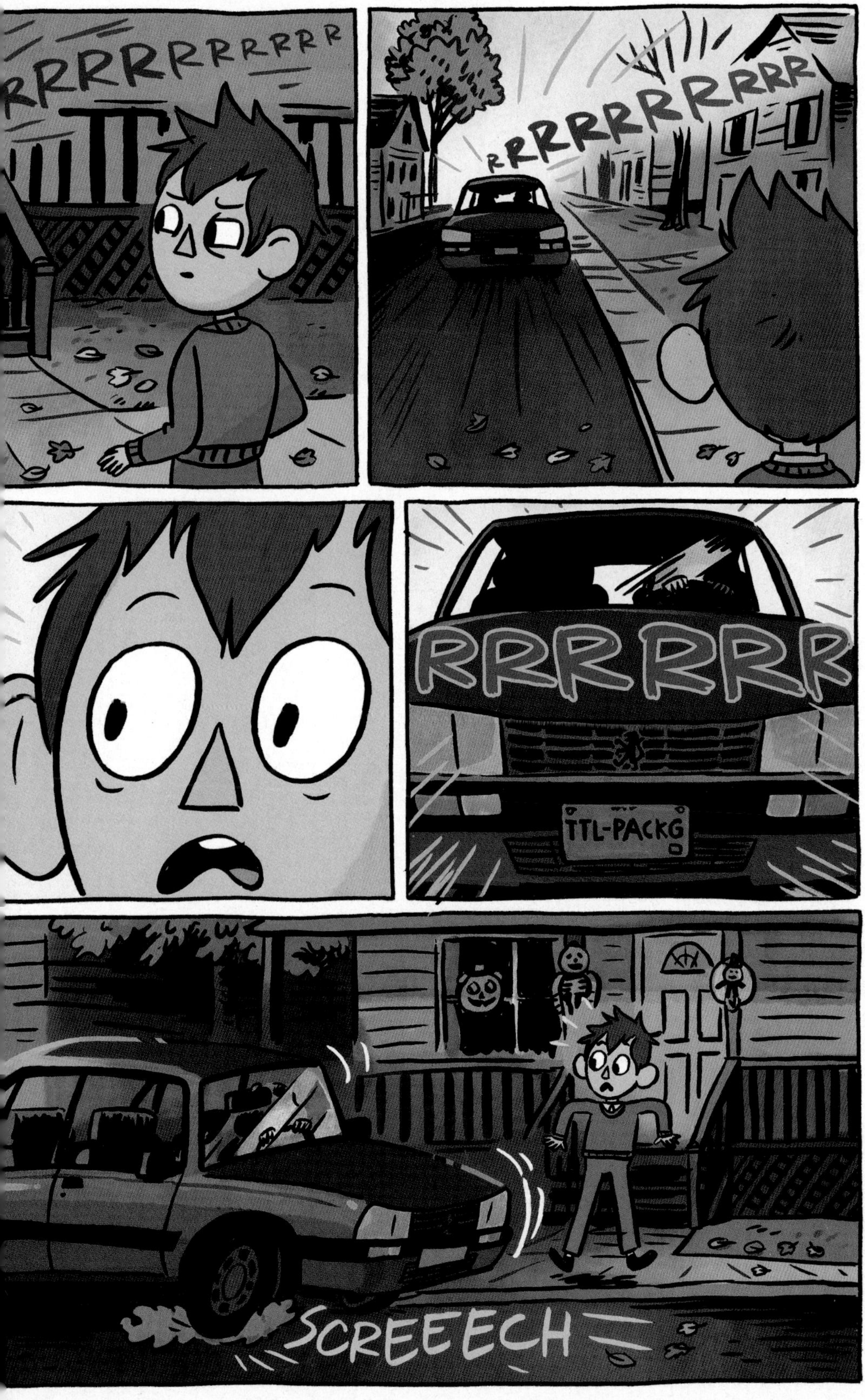
RRRRRRRRRRR
rRRRRRRRRRRR
RRRRRR
TTL-PACKG
SCREEECH

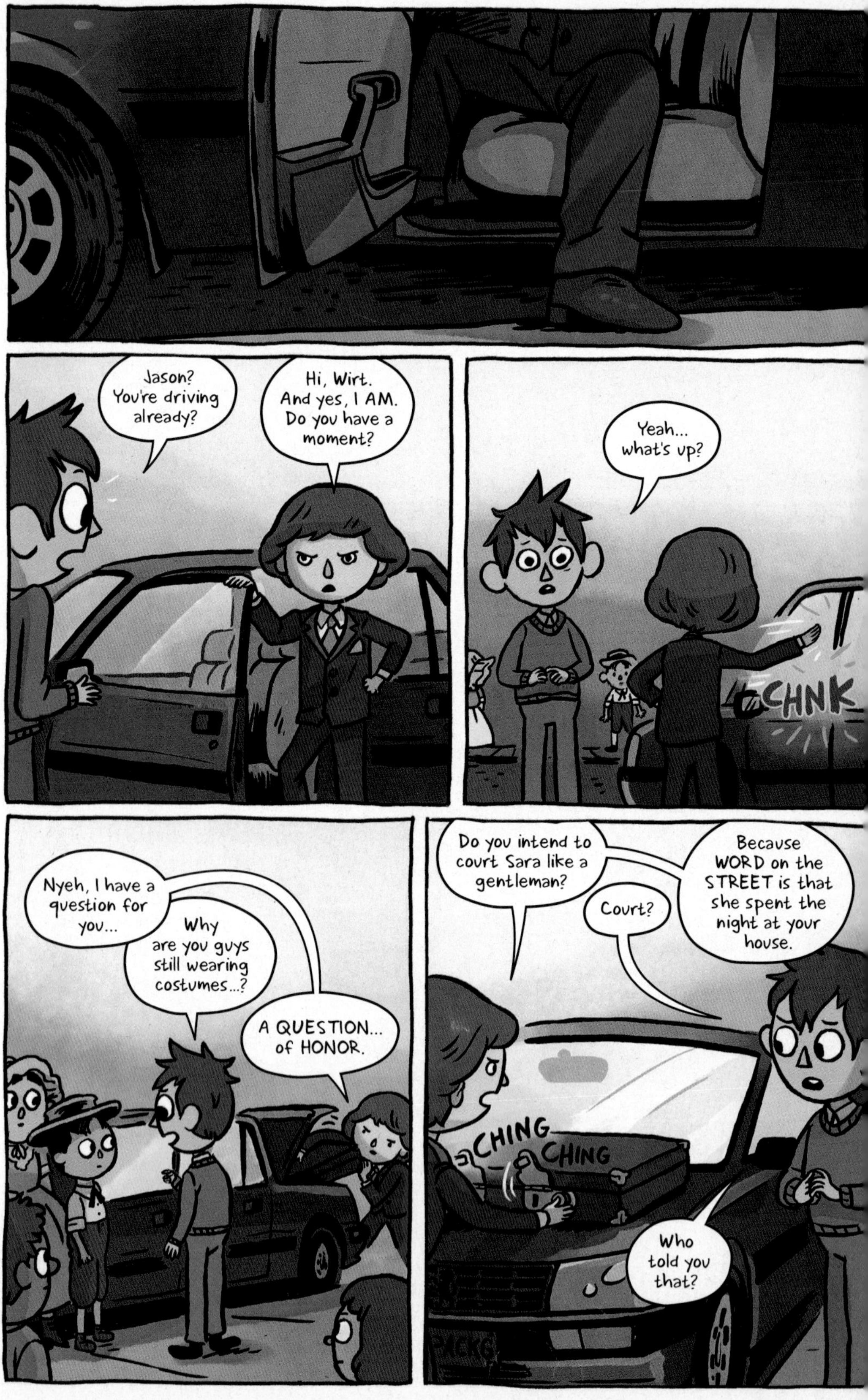

Jason? You're driving already?
Hi, Wirt. And yes, I AM. Do you have a moment?
Yeah... what's up?
CHNK
Nyeh, I have a question for you...
Why are you guys still wearing costumes...?
A QUESTION... of HONOR.
Do you intend to court Sara like a gentleman?
Court?
Because WORD on the STREET is that she spent the night at your house.
CHING
CHING
Who told you that?

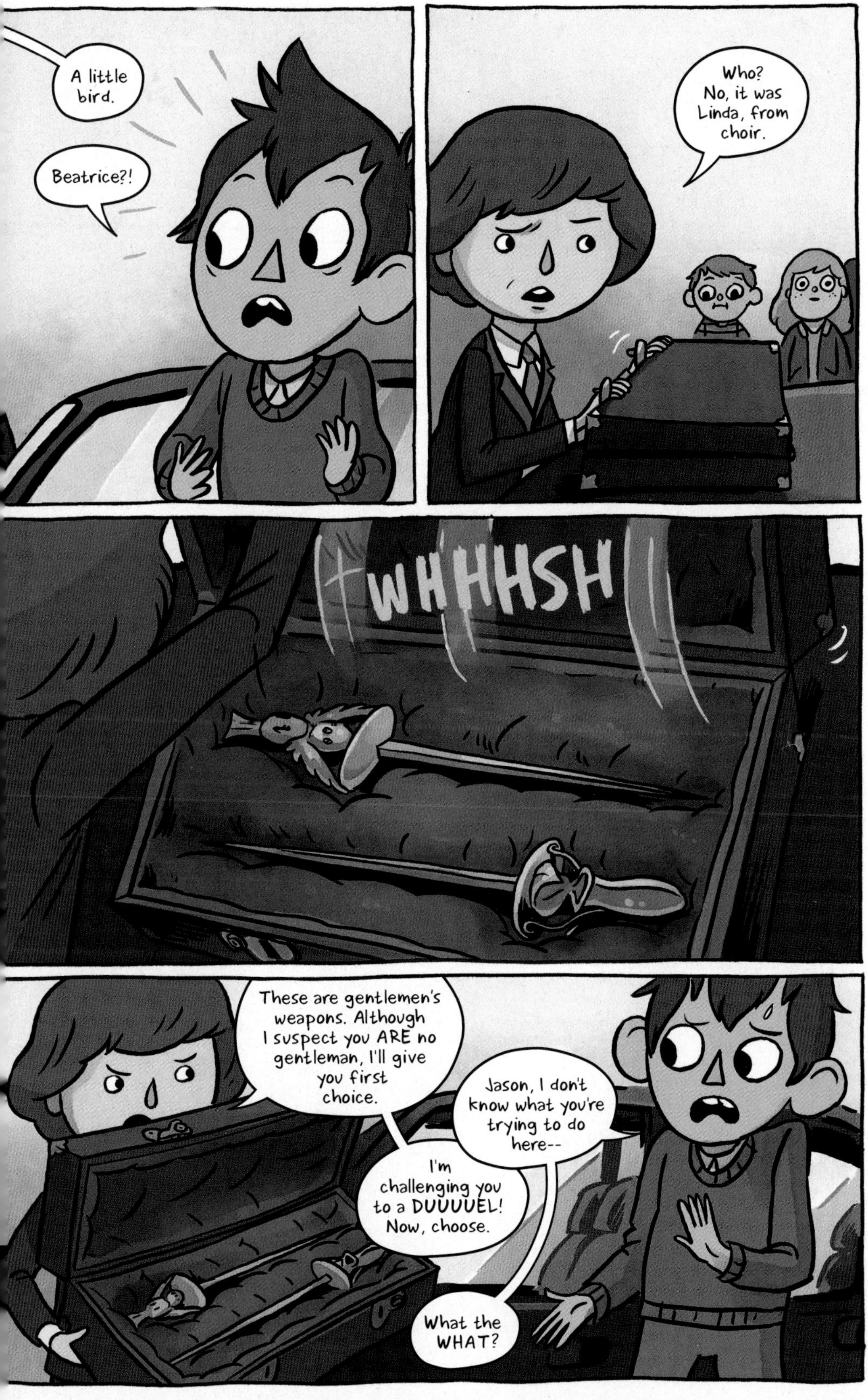
A little bird.
Beatrice?!
Who? No, it was Linda, from choir.
WHHHSH
These are gentlemen's weapons. Although I suspect you ARE no gentleman, I'll give you first choice.
Jason, I don't know what you're trying to do here--
I'm challenging you to a DUUUUEL! Now, choose.
What the WHAT?

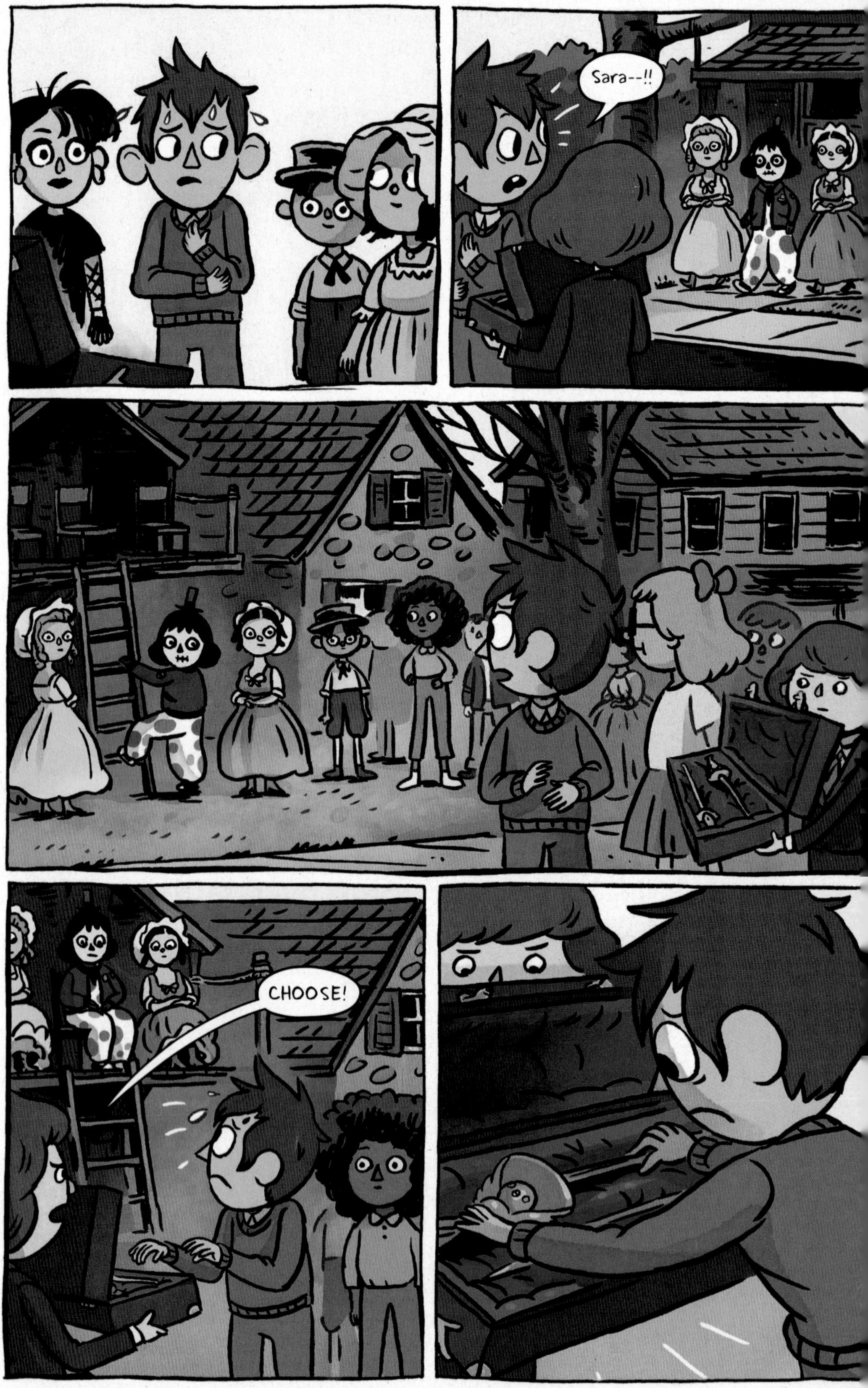
Sara--!!
CHOOSE!

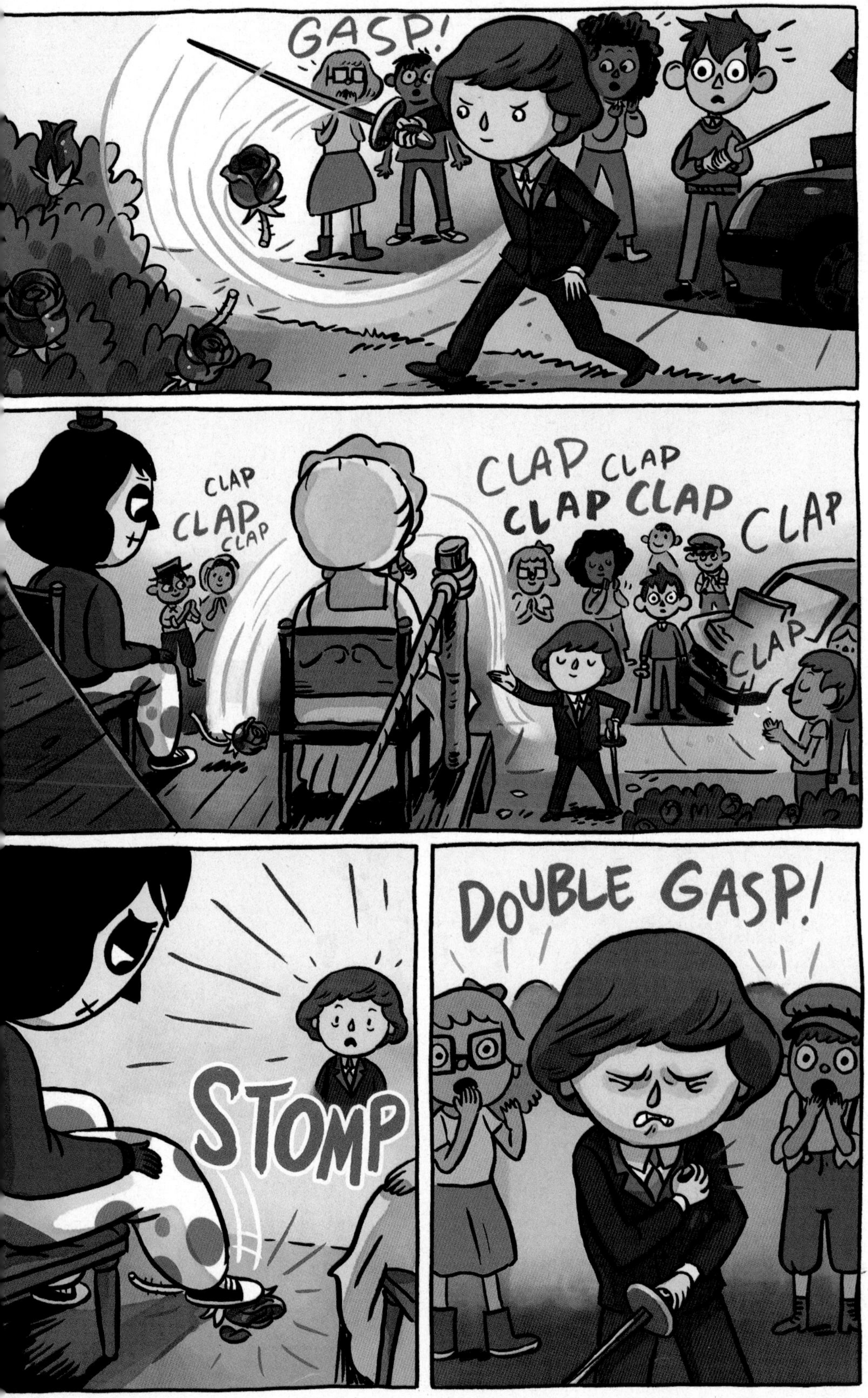
GASP!
CLAP
CLAP
CLAP
CLAP CLAP
CLAP CLAP
CLAP
CLAP
STOMP
DOUBLE GASP!

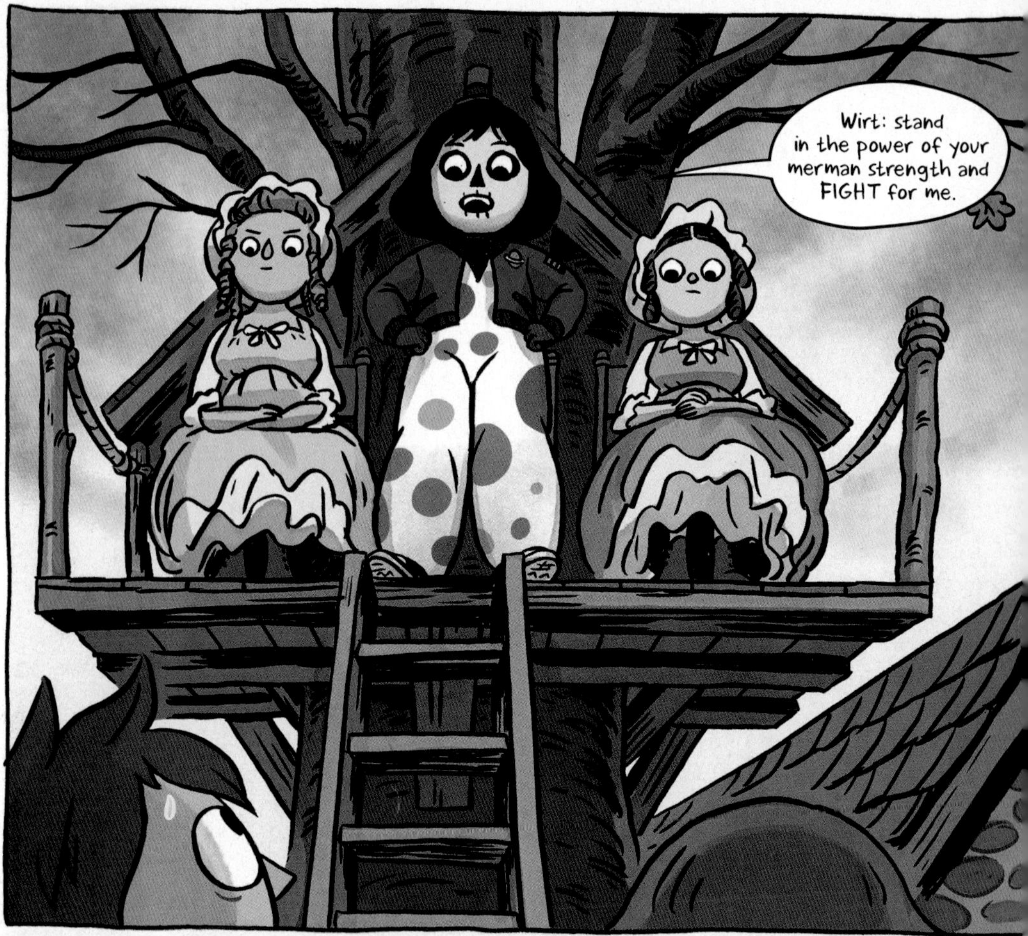
Wirt: stand in the power of your merman strength and FIGHT for me.

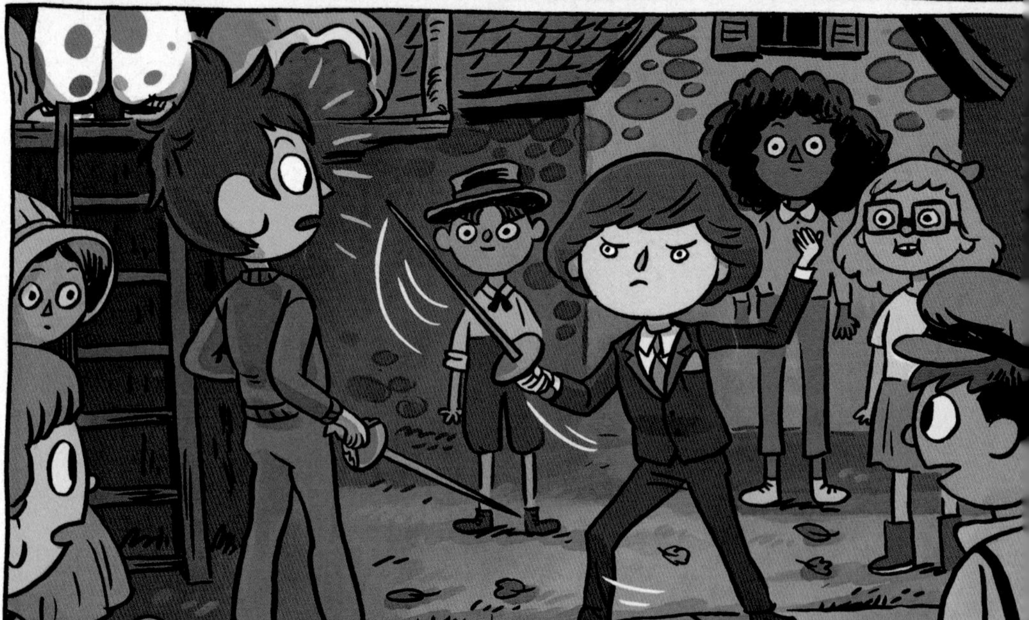

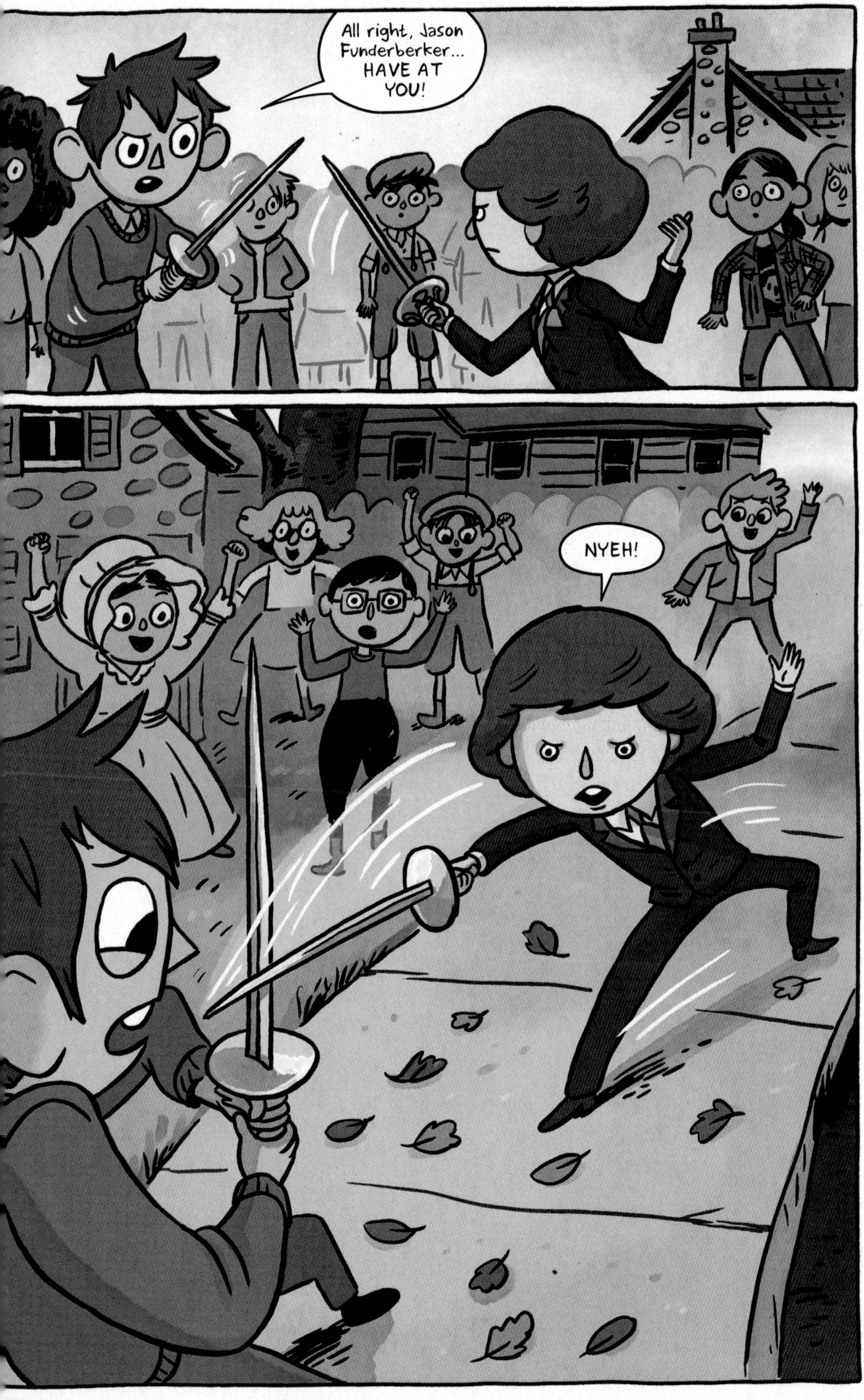
All right, Jason Funderberker... HAVE AT YOU!
NYEH!

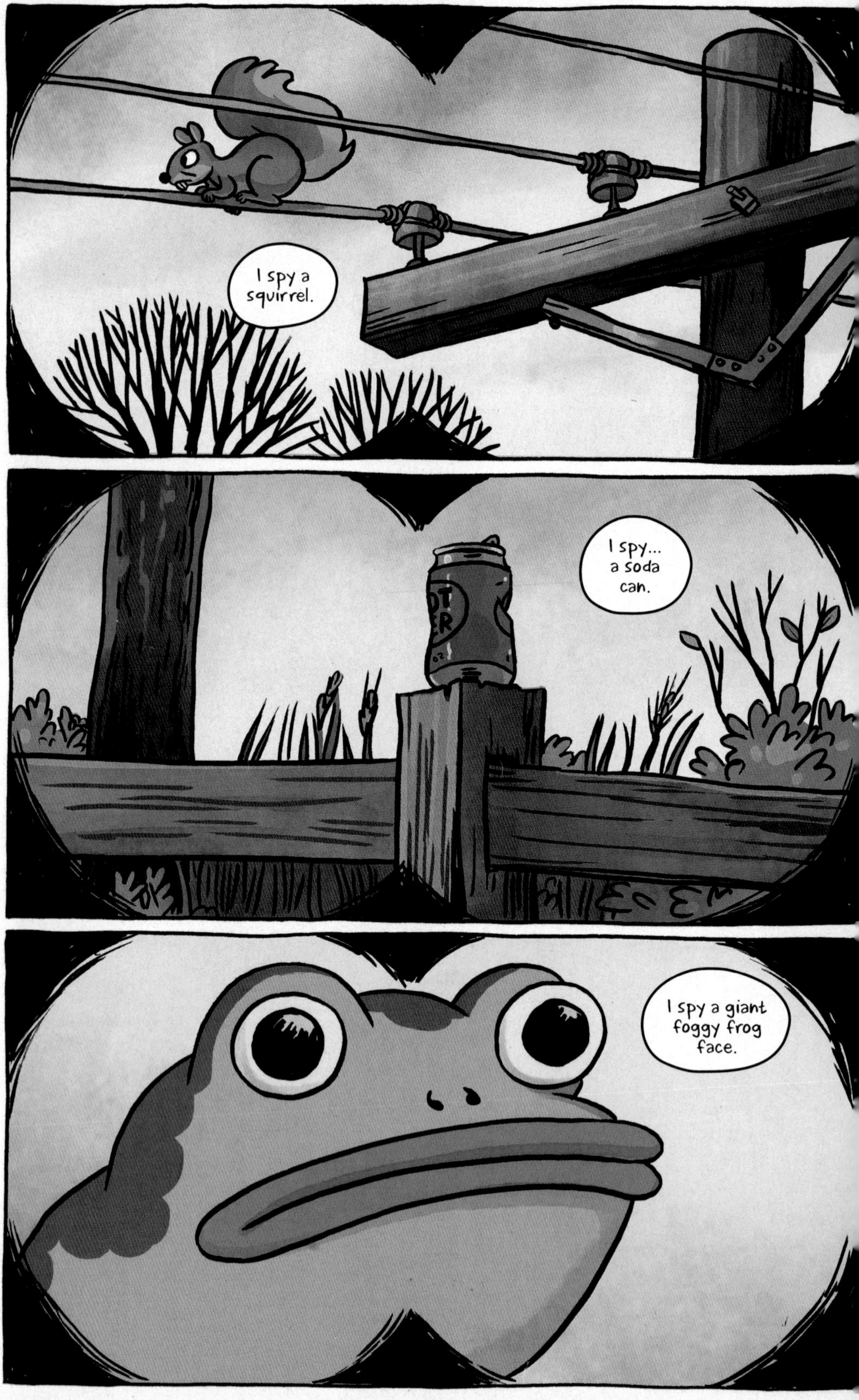
I spy a squirrel.
I spy... a soda can.
I spy a giant foggy frog face.

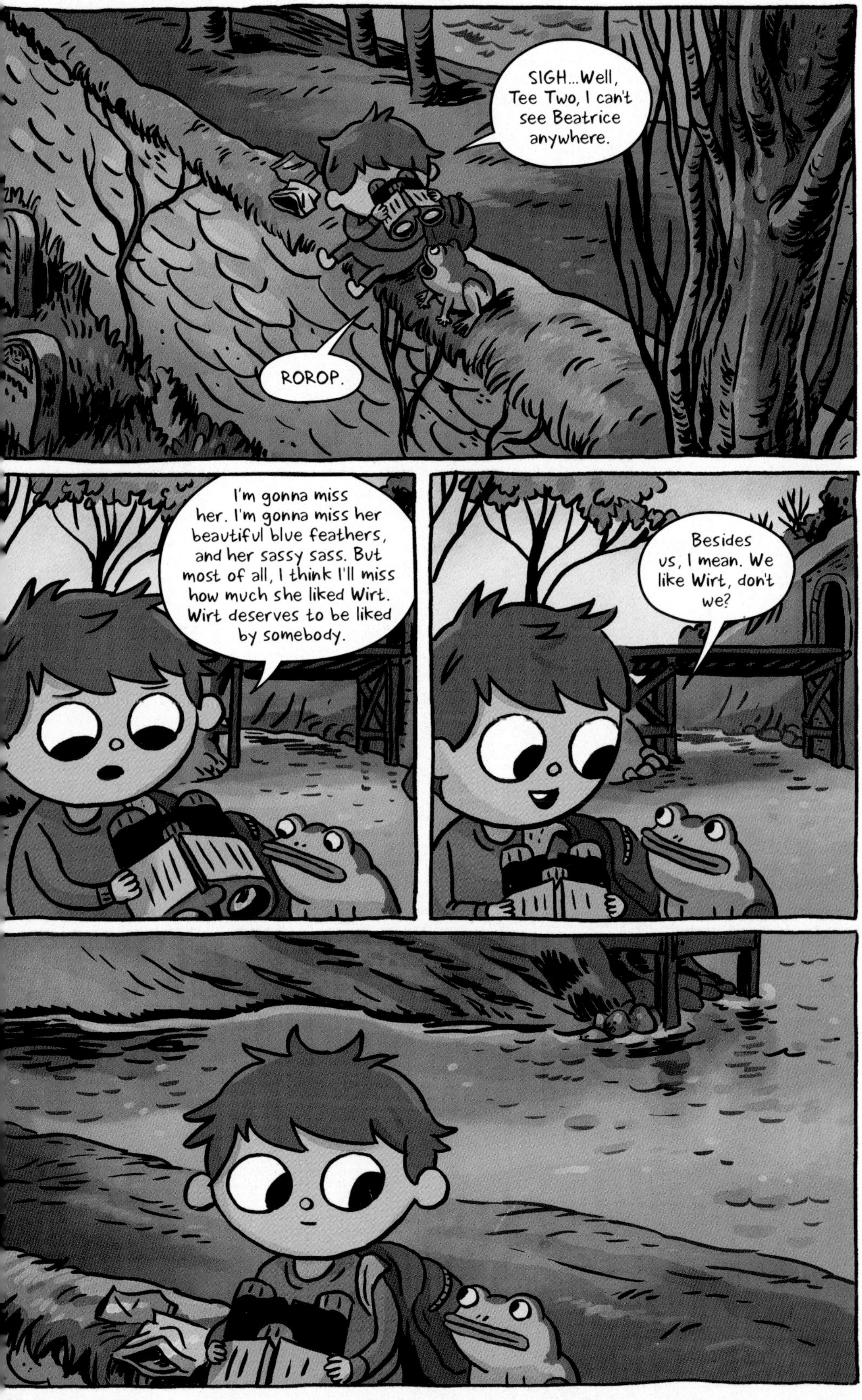
SIGH...Well, Tee Two, I can't see Beatrice anywhere.
ROROP.
I'm gonna miss her. I'm gonna miss her beautiful blue feathers, and her sassy sass. But most of all, I think I'll miss how much she liked Wirt. Wirt deserves to be liked by somebody.
Besides us, I mean. We like Wirt, don't we?

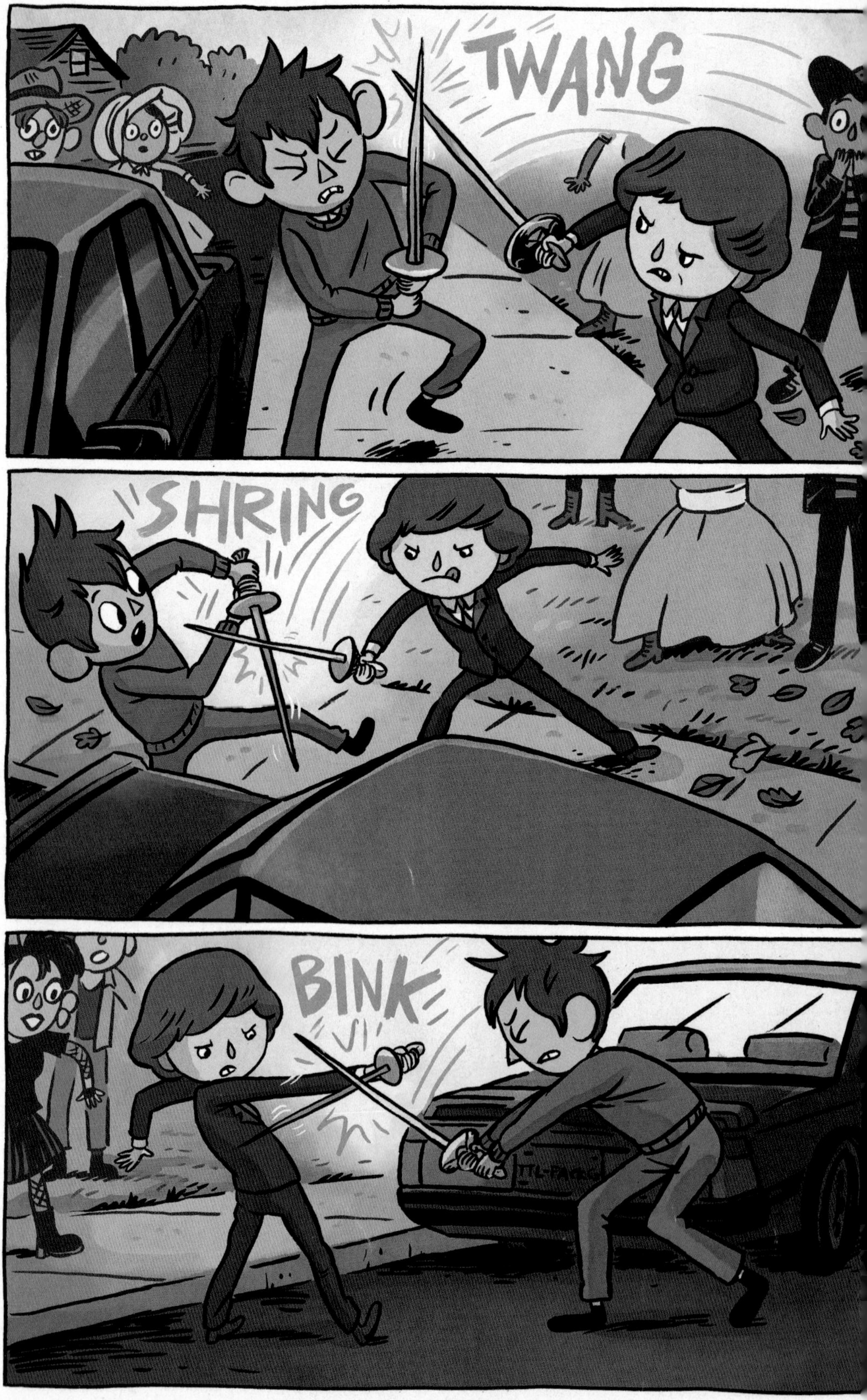
TWANG
SHRING
BINK

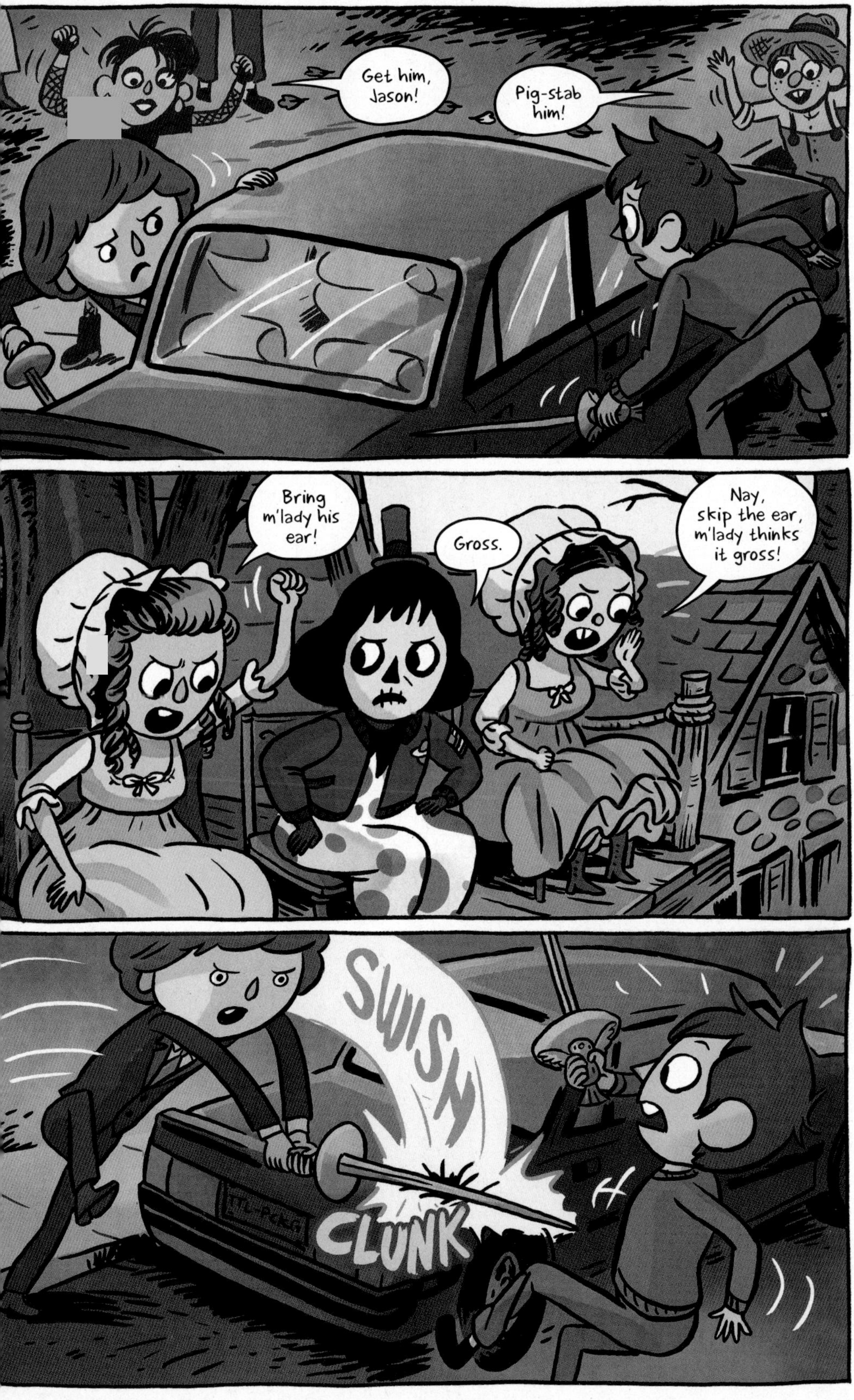
Get him, Jason!
Pig-stab him!
Bring m'lady his ear!
Gross.
Nay, skip the ear, m'lady thinks it gross!
SWISH
CLUNK

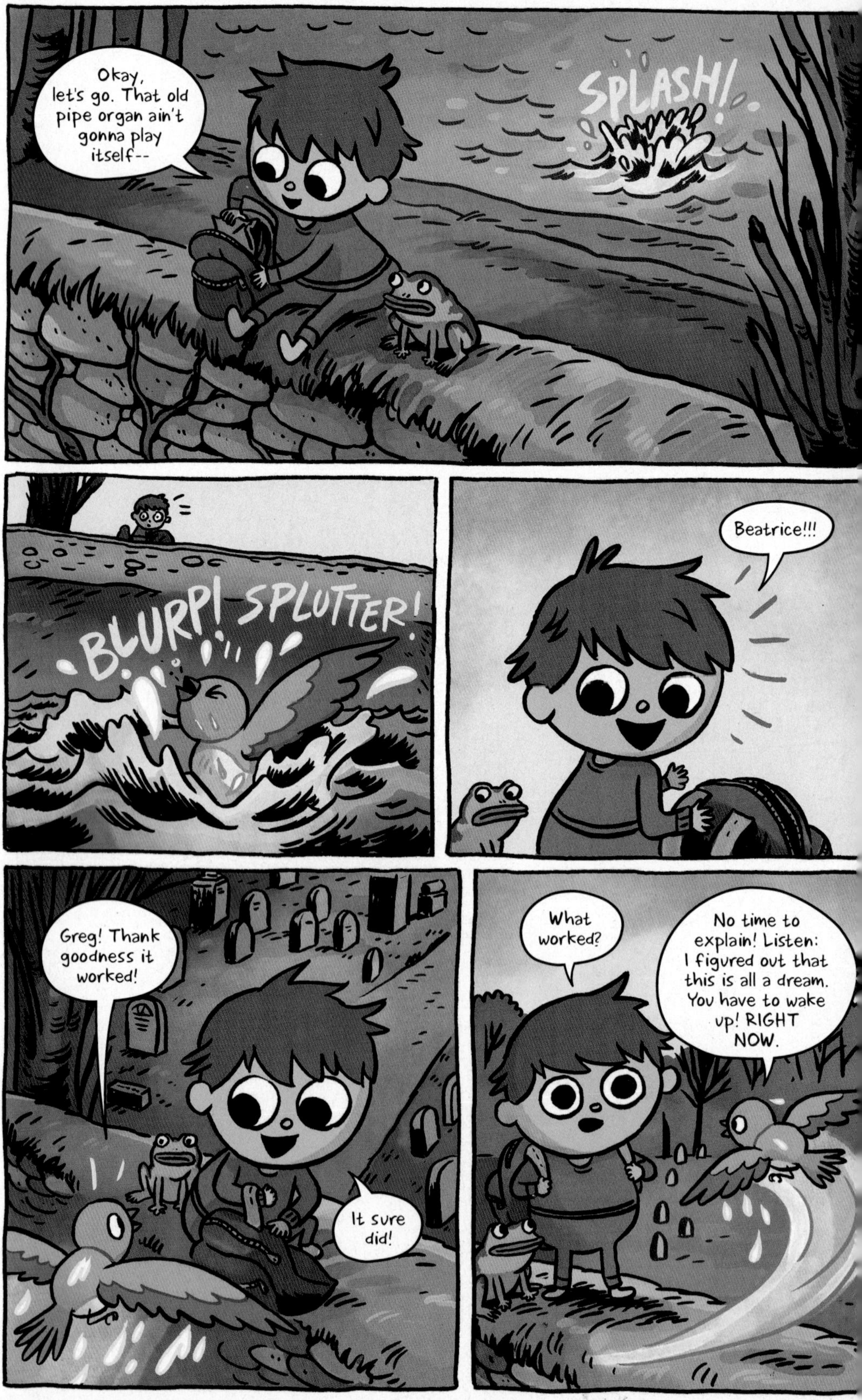
Okay, let's go. That old pipe organ ain't gonna play itself--
SPLASH!
BLURP! SPLUTTER!
Beatrice!!!
Greg! Thank goodness it worked!
It sure did!
What worked?
No time to explain! Listen: I figured out that this is all a dream. You have to wake up! RIGHT NOW.

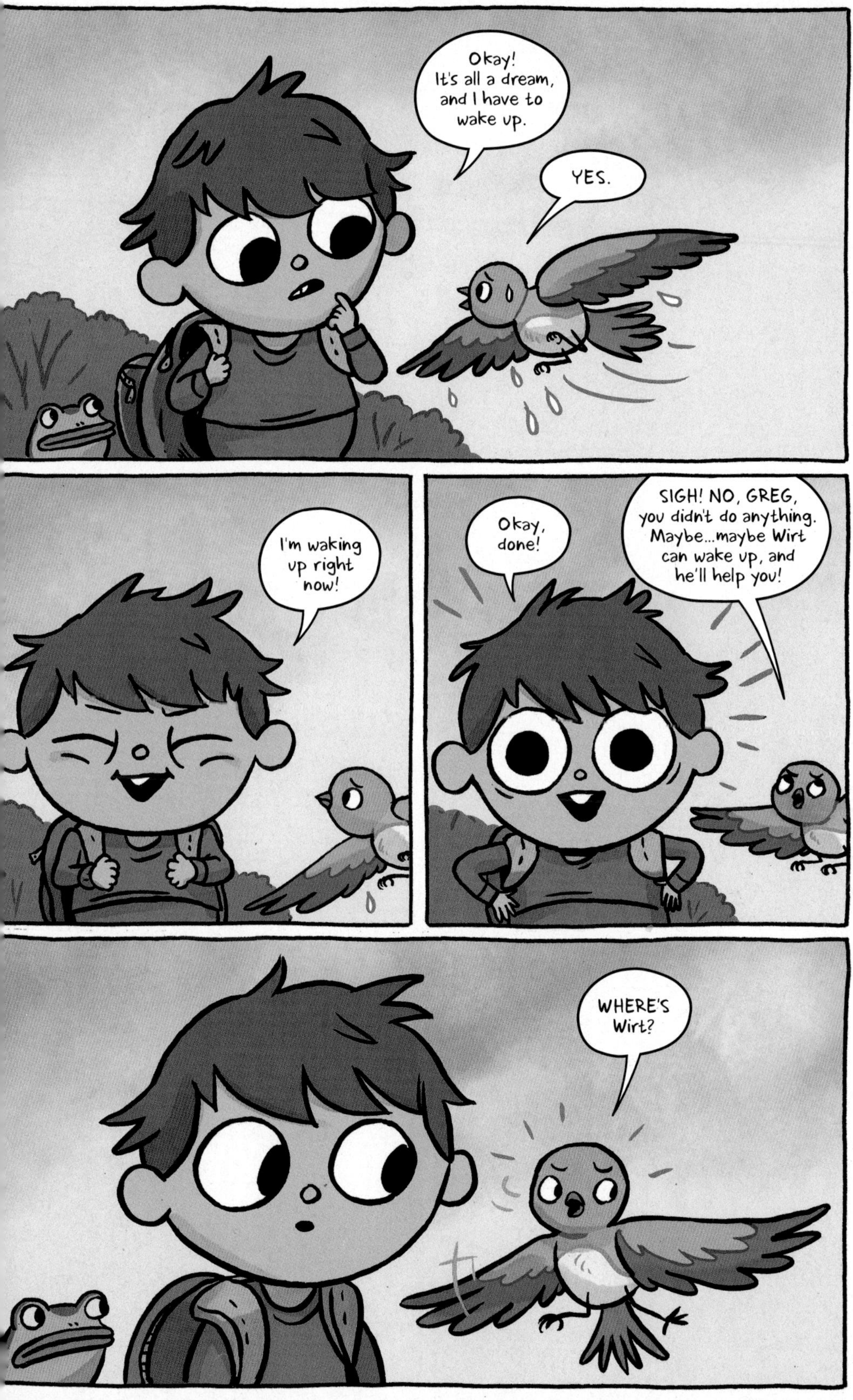
Okay! It's all a dream, and I have to wake up.
YES.
I'm waking up right now!
Okay, done!
SIGH! NO, GREG, you didn't do anything. Maybe...maybe Wirt can wake up, and he'll help you!
WHERE'S Wirt?

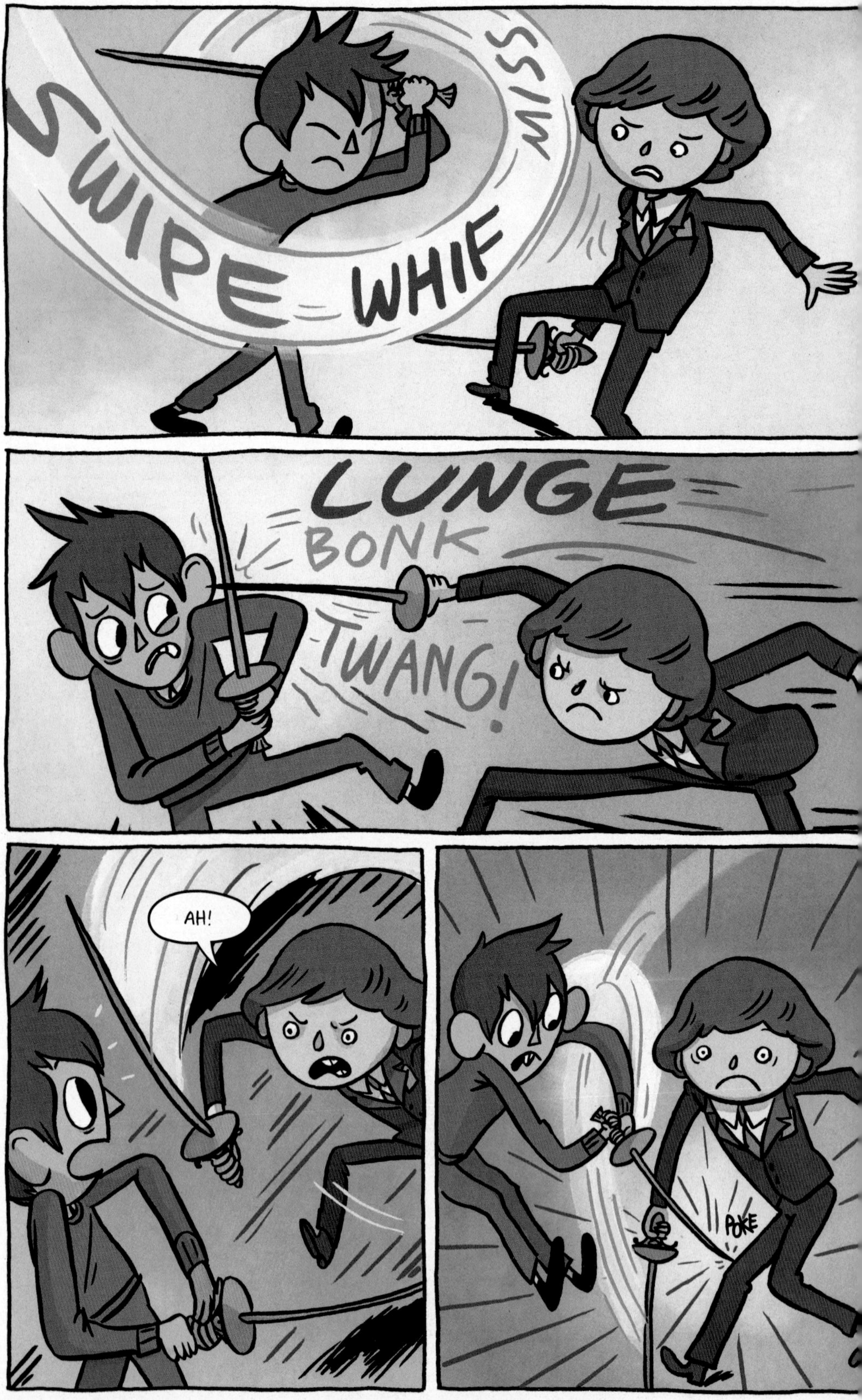
SWIPE
WHIF
MISS
LUNGE
BONK
TWANG!
AH!
POKE

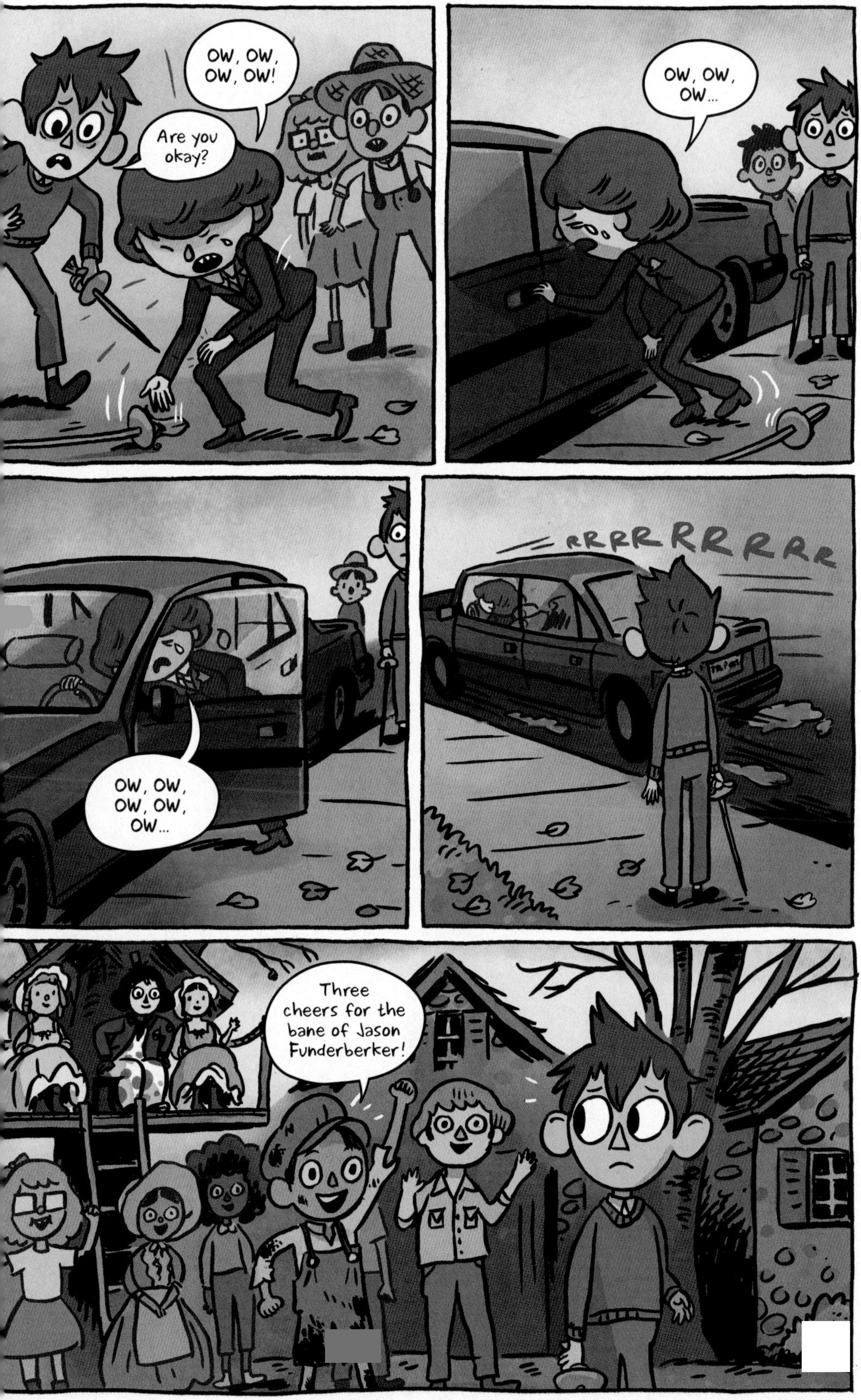
OW, OW, OW, OW!
Are you okay?
OW, OW, OW...
OW, OW, OW, OW, OW...
RRRRRRRRRR
Three cheers for the bane of Jason Funderberker!

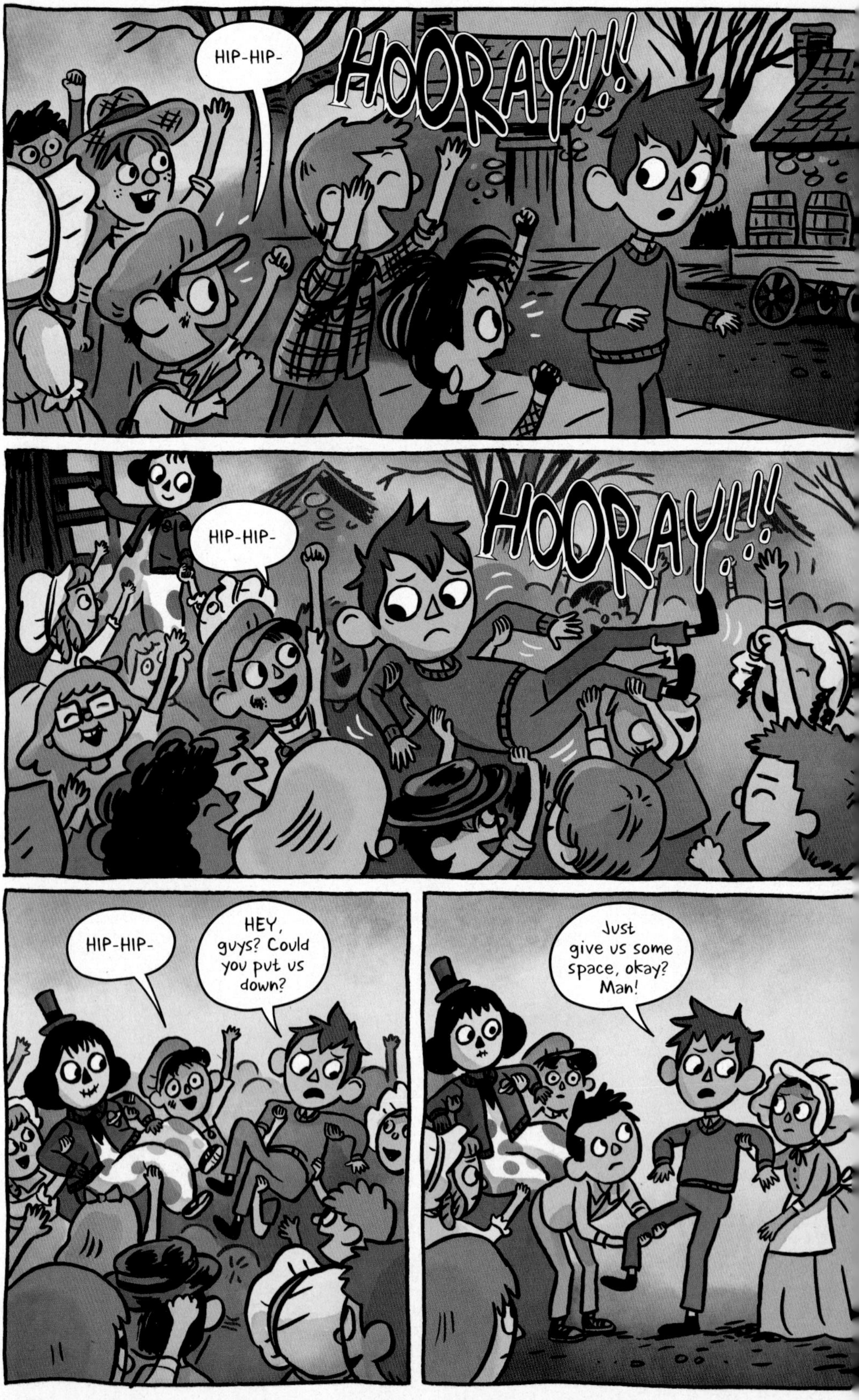
HIP-HIP-
HOORAY!!!
HIP-HIP-
HOORAY!!!
HIP-HIP-
HEY, guys? Could you put us down?
Just give us some space, okay? Man!

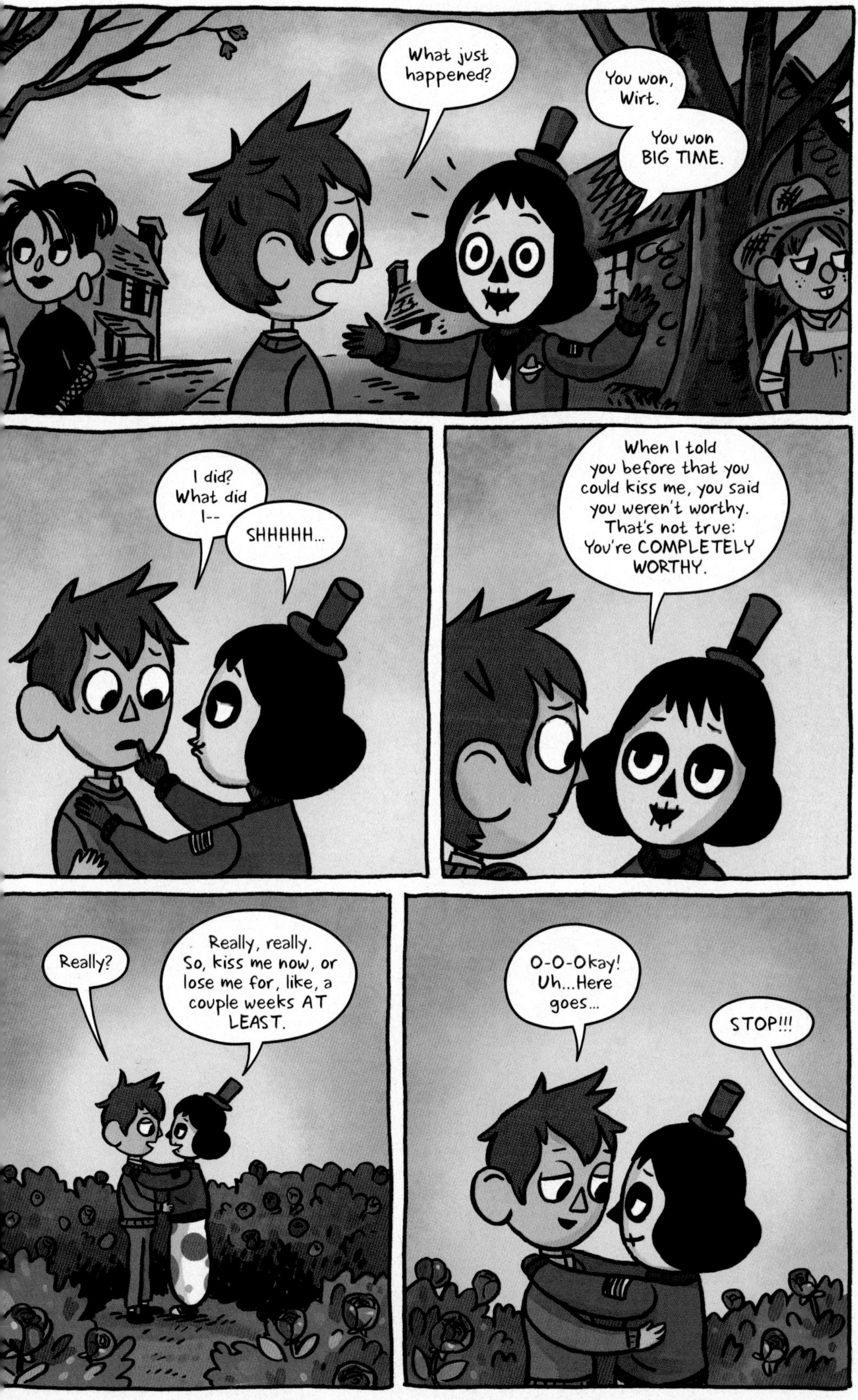
What just happened?
You won, Wirt.
You won BIG TIME.
I did? What did I--
SHHHHH...
When I told you before that you could kiss me, you said you weren't worthy. That's not true: You're COMPLETELY WORTHY.
Really?
Really, really. So, kiss me now, or lose me for, like, a couple weeks AT LEAST.
O-O-Okay! Uh...Here goes...
STOP!!!

IT'S A TRICK, WIRT! IT'S NOT REAL!

Beatrice, what are you doing?!! Sara, I can explain--

You're dreaming, Wirt! You have to wake up!

Wirt, what's she talking about?

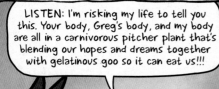

LISTEN: I'm risking my life to tell you this. Your body, Greg's body, and my body are all in a carnivorous pitcher plant that's blending our hopes and dreams together with gelatinous goo so it can eat us!!!

None of this is real: SHE ISN'T REAL!

Yes I am! Wirt??? IF YOU NEED PROOF I'M REAL, JUST KISS ME.

NO! IT'S A TRAP!

KISSSSSSS--

WIRT! Look at me!

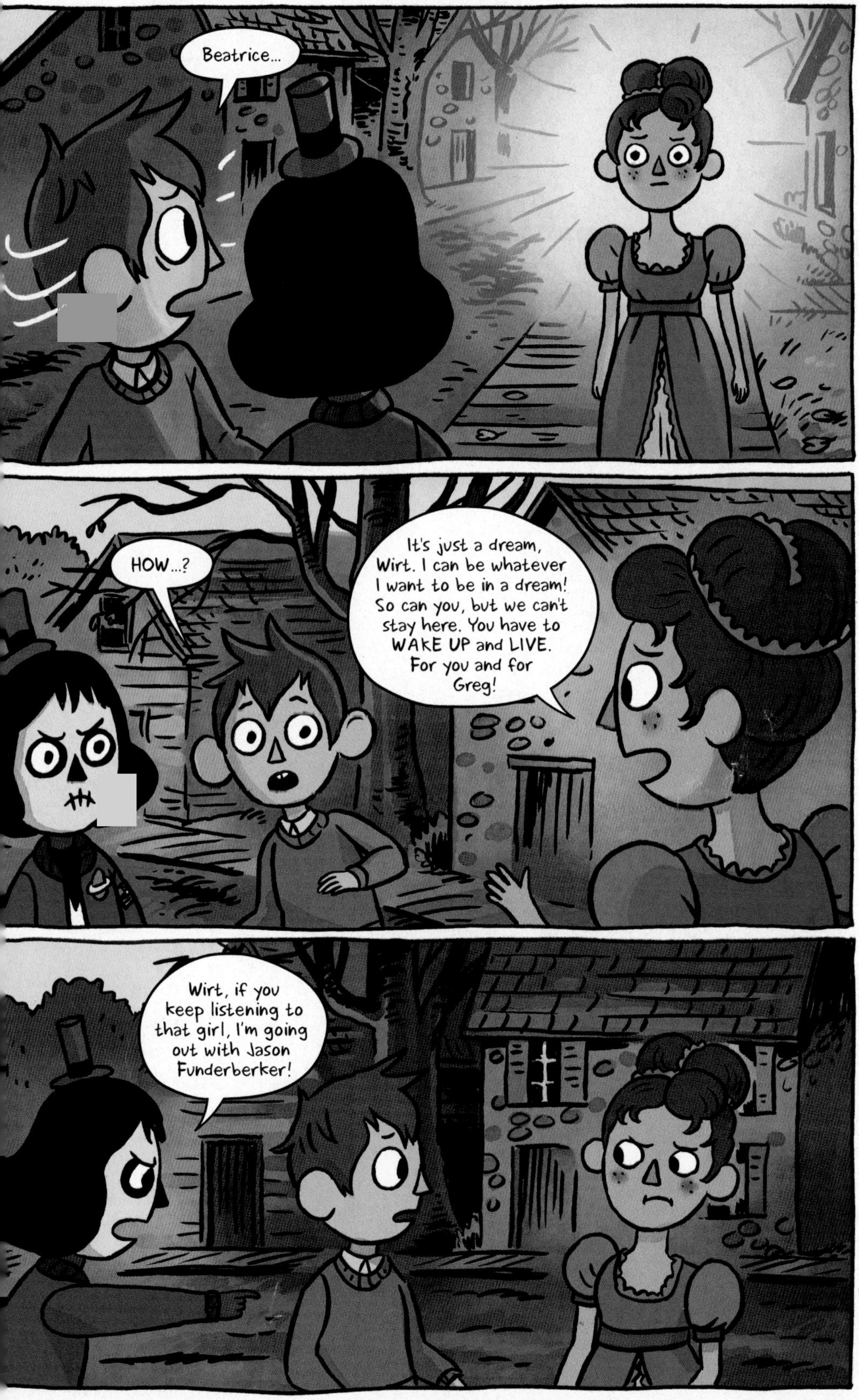
Beatrice...
HOW...?
It's just a dream, Wirt. I can be whatever I want to be in a dream! So can you, but we can't stay here. You have to WAKE UP and LIVE. For you and for Greg!
Wirt, if you keep listening to that girl, I'm going out with Jason Funderberker!

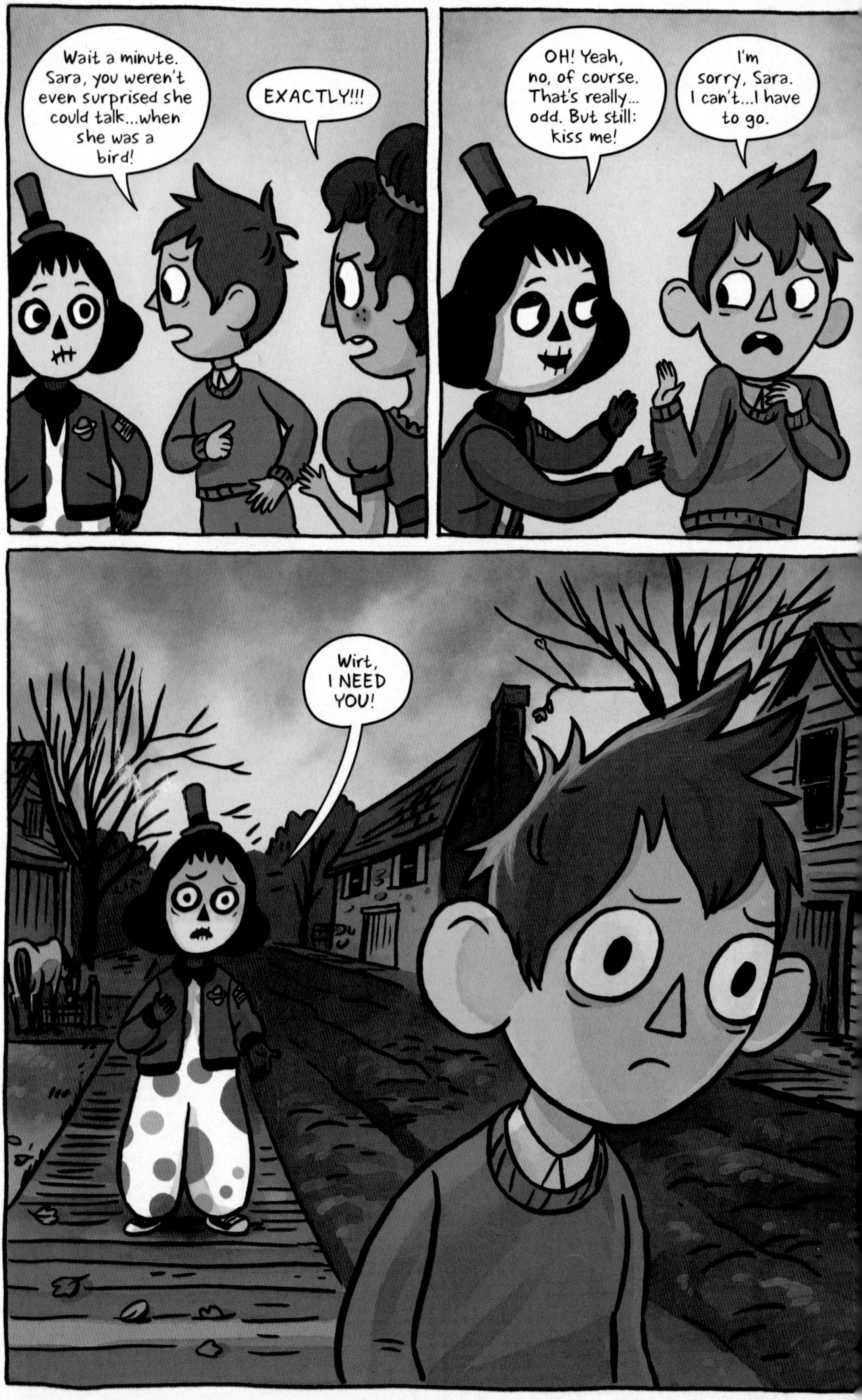
Wait a minute. Sara, you weren't even surprised she could talk...when she was a bird!
EXACTLY!!!
OH! Yeah, no, of course. That's really... odd. But still: kiss me!
I'm sorry, Sara. I can't...I have to go.
Wirt, I NEED YOU!

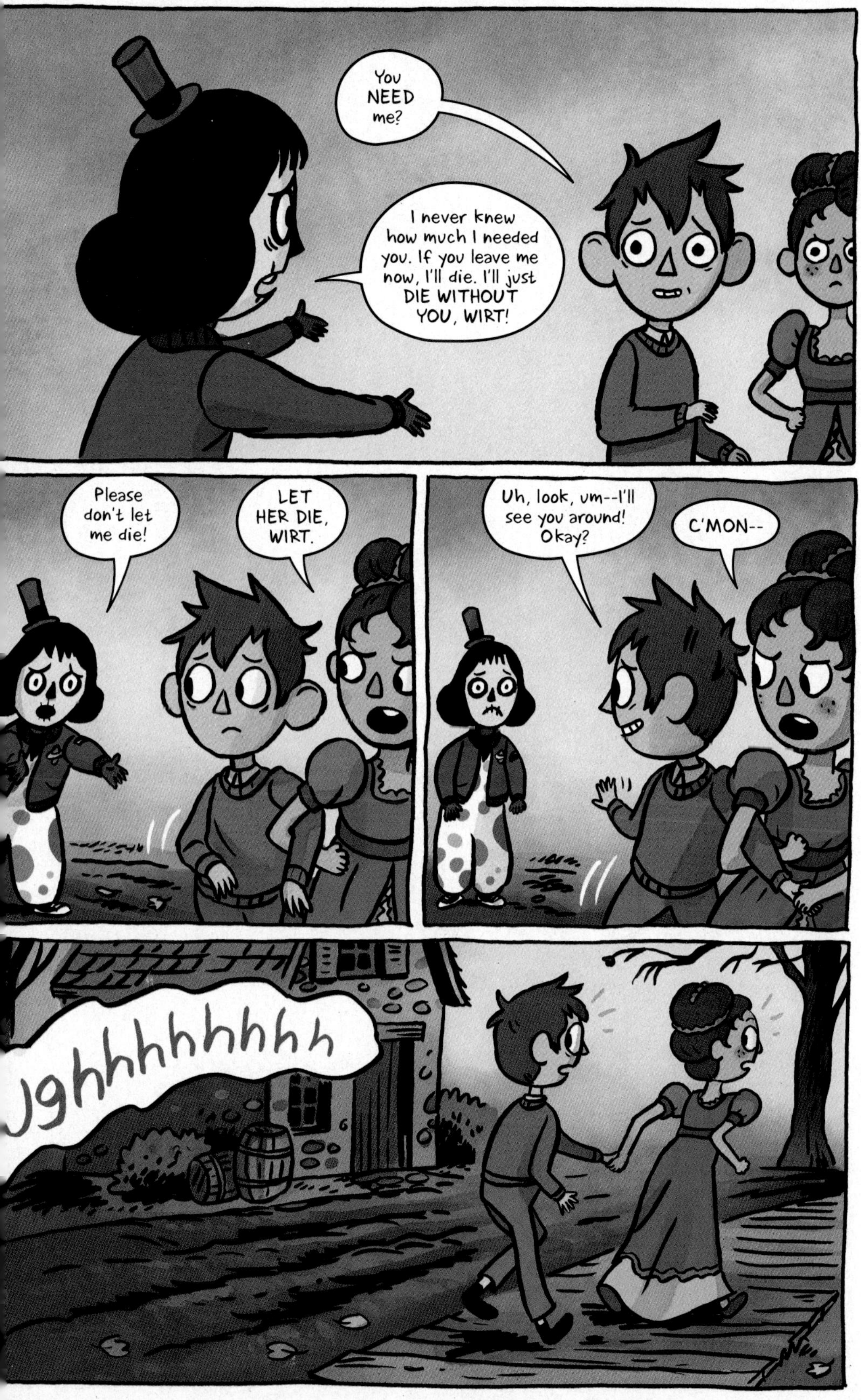
You NEED me?
I never knew how much I needed you. If you leave me now, I'll die. I'll just DIE WITHOUT YOU, WIRT!
Please don't let me die!
LET HER DIE, WIRT.
Uh, look, um--I'll see you around! Okay?
C'MON--
Ughhhhhhhh

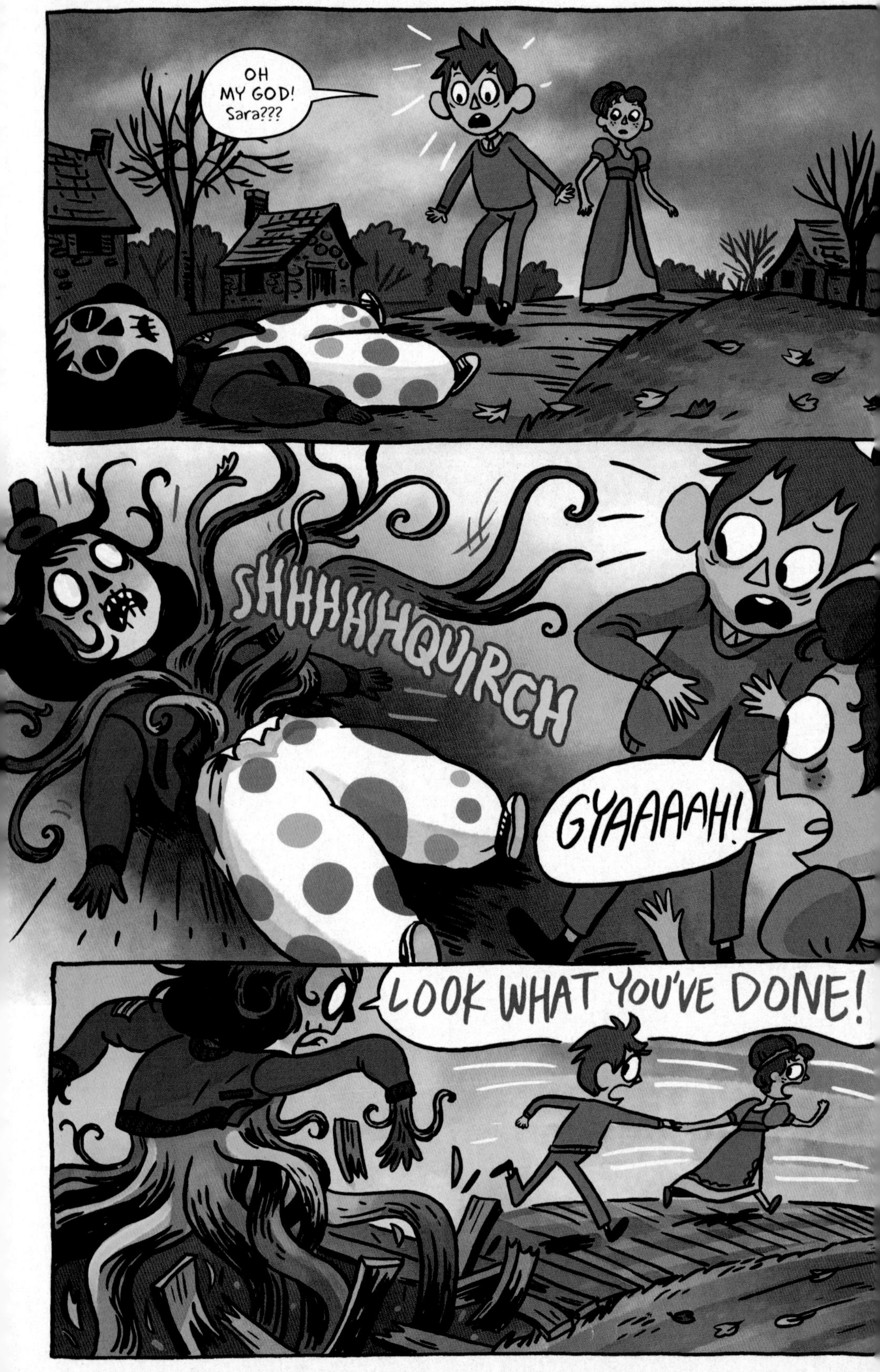
OH MY GOD! Sara???
SHHHHHQUIRCH
GYAAAAH!
LOOK WHAT YOU'VE DONE!

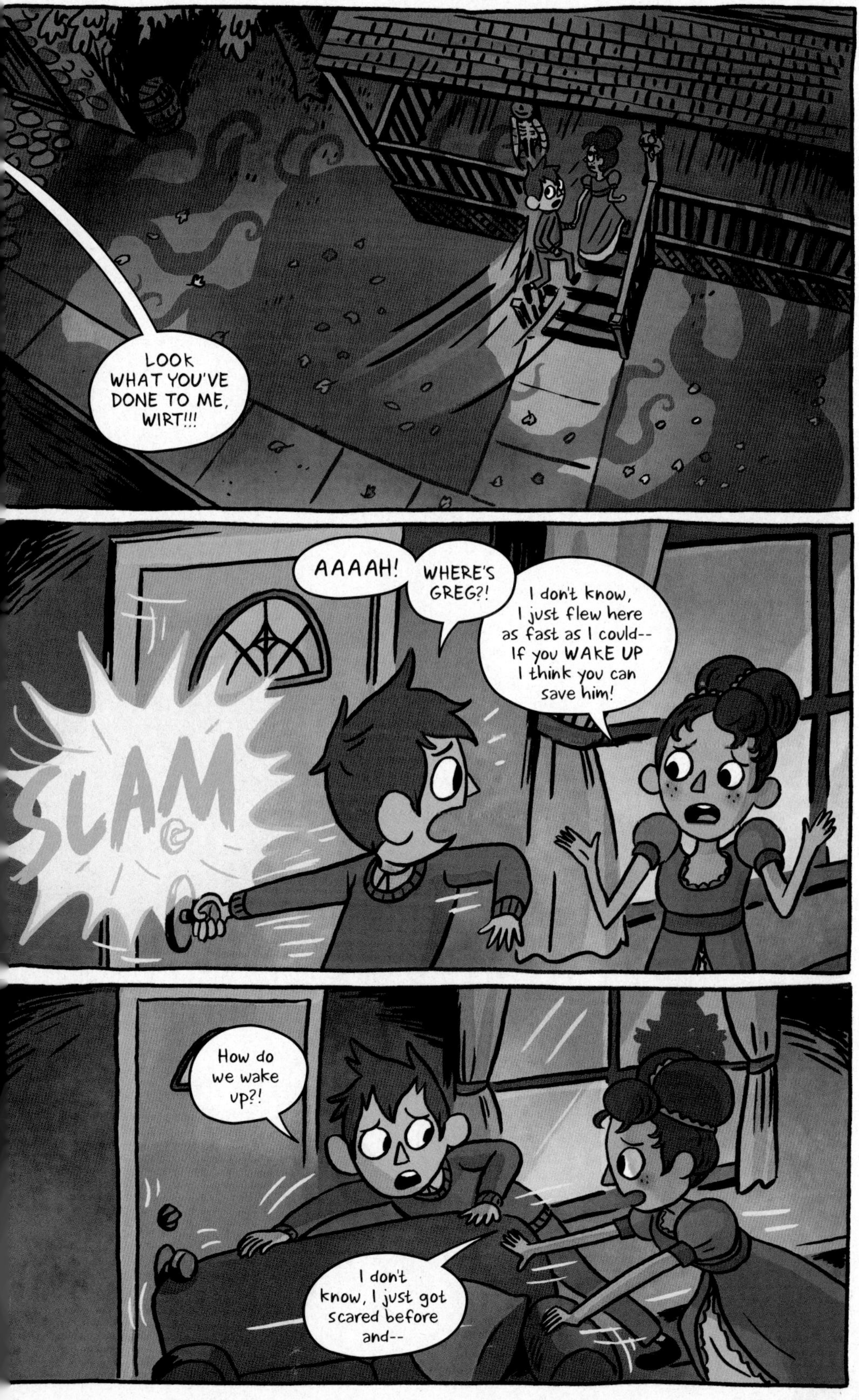
LOOK WHAT YOU'VE DONE TO ME, WIRT!!!
AAAAH!
WHERE'S GREG?!
I don't know, I just flew here as fast as I could-- If you WAKE UP I think you can save him!
SLAM
How do we wake up?!
I don't know, I just got scared before and--

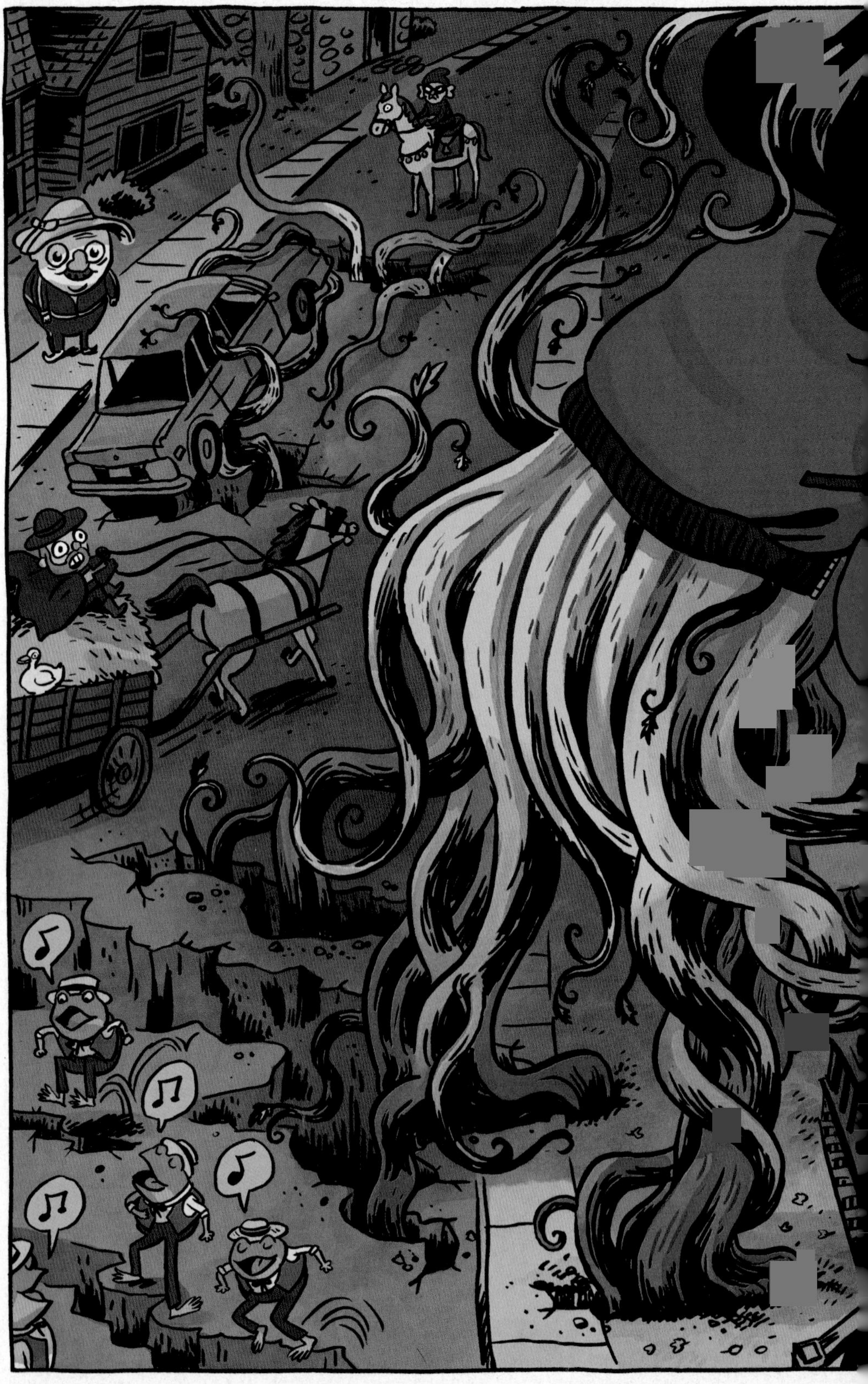

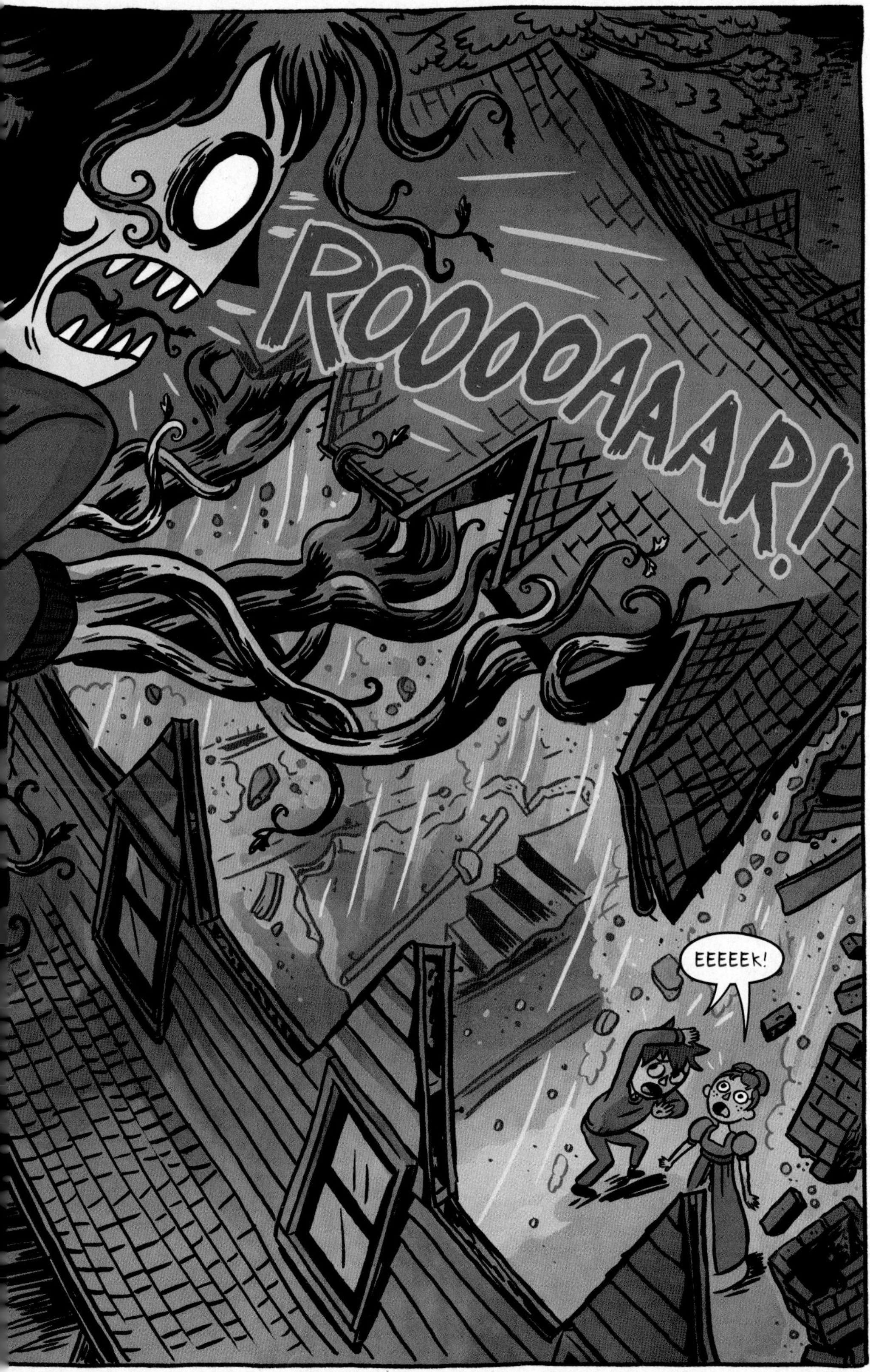
ROOOOOAAAR!
EEEEEK!

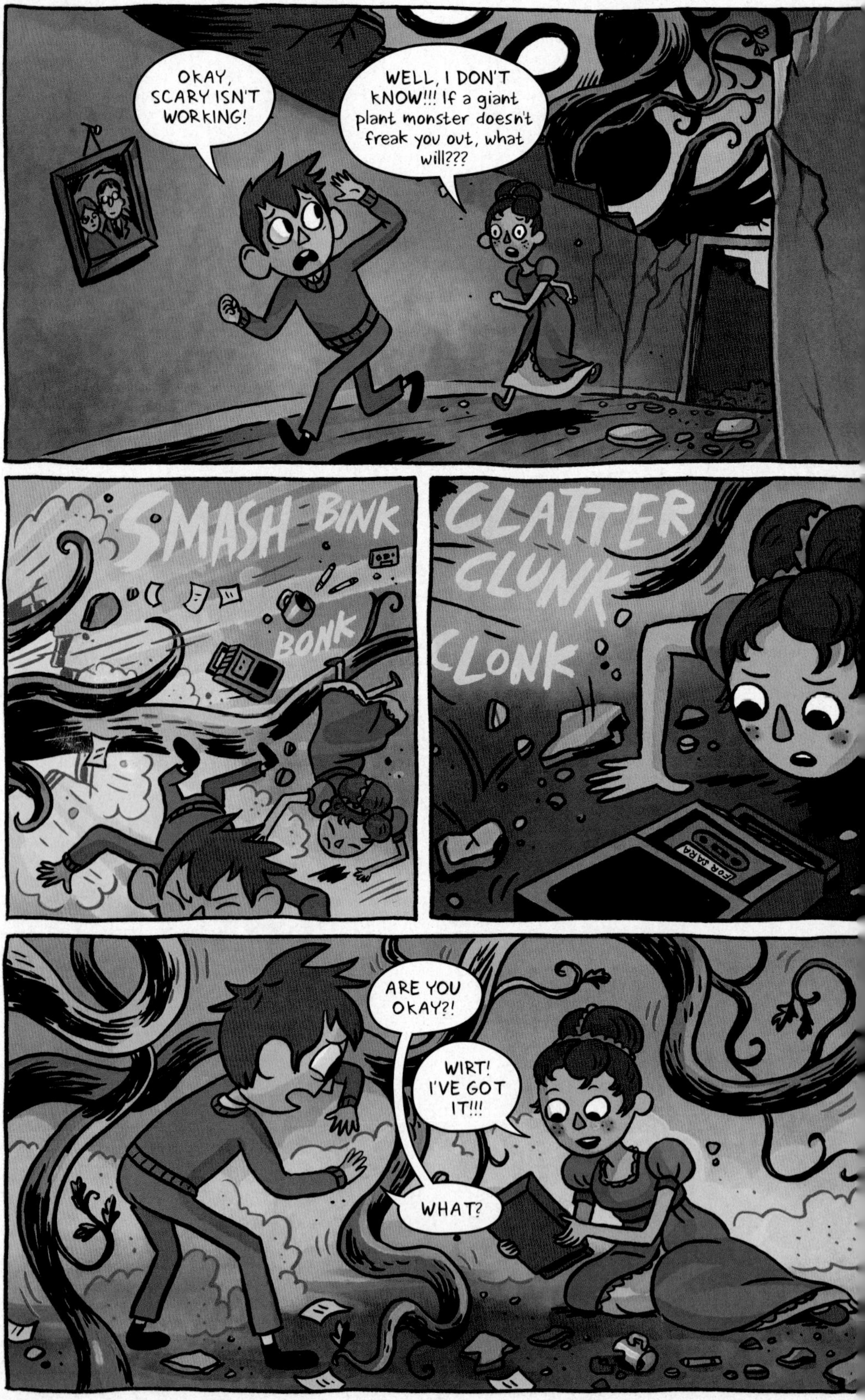
OKAY, SCARY ISN'T WORKING!
WELL, I DON'T KNOW!!! If a giant plant monster doesn't freak you out, what will???
SMASH BINK
BONK
CLATTER
CLUNK
CLONK
FOR SARA
ARE YOU OKAY?!
WIRT! I'VE GOT IT!!!
WHAT?

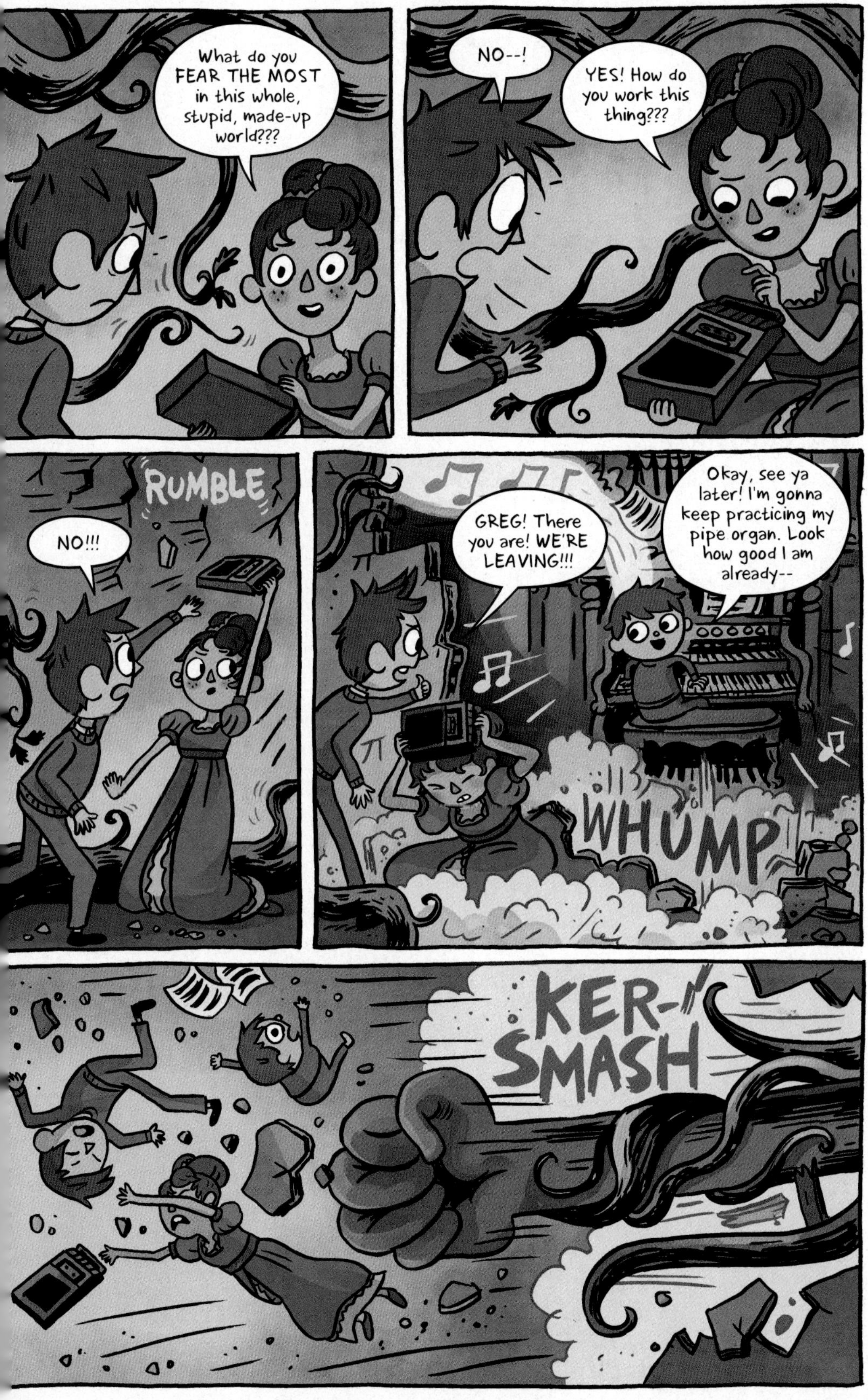
What do you FEAR THE MOST in this whole, stupid, made-up world???
NO--!
YES! How do you work this thing???
RUMBLE
NO!!!
GREG! There you are! WE'RE LEAVING!!!
Okay, see ya later! I'm gonna keep practicing my pipe organ. Look how good I am already--
WHUMP
KER-SMASH

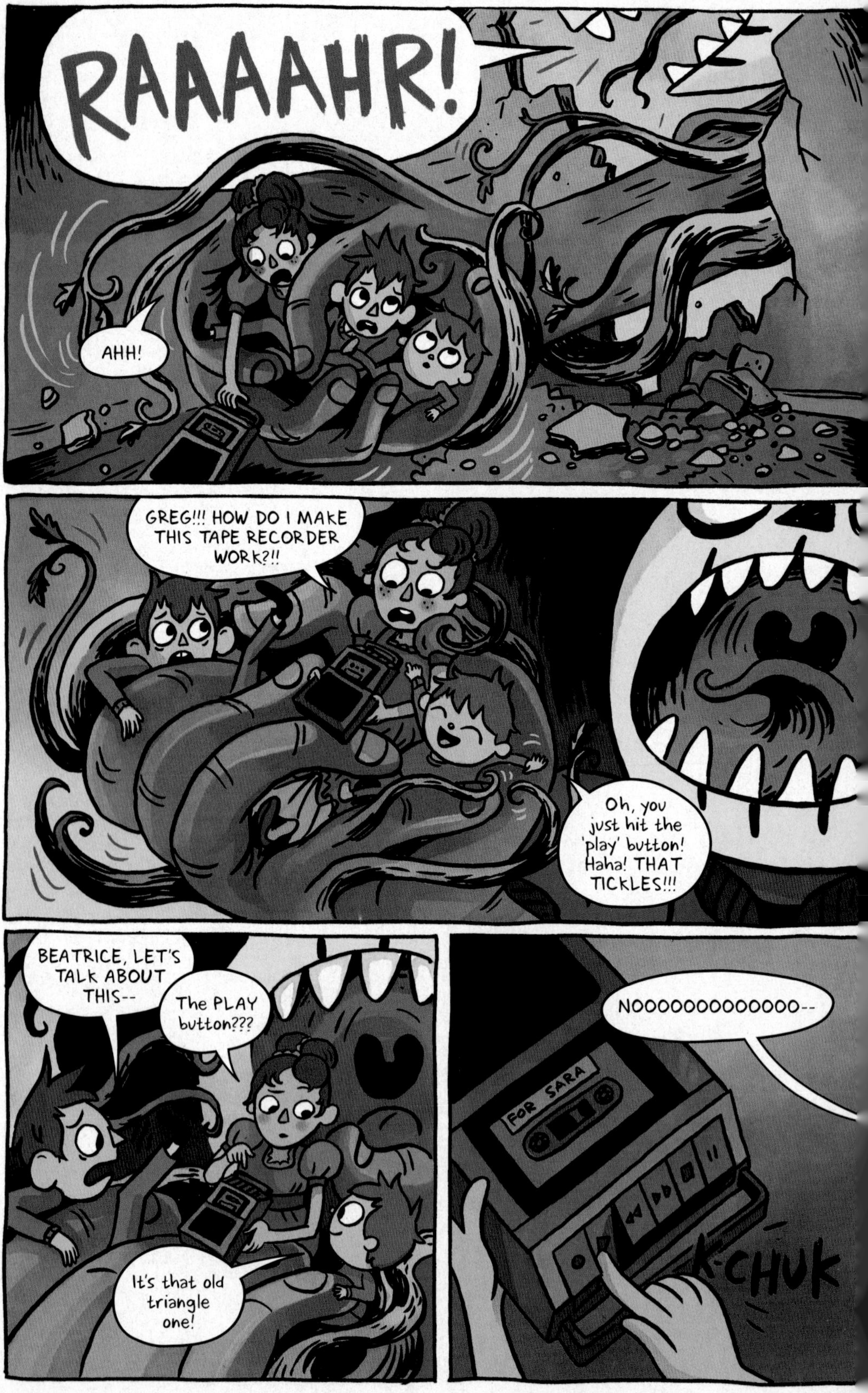
RAAAAHR!
AHH!
GREG!!! HOW DO I MAKE THIS TAPE RECORDER WORK?!!
Oh, you just hit the 'play' button! Haha! THAT TICKLES!!!
BEATRICE, LET'S TALK ABOUT THIS--
The PLAY button???
It's that old triangle one!
NOOOOOOOOOOOOO--
FOR SARA
K-CHUK

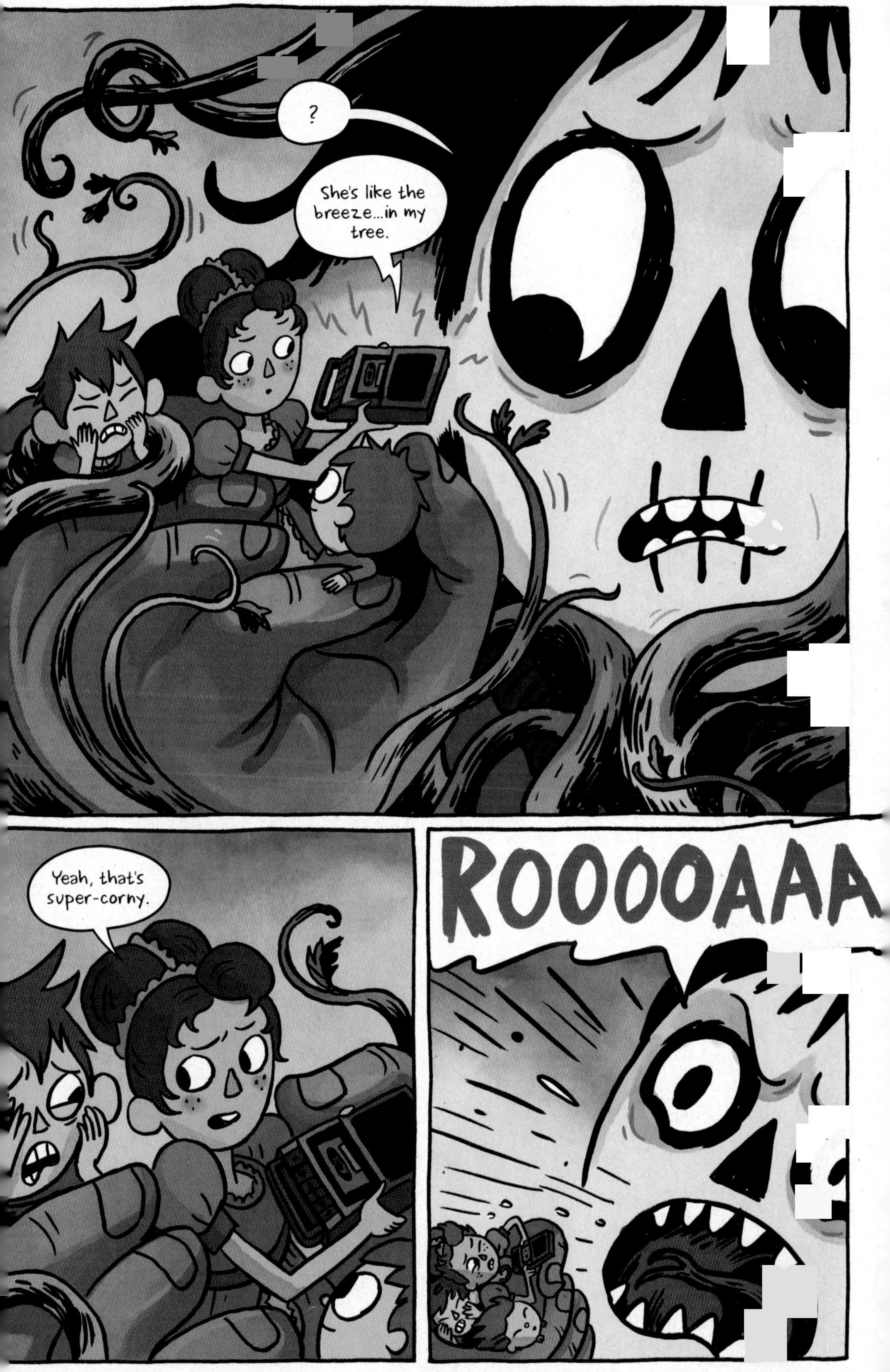
?
She's like the breeze...in my tree.
Yeah, that's super-corny.
ROOOOAAA

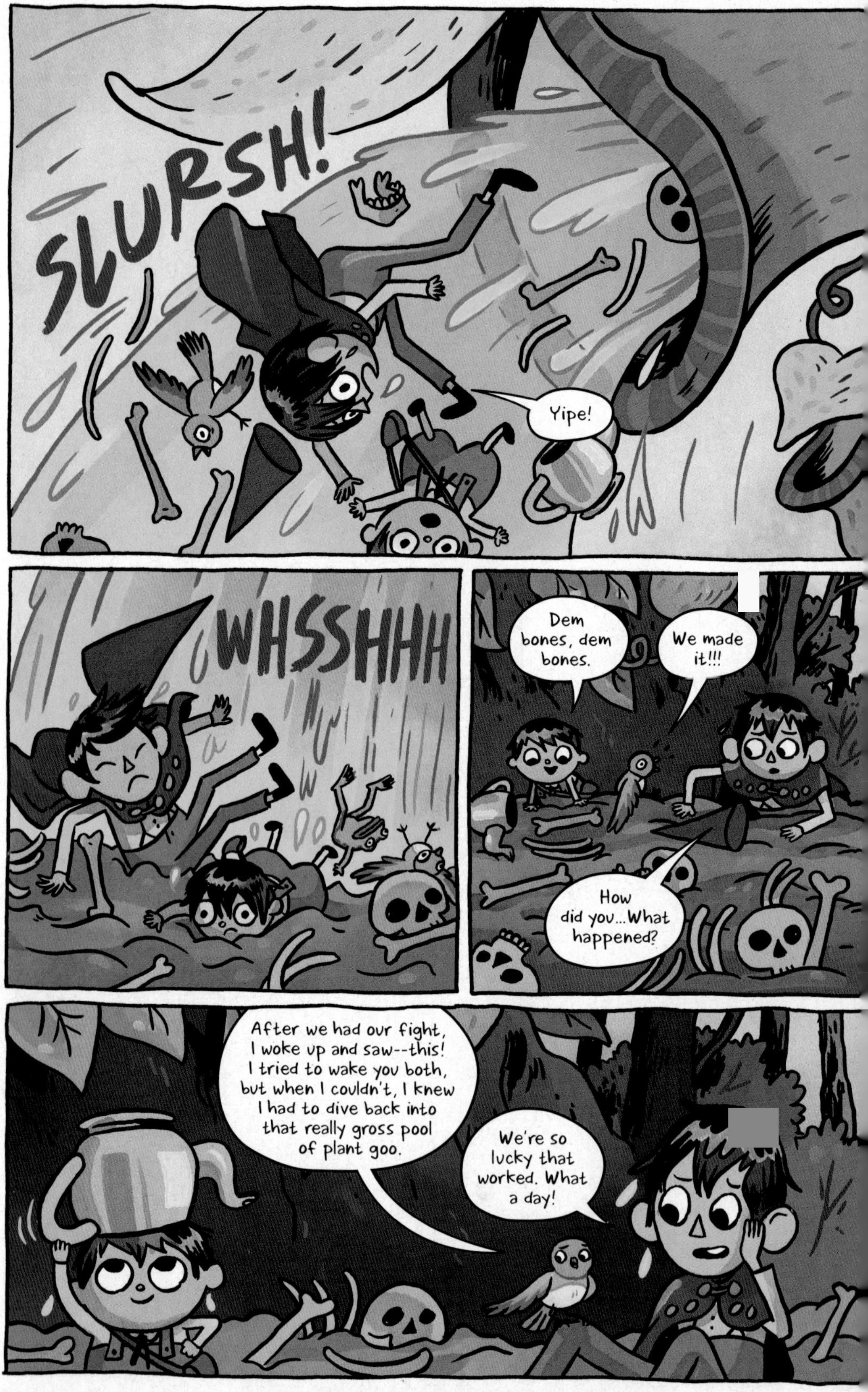
SLURSH!
Yipe!
WHSSHHH
Dem bones, dem bones.
We made it!!!
How did you...What happened?
After we had our fight, I woke up and saw--this! I tried to wake you both, but when I couldn't, I knew I had to dive back into that really gross pool of plant goo.
We're so lucky that worked. What a day!

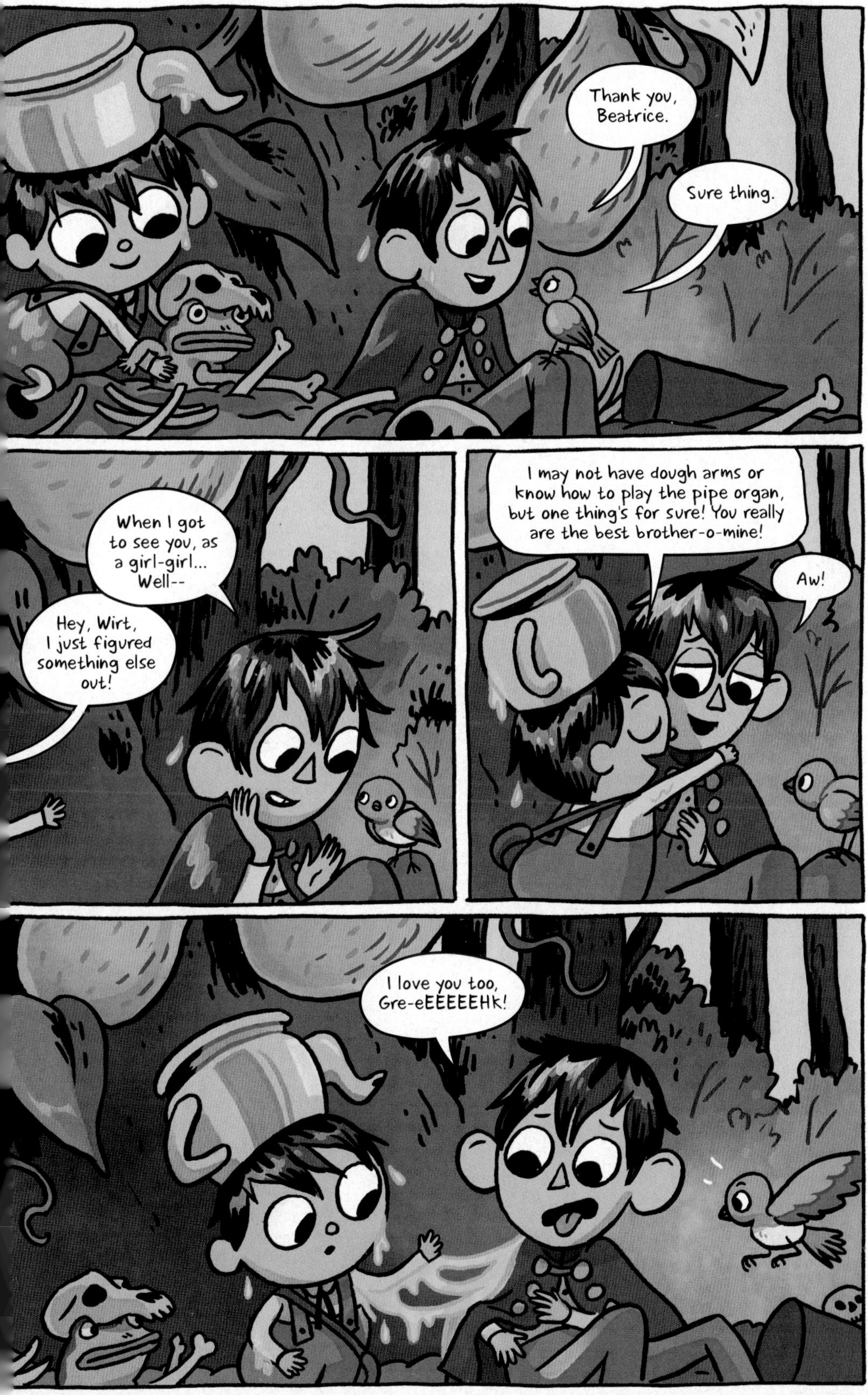
Thank you, Beatrice.
Sure thing.
When I got to see you, as a girl-girl... Well--
Hey, Wirt, I just figured something else out!
I may not have dough arms or know how to play the pipe organ, but one thing's for sure! You really are the best brother-o-mine!
Aw!
I love you too, Gre-eEEEEEHK!

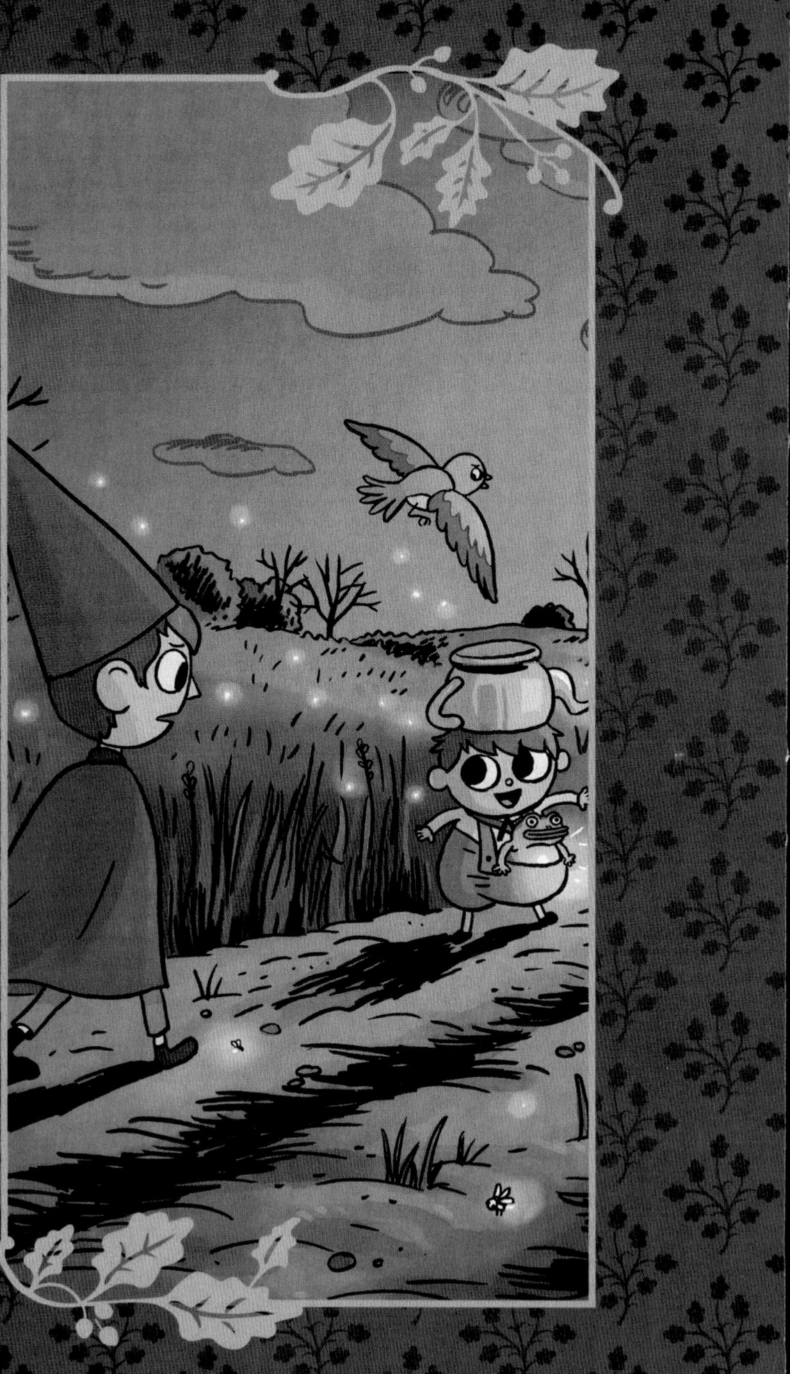

EPILOGUE

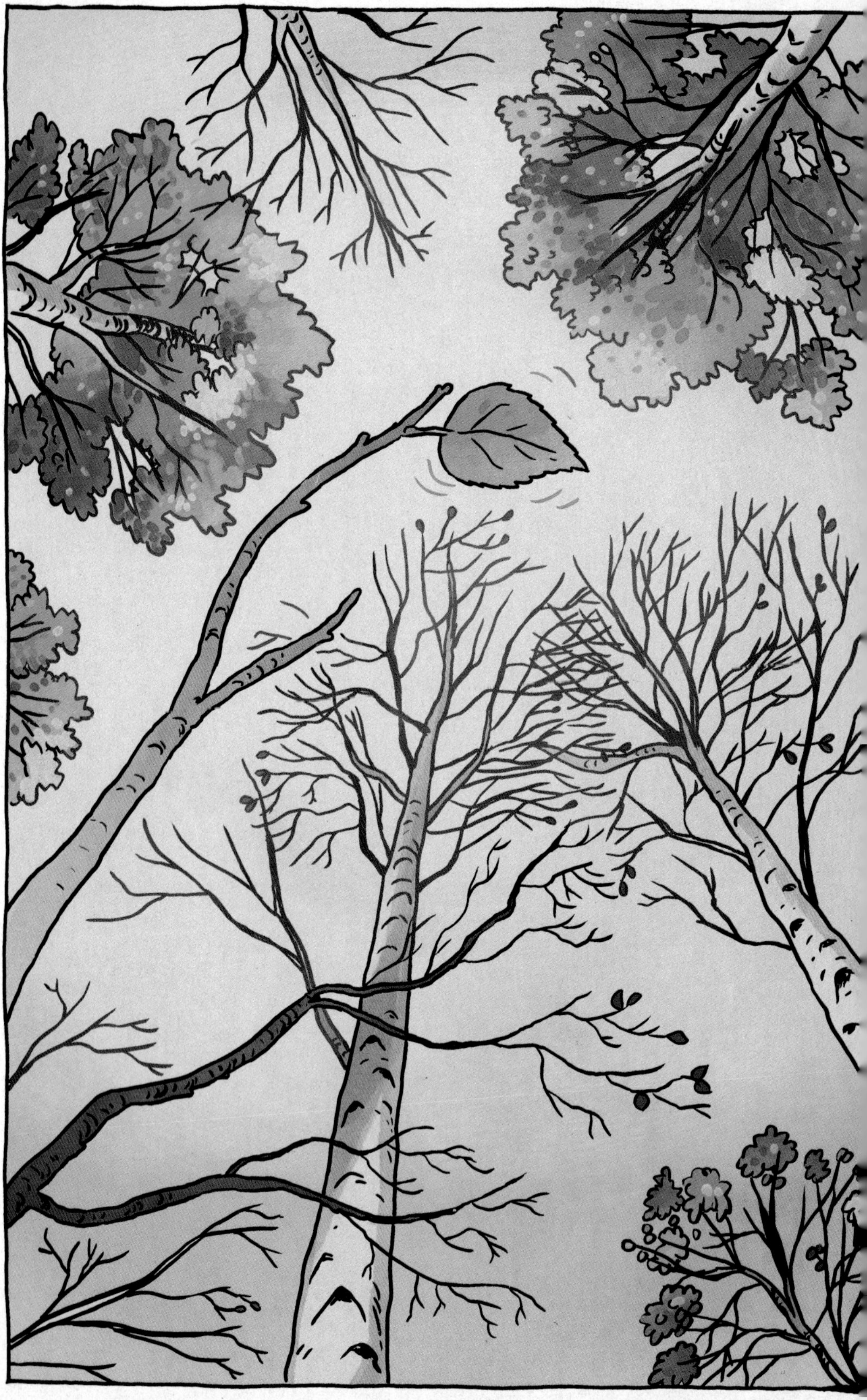

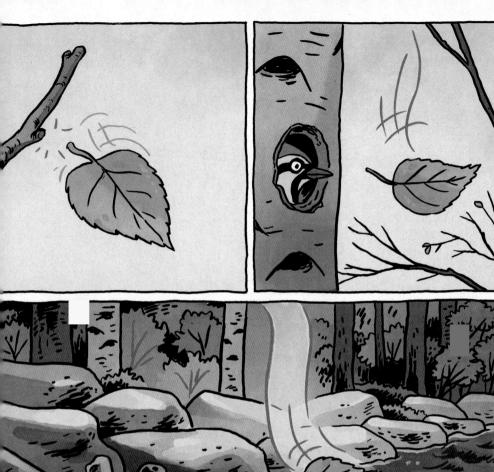

SCRUB
SCRUB
SCRUB

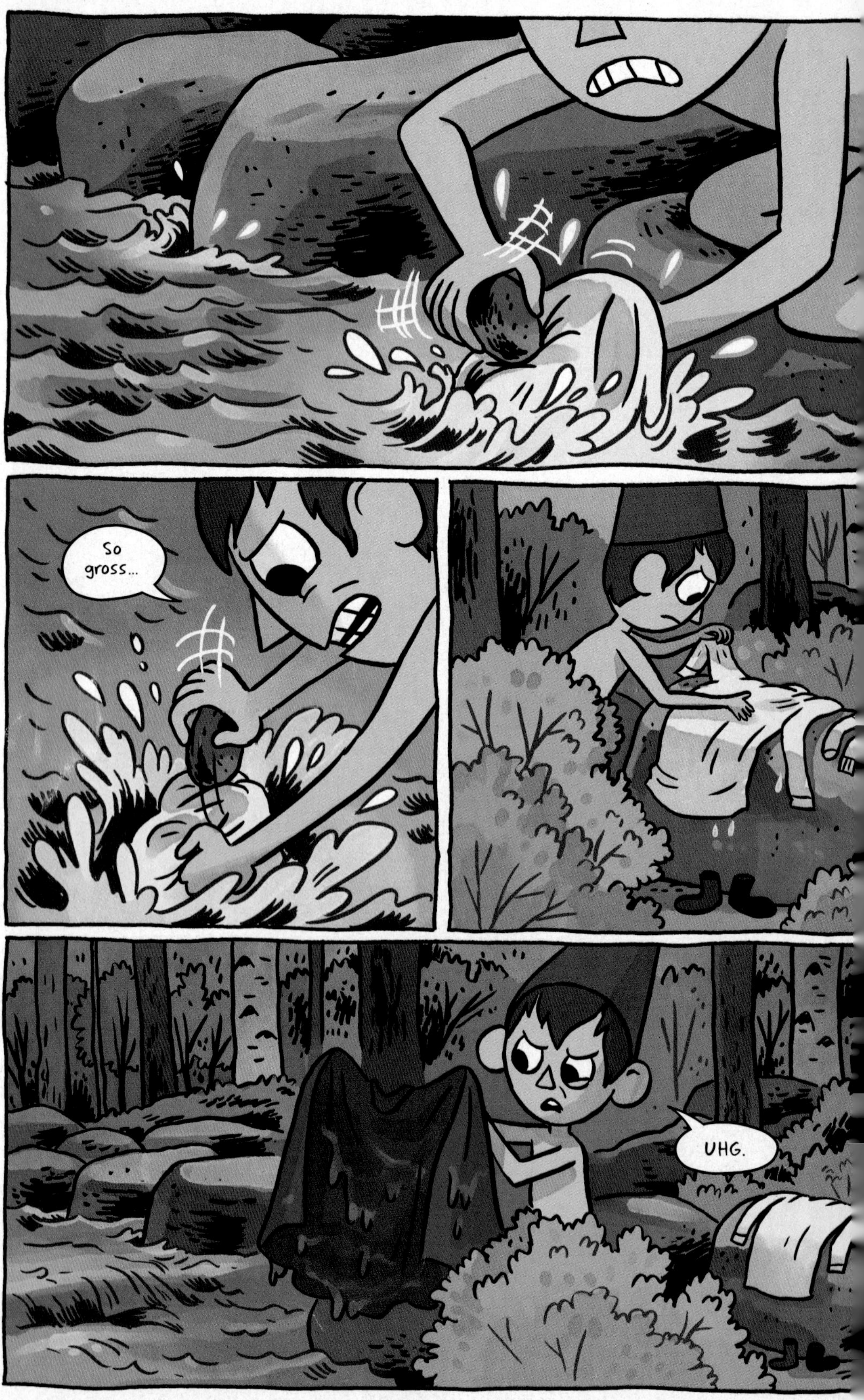
So gross...
UHG.

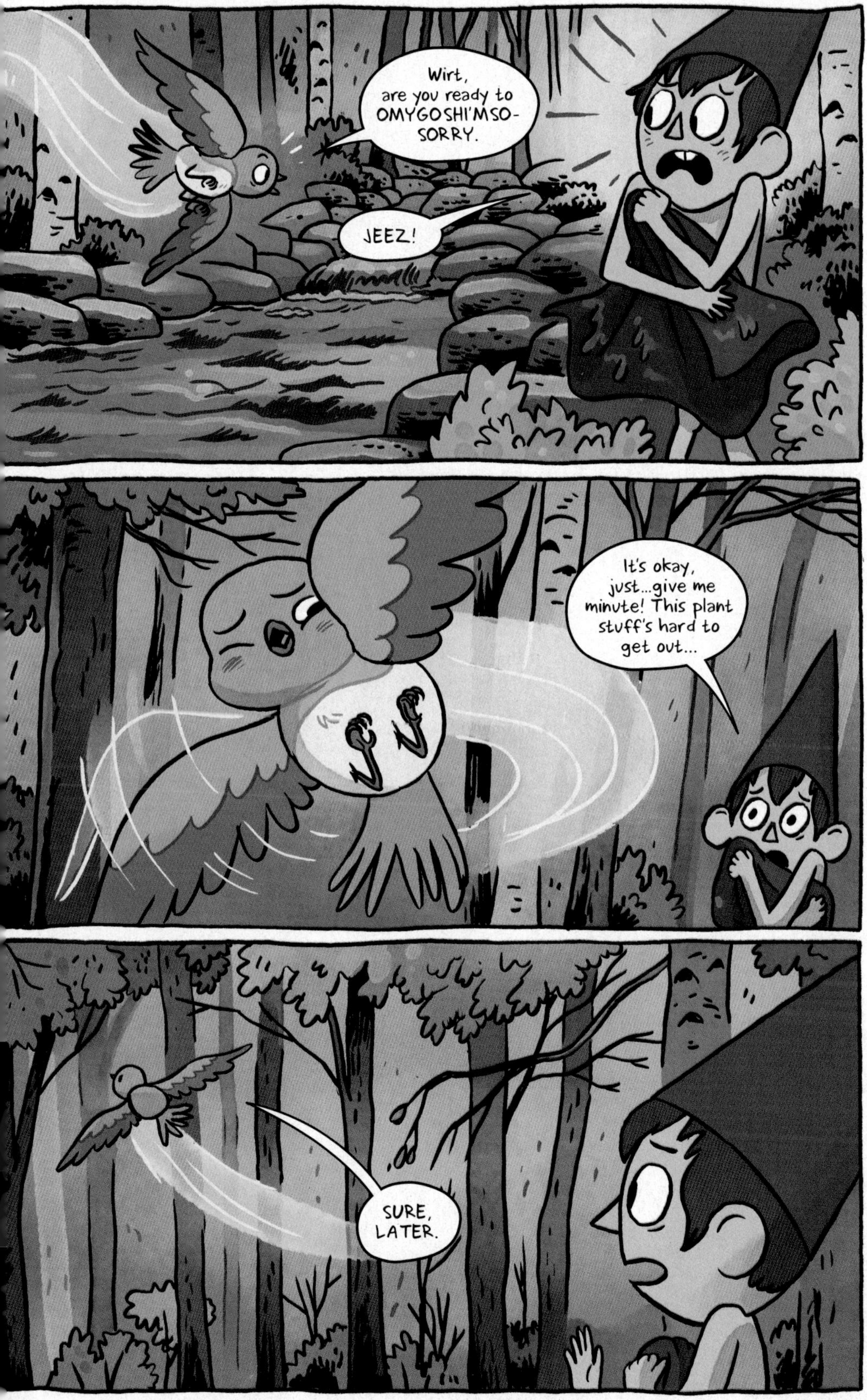
Wirt, are you ready to OMYGOSHI'MSO-SORRY.
JEEZ!
It's okay, just...give me minute! This plant stuff's hard to get out...
SURE, LATER.

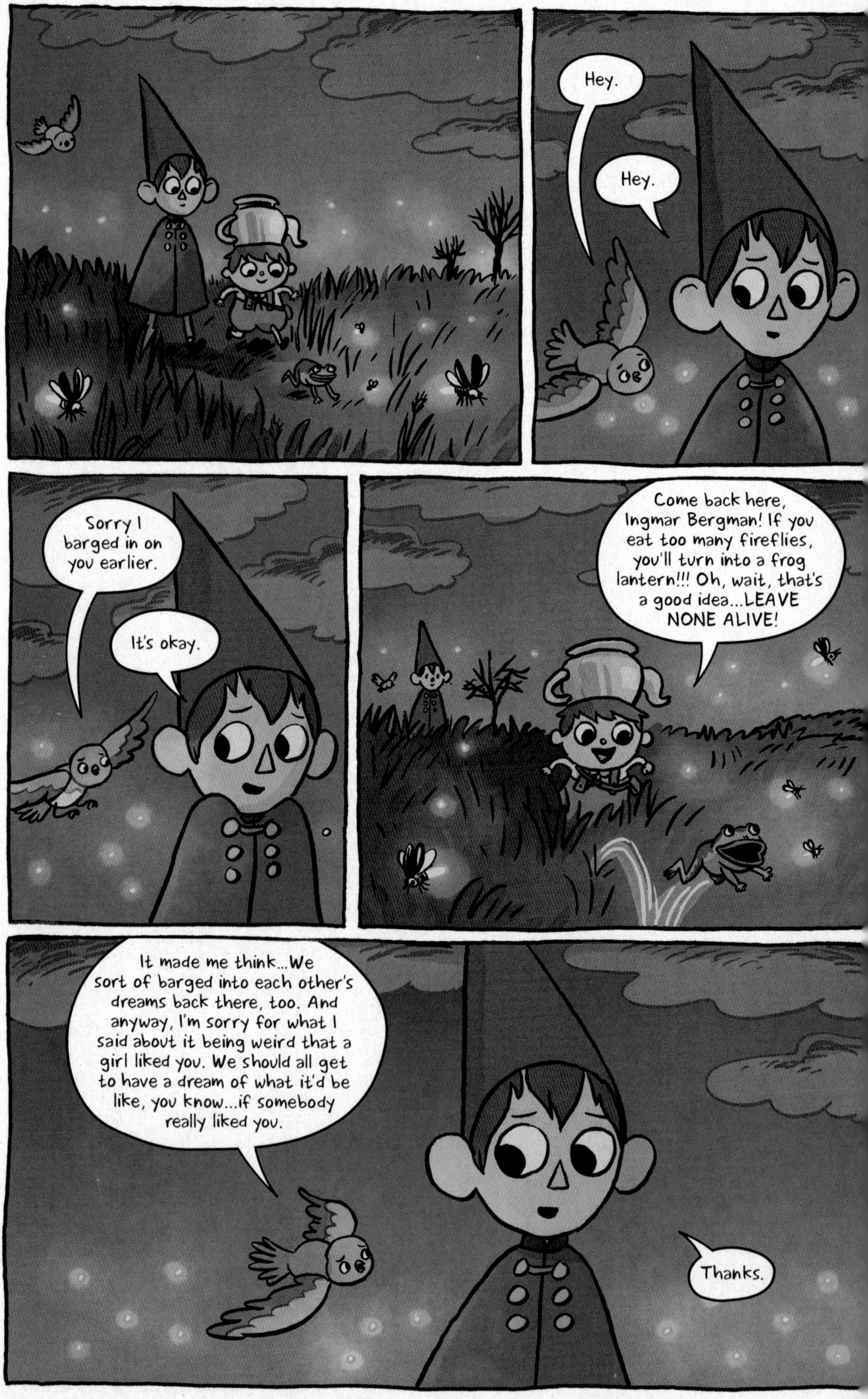
Hey.
Hey.
Sorry I barged in on you earlier.
It's okay.
Come back here, Ingmar Bergman! If you eat too many fireflies, you'll turn into a frog lantern!!! Oh, wait, that's a good idea...LEAVE NONE ALIVE!
It made me think...We sort of barged into each other's dreams back there, too. And anyway, I'm sorry for what I said about it being weird that a girl liked you. We should all get to have a dream of what it'd be like, you know...if somebody really liked you.
Thanks.

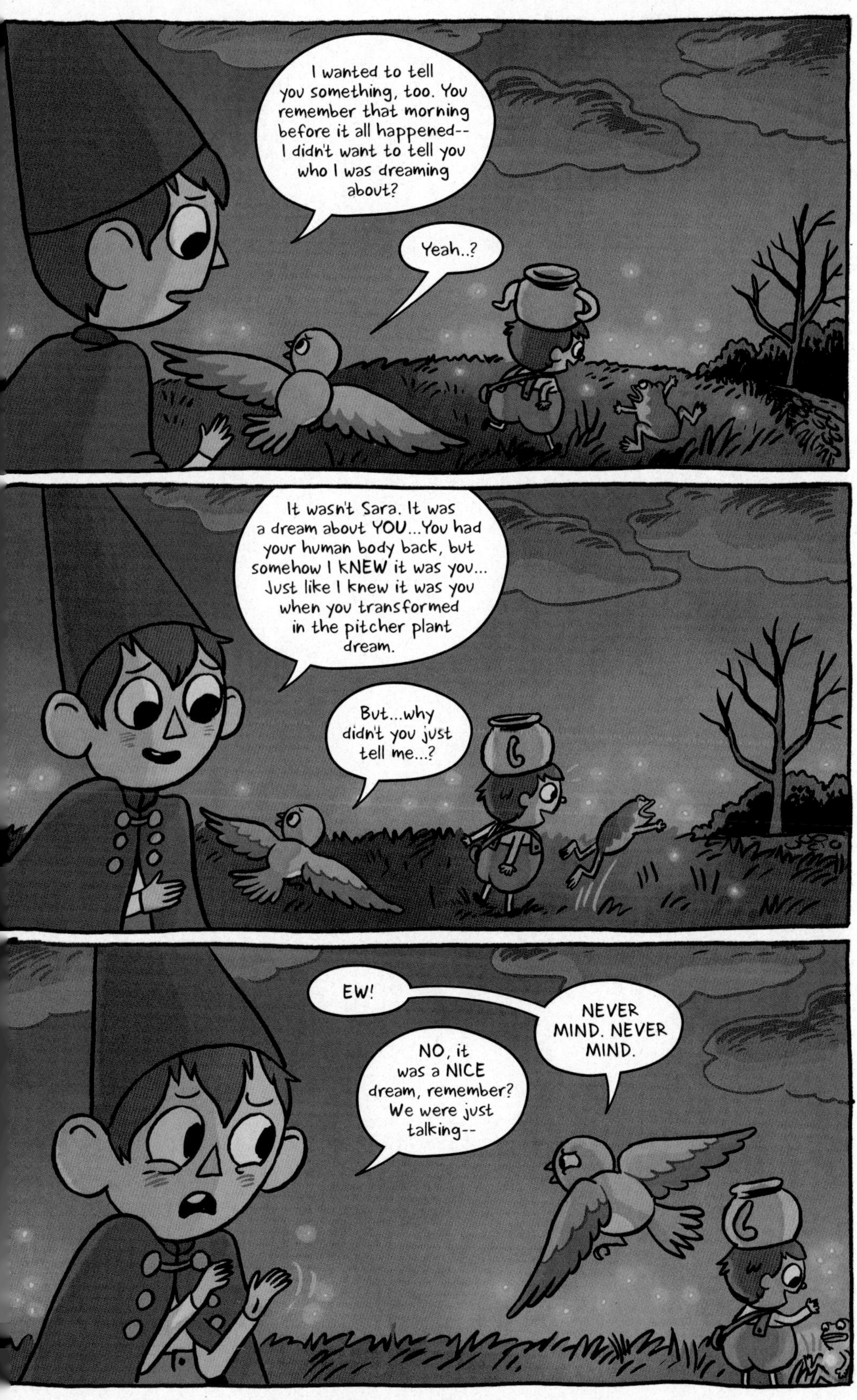
I wanted to tell you something, too. You remember that morning before it all happened-- I didn't want to tell you who I was dreaming about?
Yeah..?
It wasn't Sara. It was a dream about YOU...You had your human body back, but somehow I KNEW it was you... Just like I knew it was you when you transformed in the pitcher plant dream.
But...why didn't you just tell me...?
EW!
NEVER MIND. NEVER MIND.
NO, it was a NICE dream, remember? We were just talking--

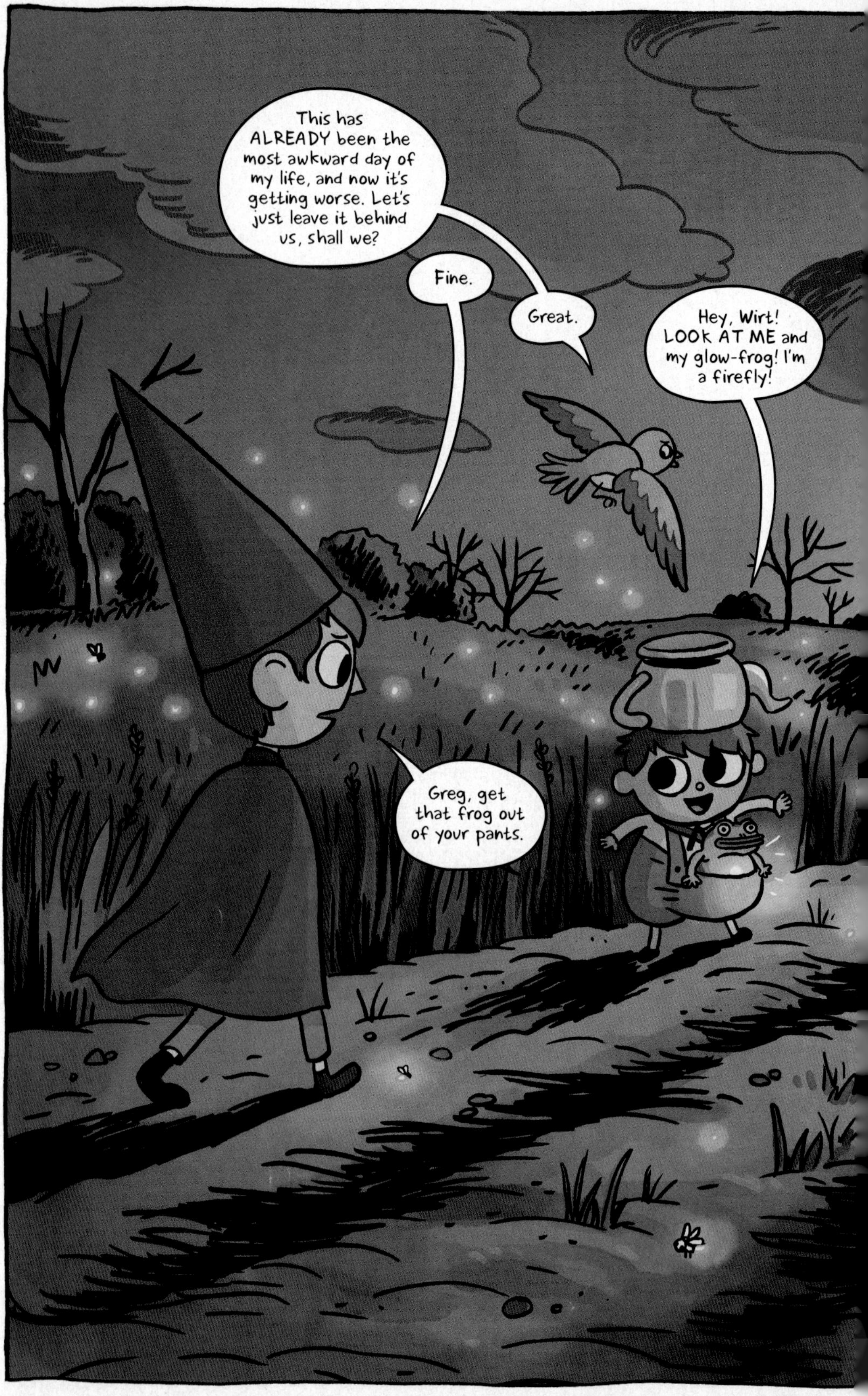
This has ALREADY been the most awkward day of my life, and now it's getting worse. Let's just leave it behind us, shall we?
Fine.
Great.
Hey, Wirt! LOOK AT ME and my glow-frog! I'm a firefly!
Greg, get that frog out of your pants.

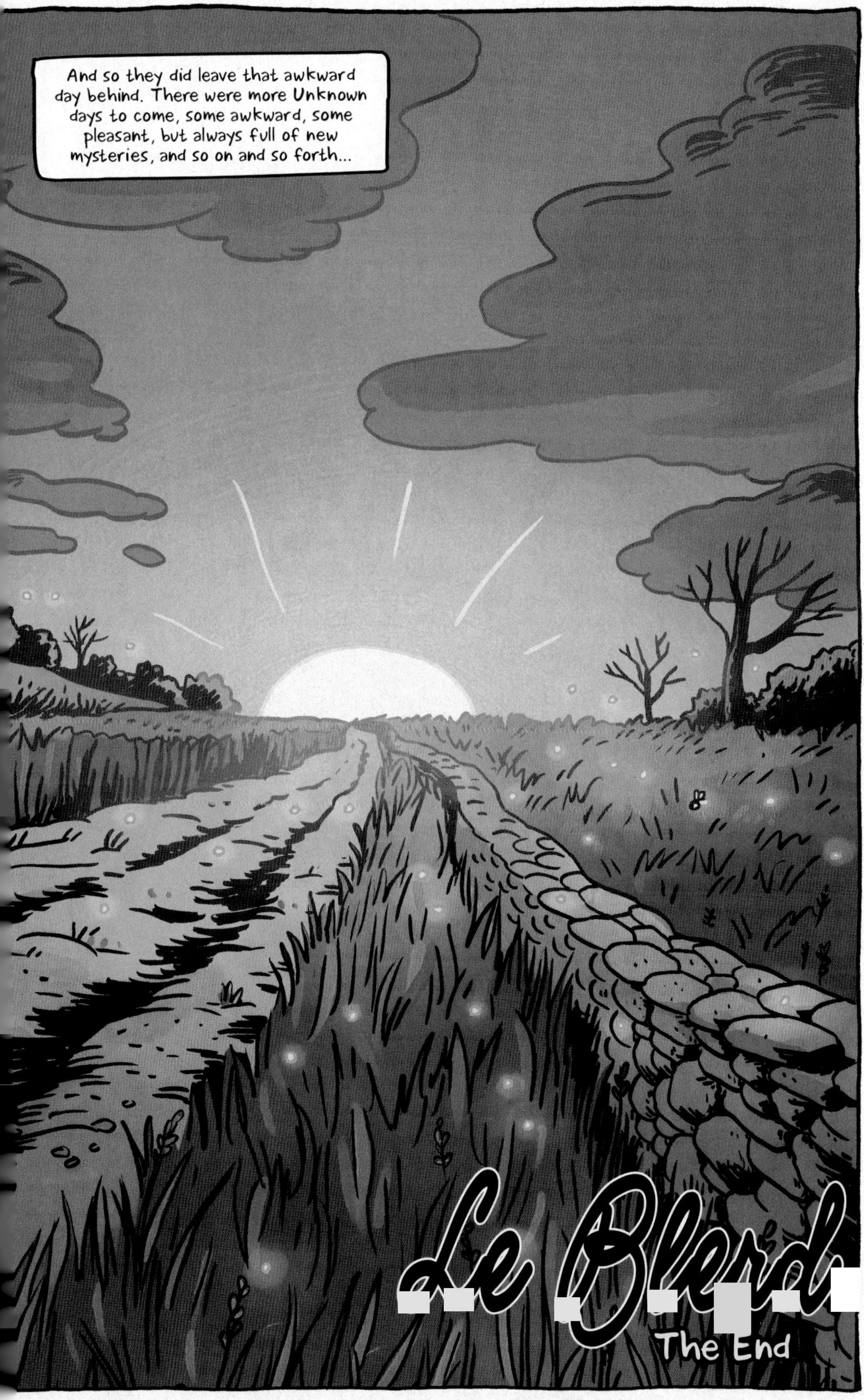
And so they did leave that awkward day behind. There were more Unknown days to come, some awkward, some pleasant, but always full of new mysteries, and so on and so forth...
Le Blerd
The End

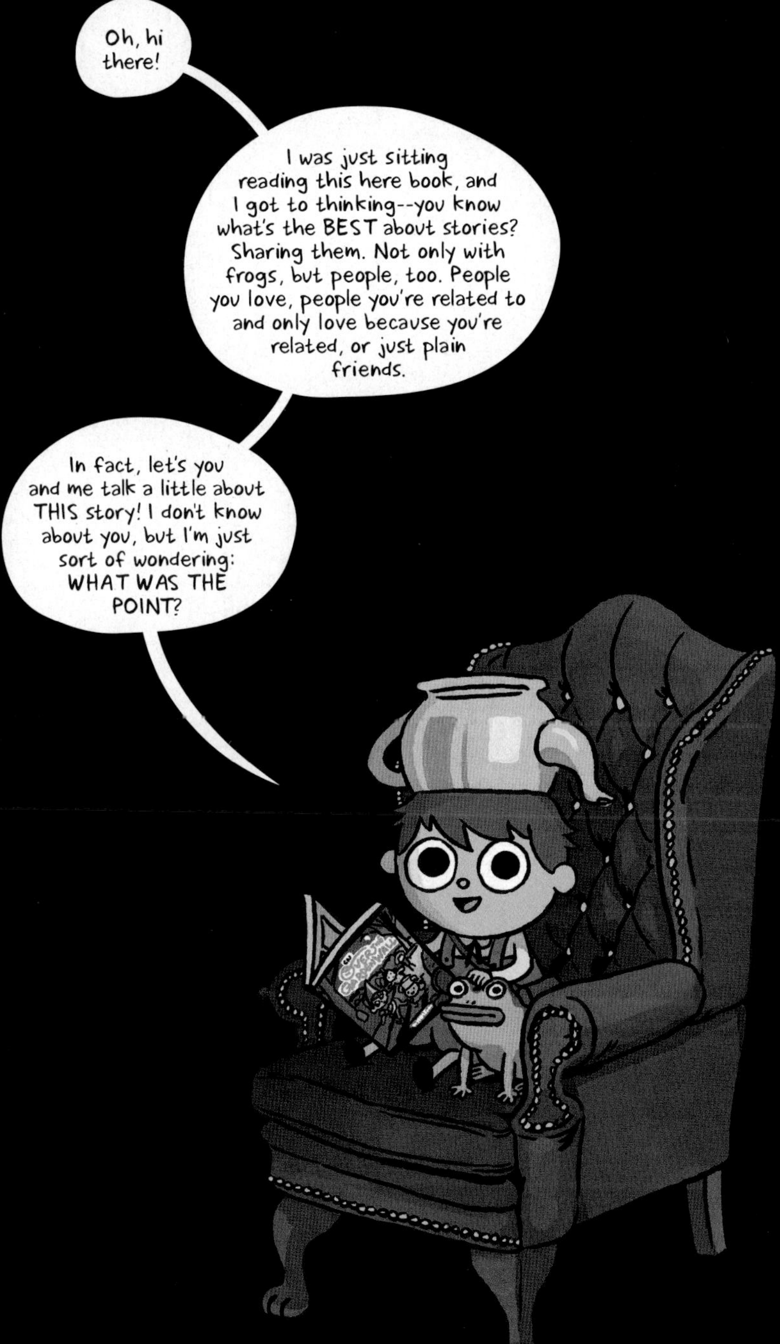
Oh, hi there!
I was just sitting reading this here book, and I got to thinking--you know what's the BEST about stories? Sharing them. Not only with frogs, but people, too. People you love, people you're related to and only love because you're related, or just plain friends.
In fact, let's you and me talk a little about THIS story! I don't know about you, but I'm just sort of wondering: WHAT WAS THE POINT?

In Distillatoria, we giggled at Wirt and Beatrice's weird arguments. We were thrilled at the sight of Jason Funderberker getting his leg poked. And when the monster sprouted out of Dream-Sara's body, we thought, HEY THAT'S NEAT!

But there was one part I really didn't think was very good. Do you remember? It was where Wirt tucked me into bed and then he tried to tell me that something I said was a rock fact.

I STILL don't understand what he meant, and I hope you don't either, because that means I'm not crazy!

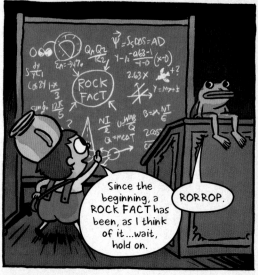

Since the beginning, a ROCK FACT has been, as I think of it...wait, hold on.

RORROP.

Just a minute. Where IS that doggone thing?

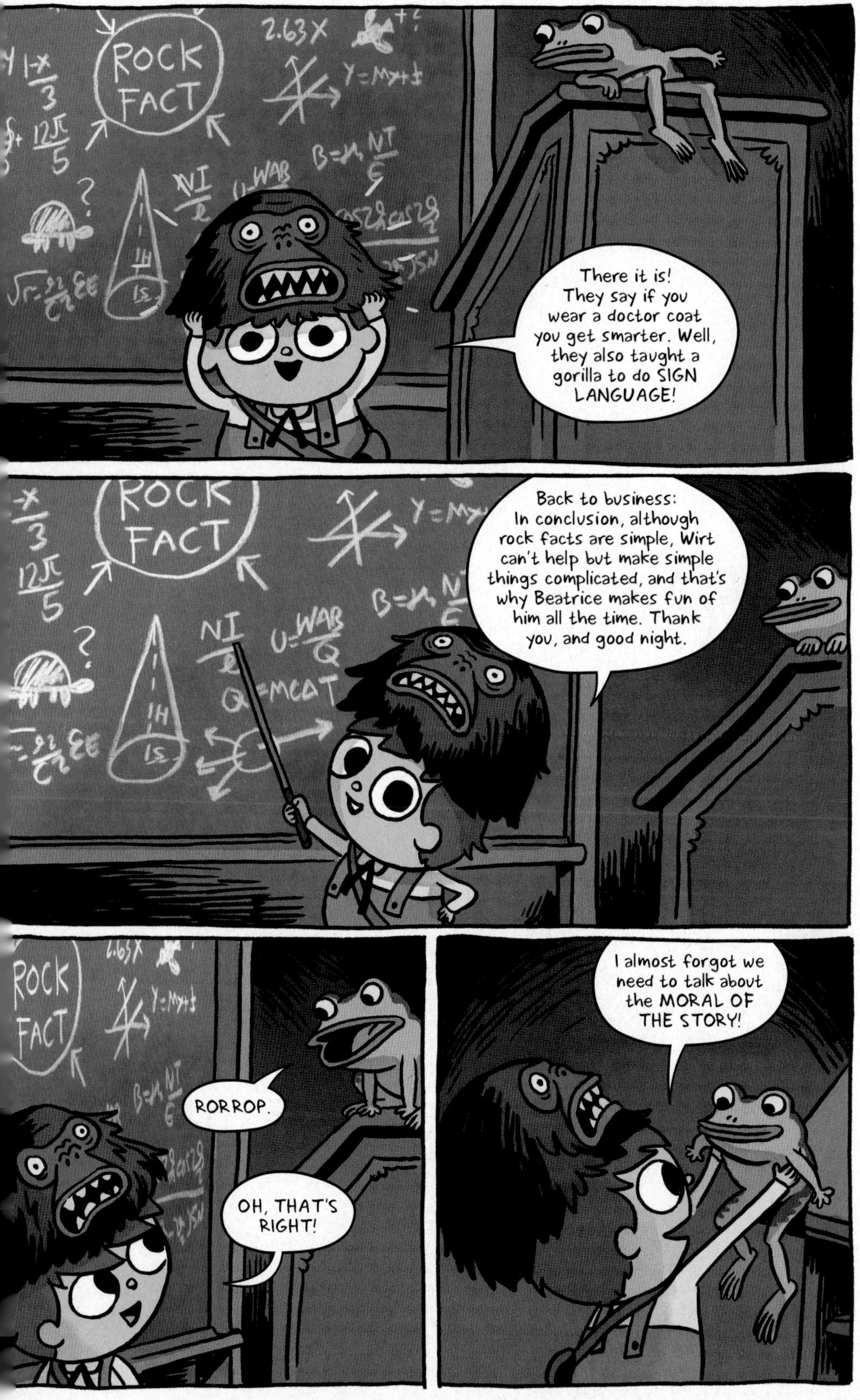
There it is! They say if you wear a doctor coat you get smarter. Well, they also taught a gorilla to do SIGN LANGUAGE!
ROCK FACT
Back to business: In conclusion, although rock facts are simple, Wirt can't help but make simple things complicated, and that's why Beatrice makes fun of him all the time. Thank you, and good night.
RORROP.
OH, THAT'S RIGHT!
I almost forgot we need to talk about the MORAL OF THE STORY!

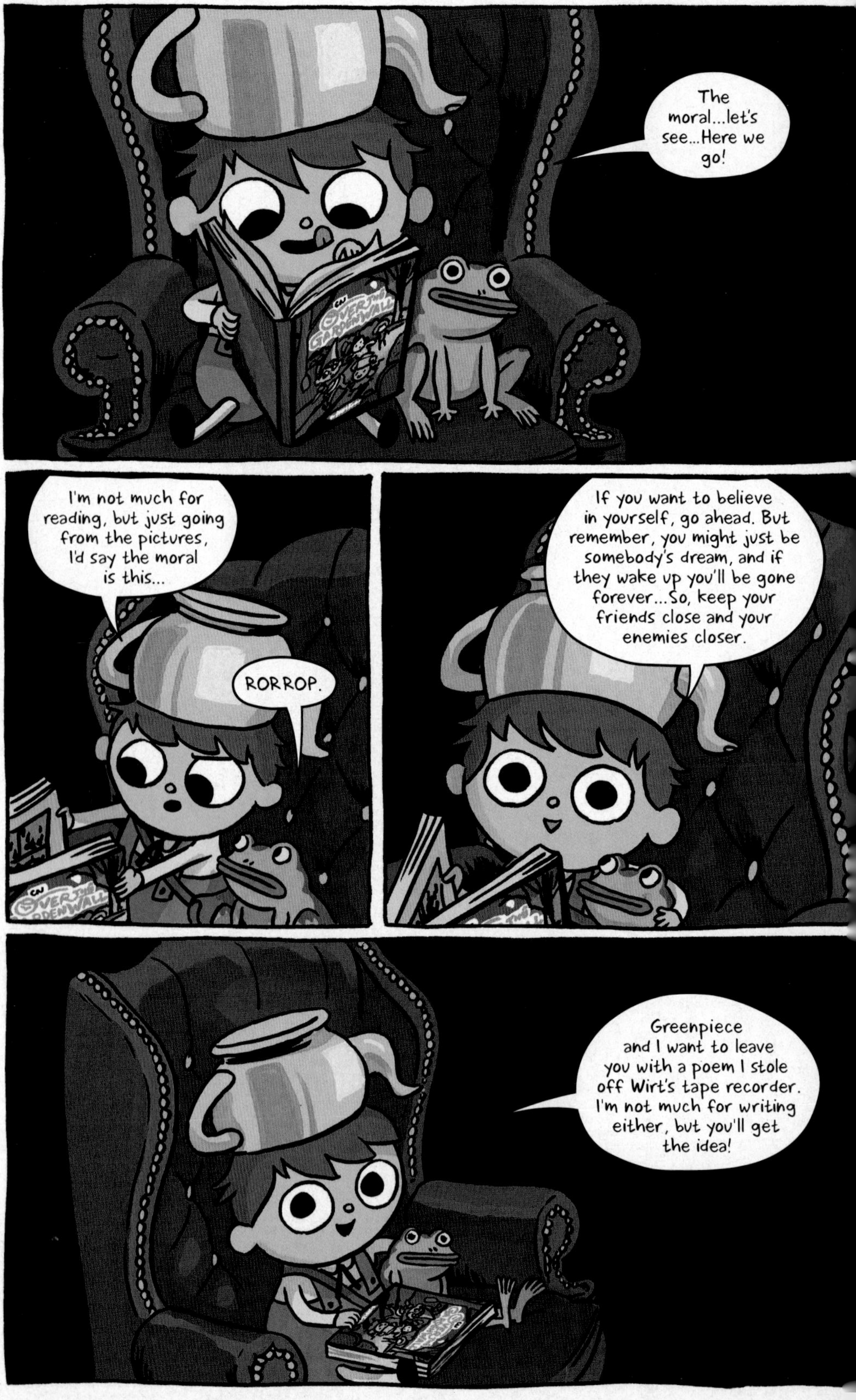

The moral...let's see...Here we go!
I'm not much for reading, but just going from the pictures, I'd say the moral is this...
RORROP.
If you want to believe in yourself, go ahead. But remember, you might just be somebody's dream, and if they wake up you'll be gone forever...So, keep your friends close and your enemies closer.
Greenpiece and I want to leave you with a poem I stole off Wirt's tape recorder. I'm not much for writing either, but you'll get the idea!

SHEEZ LYK THU BREEZE
BY WIRT

STOLEN AND WRITN DOWN BY GREG

SHEEZ LYK THU BREEZ
THRU MY TREE
SHEE FLYZ A KYT
AND ITZ MEE

SHEE GIDZ MEE THRU STORM CLONDS
OLY 2 SKORCH MEE WITH HUR SPARK
SHEEZ GOT MY HOL HART
SO WY DOO I FLY IN THU DARK

I THINK OF HER LUVLEE FACE
HER LAF SO LYT AND FREE
CANT TALK 2 HER THO
SHEEZ HI ABUV MEE

SUCH A CLOWN 2 BEELEEV
IM THU TYP OF MAN SHEE NEEDS
SHEEZ LYK THU BREEZ
SUCH A CLOWN 2 BEELEEV

(SHEEZ LYK THU BREEZ)

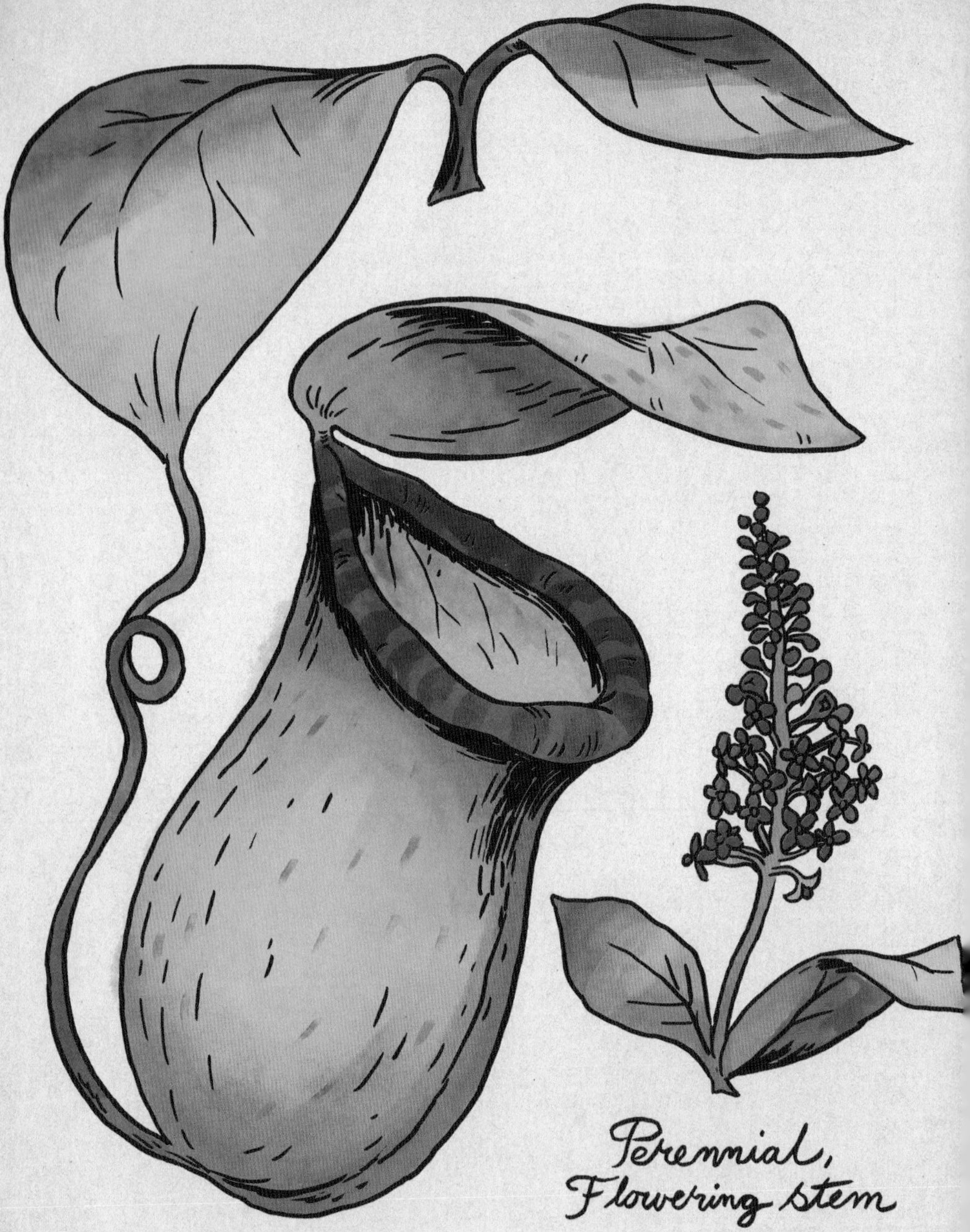
Perennial,
Flowering stem

Nepenthes distillatoria

English Name: Pitcher Plant

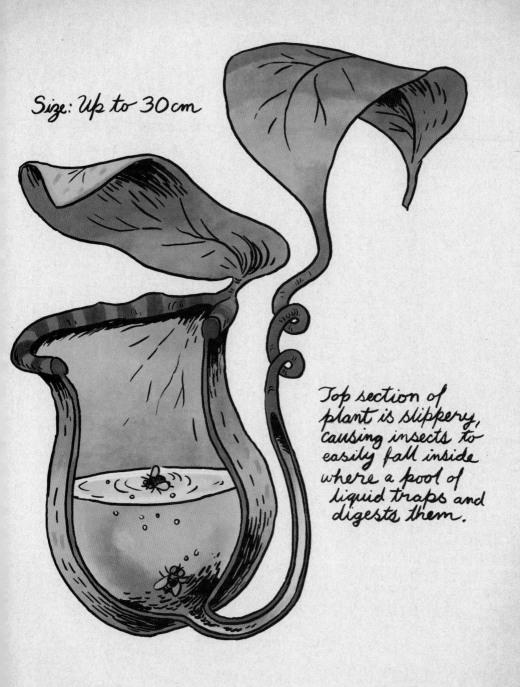

Size: Up to 30cm

Top section of plant is slippery, causing insects to easily fall inside where a pool of liquid traps and digests them.

Habitat: waterlogged open scrub, marshes, woods Sea level to 700m altitude